MW01169724

Magic Rune Academy

Landon Scott

Adam Sage

ROYAL GUARD

Copyright © 2024 by Royal Guard Publishing LLC

All rights reserved.

No part of this book may be reproduced in any form or by any electronic or mechanical means, including information storage and retrieval systems, without written permission from the author, except for the use of brief quotations in a book review.

Chapter One

It was a dreary evening as the rain pelted against my windshield, the wipers struggling to clear my view long enough for me to navigate around the tight streets of Boltan University. The weather, though dull and depressing, was actually quite fitting and a perfect outward representation of my recent mood.

"I'm telling you, Nate, this is exactly what you needed!" Tara blurted out from the passenger seat for about the third time since we left our dorms, just ten minutes ago.

"A trip to a card shop on the first Friday night of the school year? Yeah, it's a foolproof solution," I sarcastically said.

Tara scoffed. "It's not just a card shop! We're talking about a full-on—"

"Magic shop. I know, I know. I've heard the *crazy* stories." I couldn't help but let a grin slip as I finished her sentence.

"Uh, yeah! I mean, they've got all kinds of cool things—crystal balls, wands, Ouija boards, fortune teller cards, even cosplay stuff! The list goes on and on, really. And you can't forget about all the premium Kingdom Monster cards they have! I'm gonna *dominate* the next card club once I finally

1

get my hands on Drakthor the Tormentor," she muttered that last sentence to herself, clearly now in her own world.

My grin had turned to a full-blown smile as I tried to suppress a laugh. It's always been one of my favorite things about Tara. A short, spunky girl with platinum blonde hair and big glasses, she'd been my best friend since we were kids, to the point where we even decided to go to the same college together. The girl never seemed to care about what others thought, just doing what she enjoyed doing. And I respected the hell out of her for that. However, though fun when we were younger, the card games and magic stuff just weren't exactly my cup of tea these days.

And maybe it wasn't just the cards I was bored with. Anymore, reality just felt so dull and repetitive to me, almost like the feeling you get after beating a video game or something. And at just nineteen years old, that's kind of a scary thought. I mean, I even majored in General Studies because nothing else interested me.

I don't know, I just wanted more from life than what it seemed to offer, not to mention I always felt different in some way that I could never explain, like everyone around me was on autopilot, content with their daily lives. I recently wondered how they can just accept this shit.

Maybe that's just what it means to merge into adulthood: accepting reality for what it is. Or maybe I was still upset over the fact that I had just recently ended my relationship with my now ex-girlfriend.

You never do seem to entirely forget the mark that a first girl-friend leaves on you. It's always such an amazing time, until it's not. We had dated through most of high school, and even all freshman year of college, but it just got to the point where it became, I don't know, stale. It was a mutual break up by the time it finally happened right before the start of this semester, but that doesn't make things any easier. I mean, you share a huge chunk of your life together with one person and all of a sudden, they're just gone? It's kind of hard to accept at first.

"They'll have those candies you like too, you know, the ones that pop while you're eating them!" Tara continued, her green eyes practically gleaming with excitement through those geeky-looking glasses of hers. Her hair was put up in a messy ponytail with a couple strands of her bangs cascading down her face, and she was wearing a loose hoodie and black yoga pants, which were surely hugging her tight, thick thighs as she sat Indian style in the passenger seat.

Growing up, Tara always had a cute look to her, but she was never really "the girl who'd turn heads everywhere she went." That is, until maybe about a year or two ago. A late bloomer, no doubt, she now easily pulled off that whole cute, nerdy vibe, while also somehow looking equally sexy, and I often wondered if she really had no clue just how hot she was these days.

"All right, all right, you already got me in the car, no need to oversell it." I said with a grin, parking into a snug spot on the side of the street.

We both exited the car and stepped out onto the soaked sidewalk. Just as two typical college students would do, we forgot our umbrellas, which meant we were left to be shielded from the persistent rain by only our hoodies.

"You've got to love September in Maine, right?" Tara hollered out from the other side of my car before starting down the sidewalk of East Street.

As expected, the streets were pretty vacant. All the shops, bars, and breweries were open, of course, but most students were likely pre-gaming in their dorms or apartments at this time of the evening, staying dry and warm while getting ready for the first weekend of the school year; it was pretty much a rite of passage to get completely hammered after being bored to death all week from professors drilling class syllabuses through their heads. So surely, they'd come out later tonight to drunkenly endure the rainy weather.

We continued treading down East Street for about five minutes before Tara abruptly stopped in her tracks and pointed across the street at an old-looking brick building. The entrance door was an ugly bright red, and the words *Magic Gateway* were painted over the large, dirty window in a yellow cursive font. It was one of those buildings you wouldn't even notice driving through town.

As we got closer, I could make out the rest of what was painted over the window:

> *Welcome to the Magic Gateway!*
> *All are welcome to visit, but few are worthy to stay.*
> *Enter if you wish it, and find a home, you just may!*

I couldn't help but cringe a bit.

Tara didn't miss a beat, though, so I followed her into the *magical realm of possibility*, or whatever.

As the ringing from the shop door let out from behind us, the girl working at the front of the counter briefly looked up from whatever it was she was reading, and it was like a switch turned on inside of me. My attitude about this place immediately shifted, and it had nothing to do with magic cards. This girl was absolutely stunningly beautiful, in a captivating way that I just couldn't quite explain. It was a feeling I'd never experienced before.

"Check it out, Nate. They've got the newest sets!" Tara's voice rang out, bringing me back down to reality and forcing my gaze away from the front counter.

I walked over to her and began fiddling through the packs of cards on the nearest shelf, pretending to be interested. "Yeah, these are pretty cool," I nonchalantly said.

"I know, right?!" Tara responded as she enthusiastically shuffled through all the packs. "They *have* to have it in here. I just know it!"

"Have what?"

She gave me an incredulous look. "Drakthor, duh!"

"Oh, yeah that's . . . that's great. Hey, check out the girl up front," I quietly muttered to her.

That was enough for her to briefly pause her shuffling as she craned her neck toward the front of the shop. "Eh, she's okay," she mumbled indifferently.

"Just okay? You're crazy," I whispered.

Tara went back to her shuffling. "What? I just think you could do better, that's all." She didn't look up at me as she said it. Her mood seemed off now, and I couldn't help wondering why. It wasn't like her to be discouraging when it came to me and other girls.

She glanced up at me from the packs of cards, blushing a bit. "What?" she asked. I had been giving her a curious look, but quickly shook it off.

"I'm gonna go talk to her," I said.

"That's fine, but don't come crying to me when she ruins your life. Just look at her, she totally gives off the life wrecker type of vibe."

I chuckled. "She's just innocently reading a book up there. I'm going for it, wish me luck."

I started casually walking around the store, taking in all of what it offered before jumping into things with the girl up front. It really was quite the sight. Every inch of space on the walls was covered with different magical items, from your basic playing cards to unique artwork. A ridiculous number of various graphic tees were hung up on clothing racks throughout the middle of the store, and the shelves along the walls were stocked up to the ceiling with wands, hats, board games, and other collectibles. In the back of the store behind the counter were two large bookcases blocking the wall behind it, each of them seemed to be filled with all kinds of books, from your traditional novels to comic books and manga. I had to admit, the place really did make me feel like a kid again.

Although, my primary focus didn't revolve around *what* was in the store, but rather *who* was in it. The place was completely abandoned other than Tara, me, and the girl working the front desk. Somehow, she had a sort of hold on me, and yet I hadn't even gotten a close look at her yet.

As I moved toward the front register, I managed to steal a glance. She was even better up close. Her face was flawless, other than a tiny little mole on the lower part of her left cheek (if anything, it just added to her appeal). Her hair was jet-black, but with dark maroon highlights running through it, and shorter in length, ending just above her shoulders. It was cut in a way that gave it that choppy type of texture, and her bangs fell over her face so that they covered one of her eyes. Her skin was pale, but damn, could she pull it off; her dark hair, eyes, and the deep maroon colored lipstick she was wearing to match her highlights all somehow perfectly complimented her skin complexion.

And that was only her face; her body was what really brought the whole thing home, which was only emphasized even more by the way she was smoothly leaning over that counter while flipping through the pages of her book. Her slender curves were on full display, wearing this tight white top that only went down to her bellybutton, and skin-tight jeans that hugged her slim legs and surprisingly thick ass for an otherwise petite girl. The shirt was hanging low up top, even lower with how she was hunching over, and I couldn't help noticing the upper gap between her breasts. They weren't too big, but fuck, were they perfectly shaped. She couldn't have been any taller than maybe five feet or so. She just had this tight, little appearance to her, which I was absolutely loving.

It was kind of odd in a way, because there was no doubt she had a bit of a goth, punk thing going on, which was never really my type. And yet, she was easily pulling it off, even turning the look into a certain something I never knew I needed until this very moment.

I had to talk to her.

I continued my way over to her, all while trying to think of some excuse to spark up a conversation. When I reached the counter, I paused for a moment, waiting for her to look up.

The problem was, she didn't. Her eyes remained fixated on whatever she was reading. Finally, feeling kind of dumb just standing there, I spoke up, "You guys have any of those pop candy things? You know, the ones that crack when you start eating them?" It was kind of a stupid line to open with, but I figured it'd be better than asking for their finest potion sets, or something like that.

She still didn't look up to make eye contact with me though, which was now kind of irking me. Instead, she pointed to the side of the counter, and of course, there they were, stacked among other fun types of candies.

Yep, I had to ask for the one thing in the store that was directly in front of my face.

For some reason, maybe for the simple sake of redeeming myself, I decided to still try my hand at this.

"I like your hair, those highlights really compliment your whole look," I said.

Finally, this got her attention enough for her to look up at me, and as she did, I couldn't help but feel mesmerized glancing into those dark eyes of hers.

"Thanks," she replied, and then went back to her book.

So much for the mesmerized feeling. That was all I needed to get the gist, so I said fuck the candy and quickly turned around to take my leave, but as I did, I bumped into someone else.

"Nate, check out the–" was all Tara got out before I accidentally knocked the deck of Kingdom Monster cards out of her hands, causing them to all separate and fall to the floor.

"Shit, sorry Tara" I muttered, bending down to help Tara pick up the cards, who looked a bit flustered.

"Ugh, really?" the girl behind the desk groaned.

I gave Tara a quick look of foreboding while the girl came walking around the counter.

"Don't even worry about it," the girl groaned, bending down beside me to help pick the cards up before trailing off. To make things even weirder, I could have sworn I heard her making a sniffing noise before she paused.

I did my best to ignore that strange act, though, and continued picking the cards up off the floor. Yet, I couldn't help noticing in my peripherals that she was still staring at me, frozen in place.

"Are you good?" I abruptly looked up at her. She remained paused in place, staring blankly away at me; it was like she was looking at me for the first time all over again, almost like our previous encounter never had occurred.

She blinked a few times. "No, no, sorry, I uh, what did you say your name was again?"

"I never . . ." I continued staring into those dark eyes, which seemed to have an entirely different feel to them now, more innocent than before. "Nate, Nate Gannon."

For the first time, I saw her smile, and it somehow transformed her entire look. Before, she was giving off that fierce and cool type of beauty, but now that she was smiling, she radiated a surprisingly warm aura, showing off a very cute side to her that had been hidden away up until now.

"Nice to meet you," she began, "I'm—"

"Dawn," I said, pointing to the name tag on her shirt and giving her a kind smile back.

She lightly chuckled. "Yeah, duh." Her eyes shifted to the floor and she blushed a little, which really stood out against her pale skin complexion. I couldn't help but take in just how cute she looked now that she was suddenly showing a vulnerable side.

"Well, this has been fun!" Tara blurted out, breaking the silence. "Sorry again about the cards, we'll just be going now!" she finished with an awkward laugh that seemed forced.

"So, you play?" Dawn asked, completely ignoring Tara as she stood back up.

My face went blank, not sure if this was a trap or not. She was either a full-on nerd, or testing to see if I was, for better or worse.

"Nope! No playing at all!" Tara jumped in again. "Just looking, actually. What were these called again? Oh—Kingdom Monsters—kind of a dumb name if you ask me!" Tara had grabbed my arm and was tugging at it while trying to make her escape.

At this point, Tara's behavior had me completely perplexed. It wasn't like her to lie for no reason; she and I would play the game together all the time when we were younger, before I started dating my last girlfriend, at least. I'd usually win, too, often finding a way to pull the exact cards I needed from the deck when it mattered most.

"I dabble a little. It's been years, but when we were younger, I'd whoop her butt all the time." I gestured at Tara, who playfully slapped me on the shoulder.

I wasn't sure how exactly Dawn would take that, so I was relieved when a smile forged across her face. It was actually more of an ornery grin, and I wasn't sure why until about a second later. "Oh yeah? What's *she*, like your sister or something?" she asked.

"Sister?!" blurted Tara

It didn't seem to faze Dawn though in the least bit. "Nah, I'm just messing. I know you wanna bang him."

Tara spluttered with a complete loss for words.

I rubbed the back of my head, trying to fight the sheepish look that was undoubtedly painted all over my face. I couldn't help feeling a bit guilty from not interjecting, but I figured it was all in good fun.

Dawn turned to me, holding out the cards and biting her lip with a tempting look in her eyes. I could have melted on the spot. "Well, are you game?"

This confirmed the fact that Dawn indeed had a bit of a nerdy side to her. And to be honest, it was kind of a turn on. "Can't say no to that!" I replied. "But really, I may need a quick review."

Dawn grabbed a couple of card decks from behind the counter and led us over to a table in the corner of the shop before we all took our seats around it, though Tara did so a bit reluctantly.

"Okay," she began, impressively shuffling away at the cards, "I'm sure you remember the basics since it's your typical life point system. We'll play with 1000 LP instead of the standard 2500 to make it go a bit quicker. There are monster cards, trap cards, magic cards, and each monster has attack, defense and health stats . . ."

Seeing her go on and on about the rules so enthusiastically had me appreciating her on an entirely new level. While only minutes ago she was just a pretty face and a smoking body, I was somehow already finding myself feeling even more intrigued by this very eccentric girl who seemingly wanted absolutely nothing to do with me at first.

What could have changed her opinion of me so quickly, and so drastically? Not that I was complaining.

". . . and then each monster has an element stat, too, with specific weaknesses for each element. Are you getting all this?" she asked.

"Yeah, I think it's coming back. Let's do it," I said, not really remembering everything to it, but I figured her winning wouldn't exactly be the worst thing for my chances.

"Oh, yeah?" she purred. "I'm cool *doing* it, if you are."

Tara scoffed and rolled her eyes as Dawn began rapidly handing the cards out like some sort of professional casino dealer.

It wasn't long at all before we each had three separate decks of cards: one for monsters, one for trap cards, and another for the magic cards. We both randomly drew three cards, one from each pile. My monster card was a water elemental knight by the name of *Oosharoo Sir Floatsal*, with 300 attack points,

250 defense points, and 200 HP points—an average card from what I remember, so I went ahead and played it face down so that it would cause Dawn to hesitate on attacking it.

"Playing it close to the chest, are we?" she asked.

"Nothing wrong with being close to the chest," I responded, quickly glancing down at her own perky set.

Dawn smirked. "I'd have to agree with you there," she said before throwing a monster card down of her own, a fire type bird by the name of *Phoenix Queen Ashara* (I couldn't help getting a kick out of these names). With an attack stat of 450, she decided to attack my face down card. I was then forced to flip the card up and discard it from the field, losing 200 HP points of my 1000 total.

We continued going back and forth, throwing various cards down on the table while Tara watched eagerly from the side. Her nerdy nature and love for the game couldn't stop her from enjoying the match, no matter how indifferent she was clearly trying to act. And I had to admit, I was actually having fun, too. Not only were Dawn and I going back and forth on the table, but the banter was also starting to heat up.

"I thought you said you were good at this," she teased after eliminating another one of my monster cards with a magic card. The score was now 700 to 200 in her favor, with no signs of winning in my sight.

"Yeah, yeah." I pulled another card at random from my monster deck: another shit card called *Dooey the Oozepuff*. I played it faced down.

Dawn then drew a card from her deck and smiled. "Damn, I was really looking forward to getting bent over tonight, too," she said, throwing back in my face something I had said earlier in the match during our jesting.

As Dawn placed the card on the table, Tara let out a small gasp before quickly putting her hands over her mouth. "That's the Drakthor card you were talking about earlier, isn't it?" I whispered to Tara, who quickly nodded, her eyes wide and hands still placed over her mouth. "Shit," I muttered to myself.

I had to admit, it *did* look pretty cool. A red dragon with huge, spiky wings and glowing yellow eyes, it had an impressive attack and defensive stat of 1000, and 850 HP. Not only that, but it was the rare cosmic type, which had no elemental weaknesses other than another cosmic type.

"But I think *I'll* bend over whatever it is you've got over there." Dawn pointed at my card.

And with that, I was down to just 50 life points, so I figured I'd take a chance on trying to pull a magic card this time. I looked at the three stacks of cards in front of me and held out my hand, trying to carefully decide which to randomly draw. I closed my eyes, concentrated on getting lucky, and pulled a single card from the lot.

I was pleasantly shocked by what I was looking at; it was almost humorous. I had somehow pulled a magic card that allowed me to delete any cosmic type card—totally useless in almost any other situation, yet exactly what I needed in my specific predicament. I couldn't help but grin, and Dawn seemed surprised, yet very intrigued.

I threw the magic card down, and Dawn's eyes went wide. Tara let out a high-pitched squeak.

"How did you do that?" Dawn asked.

"I think that's the game, right?" I asked, fully knowing that I'd won. "The bigger and badder the card, the bigger the risk. That dragon had a whopping 850 HP, and well, I'm pretty sure you had less than that left in your total life points, right?" I couldn't help myself, and she seemed the type to like a bit of the shit-talking anyway.

Dawn still appeared to be trying to wrap her head around something. "You do realize there's only one counter to Drakthor in this entire game, right?"

"Nope, but I do now." I grinned.

"And you pulled it, exactly when you needed it. And out of that whole stack of magic cards."

"Just dumb luck, really," I said.

"Dumb luck, *right*." She was giving me an interesting look—a little too intense of a look for just a card game, if you asked me.

After our match, I helped Dawn clean the cards up and put them back underneath the counter. The rain had finally lightened up, and we had been in the store for a little over an hour by then, so I figured it was a good time for us to take our leave.

"Hey, this was fun," she said.

"It really was," I agreed. "It's kind of weird, I haven't played that since before—" I stopped myself from ending the night on a terrible mistake, the last thing a girl wants to hear about is your ex. "Well, it's just been a while, and this was surprisingly refreshing."

"Well, maybe come and play again sometime? I'm here pretty much every night," she responded as she was starting to blush again.

Hearing her say that made my evening. To be honest, I was kind of bummed to be leaving with no further commitments on seeing each other again, especially after how much unexpected fun I ended up having, but now any remaining doubts had been erased.

"Yeah, I'd really like that. My phone's dead, but I'll write down my number for you."

"Old school, huh? I like it," she said, handing me over a pen and a notebook.

I wrote my number down and ripped the paper out. "Well, I should get back to my friend before the rain starts up again," I said, glancing at Tara through the shop window. She was standing outside with her arms folded. "I'm kind of surprised she was so eager to leave. Usually, she could spend all day in stores like this. She didn't even bother trying to buy that dragon card she's been going on about."

Dawn smiled. "You *do* know she's crazy about you, right?"

"Tara?" I asked incredulously, holding back a laugh at her assumption. "Nah, we just go way back, me and her."

"Trust me, a girl knows." She grinned. "And you're into her, too."

My eyes widened for a second before I caught myself. That was the last thing I expected her to say.

She chuckled. "It's totally cool, you don't have to hide it."

"It's just—"

"Complicated, I know." She smiled at me, seemingly unbothered by my apparent feelings for Tara, which kind of bothered *me*. Perhaps Dawn wasn't into me the way that I thought she was.

"Well, we're really good friends," I admitted. "Best friends, to be honest. So, it would never really happen."

Dawn's smile didn't falter, though. "Never say never." She winked.

I was very confused at this point.

"But before *never* happens," she purred, "stop by again. I've got plenty more games we can play in the back." She shifted her hips, emphasizing her thick ass in those tight jeans. I had to do everything in my power not to get hard in the middle of the store.

"Oh, you've got yourself a regular customer, don't worry," I said, handing her over the piece of paper with my number on it. As I did, my hand grazed hers for just a moment and I couldn't help but note that her skin was so soft.

I then started heading over to the exit but remembered something else I wanted to say. And as I turned back around to address her, I was astonished at what I was looking at. Dawn had two furry ears poking through her hair, jet-black in color, they looked like the ears of a cat.

I smiled brightly, completely forgetting about what I wanted to say. "No way, that's so cool," I said.

She looked confused. "What?"

"Those ears!" I chuckled. "You really are good at this magic trick stuff, aren't you? What are those, like some sort of retractable ears on a headband or something?"

For some reason, she still looked a bit unsure as she raised her hands to feel them. And when she touched them, I could have sworn she had a flash of a startled expression before catching herself.

"Yeah," she giggled in a way which I hadn't heard from her yet that night. "You like that, do you? Well, I've got all kinds of tricks up my sleeve—you'll see." She gave me kind of an awkward wink. It was like she suddenly forgot how to be cool and confident, which I found to be pretty cute, actually.

I finally left the Magic Gateway, feeling loads lighter and way more hopeful than I was when entering the store just an hour ago. Yet, as I was walking back to the car with Tara and she was rambling on about how happy she was that I beat "the little tease" in the card duel, I couldn't help but replay that last scene with Dawn back in my head. The more I thought about it, the more I started convincing myself that those ears actually twitched a little when she went to feel them.

Then again, the lighting in that store wasn't entirely the best.

Chapter Two

I woke up the next morning feeling better than I had in weeks, and much more hopeful, too. Even the weather seemed to be reflecting how I felt. The rain had come and gone, and the sky today was a clear blue. It was a bit colder out this morning, signaling that fall in the northeast was right around the corner, so I needed a light jacket as I left my dorm room that morning to meet up with Tara for our typical Saturday morning breakfast.

Tara and I each had our own personal dorm rooms this year, which was kind of nice not having to deal with roommates getting curious and questioning our relationship (it always seemed to attract unwanted attention and make things a little awkward). The only problem was that our dorm buildings were on completely opposite sides of the campus, about twenty minutes by foot, so we just decided to meet halfway at the campus dining hall. I didn't mind the walk over, though, as the brisk weather was a refreshing change after having such a hot and humid August.

Once I arrived, I could see Tara waiting for me out front of the dining hall. Oddly enough, she looked even more amazing than usual, like she actually tried to look good for once. Her hair was still up in the usual messy bun, her glasses still thick and nerdy looking, but she was dressed up a bit, especially for a casual Saturday morning. She was wearing a pair of tight black jeans which really highlighted the curves of her legs nicely and a snug white sweater that emphasized her large, perky chest. She was holding a plastic white coffee cup in one hand and looking down at her watch on the other; she must have been up for a while.

"Hey, Tara! At least, I think you're her," I said. "Look at you, all dressed up this morning and stuff."

She looked up from her watch. "Just had some time to kill this morning!"

Now that I was closer to her, I noticed another surprising difference. "Is that makeup you're wearing?" I asked.

She blushed a little. "It's not like it's the first time, you know!"

I raised an eyebrow, trying to think back. "You don't usually wear makeup though."

"Come on, let's just head in." She rolled her eyes in a playful sort of way.

Once inside, we swiped our badges at the front gate and headed straight for the buffet lines. As usual, a variety of foods were sorted along the many buffet trays. I decided to go all in on breakfast. I made a plate with pancakes, sausage gravy with biscuits, and a heaping side of bacon. Tara chose a breakfast sandwich and a colorful parfait cup.

"You know, I'd like it if you actually made it to your late twenties one day," Tara joked, eyeing the many slices of bacon piled on my plate as we sat down at a table by the window.

"Hey, it's my life," I said with a grin.

As I dove into my large breakfast, I couldn't help sneaking some occasional glances at Tara's new appearance and wondering what the reason or occasion was for it all, and then what Dawn said to me yesterday resurfaced in my mind.

Did Tara have feelings for me that were more than just friendly? And if so, for how long? We've been friends since we were kids, and I never noticed anything that suggested anything more until maybe yesterday.

And then, what if she did? What would my next move be? I mean, there was no doubt that I found her to be more attractive than ever these days, and we've always gotten along great, it was just so easy and natural with Tara. So of course I had feelings for her, but to take it to the next level was another question entirely. With any other girl I was attracted to, there would be no second guessing. But with Tara, if I lost her, well, I'd lose our friendship too.

"What?" she asked, covering her mouth and holding back an embarrassed smile.

"It's nothing, don't worry," I said.

"It's definitely something, so just come out with it already, Nate."

"Well, you have plans today or something?"

"Plans?" she asked, pausing mid-bite. "Nope, other than just chilling with you. Why?"

"I just couldn't help noticing that you're all dolled up this morning, is all."

She blushed again. "I told you, I just had some time to kill this morning."

"You've had 'time to kill' plenty of mornings, and this," I gestured at her appearance with my hand, "is a first, Tara." I could tell she didn't really know what to say. "Not that it's bad!" I quickly caught myself. "I mean, you look great. Well, not that you don't usually look nice, too."

Tara was blushing even harder, which was starting to confirm my suspicions. "You think I look nice?" she asked, then quickly glanced down at her parfait cup.

"Well, nice is an understatement, if I'm being honest." I smiled at her.

She reciprocated a brave smile of her own. "I'm glad you noticed."

We continued finishing up our meals, moving on from the topic and instead talking about our plans for the day and what we wanted to do that night. I could have continued pressing the subject, but figured there was no rush. I had all day to spend with her, not to mention plenty of time after that.

We remained sitting at the table for a while after finishing up our meals, catching up on how our first week of classes went. It wasn't until past noon before we finally got up to leave the dining hall. From there, we proceeded with our lazy Saturday. First we went grocery shopping, then we hung out by the campus pond where we simply sat on a bench and reminisced about the times when we'd gone fishing with my grandparents as kids, before finally heading back to her dorm to chill out and watch a few movies.

It was a pretty great day, but I couldn't help shaking the feeling that it kind of felt like a date, which was weird because we've done things of this nature plenty of times before, almost every weekend, actually. And yet, today just felt different. Maybe it was the fact she was dressed up a bit more, or how I brought up her looks earlier, or even just the simple fact that I was starting to really become aware of her feelings now, but *something* felt different about all of it this time around.

Regardless, I was happy, happier than I'd been in a very long time. Whether that was from my time with Dawn yesterday, or my day with Tara today (maybe even both), I wasn't yet sure.

We were watching our final movie of the night in her room, when things became very real and very clear, though. Tara and I both had gradually shifted closer to one another as the night went on, and we were now basically laying together on her couch, her head resting upon my shoulder. It was all I really needed to confirm that my feelings about today being different weren't just in my head, and I began to mentally wrestle with my own thoughts.

If I were to make a move, everything would change. Going back to just being friends after taking things to the next level is never really an option that bodes well. But a part of me couldn't help myself from wanting this. She looked so good these days. My insides began to stir with some nerves as the realization set in, my thoughts about to become actions. Fantasy was now possibly becoming reality, for better or worse.

There was no point in fighting it. I wanted her, and I was pretty sure that she wanted me.

No better time than now to take the jump.

As it would turn out, there would have to be a better time. After glancing down at Tara, who was still resting on my shoulder, I noticed she was doing more than just resting— she was out cold. For how long, I'm not sure, but I got the feeling that this entire time I was struggling with my internal thoughts, she was dreaming away. I couldn't help but smile, she just looked so at peace, snoozing away on me like that.

I decided to sit in silence throughout the remainder of the movie, not wanting to wake her, and it wasn't until it ended, about an hour and a very sore shoulder later, that I decided to carry her off to her bedroom. She must've been exhausted from our day together, because she didn't wake up even a little from the couch to her bed. I gently placed her on the mattress, turned on her bedroom TV (she always preferred sleeping with it on), and took my leave for the night.

As I left her dorm building, embracing the very brisk night air with only a light jacket on as an extra layer, I couldn't help feeling kind of torn with how the night ended. I was bummed, but also kind of relieved. This would give me a bit more time to think things over. At the same time, though, I couldn't wait forever. With the way she looked today, it wouldn't be long before a whole flock of dudes would be gravitating toward her. If I was going to make a move, it needed to be soon.

It was shortly after this thought occurred that I was abruptly brought back to reality. Something had caught my attention to my far right, deep within the thick tree line just off the sidewalk. And I suddenly was reminded that I was walking entirely alone out here. It was around 2:00 am by now, the only light coming from the bright, nearly full moon way up in the sky. The only people out right now were likely in town at some house parties, certainly not on campus. And yet, my thoughts weren't fixated on them, or on *people* at all.

No, I could have sworn that whatever I saw in my peripherals, for only just a second, didn't belong to a human. It was a pair of big, bright yellow eyes.

Goosebumps arose along my entire body, but not from the cold. The hair on the back of my neck stood up as I continued gazing into the deep, dark abyss through the thick trees. I stood there, paralyzed for a few minutes. But nothing presented itself except darkness.

Could I just be seeing things?

I decided it was probably in my best interest to move along, so I continued my walk back, albeit a little swifter than before, and I made it about halfway back to my dorm, to the campus quad, before seeing anyone else. Unfortunately, *anyone else* ended up being three guys who looked like they were up to no good. All of them were wearing hoodies and standing by the small statue at the center of the quad, where all the pathways intersected with one another.

"Hey, man, what's the rush?" one of the hooded punks said as I walked by them, trying to mind my own business. But, as I knew by now in my life, when conflict wants to come it'll come, whether you try to avoid it or not.

I continued walking away, but I heard their footsteps picking up, and it wasn't long before they had sped past me and cut me off. "Hey, I was talkin' to you," said one of the goons. "I said, what's the rush?"

"Yeah, he said 'what's the rush,'" a smaller hooded guy echoed his buddy.

"I heard what he said," I began, "but thanks for reconfirming it for me. What are you, his parrot?"

One of them snickered. But the first dude spoke out again. "We got a funny guy, here? Well, I bet the funny guy's got a fat wallet in those pants."

"There's something fat in there, but it's not the wallet." They were making it too easy. I had to.

They went silent for a moment, clearly not sure how to respond to that.

"Look, guys," I went on, "I don't think you're really cut out for this gig, but if you're in need of some extra cash, I hear the McDonald's in town is hiring."

That was all it took. The guy who seemed to be their leader stepped forward, and my adrenaline started to pump.

But before any punch was thrown, a distant noise from the other side of the quad stopped all four of us. It sounded like racing footsteps, but faster, heavier.

I turned to look, and my eyes widened.

Tearing through the yard of the quad, was what looked to be an extremely large, very black cat—almost like the shadow of a tiger.

Within seconds, it was already right in our faces, lunging at us and breaking the skirmish apart. I fell back to the ground, and the other three stumbled along and took off in the opposite direction. One of them almost tripped over his own two feet, while another was desperately trying to pull up his oversized pants while trotting away.

I would have laughed if it weren't for the predicament that I was now in. The large cat let out a high-pitched, ear-splitting roar before slowly turning to face me. I was completely helpless as I sat on the cool, damp yard.

I still could not believe my eyes. I wasn't sure whether to be amazed or terrified. Now that the cat was closer, I noticed that it wasn't a tiger, but instead a rather large, black panther. Its bright yellow eyes seemed to look through me, and then it hit me. This was what I saw in the woods just moments ago.

It slowly prowled closer to me, baring its four large fangs. "Nice kitty," was all I could think to say. I tried my best to remain calm, knowing that panicking would do nothing for me at this point. If this thing wanted to take me down, there wasn't much I could do to stop it.

I hesitantly stuck a trembling hand out. Then, to my great surprise, the cat seemed to respond to my gesture, its expression changing from fierce and hungry, to more innocent and welcoming. It then lowered its head before me, gently purring.

The sudden shift of the cat's attitude had me completely perplexed. It was as if it was familiar and comfortable with my presence.

My heart rate finally leveling out again, I decided to take a chance on what I hoped was an invitation to pet it, and as I did, the panther purred even louder. It was almost humorous. I could have sworn it was smiling at me with those bright yellow eyes.

"You're not so bad, are you?" I whispered. "What the?"

As if I didn't think the night could get any weirder, what happened next made my head spin. The cat first backed up a few feet, then began to morph into something entirely else. The fur receded as it began to stand on its hind legs, the two front ones becoming smaller and much thinner. It craned its neck a few times like it was sore and needed a good stretch. The panther was growling as it morphed, but the growls began to sound more familiar, more human-like, and suddenly it sounded like a woman groaning.

When this unbelievable transformation ended, I was staring at a girl wearing nothing but a pair of tight black spandex shorts and a thin black sports bra. But it wasn't just any girl.

"Dawn!?" I blurted out.

She let out a moan of relief and stretched her arms out above her head. "Ugh, I still can't seem to shift back smoothly enough," she said, way too casually, given what had just occurred.

I stood frozen in place, still sitting on the damp grass, no doubt looking completely dumbfounded.

"You good?" she asked. "I mean, you seemed like you had everything under control with those goofs, but they were starting to kinda piss me off. Can't stand Lackers."

"What? I don't, what?!" was all I could get out.

"Need a hand?" she reached out.

"No, no, I think it's probably best that I stay down here for a minute," I admitted, my head still spinning over what couldn't possibly be real.

But Dawn laughed. "I promise I won't bite. Well, unless you're into that kinda thing."

"Dawn, what the hell just happened?" I finally found my words and my head, slowly making my way up to my feet.

"I'll explain everything to you in a bit," she began, crossing her arms and rubbing her shoulders, "as soon as we're somewhere a little less brisk." Her teeth were chattering.

"Here," I took my jacket off and wrapped her in it, "We can head back to my place. That should keep you at least a little warmer on the way over."

"Thanks," she softly said.

"If you don't mind me asking," I broke the silence after walking for a few minutes, "what's up with that getup, anyway? Not that it doesn't look great," I couldn't help myself from eyeing her up and down, "but it's sort of chilly out tonight."

"Yeah, I probably should've just stayed in my primal form. At least I'd have the fur coat," she muttered.

"Right," I agreed, trying to sound like that was a perfectly normal thing for someone to say.

"But these clothes are designed in a way to stretch without ripping when I shift back and forth. They stretch so thin when I'm in my primal form that they become completely concealed by my coat, but also fit right back in place when I return to my base form."

I didn't know what to say to that. To be honest, most of my head was still spinning. This kind of stuff doesn't happen, at least not in real life. And yet, here she was just talking about it like we were conversing about final exams over coffee or something.

"Look, I can't even imagine what must be going through your head right now," she said.

I scoffed in a playful sort of way.

"This wasn't how I intended for you to find out. Not at all."

"I saw you in the woods earlier. That was you, wasn't it? You're not like stalking me or something, right?"

Dawn chuckled. "Stalking, nice choice of words, there." She playfully leaned into me. "But no, I wasn't *stalking* you. The truth is, there's something I need to tell you. But I knew you were with Tara today, so I didn't want to interrupt your guys' date." She winked at me.

I gave her a kind of sheepish look.

"So, I just figured I'd wait it out 'til you left her dorm before I gave you the news. I was beginning to think I'd have to set up camp for the night! Must have been a pretty fun night?" She grinned.

"Nothing happened, actually."

"Hey, none of my business. But anyway, then I saw those dumb Lackers up there while you were heading out, so I figured it couldn't hurt for me to be in my primal form, just in case."

"You said that word before, 'Lackers,' is that some new lingo going around or something?" I asked. "Also, what news?"

"Oh, Lackers is just slang for people who don't have any mytosomes."

I stopped in my tracks, staring at her. It took her a bit before she realized I was no longer walking.

"I promise," she began, skipping back to me. "I'll tell you everything when we get back to your place. Same goes for the news, too. And it's great news!" She smiled at me. I could just barely make out her eyes in the dark night, which were now back to that deep brown, almost black color instead of the bright yellow ones I saw earlier in the woods.

I figured I'd take her word, so I put off my many remaining questions for the time being. It was about another ten minutes or so before we made it back to my dorm building. Once inside the first set of entrance doors, I scanned my badge to get through to the rest of the building. From there, we continued walking down the empty hallway until finally making it to my dorm room at the very end.

As soon as we entered, Dawn plopped herself on my bed. "Nice place!"

"It's basically just a bed," I laughed.

"Exactly." She had that ornery grin on her face. As tempting as it was to play along, I needed answers.

"Dawn . . ." I gave her an impatient look.

"I know, I know," she began, rolling on her stomach and resting her head upon both her hands, "the question is, what would you like to know?"

I scoffed. "What would I like to know? Well, where do I even start? I just came face to face with a panther that ended up transforming into a girl, a girl who I figured the biggest thing I had to worry about was when to ask her out!"

"Awe," she muttered, smiling.

I smiled back. "Well, yeah." I shook my head, reminding myself to stay on track. "That's a conversation for another time. Dawn, please just tell me what the heck is going on before I lose whatever's left of my mind?"

"Of course." She sat up on the bed. "Okay, well, what if I were to tell you that everything you think you know about the world, no, the universe, even, was just the tip of a very large iceberg?"

"Well, earlier today I'd maybe question it, but not so much after what I just saw."

"Good, at least you're open-minded, this will be easier that way." She stood up from the bed and began pacing back and forth. It was clear she was trying to be careful with how she delivered her next sentence.

"So, yesterday, at the Magic Gateway, there's a reason I was there. I'm an employee there technically, but not in the way you might think."

"Okay?"

"You see, I'm doing my internship right now for my school."

"*Your* school? But I figured you went here."

"Not quite," she said. "Actually, not even close. I attend a school very far away from here, but also not far away at all, in a way. I know, I know, but just listen, it's called Magic Rune Academy, and it doesn't reside in this dimension. Instead, it's located in what's called the Rune Realm."

She paused to make sure I was still with her, but to be honest, I was struggling to keep a straight face. I knew it was too good to be true: finding a cute girl who was also a bit nerdy and really cool at the same time. It was becoming clear that she was off her rocker.

But then again, I witnessed something unbelievable with my own eyes just moments ago. Maybe *I* was off my rocker.

"Okay, so where is this *Rune Realm*?" I asked. I figured I might as well play along for now.

"Like I said, it's in another realm entirely. In this realm, you have your own universe with its own stars and planets and all that, but the Rune Realm exists in a dimension of its own. Think of it as an entirely different universe, but we're able to commute to it from what are called rune points."

"So, the Magic Gateway is an actual gateway." I put two and two together.

"You catch on fast!" Dawn said excitedly. "It is, well, a rune point is in the back of the store, at least. That's how I'm able to commute from one realm to the next so quickly. Rune points are placed sporadically across Earth. But it doesn't stop there, we have them on other planets, too."

"Other planets? So, there are aliens who can also access this world?"

Dawn giggled. "Aliens, sure, if you want to call them that. We have a few different races that inhabit the Realm: humans, of course, but also orcs and elves. They live there all thanks to the rune points placed on their own planets."

"Okay, but that still doesn't exactly explain how you can turn into a big ass cat." I added carefully, trying to make sure it didn't seem like I was coming off rude.

"Oh, but it does," she said, shuffling closer to me. "How to put this," she pursed her lips, tapping a finger to her cheek, "well, what's often referred to here as magic, that's what's known as rune in our world. The entire realm is made up of it. It's like energy, or air. You can't see it, but it's there."

"And people who have mytosomes in their blood can manip-ulate and use rune to do all sorts of things you'd never even imagine were possible. The mytosomes reside within the cells of certain individuals, individuals like me, don't worry, they're perfectly harmless, though," she quickly added after taking note of my expression.

"Ah, the mytosomes," I said after a brief pause, "something those Lackers didn't have?"

"Yeah, and that's where you come in, Nate, because you have them, too, an enormous amount of them, actually. That's why I started to shift into my hybrid form yesterday without even realizing it, right before you left. It was when you touched my hand. To make me shift like that, just from your touch, that's something only someone with an enormous amount of mytosomes could prompt."

I thought back to how I left things with her yesterday. So those ears, they *did* move on their own! They weren't a prop after all?

"And guess what," Dawn continued, "It doesn't stop there. Your girlfriend, Tara, also has them!"

I remained standing in silence, ignoring the "girlfriend" comment, before slowly making my way over to sit down on my bed.

"That's part one of the good news, you know." She sat down next to me. "Kinda thought you'd be a bit more excited about that."

"Look," I began, trying not to sound too harsh, "I really appreciate seeing you again. And you're great, really. I mean, you're cool, pretty, obviously creative, but . . .'

Dawn rolled her eyes. "You still don't believe me?" she nonchalantly asked with an unwavering smile. "And I thought you were open-minded. I mean, I know I'm not the best at explaining stuff but still."

"No, it's just I think I would have known by now if I had these mytorones, or whatever they are called, in my blood. I'm sure I would have accidentally transformed by now or they would have shown up in a routine blood test or something."

The truth is, I just couldn't wrap my head around the idea of me being special in any sort of way. My entire life, I was average at best with anything I did. So, even though I really wanted to be excited over Dawn claiming that I had an unusually high number of these, whatever they were, it unfortunately didn't seem to line up with my history.

Dawn laughed. "They don't work like that, Nate. First, not everyone is a shifter like me, some people are rune-knights, or sorcerers. But also, you wouldn't know you have the myto-somes until you interact with rune, which believe it or not, has happened to you before, you just haven't realized it yet."

"What do you mean by that?"

"Kingdom Monsters," she casually said.

"The card game?"

"Yep! How long has the game been around?" she knowingly asked.

"I don't know." I pondered the question. "Well, my whole life, now that I think of it."

"Exactly. That game was created ages ago. In the Rune Realm. Some of the monsters on the cards are actually based on creatures that live in the Realm, and the cards themselves are made of material from there, so they have small amounts of rune in them as well. And I'm guessing from our duel yesterday that you can actually sense rune."

I was giving her another weird look.

"Think about it—you *randomly* pulled that card against me, and exactly when you needed it, too. I'll take a wild guess and say that's not the first time that happened."

She had me curious now. It was true, but I always boiled it down to dumb luck. Could this all actually be real?

"That's what I thought," she said.

I looked up to see her smiling even brighter at me, and I couldn't help but crack a small grin back.

"Now," she went on, "I already have an idea of what class you belong to from that information alone. I won't spoil anything just yet, but you're probably not a shifter."

"You said you're doing an internship," I said after a few more moments of silence, now becoming genuinely interested in this.

"Yeah, I'm doing my internship with what's called the Guard. It's an organization that helps find and recruit outsiders to our world."

"It's all making sense now," I said. "So, does the owner of the Magic Gateway know you're a double agent?" I joked.

"The owner of the Magic Gateway lives in the Rune Realm, you goof," chuckled Dawn. "He holds a prominent position with the Guard. You see, one advantage of being a shifter, particularly a shifter who can shift into an animal with heightened senses, is being able to sniff out mytosomes in people. So, I figured why not do something I'm already naturally good at, right? I was starting to think I'd never find *anyone*, though. It was getting boring as hell. But then, go figure, I found two runics at once!"

"And just so we're clear, runics are . . . ?"

"People who can manipulate rune due to the mytosomes in

their cells. People like you and Tara. Or *magic people*, as the Lackers would say." She rolled her eyes.

I thought back to yesterday. "You were sort of standoffish with me at first," I said, putting something together. "You thought I was a Lackey or whatever you call them?"

"A Lacker, yes."

"And then you bent down close to me," I continued, "I knew I heard you sniff me!" I was smiling. Things were actually starting to fall in line with what she was saying.

"I did," she admitted, looking a little embarrassed. "I'm sorry, Nate. I just . . ."

"You clearly don't like normal, I mean, Lackers," I slowly said to myself, piecing another thing together. "You assumed I was just another Lacker at first, and *that's* why you were brushing me off when I first met you!"

An awkward silence filled the room. "Well, the bottom line, and the main reason I'm here, is to give you this," she said, reaching into the back of her tight spandex shorts and pulling out two very crinkled envelopes. I couldn't help but laugh.

"I've arranged everything with the dean of Magic Rune Academy," Dawn began, her tone unusually formal, it was kind of cute. "And I, uh, hereby am very pleased to announce that both you and Tara are officially invited to attend Magic Rune Academy for the fall semester this year!"

"Nice delivery," I said, marveling at the envelopes she had handed me. Could this all really be happening? This sense of yearning I had for something else, something different, could it have been for a whole new world? And were these envelopes my ticket, my answer? Or was there a gas leak in my place, and was I just tripping balls? I still wasn't really sure, to be honest.

"Thanks," Dawn replied proudly. "I was working on it earlier while waiting for you to finish your *love-making* with Tara."

"I wasn't—"

"Come by the Magic Gateway tomorrow, okay?" She stood up and started making her way over to the door. "I can't wait to show you both the Realm. You two will fit in perfectly!"

I was kind of sad to see her leaving, even though it was almost half-past three.

"Uh, you don't have to go. I mean, are you heading back into town to go back to your world? It's late, and that's a far . . ." I thought about it for a second. If she wanted to, she could probably transform and make it there in just minutes, not to mention nobody will fuck with a big ass panther storming through the streets.

"I think I could handle my own, but I appreciate it."

"Hey, real quick," I blurted out, a thought coming to me.

Dawn paused, one hand on the doorknob, and then turned to face me.

"You mentioned a hybrid form earlier. So, you have another form?"

"Oh! Yeah, of course."

And then, almost instantly, those same furry black ears sprung out from underneath her hair. But that wasn't all: Her eyes changed from black to bright yellow, her pupils elongated to thin black slits, and then finally, a long, thin, furry black tail wiggled out from her spandex shorts.

"This material," she tugged on her shorts, "is flexible enough to where my tail can easily slip through when I shift. The clothing is designed specifically for shifters. Gotta love it."

She gazed at me with those cat-like eyes, smiling, and I couldn't help thinking how cute she looked. Aside from those few features that changed, everything else about her was the same as when she was in her human form.

"Well, this is quite a look for you," I breathed.

Almost instantly, she shifted back. "It's not all for show," she purred, opened the door, and was gone.

Just like that, I was left sitting on my bed alone with my thoughts, still clinging to the crumpled-up envelopes, the only proof left that confirmed I wasn't imagining it all.

Chapter Three

"I JUST DON'T UNDERSTAND why you have to bring *me* along on your precious little date with little Miss Tease-a-lot!" Tara repeated herself for about the third time.

I had been texting Dawn earlier that morning and we arranged a time for us to stop by the Magic Gateway. So now Tara and I were heading back down East Street, which was again abandoned, but this time due to it being a Sunday morning (most of the students were probably still nursing their hangovers), and not because of the weather. It was looking like it would be a sunny day, not a cloud in the sky.

The temperature was crisp yet again, warranting another light hoodie for me. Tara decided to wear a tight red flannel top and her typical black yoga pants. She had some messy bedhead this morning, but that didn't make her look any less attractive.

"Tara, really, it's not a date," I replied, trying not to sound too exasperated over repeating myself again. "She asked both of us to come here today. I even have the two letters as proof." I held them up once more.

"Let me see those again." She snagged them both from my

hand and began skimming through the fancy purple print for the third or fourth time today.

"I know it sounds insane," I muttered.

"Insane is putting it lightly! I can't believe this girl would go through the trouble of making these. It's kind of sad, in a way."

"Look," I began, coming to a halt on the sidewalk, "I don't think that's what's going on here."

"Nate—"

"No, seriously. No matter what happens here this morning, I just need you to stay calm and don't freak out."

Tara's face was a mixture of startled and skeptical. "Okay, now *you're* starting to freak me out. You can't really believe this, right? This letter? The whole thing about how we have cells or whatever that make us able to do magic? When you were telling me earlier, I thought you were joking! She's obviously out of her mind to go through all the trouble. I mean, I figured you were just overlooking it all because you really wanted to get some," she muttered.

"Tara, I saw it with my own eyes. The girl was a freaking panther and then changed back to herself right in front of me!"

"I thought you were joking about that, too! Nate, this isn't okay. I've known you my whole life and this is just not you!"

"Tara—"

"No, listen! If you want to have a fling or whatever with this girl, then fine, I won't stop you, but please don't let her warp your mind into whatever it is *she's* into . . ."

She had a genuine look of concern on her face, so I figured it would be best to just drop it for now. All I had to do was get her to the shop, and then hopefully, her seeing it with her own eyes would help things.

"Okay, yeah. I'm sorry," I said. "Let's just go. I told her we'd come, so we shouldn't leave her hanging."

Tara sighed. "All right, fine. Maybe she'll give me a deal on that Drakthor card if I play along."

As we entered the Magic Gateway, I could see Dawn was organizing some shirts in the middle of the shop. She was wearing what looked to be another pair of her shifter clothes, a sports bra and spandex shorts, tight and revealing as they were last night, but this time navy-blue. It was sort of hilarious seeing her wear something like this in the middle of the store during the day. She clearly couldn't care less about what others thought, which made her even more attractive.

The bell rang out from behind us, which grabbed her attention. She looked up, beaming at the two of us. "You made it!" She hastily hung the remaining shirts on the rack before running up to give us both a hug. Tara's eyes widened, and she mouthed "What the fuck" as Dawn hugged her.

I waved a hand in a way that told her to just go with it.

"I'm so happy you guys showed up. Wasn't sure if I scared you away or not last night, Nate," said Dawn, and she gave me one of her winks.

I had a sheepish expression on my face, being sure not to make eye-contact with Tara. "Nah, I'm bulletproof," I replied.

"I bet you are." Dawn skipped over to the shop entrance and locked the door, then she gestured for us to follow her over to the front counter.

"Okay, what the fuck was that all about?" Tara whispered.

"What?" I muttered back.

"The hug? Her choice of clothing? Or should I say, lack thereof?"

"Since when do you care how people are dressed?"

"I don't. I just . . ."

"I'm glad you brought your letters of acceptance," Dawn began, pondering over the bookcases behind the counter. "I take it you told her everything, then?"

"Yeah, basically." I glanced at Tara, who was clearly already amused, looking like she was trying to keep a straight face. "But I think she'll need some more convincing."

Tara scoffed.

"Ah, not a believer? I have to say, I'm a little surprised," Dawn replied, still with her back to us as she began to reorganize some books on the shelves.

"I wouldn't say I'm not a believer," Tara retorted. "Just a little skeptical of magical kingdoms and people turning into animals and stuff."

"I totally get it, no worries," said Dawn casually, now kneeling down while still moving some books around on the lowest section of the shelves. "Also, I'll give you guys the code for the specific book placement on these shelves for future reference. And a key to the shop, too. That way you can come and go as you please." She stood up and took a few steps back, still considering the shelves intently. "That should do."

I only had about a split second to be confused, because almost immediately after she said that, the shelves started to tremble. Then, they both began to slowly slide open, revealing what looked like the opening to two long, dark tunnels. They appeared to somehow be carved into the back of the building.

"We can enter and exit through either one. They both lead to the same room," said Dawn, and she started down the tunnel on the left side.

I looked down at Tara, who gazed back at me with a hesitant expression. "This doesn't mean anything," she said, quickly straightening her face. "It's a magic store. I shouldn't be surprised."

I tried not to grin at her resistance, and then followed Dawn through the tunnel on the left. Tara was practically hugging me from behind as we entered. Oddly enough, the tight tunnel seemed to go on for a while, even though the store didn't look that big from the outside; I couldn't see the ending of the pathway, only darkness.

The walls were stone, and the floor cement, which was entirely different from the front of the store. It was like we suddenly went back in time to the Middle Ages and were walking through a dark dungeon, the only light coming from the occasional torch hanging on the dirty stone walls.

We continued walking for maybe twenty or thirty seconds before the floor started sloping downward, then finally came to the top of a spiral staircase. We walked down the steps, and I couldn't believe what was presented before me once the lower level came into view.

We were entering from the left side of what looked to be a huge cavern. In the center of the cavern floor was a bright pool of water, as clear and pristine as water could ever look. It seemed to be emanating a silvery glow, illuminating the entire cavern. A small, circular concrete platform was in the very middle of the pool, with a cement pathway extending from it. And placed in the center of the platform was what appeared to be a stone arch.

Dawn was already down there, leaning up against the stone arch, waiting patiently for us.

"What, you get lost on the way here or something?!" her voice echoed up to us. "There's only one way to go, you know!"

"Just wasn't expecting to be entering the Batcave today!" I shouted back, carefully treading down the remaining steps.

Once we reached the bottom of the slippery stairs, we headed over to the large pool of water. Tara and I carefully tip-toed along the cement path that led to Dawn and the stone arch.

"All magic shops have these, I'm sure of it," Tara said quietly behind me.

"So, what do you think?" asked Dawn when we finally reached her.

"This is . . ." I began, looking around and taking in my surroundings. Large stalactites were hanging down from way above, and six huge stone pillars with interesting carvings connected the floor to the high ceiling. They were strategically placed throughout the open room, most likely for structural support.

"What is all this?" Tara sputtered from behind me. "Extra storage space for inventory or something?"

"Still not convinced?" chuckled Dawn. "Those acceptance letters in your hand aren't just for show. Everything I've told Nate so far has been the honest truth."

Tara looked up at me for reassurance. I gave her a smile.

"You two are what are called runics. You're a part of a very unique society of people who can bend and manipulate what we call rune, the energy within our world."

"I just, there's just . . . this can't be!" Tara stammered.

"Well, if you still need convincing." Dawn proceeded to shift into her hybrid form. Once more, her black cat ears sprung up from beneath her dark hair, her eyes turned yellow with the black slits, and her tail squeezed out from her spandex shorts.

"What the?!" I heard Tara's voice ring out.

"They're real, trust me," Dawn calmly said, bowing her head and moving her cat ears without touching them. "Feel free to pet them, if you'd like."

"Um, I think I'm good, thanks!" Tara's voice cracked. "What is she?" she whispered to me.

"I'm a shifter!" Dawn enthusiastically replied, unbothered by the question. "These ears aren't just for show, either; I can hear pretty well."

"S-sorry," Tara softly said.

"No worries! But yeah, I can shift into a panther as my primal form. There are all kinds of different shifters in the Rune Realm, with different forms."

"Right," said Tara.

"You may just be one yourself," Dawn added, indicating Tara, "although it's hard to tell with you. I actually didn't even catch your mytosome scent until much later. Not like this one," she nodded at me, "whose mytosome scent nearly knocked me out at first!"

"Thanks, I shower pretty regularly," Tara said, proudly stroking her hair.

I tried not to laugh. "Do mytosomes stink or something?" I mumbled to Dawn.

"Nah, you're good. Don't worry," she whispered back with a reassuring smile.

"So," Dawn continued, spreading her arms out toward the stone arch in the middle of the platform, "what do you think? I bet you've never seen a rune point before, have you?"

I gazed at the large arch. It had similar unique carvings on it as the stone pillars placed throughout the cavernous room. And now that I was closer, I noticed that the gap in the arch appeared to have some sort of clear layer over it. It looked as if the air was rippling inside it, making the surroundings on the opposite side of the gap appear distorted and wavy. But whether this layer was liquid, solid, or even gas, I couldn't quite tell.

"I promise, it doesn't bite," Dawn said, trying to hold back a laugh, likely because of the nervous looks on mine and Tara's faces.

I carefully walked closer and closer to the arch until I was only a few feet from it, and as I slowly reached an arm out, I could hear a subtle whooshing sound, as if it were whispering to me.

A soft hand gently caressed the back of my shoulder. "Are you ready to take your first steps into the Rune Realm?" Dawn whispered into my ear in a seductive sort of way, goosebumps arose on the back of my neck.

"Nate, I'm not so sure," Tara said, failing to hide the fear in her voice.

I turned to her. "You trust me?"

"Yes, but—" Her nervous eyes quickly darted to Dawn, who was still in her hybrid form.

"It'll be okay." I gave her a confident smile, but to be honest, I was a little nervous myself. I mean, all things considered, I really didn't know Dawn that well. And yet, something just seemed strangely natural about all of this. I couldn't quite explain it, but it was like this portal was somehow familiar, like a long-lost friend, even. "I'll go in first," I continued, "then you follow me shortly after. Sound good?"

Tara gave me a quick nod, her knuckles white, as she nibbled on her fingernails (it was always a nervous habit of hers).

"I'll bring up the rear," Dawn confidently added. "Whenever you're ready, Nate, just step through. Keep walking until, well, you'll know when to stop."

I nodded and turned to face the stone arch, then let out a deep breath and walked through.

It was like plunging myself into a refreshingly cool pool, but at the same time I knew I remained dry. As soon as I entered, my view of the other side of the arch had warped and blurred, even fading in color until all I could see was a bright silver light, which had a subtle wave to it that made my surroundings feel like they were in motion.

The whooshing sound that seemed to be whispering before was now all I could hear, almost engulfing me. But I continued to tread forward, trying my best to ignore the swaying surroundings for the sake of not falling over. Until suddenly, my legs almost gave out as I abruptly emerged into a quiet back room. The walls were a bright purple, and there were cardboard boxes upon more cardboard boxes stacked up to the ceiling. It looked as if I was in a storage room.

I turned to see the same stone arch directly behind me, but to my surprise, there were two others just like it to the left and right. They appeared to have slightly different carvings on them, though. Suddenly, the arch in the center made a warping noise before Tara quickly and clumsily stumbled out from it. I managed to catch her just in time.

"Hi. That was a trip," she whispered, breathing heavily.

"But we made it." I smiled, still holding her close.

Another warping sound, and then Dawn smoothly emerged from the arch. "I can come back in a bit, if I'm interrupting something?" she said with a grin.

Tara and I smiled sheepishly, but then broke apart.

"Where are we?" asked Tara.

"Glendor's Cards," Dawn said, but we remained silent. "Oh, duh, I keep forgetting you guys are brand new. I'm so terrible at this. Glendor's sells Kingdom Monster cards. It also houses rune points for our world and the others, as you can see." She pointed to the three stone arches behind us. "Think of it as the counterpoint to the Magic Gateway. Now come on, I can't wait to see the looks on your faces!"

We exited the back storage room through another door, emerging out into the front section of the card shop.

"Ah, finally found some recruits, Dawn?"

Tara jumped back and nearly fell over as we turned to see an older gentleman standing behind the counter, smiling at us. He was stocky and slightly on the shorter side, but with arms bigger than any man I've ever seen. It looked as if his shirt was about to rip open. His hair was white and he had a long white beard, yet I knew that none of those features were what made Tara leap back. But instead, it was the fact that this *man* had two tusks protruding upward from the bottom of his mouth, orange eyes, and finally, bright green skin.

"You know it, Glendor!" said Dawn, smiling proudly at us. "Guys, this is my boss, Glendor!"

"Very good, very good," Glendor muttered with an unnaturally low and hoarse voice. "Nice to meet you folks. I'm head of the Guard, but I also run the Magic Gateway, as well as this old card shop here. Do you play much Kingdom Monsters?" He offered me a very large handshake.

I stepped forward to firmly shake his hand, which practically disappeared in Glendor's grasp; his hand must have been about three times the size of mine, and it's not like I'm a real small guy or anything.

"Nice to meet you. Yeah, we play now and then," I began, "so I'm sure you'll be seeing us around. My name's Nate Gannon. This is my friend, Tara." I turned to address Tara, who was still pinned to the wall, looking a bit pale.

"N-nice to meet you, sir," she said shakily.

Dawn gently grabbed hold of Tara and nudged her along. "Well, lots to do today, Glendor. But we'll be back, I'm sure. I know this one's eyes lit up when I pulled out a Drakthor right in front of her."

Glendor let out a hearty laugh. "Well, I only got a few of him left in stock, but I'll be sure to try to save one for her if she's interested!"

Based on Tara's reaction after meeting Glendor, I became concerned that she would be passing out at any moment once leaving his store because it only got weirder from there. We emerged onto a red brick street in the middle of a village, but it was a village like I've never witnessed before, besides in movies, maybe.

The streets were lined with shops, breweries, restaurants, and plenty more from the looks of it. But that wasn't the strange part. What was strange was what the shops were selling. I could have sworn that long broadswords were on display in the windows of a store a little way down the street, and the clothing worn on some mannequins across the street from us looked like something worn at renaissance fairs.

Unlike East Street, which was dead earlier this morning, this street was booming with residents, very peculiar-looking residents, some human, some definitely not human, who all seemed to be enjoying themselves to the fullest. A gang of large green men strolled past us, all holding big mugs. An unusually tall woman with pale blue skin and long pointy ears was chatting it up with another lady who looked to be human, both carrying large shopping bags seemingly stuffed with a bunch of new clothes. And a trio of three men outside a music shop, one green and stocky, one with dark-red skin and pointy ears, and another with blue skin, all wearing funny-looking caps and matching outfits, were playing a tune with their individual harps that sounded like a melody straight from the medieval times.

"Welcome to Hearthvale," Dawn said. "Think of it as the college town for Magic Rune Academy. Shall we?"

I happened to glance at Tara, who was in complete awe at the moment.

As we followed Dawn along the brick road, I couldn't help noticing how the air smelled of homemade bread, and just how clear and blue the sky was, shimmering even brighter than I've ever seen it do before. The longer I gazed at it, the more I could have sworn it was glistening, even. There was a combination of different looking clouds scattered throughout the bright blue canvas, from white streamlines to fluffy pillows, somehow all of them looking whiter and cleaner than any cloud I'd seen in my life.

To my left, way off in the distance, enormous greenish-blue mountains towered over the village.

As we continued venturing down the bustling street, I caught glimpses of what looked to be either an exceptionally large lake, or maybe even the ocean (if the Rune Realm had oceans) down the thin alleyways between the many apartments and shops to my right. It appeared to be a bright teal color, and clearer than any body of water I've ever known. The beach leading to it was a bright white, as white as the clouds above us. I had just arrived, but already everything just seemed brighter and happier in this world.

"You know, you two are holding up pretty well, actually!" Dawn shouted out from ahead. "It's not entirely uncommon where you'll find noobies passed out along the streets of Hearthvale. Just a lot to take in at once, you know?"

"You don't say?!" Tara replied.

Dawn chuckled as we turned a bend, and from here I could see a long canal which looked to run through the entire center of the village, with more shops and restaurants placed along it. "You guys hungry at all? Let's make a quick pit stop at the Bronze Dragon for a bite and some drinks? It's been a minute since I had a good runic ale."

We ended up sitting in an outside patio section, right off the canal. Colorful birds flew by as we sat waiting to be served, the hanging planters above us most likely attracting them.

"So, what do you think so far?" Dawn asked us both from across the table.

"I still think I'm dreaming," I said.

"I don't think my dreams could even make this kind of thing up," Tara added.

Dawn smiled. "You've only seen the tip of the iceberg. This realm is beautiful through and through. It puts ours to shame, really. Give it some time, and you won't ever wanna go back. Which reminds me—if you don't mind me asking— what are your living situations like back there? If you accept your invitation to Magic Rune Academy, then you'll be spending a lot of time here."

Tara and I exchanged uncomfortable looks, and I knew why.

"My, uh, I lived with my grandparents my whole life. They're both gone. I lost my grandfather before the start of freshman year last year."

Dawn's face went flat. "Oh, I'm sorry to hear that, Nate."

"It's okay, really." I quickly said. "He was old and sick for a little while before he passed, so it was all for the best. He's not suffering anymore. But to your point, I suppose I don't have much incentive to leave here anytime too soon, especially if it's like this!"

Dawn's eyes seemed to glimmer after hearing that. "What about you, Tara?"

"My parents wouldn't mind. I mean, I suppose I don't even have to tell them. I barely visit home as it is."

"Well, you could let them know if it ever comes to it. Immediate family members of runics are allowed to know. But they just have to sign a contract of secrecy that literally does not allow them to spill the beans. If they tried, they'd go mute."

Tara had a skeptical look on her face. "I think I'll just keep this to myself for now," she drawled. "Thanks, though."

At that point, our server came over to take our orders. I almost fell over when I saw her: She was maybe the cutest girl I've ever seen. She appeared to be human, but must have been a shifter in her hybrid form, which looked to be some sort of fox, maybe. She had pink hair that was fashioned in a long braid, and adorable, fluffy pink ears that sprouted from the top of her head. Her eyes were a bright green.

She was incredibly short, but not petite by any means; she had nice, thick curves and her breasts were practically popping out from the red and white blouse she was wearing. Her tails (she had two of them) were fluffy and pink, poking out the back of a short skirt.

"Um, hi, hello, may I take your orders?" she asked in a soft and high voice.

"Are you guys good with just some apps and drinks?" Dawn asked.

As Tara agreed to Dawn's recommendation, I stole another quick glance at the girl, and noticed that she was carefully gazing back at me. But as my eyes met hers, she quickly looked away, blushing.

"Nate? You're up," said Dawn.

"Oh, right. Let's see, I think I'll do a . . ." I tried to meet Dawn's gaze before finally muttering, "What's the drinking age here?"

"It's sixteen, actually," replied Dawn. "Go for it!"

"Don't have to tell me twice!" I happily said. "I'll try a runic ale and then, let's do one of your wyrm pretzels—they're not actually made of dragon, right?" I quickly asked Dawn, unsure about pretty much anything at this point.

The fox girl let out a quiet giggle before catching herself and immediately covering her mouth. She blushed some more when I looked up at her with interest.

Dawn was chuckling, too. "It's just a soft pretzel, don't worry. And the beer cheese is to die for. Good choice!"

I handed my menu to the fox girl, noticing the name on her name tag. "Thanks, Sakura. I like that." I smiled at her.

She looked stunned, wide eyed and suddenly very stiff. She remained standing there for a good few seconds, and then suddenly darted off toward the kitchen. I felt kind of bad, and a little confused, too.

"Huh, I hope she got all our orders," said Dawn, a concerned look on her face as her yellow eyes followed after Sakura.

I turned to Tara, who was glaring at me for some reason.

"So," I said, trying to move past that awkward moment, "yesterday you mentioned there are orcs and elves in the Rune Realm, I take it that Glendor is an orc, then?" I tried to keep my voice down, as there were what looked to be orcs and elves sitting around us, and I wasn't entirely sure if I was being rude.

"You bet," Dawn replied. "Orcs are easy to spot by their, well, the green," she whispered.

"Not to mention they all look like they're on steroids," I added.

"Yeah, you don't want to get into a skirmish with an orc, especially if all you have are your fists to do your bidding. Now, elves can be a bit trickier to identify, but usually they have a pale blue or dark red skin tone. They're typically on the taller side, sometimes very tall, and have long pointy ears. Oh, and their hair can be all kinds of flashy colors, too, from bright green to light blue and purple, you name it."

"Good to know," I said.

"I just still can't believe this is real," Tara said. "And it's been here for ages? How did all of this even come to be?"

"Ah, we're getting into the deep stuff now." Dawn leaned forward. "Well, nobody can confirm for sure, but legend has it that the Realm was created from just one being, an ancient, all-powerful mother. A goddess, even, and that she still watches over the Realm to this day, but now as a great, big tree. But again, nobody knows for sure. Those are all just stories passed down from generations."

"Heavy stuff," I said.

"Sure is," Dawn agreed. "But it's said that the mytosomes originated from this all-knowing goddess—they were originally unique, tiny molecules in her own cells—and were then passed down from generation to generation. The same goes for the rune in this whole realm—the rune was originally a part of the goddess' soul or energy, or whatever you want to call it, and she continues to breathe life into this world today as a tree, by spreading her energy, or rune, into the Realm. Apparently, that's why people with the myto-somes can manipulate and bend rune for their own magical advantages—it's all connected to her."

"So," Tara slowly began, "this goddess, or whatever, she turned into a tree?"

"That's what they say! Even our calendar years here are based on it. It's currently 2953 AT."

"AT?" I asked.

"After Transformation." Dawn casually replied.

"Ah, on account of her transforming into a tree." I put two and two together, trying not to sound too skeptical of it all.

"Wow, you said it's all a story, though?" Tara asked.

Dawn shrugged her shoulders. "Nobody knows for sure, but that's the beauty of it, right?"

"Yeah, I suppose," said Tara, clearly pondering something. "But then, how come people like Nate and me have the mytosomes? As far as I know, we were both born on Earth."

"It's a more common occurrence than you'd think," Dawn said. "That's why the Guard was established."

"The Guard is where Dawn is doing her internship," I said to Tara, proud that I actually knew something for a change. "They basically recruit outsiders to the Rune Realm."

"Wow, look at you, remembering stuff." Dawn winked. I shrugged my shoulders. Tara scoffed. "But yeah, Nate hit the nail on the head, we recruit outsiders. You see, nobody is bound or forced to stay in the Rune Realm; people can head back to their home worlds as they please. And sometimes, they decide to stay there, eventually having kids of their own. When that happens, there's a chance for the myto-somes to get passed down to future generations."

"So, you're saying our parents were magic, too?" Tara asked.

"Possibly, but not necessarily; sometimes the gene skips a generation, so it could have been your grandparents or even great grandparents and beyond. The Realm has been around for ages, so it only takes one of your ancestors to have been a runic for the gene to get passed down to a future generation. And that's how outsiders come about. The only thing is, the outsiders would never know otherwise until they interacted with the rune, and usually the only way that happens is if they come to the Rune Realm, hence why the Guard is so important."

"So, someone can be a runic and go their whole life without even knowing?" asked Tara.

"Pretty much!" replied Dawn.

At that moment, Sakura came back with our beers and a big, dragon-shaped, soft pretzel with beer cheese; it looked amazing. Interestingly enough, the runic ales were a shade of light blue.

"Thank you." I raised my beer to Sakura, smiling. But as I did so, she let Dawn's beer slip out of her grip; it clanged on the table and doused Dawn a little, but otherwise was fine.

"Oh, no! I'm so sorry!" squeaked Sakura. "I'll get a rag."

"No, no, it's okay. Really!" Dawn reassured her. "It barely got me. I needed to cool down a bit, anyway." She smiled.

Sakura let out a nervous little laugh, her big green eyes shifting back at me for just a second. "Well, enjoy your meals!" She quickly ran off again.

"Stop doing that to the poor girl!" whispered Tara.

"What? Talking to her?!" I retorted.

Dawn appeared to be working something out in her head

before a grin appeared on her face. "Well, I guess let's dig in!" she finally said, changing the subject.

I took a piece of the pretzel and a big swig of my aqua-tinted beer. It was easily the best tasting beer I've ever had up to that point; it had a unique, refreshing flavor to it, with a very subtle hint of fruit at the end, which was surprisingly delicious.

"It's brewed with a specific wheat that grows here in the Realm." Dawn nodded at the beer.

"These bad boys can be dangerous. That's good beer!" I said.

Dawn's eyes trailed from my beer to Sakura, who I could hear was at the table behind us. "I have a hunch that you're gonna love it here, Nate." She grinned once more.

We left the Bronze Dragon with some food in our stomachs and a nice little head buzz, and from there headed toward the opposite side of the village, furthest from the shore. I could see a huge stable up ahead, filled with a bunch of, what looked like, giant ostriches.

"Axe beaks," said Dawn. "Wait 'til you guys ride one of these babies for the first time, one of the fastest creatures in the Realm."

As we got closer, I could see that they were all different colors. Some had beautiful blue feathers, others a fierce red or an emerald green. There was even an odd-looking one, a scrawny-looking male with purple colors. For the most part, (other than that purple one, maybe) they looked very distinguished, standing tall and proud with their big axe-shaped beaks. They had two long legs, with big talons on the bottom of their feet, but their wings were very small and clearly these large birds didn't specialize in flying.

"No way!" Tara shouted out. "Is that . . .?"

"Legalon the Quick! From Kingdom Monsters. Nate, you didn't tell her that certain Kingdom Monster cards are based on actual creatures in the Rune Realm?" Dawn asked, smoothly hopping on a red axe beak.

"It may have slipped from my mind," I replied.

"No wonder she wasn't as excited as I thought she'd be. Well, you guys going to pick one? It's a bit of a hike to Magic Rune Academy from here. Just over the mountain. Much easier to ride there."

"Can I?" Tara began, creeping over to what I assumed was Legalon; it was black with streaks of orange in its feathers. Its eyes were a fierce red, and it was by far the biggest of all the axe beaks in the stable.

"I would suggest picking a different one, Tara." Dawn quickly said. "I don't mean to spoil your fun, but that guy will go zero to ninety in a matter of seconds, and for someone who's never rode one of these, well, he'll make it there, but no guarantee that you'd be with him when he did."

"Yeah, I guess that makes sense," Tara said, looking very disappointed before choosing a calm green one.

I took my time picking my axe beak, strolling back and forth among them, sizing them all up. But for some reason, I just couldn't get over that goofy-looking, skinny purple one. I felt kind of bad for it; I doubt anyone ever picked it as their first choice. So naturally, that's exactly what I did, and I could have sworn that its eyes lit up with joy as I climbed up and took my seat on its saddle.

"All right, y'all guys ready?" Dawn shouted back to us with a very poor attempt at a southern accent. "Just be sure now to give 'em a good two taps on the side with your foot and shout 'zapzap' when y'all wanna go. Oh, and hang on tight!" She lost her fake accent with that last part.

No point in waiting around.

"Zapzap!" I immediately yelled out, feeling sort of ridiculous, and then tapped the purple axe beak twice with my right foot.

I almost fell backwards off the bird. It instantly bolted past Dawn and Tara before striding off toward the mountains. It seemed as if I had no decision on where it was going, like it was trained to know its way to and from the school. It wasn't long at all before I had left the outskirts of the village and was on my way up the winding hillside.

The rows of apartments and houses all blurred together as the cool air rushed against my face, which felt soothing against my skin, comforting, like it somehow belonged to me.

Before I had even really noticed, the scenery changed to rural countryside as we continued traveling up the mountain. The red brick road had now turned into a dirt path, the houses had disappeared and been replaced with wild-looking, bluish-green grass and massive trees.

There was nobody else in my immediate sight, and I was riding for about five minutes before I saw Tara again, who came striding alongside me with her green axe beak. She seemed to be in her natural element, a huge smile on her face as her platinum blonde hair flowed in the wind.

"I think we're a long way from Maine!" she hollered over to me.

"You think so?!"

We continued riding for a few more minutes before we finally made it to the top of the mountain, and now I could get a full view of the campus from below. It sat in a vast, flat prairie, surrounded by more tall mountains from every side, some of which had long streams of water flowing down from them. Buildings of all shapes and sizes were scattered throughout the huge, blue-green prairie. I could see a big clock tower, multiple modern-looking buildings, more apartments, an enormous stadium, what looked to be maybe lab buildings, a student center, and a very impressive quad in the center that, from here, looked more like Central Park than a campus quad.

Our axe beaks had come to a halt, (I assumed to catch their breath for a second) which gave Tara and I the perfect opportunity to take it all in.

"There she is," Dawn said as she came slowly riding up next to us. "What do you guys think?"

"It's beautiful," Tara whispered (it seemed like she was finally over being skeptical).

"I know, right?" Dawn agreed. "Puts anything back home to shame, just another reason I hate going back there. Come on, it's waiting for us."

A few minutes later, we had reached the bottom of the mountain, and the wild, dirt path had come and gone. We were now presented with a pearly-white stone walkway that led to the entrance of the school up ahead.

To my left, was a huge stable filled with other axe beaks waiting to take their future riders back to the village.

Dawn hopped down from her bird. "This is where we part ways, big guy," she said, patting her ride.

I sort of clumsily got down from my purple axe beak and gave it a pet on its head before it trotted over to the stable.

Tara and I followed Dawn down the long stone path, which eventually led to a big plaza in front of a large entrance gate. A bunch of students were hanging out here, I suppose just enjoying their leisurely Sunday. In the middle of the plaza was a large fountain. It had similar carvings on it as the stone archway and the pillars at the bottom of the Magic Gateway.

Placed inside the fountain's pool were four statues of different creatures I'd never seen before, all of them trickling streams of water into the pool.

We walked past the intriguing fountain, and Dawn stopped at the entrance gate, which was already open for students to come and go as they pleased.

She spun on her heel to face Tara and me, her hands clasped together and an excited smile on her face.

"Well," she began, forcing her voice to sound all formal again, "I'd like to officially welcome you both to Magic Rune Academy."

Chapter Four

WHILE RIDING through the hills on the axe beak, I wasn't sure if I'd ever find a more beautiful scenery again in my life. I was wrong. The campus of Magic Rune Academy somehow took the natural beauty of this world and put a bow on it.

The pearly-white stone path that led us into campus extended throughout it as well, lined with light posts and veering off in various directions dividing the perfectly land-scaped blue-green grass. We passed a few tranquil-looking ponds, with this world's version of what looked to be weep-ing-willow trees, which were also the same bluish-green color of the grass, planted alongside the borders of the water. A few benches were placed around the ponds as well, some of them occupied by happy couples.

"So, something I've been wondering about," I turned slightly to ask Dawn, who was letting us lead the way. "Why are all the trees and the grass this blue-green color here?"

Dawn laughed. "That's like asking why the grass is green back on Earth. I don't know—it just is."

"Fair enough," I chuckled.

As we continued walking through campus, passing all kinds of different buildings along the way, from old stone buildings to modern skyscrapers, there was something else I picked up on that I thought was a bit unusual, and it wasn't the fact that half the students were wearing robes, or shifter clothes, or even full sets of armor. No, it was that I seemed to be catching the eye of many people walking past us, all of them being women. And I knew this wasn't all in my head, because Tara seemed to notice too; she was walking almost unnaturally close to me.

It was happening often enough that I was starting to think something was on my face, or that maybe it was the way I was dressed. But if I didn't know better, I'd say they all had the same look in their eyes: a look of seduction.

It was a little strange. I mean, it wasn't like I thought I was ugly or anything (I felt like I did all right for myself back home), but to have just about every single girl we walked by eyeing me in the same way, it was almost unnatural.

"Yep, you're definitely going to love it here," Dawn mumbled quietly to herself from behind us. "Hang a left here, guys."

We continued walking until reaching the vast quad. From way up on the mountain, I could take in its sheer size entirely, but I didn't fully appreciate it until being down at level footing. I could just barely make out the end of it from where we stood.

The white stone pathway paved its way through the entire quad as well, coming to an intersection with its counter points at the center, where they formed a sort of mini-plaza, similar to the one outside the entrance gate. At the center of the plaza was a tall, fascinating statue, an abstract one that almost looked like a woman with wings, or some sort of butterfly lady.

A plethora of different activities were going on throughout the quad. Tents had been pitched all around with people trying to recruit others to their clubs or sororities and fraternities. A team of cheerleaders were practicing (some of them became distracted as we walked by), and there were small groups of students either studying together under a tree, or even appearing to be fighting amongst one another, for some reason.

"They're part of the Quester program—it's pretty popular at this academy," Dawn said, noticing that I was staring wildly at them. "It's a profession in the realm, like how I'm part of the Guard; they complete missions or requested tasks from civilians in small groups, and you get paid after completing them. The more difficult the mission, the higher the payout."

"Oh, nice! Sounds like a fun way to make a living!" I replied enthusiastically.

"Definitely better than washing dishes at the Cheesecake Station," Tara said. "I swear, I'll never look at cheesecake the same way."

"You worked there for three days," I laughed.

"And that was all it took for me to never want to eat cheesecake again!"

It took us about fifteen minutes just to get to the other side of the quad, and as we did, I noticed that the infrastructure on this side of campus seemed to be older. A higher number of buildings were made from stone, some even resembling small palaces. The pathways remained pearly white and modern, though, and were now lined with rows of small trees as we continued along them.

Up ahead, I noticed a building that looked very distinguished, standing out from even the most impressive structures on campus. A large, pristine-looking courtyard preceded it, followed by two wide flights of stone steps. It looked like a small castle, or a fort, even. The center part of the building was the tallest, peaked with a large spire and four smaller ones right beneath it, and exterior corridors branched out from the main section to the left and right wings, which ran perpendicular down the courtyard.

"That's where Dean Celestine's office is located," explained Dawn as she pointed at the impressive building ahead, "in that building—the Cathedral of Tranquility. Mainly sorcerers and healers have classes there." She had just a hint of jealousy in her tone.

The courtyard had a serene look to it. The pathway was bordered with neatly trimmed hedge lines, and in the center of the yard was a long, square pool of water. I was barely paying attention to where I was walking and almost tripped up the flight of stone steps leading to the upper lawn, which also had a pool of water in the center of it, this one perfectly circular.

"This is beautiful," said Tara, mesmerized. "It's just so peaceful."

"Yeah, it really is something," Dawn replied, gazing up at the highest spire of the building. "Well, I'll show you guys inside and take you to Dean Celestine. That's where you'll get categorized into your classes. You'll also get assigned a rank based on your mytosome count," her eyes lingered on me while she said that, "so that you can get an idea of your potential compared to other runics. I'm so excited to find out what you both are! I hope at least one of you is a shifter! It'd be nice to have someone to talk about shifting with."

The Cathedral was as impressive on the inside as it was on the outside. The floor of the main entrance lobby shined with marble, the ceilings were high, and the tall windows allowed plenty of natural light to come in. There were what looked to be classrooms to the left and right, and straight ahead was a big staircase that led to the upper levels. Tara appeared to be in some sort of trance as she gazed up at the big chandelier hanging down from the ceiling.

"The professors' offices for the sorcerer and healer classes are on this floor," Dawn panted, after we finished treading up the big, fancy staircase to the third floor. "And at the end of the hall is where Dean Celestine's office is. This is where we part ways, at least just for now. You'll each be examined separately. A runic's mytosome count is *technically* supposed to be confidential information, though barely anyone keeps it to themselves. Head in one at a time with your acceptance letters. I'll be waiting for you both outside when it's done. Good luck!"

"But wait!" Tara nervously called back to Dawn. "I still have questions. What's considered a high mytosome count? And what happens if it's low? What are all the classes a person can be categorized into? This is a lot of info, and I need to be prepared before meeting the dean!"

She was fiddling with her fingers, a sure sign that she was about to start biting at her nails.

But Dawn simply waved a hand at her. "Don't stress, Tara. Dean Celestine will explain all of it to you. I'll be outside waiting for you guys!" And then she departed back down the staircase, leaving me and Tara alone for the first time in what felt like awhile.

"That girl is way too lax for me," Tara muttered.

But I had to agree with Dawn—no reason to stress if we didn't need to. So I shrugged my shoulders and shot Tara a convincing smile before we continued down the long hallway.

Tara insisted that it be me who went in first. I could tell she was nervous, so I had no problem obliging.

I gave the wooden door with Dean Celestine's name on it a few good knocks and waited a moment, but there was no response.

"Maybe she's in a meeting?" asked Tara softly.

"It's a Sunday, though. You think she's that busy?"

"Well, she is the dean after all."

I pressed my ear to the door. "I don't hear anyone."

Tara shrugged her shoulders.

"Hell with it," I muttered, and gently opened the door to head on in.

It automatically shut behind me, enclosing me in the room.

Just as I suspected, nobody was there. A big, vacant desk cluttered with paperwork sat in the middle of the room, many framed portraits and awards covered every inch of the surrounding walls, and there was a door on the back wall, which I guessed led to another room. But it looked more private, so I figured it best not to enter that one.

I waited for about five minutes before finally concluding that she wasn't here, and I had just turned around to take my leave when a warping noise sounded out from behind me.

"Ah, there you are. I was waiting for you, Nate Gannon," a smooth voice rang out.

I spun around and was looking at a middle-aged woman, maybe in her sixties. Appearing to be human rather than orc or elf, she had dark skin, short silver hair and deep blue eyes behind a pair of sophisticated-looking glasses. She was wearing a gray overcoat, with a tight black undershirt, slim black pants, and black heels.

"Oh—I was here, actually," I began. "I didn't see anyone."

"I am everywhere, Mr. Gannon. And someone who is everywhere can never be late, nor early, but rather, always perfectly on time. Now have a seat."

"Uh, yes, ma'am."

"Do I look like a ma'am to you?!" She gave me an incredulous look.

My eyes shot wide open and my mouth dropped. I wasn't entirely sure if that question was a trick or not. She definitely appeared to be all woman to me. To be honest, she wasn't bad looking at all for her age. She was average height, with a surprisingly tight body; the heels and the black pants were only emphasizing this even more. But to be honest, I was completely taken aback by her attitude. If this was how the dean of Magic Rune Academy was, then maybe it wouldn't be worth attending.

"I, um, I think so?" I finally said.

A moment of silence went by as she continued to glower at me. But then, to my surprise, she burst out into laughter.

"I'm just messing with you, Nate!" she blurted. "You should have seen the look on your face."

Still off guard, I laughed back halfheartedly.

"Oh, my," the lady sighed, "have a seat, Nate, please," she repeated, this time in a much less demanding tone.

I sat down on the opposite side of the lady who I assumed to be the dean of Magic Rune Academy, but to be honest, her demeanor had me unsure.

"I'm Dean Celestine. First name's Selene. You can call me whatever you like." To my surprise, she winked at me.

I tried to hold back the smile on my face, but it must have slipped.

"Something funny, Nate Gannon?"

"Just Nate is fine, thanks. But no, sorry ma'—sorry."

"It's okay," Dean Celestine began, "you can tell me," she insisted.

"It's dumb, really," I started, unsure if I should be honest in this case, "it's just your name. Dean Selene Celestine. That's a whole lot of rhyming, right?" I started laughing, but to my unfortunate realization, Dean Celestine wasn't laughing with me.

"Something funny about my name?" she said, glaring through me.

I paused, not knowing how to respond again.

But her fierce stare broke once more, and she let out another hysterical laugh. "You're right—it's ridiculous! Made the same joke about it myself after I first took the position. And the fact you had the guts to say it to my face. I like you, Nate."

"Uh—thank you, I think."

Dean Celestine drawled out another sigh. "Good stuff, good stuff. Well, Nate, I see you have your letter with you."

"Oh, yes, I . . ." The letter somehow flew out of my hand and directly into hers (I took it as her doing).

"No need for that anymore." She threw it over her shoulder. "The others will be here soon enough. I've got a really good feeling about what you are, Nate. And as far as your mytosome count goes, I think you're in for a treat."

At that moment, the door opened again, revealing two other people. One of them was a young woman with light red skin, silky long blue hair that came down below her ass, pointy ears, and bright purple eyes. She was slender and about my height, which was pretty tall for a girl. Going off of what

Dawn was saying earlier, I guessed she was an elf. She couldn't have been teaching for very long, because she didn't appear to be much older than me.

The other person was definitely human; he was a tall and muscular middle-aged man, with pale skin and long, curly black hair. His rough, burly exterior was only further emphasized by his thick black beard.

The young woman was carrying a small black box. "I've retrieved the Reader, ma'am."

"Ah, thank you, Keerla."

"Of course," she quickly replied, placing the small black box on the table.

"Nate, this is Professor Keerla Morran and Professor Ivan Kravitz," Dean Celestine said.

"It's nice to meet you." I stood up to shake both of their hands.

"A pleasure," Professor Morran quickly said.

Professor Kravitz firmly shook my hand, but said nothing.

"This," Dean Celestine opened the small box, revealing a clear glass ball about the size of my palm, "is a device created way back in the day. It's called the Reader, and it measures the exact type and volume of the mytosomes inside an individual. It's how we determine new students' classes and tiers."

I leaned over, gazing into the glass orb. "What do I do with it?"

"It's a simple process, really," Dean Celestine explained. "All you need to do is hold the Reader in your hands and empty your mind. It will do the rest."

I was a little skeptical—it seemed too easy. And to be honest, I still had my doubts that I even belonged in this world. What if I grabbed the Reader and nothing happened at all? Would they have to escort me off campus, forcing me to leave the Rune Realm and never return? And then what would happen to me and Tara? Would she stay here if I had to leave? I assumed she'd want to come back with me, but then I'd be hindering her from potentially having an amazing life here!

Noticing that my thoughts were starting to spiral, I shook my head slightly to try and regain my composure. Then I let out a deep breath, gently picked the Reader up, closed my eyes, and simply hoped for the best.

It became eerily quiet in the room. Even though my eyes were shut, I could feel Dean Celestine, Professor Morran, and Professor Kravitz all gazing at me. For some reason, they seemed very interested to receive my results. I wasn't sure if this was how it was with all students, or if I was an odd case, but I was starting to get the feeling that it was the latter.

For a minute, nothing notable transpired, and my worst fears seemed to be coming true. But then, a warm sensation arose from my gut; at first, the feeling was subtle enough to the point where I thought maybe it was all in my head, but then it became much more prominent, diminishing any remaining doubt.

The warmth intensified before spreading throughout the rest of my body, and it wasn't long before it enveloped me. It was a strange sensation, almost like I pissed myself, actually. And then a gasp came from one of the professors in the room, which made me start to worry that I actually *had* pissed myself.

I opened my eyes, and to my pleasant surprise, the orb had turned to a solid blue, and I assumed that had to mean something good. From there, the color only continued to become more evident. The blue became bluer until, to my *unfortunate* surprise, a crack emerged at the top of the glass orb. It started as a little thin line, but then continued to spread and feather down the Reader.

I looked up at Dean Celestine, wondering whether to put the Reader down or not, since the last thing I wanted to do was break this valuable tool that they apparently had for ages. Oddly enough, though, Dean Celestine remained unbothered, a curious look on her face as she peered into the broken orb.

"I knew it," she muttered to herself. "I absolutely knew it." She clasped her hands together, smiling.

"Knew what?" I asked.

Professor Morran and Kravitz huddled around me as they gazed into the Reader in my hands.

"It can't be . . ." Professor Kravitz groaned.

Professor Morran remained silent, her eyes shifting from the Reader to my own. She looked astounded.

Finally, and to my much-needed relief, Dean Celestine grabbed the Reader from me. As she did so, she hovered a hand above it and twiddled her fingers. The crack in the glass orb immediately disappeared. She then placed the orb back in the box, closed it, and sat back in her seat, considering me with an intrigued smile.

"If you will be so kind?" she said to Professor Kravitz and Morran, gesturing to the little black box and then to the door.

"Yes, of course," Professor Morran said, before taking the box and leaving the room. Professor Kravitz followed her out, but not before giving me, for some reason, a disapproving look.

"Did I do something wrong?" I asked, genuinely concerned by the reactions.

Dean Celestine chuckled, still smiling. "On the contrary, Nate." She stood up and came closer to me, sitting on the corner of her desk in a way that caught my attention for all the wrong reasons. But I tried to keep those thoughts at bay.

"I knew when Dawn told me that you made her shift from just a simple touch that you were potentially special. And that was only reconfirmed once we met. I could sense a significant presence of mytosomes coming from you."

"Oh, okay. That's good, then, right?"

"But exactly how much, I still wasn't quite sure," Dean Celestine went on. "That's where the Reader surpasses even *my* prowess."

"So, what did it say?" I asked.

She smiled warmly back at me. "I take it that Miss Hillman didn't tell you quite all the details about how the Reader works. And classes, too."

It took me a minute to realize that she was referring to Dawn, and that I never happened to get her last name before now.

"That's okay," Dean Celestine continued, "she's still a little green around the kitty ears, that one."

"She gave me a good rundown of things, though," I genuinely said.

"I'm sure she did." She beamed. "But just so you know, runics are typically categorized into four different classes: shifters, who can use rune to transform their own myto-somes, mimicking the mytosomes of certain beasts in the Realm, and therefore turning into the beasts themselves; sorcerers, who excel at sensing and manipulating the rune around them to where they can eventually even bend it to their own will, wielding it as their most lethal weapon; rune-knights, who specialize in using weapons and taming beasts in the Realm to do their bidding; and finally, healers, who use rune to heal wounds and replenish the energy within one's body."

I counted everything off on my fingers, trying to keep up.

"The Reader," Dean Celestine continued, "categorizes every runic into one of these classes based on the specific type of mytosomes within their bodies; the color that the Reader gives off represents these classes: green for shifters; yellow for healers; red for rune-knights; and finally blue for sorcerers."

"All right, so I'm a sorcerer! That sounds neat," I said, just happy to be categorized at all, really.

"As am I," she noted, smiling, "and so, as the head of the sorcerer department, I look forward to working very closely with you. But that's not the cause for the looks of bewilderment just now, which I am sure you picked up on, nor the reason the glass began to crack on the Reader.

"You see, Nate, the Reader also puts individuals into one of four ranks based on their mytosome count, thus identifying their *maximum* potential: D-tier, C-tier, B-tier, A-tier, and finally S-tier. By far the most common being C and B-tier."

"So, how do I know what I am?"

"The prominence of the color displayed is what determines the class. There is a whole course on Reading that we offer here at the Academy, where graphs are studied and examined closely to ensure no mistakes are made when establishing ranks. But I shall spare you the details. In short, the denser the color, the higher the rank. For example, if you were a D-tier, the blue you saw in that orb would be very faint—"

"But mine was . . ."

"That's correct, Nate," Dean Celestine concluded. "Yours was a very strong color blue, and so immense that even the structure of the Reader was fragmented, was it not?"

"Well, yeah, I suppose."

"Nate, you are a sorcerer of the highest tier, the S-tier."

I blinked a few times, trying to take in her words. I was an S-tier? The highest rank possible? Was this really happening?!

Excitement began to swell through me as I tried to keep a straight face.

"To put things into perspective," she went on, "there is only one other S-tier runic on this campus, who also happens to be a sorcerer, well, sorceress, technically—and you're looking at her."

"There's only . . . you're . . . ?" The magnitude of this news was now starting to hit me for what it really was.

"That's right, Nate," she replied as she uncrossed her legs and walked back behind her desk to sit in her chair again, "you and I are a lot alike. And I think you're going to love it here."

"That's what Dawn told me earlier! I can't disagree, this world seems like it has a lot to offer. I mean, even just the landscape is really—"

"Yes, yes, the land and flowers are pretty. Listen, you're about to get more action here than a bee falling into a jar of honey."

I went silent, my face blank. "I'm what?"

"It's one of my *favorite* perks that come with being an S-tier runic. Members of the opposite sex desire us with a fiery passion, Nate. Hell, even the men of this realm who have lower tier rankings will have a natural inclination to follow and befriend you."

"But how? I mean, yeah, I guess the girls *would* like that I have a high rank or whatever."

"Oh, it's more than just the fact you have high potential," Dean Celestine explained. "It's biological. It has to do with the mytosome count in your body. Mytosomes are attracted to mytosomes, so since you have a bunch of them in your body, these poor runic lasses won't be able to keep themselves from wanting you. It's practically in their DNA."

It was all becoming clear now. I thought back to the girls staring at me as I walked by, our server, Sakura, acting all funny and clumsy around me earlier (though that may have just been her), and even Dawn. Could she be attracted to me only because of my mytosome count?

"Trust me, it'll be like fishing with dynamite. And the best part is, that it's almost expected from S-tier runics to have their own harem." Dean Celestine winked.

"My own . . . ?"

"Harem, yes. A group of girls, all of whom will be happy to share romantic relations with you—sexually too, of course."

"Thanks, I kind of figured that last part," I sarcastically said, still trying to wrap my head around all of this.

"I'm telling you," Dean Celestine continued, "it's one of the *best* perks of being an S-tier runic—"

At that moment, someone came barging out from the back room: a young elf, maybe in his thirties. To my dismay, he was only wearing boxer briefs.

"Uhm, Ms. Celestine, ma'am," he carefully started, "are you almost done with—"

"Did I say you could come out yet, Kevin?!" she blurted out, avoiding eye contact with the man.

My mouth had dropped to the floor without even me realizing it, as I made sure to keep my own eyes fixated on the opposite side of the room from whatever this was that was transpiring in front of me.

And then, Dean Celestine lazily flicked her wrist causing Kevin to shoot backward into the room where he came from, seemingly being pulled by an invisible rope. The door slammed shut without anyone touching it.

There was a moment of very awkward stillness where I had to bite my lip to keep a serious face.

"Anyway," Dean Celestine broke the silence, looking very sheepish, "it's one of my favorite perks of being an S-tier. Take that one in there. Why else would I have shown up late when you arrived? Had to port myself in here just to save a bit of time."

I remained silent and, with all my mental-strength, expressionless.

"You keep this one between us and I'll give you an A on your first test," Dean Celestine concluded.

"As far as I'm concerned, I'm a mute."

"Good boy," she said, "then the A is yours, which reminds me." She flicked her wrist again, and for a second, I feared that Kevin the elf was about to get flung back into the room. But instead, she conjured a piece of paper out of thin air and gently floated it into my hands. "That is your schedule for the first semester," she clarified, "specifically designed around a sorcerer of your stature."

Reading it over, the classes seemed way more interesting than anything I would have learned back home. I wasn't sure if there was a formal decision process that needed to be made for me to start here or continue at my old school, but I assumed Dean Celestine and I were on the same page. There was no need for an official acceptance—I was already sold.

"Now," Dean Celestine continued, "I'll be giving you and your friend outside the day off tomorrow, as well as Miss Hillman. That way she can escort you both through town, so that you can pick up your supplies and books."

"Thank you, Dean Celestine." I smiled. Even though I was excited to start the program, having the first day off sounded perfectly fine to me. This way I could have a moment to at least take all of this in before jumping right into classes. It was a life changing last few days, after all, and this meeting with Dean Celestine just took it to a whole new level.

"Of course." She smiled warmly back at me. "We are going to have a lot of fun, you and I. Now, if you'd be so kind as to let your friend in next."

I stood up to let myself out, not entirely sure if I wanted to take part in Dean Celestine's ideas of "fun."

Even though it was maybe only ten minutes or so, it seemed like an hour as I waited for Tara to come out from Dean Celestine's office. When she finally did, she looked a bit down for some reason.

"Hey, how'd it go?" I asked.

"Um, it was fine," she said.

"She's a pretty . . . intriguing woman, isn't she?" I said.

"Definitely 'intriguing'," Tara chuckled. "But I liked her. She was nice."

"Yeah, I agree. So, what were your results?" I asked, anxiously wondering.

Her face dropped a bit. "Well, we aren't supposed to share all the details, right?"

I waved that off. "Apparently everyone does. You can at least tell me your class, right?"

"Oh, yeah, right, I guess I'm a healer."

"Nice!" I gave her an encouraging look. "You always did like helping people. It's fitting!"

"Yeah." Her eyes remained fixated on the marble floor.

"Tara, what's wrong?"

"It's nothing, really."

"Something is up, you know you can tell me."

I was getting a little worried that she'd overheard my *situation*. I figured it'd be best to keep the part about a bunch of girls in this realm wanting me to myself, especially with how things had been with her recently.

"Well, it's just . . . you know how they broke us down into rankings?"

I nodded.

"Ugh," she groaned, "apparently, I'm a D-tier, Nate! It's the lowest rank someone can get! That's why Dawn was barely able to smell my myto-whatevers. It's just fitting, really. I suck at everything in *this* world, too!" Her voice cracked a bit.

I instantly hugged her. "It's okay, Tara, really. All that does is put people into ranks based on their potential, from the sounds of it."

"I know, but," she mumbled into my shoulder.

"It's just potential," I continued. "I mean, I'm sure there are lazy A-tier people who barely live up to their full potential. I bet D-tiers surpass higher ranked people all the time! You'll just have to work a little harder, that's all. And I know you, you're without a doubt the hardest worker out there." I looked at her and gave a warm smile, which she eventually reciprocated.

"Yeah, I guess that makes sense."

"Definitely!"

"So, what did you get?" Tara finally asked as we headed down the big stairway.

My mind froze for a second. I wasn't sure how to handle this. I couldn't lie to her, but I also didn't want to go on about being an S-tier while she was still upset about her tier rank. "I did pretty well, actually. I'll tell you all about it later, okay?" I tried to brush off.

"Later?" Tara asked with a frown. "Come on, tell me. Let me guess, you got an A-tier?!" Her smile returned.

"Something like that—oh, look, there's Dawn!"

Dawn was waiting right outside for us, perched upon the side of the wall which bordered the circular pool of water. As soon as she saw us, she came running.

"Nate! I heard the news from Professor Morran!" she began, full of excitement.

My heart stopped as I tried to warn her with her eyes, but she didn't seem to notice.

"An S-tier! That's incredible! You're the only one in the entire school, other than Dean Celestine."

"Uh, yeah, I guess," I said, trying not to look at Tara, who I could tell was fixated on me from my peripherals.

"I knew you were something special when I met you, but to think you're S-tier! And I recruited you! Wow, I must have a knack for this whole Guard thing after all, right?" She smiled.

I nodded confidently, figuring it would be best not to bring up the whole "green behind the cat ears" comment Dean Celestine made.

"You got an S-tier, Nate?" Tara quietly said.

"I'm sorry, Tara, I just—"

"That's incredible! You didn't have to downplay it just for me. I'm happy for you, really!" She had a very sincere smile on her face.

I immediately felt lighter. "Thanks Tara," I said, "you're the best. But it doesn't have to be a big deal or anything."

"Man, you are going to be in paradise here," Dawn went on.

"Yeah, well, let's go," I started walking, trying to interrupt her. I had a feeling I knew where she was going with this.

"No, really! You're going to love it, Nate. You won't be able to keep the girls away. You can even start your own harem. As an S-tier, it's almost expected of you, actually," she chuckled.

And there it was.

"What?" Tara softly said, trying to laugh it off.

"It's a perk that comes with having a high mytosome count," Dawn went on, doing a poor job of reading the mood. "Other runics, particularly of the opposite sex, are just naturally attracted to people with a higher mytosome count."

"Oh, really?" Tara asked, looking unsure whether Dawn was messing with her.

"Yep!" she enthusiastically replied. "No wonder our server earlier was acting all weird around you. And, Tara, I heard you're a healer!"

"Yeah, I am," she quietly replied.

"That's great! It'll be a perfect fit for you, I'm sure. Although I have to admit, a little part of me couldn't help hoping you'd be a shifter, but I'll just have to deal with it. Come on, I'll show you guys to your dorms now. They're on the north side of campus, close to the North Gate, where we came in at. We actually passed them on the way in here."

The walk back wasn't nearly as fun and fascinating as the walk there; Tara hadn't said a word since hearing about the *perks* of being an S-tier. Dawn was still zealously telling us things about certain buildings that we walked by, or different activities held on campus, one of them being a popular event that takes place twice a year called the Questing Games, where people compete in groups of five and basically simulate battling one another until a victor is crowned.

"But it's perfectly harmless!" Dawn quickly added. "The participants wear regulators that limit how much power can be put out."

My primary focus was no longer on my surroundings, but instead on Tara. I continued to try to catch her eye as we walked back, but her stare remained fixated on the ground the entire time.

"And this is you guys." Dawn stopped us at the front of a newer-looking apartment building. It looked more like a really nice hotel, actually, having six floors and two long wings that extended out to the left and right from the main entrance.

"I got you both set up on the first floor, though you're on opposite wings. But that's no biggie, you've already been registered to the entire building. When you get your Reading, your unique mytosome structures also get downloaded and saved into the University's database, for identification purposes. This way, all you have to do is place a thumb over the scanners of the buildings that you have access to, and you're in," she explained.

"Thanks," Tara quietly said.

"Shouldn't we have signed a form or something for that to happen?" I asked.

Dawn gave me a funny look. "What? You think universities back on Earth don't track their students' data?"

"Fair point," I shrugged.

"Well," Dawn continued, "guess this is where we part ways for the day—I'm in a different dorm a little down that way. But you have my number, Nate. Here, I'll punch mine into your phone too, Tara. That way, you can quickly reach me if you need anything. And don't worry, you still get service in the Realm. We have contracts here with all the major carriers, believe it or not."

"Thanks, Dawn, really." I gave her an appreciative smile as Tara lazily handed her phone over, still looking glum.

"And you should have enough clothes and stuff in your rooms for the first week," Dawn added. "I hope I got your sizes right. Maybe next weekend you guys can make a trip back home to bring anything else you want."

From there, Tara and I said our goodbyes to Dawn until we would reconvene the following day, and then entered our dorm building. The lobby had a warm and welcoming feel to it, with white-tiled floors, plenty of furniture for lounging around, and a big fireplace in the center. Two long hallways branched out to the left and right behind a set of doors on each side, to which you needed to scan your thumb to get through.

Tara and I left for our designated rooms, leaving things on kind of an awkward note. I felt bad about leaving things like that, but figured not to press it for now.

My room was at the very end of the hall, and after scanning to enter it, I was pleased to see that it was much bigger than what I had at my old university. Whereas previously I only had a small bedroom, my twin-sized bed taking up most of that space, I now was provided with a large living room area, a kitchen, a personal bathroom, and a luxurious bedroom with a king-sized bed in it.

The first thing I decided to do was turn the living room television on and finally take a load off after the long day. From the window to my left, I could see the orange sun beginning to set over the distant horizon.

I was about five minutes through skimming the channels before I realized that I wouldn't be able to shake how I left things with Tara, so I pulled my phone out to send her a text:

Hey, could you come over? I'm in the last room on the right.

A few minutes later, my phone buzzed. I eagerly picked it up and read her reply:

Hi, yeah sure. Cya soon.

I was relieved to see that she at least still wanted to hang out tonight; I was starting to fear for the worst.

About five minutes later, there was a quiet knock on my door, and I let Tara in. She had changed out of her red flannel from earlier and was now wearing a white tank top which just happened to be accentuating her large chest amazingly.

I tried to keep my mind off that, however, because I could tell right away that things still seemed off. She was unusually quiet as we settled together on the couch to watch some romantic comedy about an orc and an elf trying to raise a human baby they'd adopted. We were about halfway through the episode when I finally decided to address the elephant in the room: "Tara, about today, and this whole S-tier thing . . ." I began.

She seemed a little surprised. "Nate, you don't have to explain anything, really."

"Well, I feel like I do. I mean, things seem off. I just want to make sure everything is okay."

"Why would things not be okay? You have every right to be with or do whatever you want. Don't let me stop you." She wasn't even looking at me.

"Tara," I began, "it's just . . ."

"No, Nate, there's something I need to tell you." She had a look in her eyes that I didn't like. "I'm . . . I'm not staying here, Nate. Dean Celestine said I had the choice to stay or go. I think she could tell I had mixed feelings about it. At first, I wasn't sure, but after thinking about it, I think it's for the best."

"Tara . . ."

"Really, it's for the best, Nate. You clearly belong in this world, and I truly think you'll be happy here. But I barely have enough mytosomes to be qualified as a runic. And not only that, but seeing you with a bunch of girls . . ." Her voice trailed off. "This is just for the best. I'm so sorry, Nate!"

She abruptly stood up and swiftly strode over to the door.

"Tara, Tara wait!" I jumped up from the couch and followed her. There was no way I could just let her go like this.

"Nate, please just—"

That was all I let her get out. I swung her around and passionately kissed her on the lips. At first, she was taken back by it, but then I was happy to notice her leaning into my embrace, even gently caressing the back of my neck with her soft hands.

Maybe it was the years of buildup, but that kiss was anything beyond what I imagined it could be, and when it finally ended, Tara looked up into my eyes and whispered, "Wow."

"Listen, Tara," I breathed. "I'm not letting you go. If you want to go back home, then I'm coming with you. I want you. I've wanted you for years now, and correct me if I'm wrong, but I think you want me too."

She nodded vigorously, smiling softly. "Mhm."

I threw my arms around her and kissed her again, this time with even more passion than before. She responded by moaning into my mouth and pulling me hard into her.

It wasn't long before things began to heat up, our tongues exploring each other's mouths as I guided us back over to my couch. Once I finally had her pinned down on the cushions, I ran my hands up and down her black leggings, which were so tightly stretched around her thick, toned legs.

We continued going at it like this for maybe five minutes before Tara finally pulled back, gasping.

"I want you," she whispered, "so bad."

I smiled and caressed her soft, glossy lips with my own again before pushing her hair back so that I could repeatedly kiss her neck.

"Oh god," she gasped.

I could feel her breathing hasten slightly as I continued suckling at the side of her neck like a thirsty vampire.

"Mmmm . . ." She let out a self-torturous moan, like she was fighting against herself. "Nate, I, I'm sorry. I just . . . I don't know if I'm ready." Her eyes fell in a way that told me everything. "It's just, it's such a big move, you know?"

I gave her a reassuring smile, fighting against myself as well. "I understand, trust me. It really is a big step for us, especially given our history." I slowly sat up.

"But please don't think this means I don't want you like that!" she quickly blurted out. "Because I do, I really, really do. Oh, I hope I don't regret this. Please don't think I'm a tease—"

"Tara," I said, still smiling, "I promise you, that's not what I think. As a matter of fact, the thoughts you're wrestling with right now are the same thoughts I've been struggling with myself for quite a while, actually."

She looked up at me with a smile of relief. "Really?"

"Definitely! Don't worry, I'm not going anywhere. We'll take things slow, okay? We'll figure this out together."

Tara nodded. "Thanks, Nate. It's just, so much is changing so fast, you know? I mean, we're going to be basically living in this whole new world where all of a sudden magic and elves are real and, well, 'slow' sounds good to me. I'd like that."

"I understand. Well—wait," I stuttered, putting something together. "Does that mean you're staying here?"

Tara nodded with a smile.

"Tara, we don't have to if you don't—"

"No," she stopped me, "If we're going to be official, then I want to support you. You're an S-tier runic, Nate, and I'm happy to just be a part of your future harem. As long as I'm the first member, that is," she giggled. "Besides, I really do find this realm fascinating. I'm going to do my best to be an amazing healer. For me, and for you."

I found myself feeling incredibly grateful for her at this moment.

"Tara, that whole harem thing, it doesn't have to happen," I said.

But she scoffed and waved her hand. "It comes with being an S-tier apparently, right? I'd feel bad if I ended up being the reason you couldn't fulfill your *duties*," she chuckled for a second, but then her expression became serious again. "Honestly, I know I've been acting kind of crazy jealous lately, but that was just because I was afraid of being left behind, Nate. That's why I was so set on leaving. I couldn't bear to watch you form a harem with a bunch of girls while I stayed on the sideline as just your friend. But now, well, I'm happy to support you."

"You really are the best, Tara," I muttered before giving her another passionate kiss, which she happily embraced again.

We ended up cuddling together on the couch for the rest of the night, finishing up the movie and then watching some random cartoons afterward. It was comforting, and still really nice. Even though we may not have gotten very far physically, it felt like emotionally we had progressed leaps and bounds.

Tara ended up drifting off into a heavy sleep during one of the cartoon shows. Between the long, eventful day and the stress she was probably putting on herself, I couldn't really blame her.

My mind, however, was playing back the whole day. It was crazy to think how different everything for me was compared to just a few days prior. I still struggled with believing this was all real—from being part of this beautiful, magical realm, to taking things to the next level with Tara. It was needless to say that I was well past just being on cloud nine.

I was deep in thought, gazing out of the living room window, when a beautiful purple butterfly flew past, glowing brightly and contrasting vividly against the night sky. It left a trail of glowing purple dust in its wake.

At first, I thought how strange it was to see a butterfly at night, but then I remembered I literally was having a conversation with an orc earlier that same day, and suddenly the butterfly at night seemed normal.

I carefully got up from the couch, making sure not to wake Tara, and strolled over to the window to try to get a better look. The butterfly was already gone, but what I was staring at now nearly knocked me off my feet.

I was the witness of a masterpiece—something you'd only see framed in art museums, if you're lucky: The night sky shimmered with a purplish, pink aurora; what looked to be thousands of bright stars of all different sizes were painted across the canvas, and three gorgeous white moons hung way above me, one of them being at least ten times bigger than the moon back home. It was clearly the big brother of the other two, which were much closer in size to what I was used to seeing in the sky.

It was like I was floating in outer space, goggling out of the window of a spacecraft, and I lost myself and all sense of time as I remained standing in place, taking it all in, mesmerized like a child seeing stars for the first time.

Dawn's and Dean Celestine's words from earlier played back in my head, I really was going to love it here.

Chapter Five

Dawn had texted us bright and early the next morning to meet her in front of the North Gate. So I got dressed, still tired from the late night before. I met Tara outside, where I was immediately greeted by the crisp morning air. The sun was barely poking up over the towering blue mountains as we strolled through campus.

The grounds were just starting to come to life with the flocks of early bird students, all of whom were heading to their first classes of the day. But being a night owl, I was still groggy eyed and half asleep, so I was happy to instead be heading into town for a leisurely morning.

Tara was always more of a morning person than me. She had a coffee to sip on as she walked by my side, wearing a white sweater with black stripes on it and a pair of tight jeans which hugged her ass nicely. Her hair was up in its usual messy bun. She looked like a cute treat this morning without even trying, and I was proud to call her mine.

"I wonder what kind of supplies we'll need," she said, full of enthusiasm. "It's kind of exciting, don't you think?!"

"Yeah, for sure," I yawned.

As we walked through the North Gate entrance, my eyes caught Dawn sitting on a bench by the fountain with the four statues. She was looking like a treat herself in her tight shifter clothes that always looked very similar to workout gear. Her outfit today consisted of a sleek, purple crop top with long sleeves. It came down just past her belly button, revealing a glimpse of her tight, flat stomach. She had a matching pair of purple spandex shorts on, too, ending about halfway down her thighs.

"Hey, Dawn!" I hollered out.

She looked up from her phone and smiled before immediately running over to us. "What's up, guys? How was your first night in the Realm? Sleep all right?"

Tara and I exchanged sheepish looks.

"Yeah, it was a good one," I said, trying to sound natural.

"Oh!" Dawn's eyes widened, and then bit her lip, grinning. "You guys had a *really* good night, didn't you? I knew it was a good idea to vouch for you both to be put in the same dorm."

"You asked for us to be put in the same dorm?" Tara asked.

"More or less. Figured you two *lovebirds* wouldn't mind." She winked at me.

"We're not—" Tara began. She glanced up at me, almost looking for approval.

I smiled back at her before turning to Dawn. "Thanks, Dawn. That was thoughtful of you, really."

"Of course! It was the least I could do."

I had to admit, Dawn sort of confused the hell out of me. I just wasn't sure if she was into me or not. Perhaps she was just a flirt, but sometimes, the way she would look at me and speak to me, it made it seem like she wanted me, badly. But at the same time, she seemed so supportive of me and Tara. She was either really good at hiding her feelings on the subject, or just not into me the way I sometimes thought she was.

Either way, I still enjoyed her company. She seemed like such a genuine person, the type of person who would be more than happy to give you the shirt off her back. And she seemed to enjoy my company, too, even Tara's, who hadn't exactly been the warmest to her so far.

"Now, let's be off!" Dawn shouted out. "Plenty to do today, starting with breakfast! Hope you guys are hungry. I know an amazing place in town."

We hitched a ride back to Hearthvale on the axe beaks (I chose my trusty purple pal yet again). And once in town, Dawn led us to the source of a delicious smell, which ended up being a little establishment right off the main street that we had first arrived on yesterday, which Dawn referred to as Hilt Street.

The restaurant was called Rise and Dine, and they had the tastiest, fluffiest pancakes I'd ever had, with a sweet, oak-flavored syrup that went with them perfectly. It made the dining hall's breakfasts back home seem like all they had was bland cream of wheat.

"So I figure we can get all the boring stuff out of the way first, like your books and whatnot," said Dawn, over the sound of silverware clanging against our plates, "which reminds me. Let me see your schedules again?"

Tara and I pulled our schedules out and slid them over to her.

"Oh, nice! They put you guys in a few classes together, that's good," she started mumbling to herself. "Oof, although they doubled you up. Looks like later in the year you'll both start taking some second-year courses to get you caught up, since you're technically transferring from your school on Earth as sophomores. If only I found you guys a year sooner." She took a few bites from her toast, still fixated on our schedules. "All in all, though, not terrible! We should be able to get you guys everything you need in no time. Then we can get you fixed up with your weapons, and cloaks, too!"

"Wait, weapons?" Tara dropped her fork on her plate.

"Well, you two being casters will get staves. Now, if you were rune-knights, *then* you'd get the really cool stuff, swords, maces, daggers, and axes, they get all the cool shit when it comes to weapons, I have to admit."

"Hey, at least we get the sissy cloaks, though, right?" I couldn't hide my sarcasm. I had to admit, it was a bit of a bummer knowing some people get to wield badass weapons and I just had a stick and a dress.

"Oh, don't you worry over there. Sorcerers are the cream of the crop when it comes to classes. Everyone knows it, whether they want to admit it or not. And you're an S-tier, of all things! You won't be needing a sword once you learn to wield rune the way sorcerers can."

"Really?" I asked, suspecting that she was maybe just trying to make me feel better. I mean, I had a feeling that sorcerers were particularly powerful, since the dean of the university was one herself. But still, wielding a cool sword just seemed more powerful to me.

"Yep! Trust me, there are plenty of runics who wish they were sorcerers," Dawn replied.

I leaned back in my chair, rubbing my nose and giving Tara a look of pride. "You hear that? Sorcerers are cool."

Tara scoffed and rolled her eyes. "Oh, please, don't stroke his ego any more than it needs to be." She grinned. "What about healers? Are we cool?" she tried to brush it off like she didn't care that much, but knowing Tara, she cared even more than I did.

"Oh, definitely!" said Dawn. "Without you guys, nothing would ever get done in the Realm. Trust me."

Tara sat back, exchanging the same look I'd just given her. "Hmph, how do you like that?" she raised her chin, grinning proudly at me before crossing her arms and looking out the window. But as she did, Dawn glanced at me, winced, and gave a quick so-so gesture with her hand before Tara could notice.

The rest of the morning practically flew by as we went to a few different bookstores, picking up a wide variety of books, some for our shared courses, others more related to our specific classes.

We even managed to stop in Glendor's for a bit, where Tara finally got her hands on a Drakthor the Tormentor card, which Glendor had saved for her, just as he said he would.

"Now, you take care of that, you hear?" Glendor hollered out as we left his shop. "And let her win for once, Nate, would you?" He gave a deep, hearty laugh.

"I'll do my best!" I hollered back to him. "Thanks, Glendor."

"Thanks, Glenny!" Tara shouted. "Now that I have Drakthor, he won't stand a chance!"

Dawn was trying to hold back a grin as we left Glendor's shop. "Yesterday, I had to practically peel you off the *wall*, you were so afraid of him. Now he's Glenny?"

"Drakthor will do that to a girl, I guess!" I joked.

Tara didn't even seem to hear us, though, as her eyes remained glued to the card the entire way to the weapon shop: Clean Sheathes.

I could already see a variety of weapons on display through the window of the shop: claymores, battle axes, shields, bows, even a fierce-looking flail with a spiked metal ball at the end.

Upon entering the store, an old human working the front desk immediately hobbled over to us. "Ah, newcomers, I see? How do you do? How do you do?" He had a soft, silky voice. "My name is Christopher Floyd, and I manage Clean Sheathes."

He was not what I was expecting for an owner of a weapon shop. Instead, he was a hunched over, balding, frail-looking older man with a long, crooked nose, thick glasses that looked more like two magnifying glasses taped to his face, and a cane to help keep him upright. He was about as opposite as it could get from the intimidating, unwavering weapons hung up around the dark walls of his store.

"Hey, Mr. Floyd," Dawn politely said from behind us.

"Ah, Dawn, is that you? I didn't even see you back there. How have you been?"

"Great! Finally got a couple of newcomers here, they start classes tomorrow."

"Nice to meet you, sir. I'm Nate." I shook his hand, making sure not to squeeze too hard.

"Hmmm," he pondered. "Firm grip, tall, with broad shoulders, strong-looking legs, too. You're no doubt a rune-knight?"

"Uhm," I began, not wanting to hurt the old man's feelings.

"Actually," Dawn said, "he's a sorcerer, believe it or not. And an S-tier, to boot!"

Mr. Floyd practically jumped back, adjusting his glasses. "Get out of town! I swear you kids are getting harder and harder to identify with each passing year." He turned to Tara. "Now, you . . ."

"Hello, there! I'm Tara." She gave him a kind smile.

Mr. Floyd had an ornery grin on his face. "Mmm, yes you are, aren't you . . . hee hee . . ." The old man blushed, looking Tara up and down.

Tara's smile immediately disappeared and turned to a scowl. "Can I help you?" she muttered flatly.

I could have stepped in, but I could already tell that this old, perverted geezer was as harmless as a caterpillar. Even Tara could knock him out, if she really wanted to.

"Hmmm," Mr. Floyd pondered her, "you are without a doubt a healer, now, aren't you?"

"And *you* are without a doubt an old perver—" Tara started, before Dawn quickly jumped in.

"Person! Yes, you are getting up there in the years, aren't you, Mr. Floyd? But all the wiser for it!" Dawn nervously laughed before abruptly turning to Tara. "Do you want your weapon or not?" she muttered into Tara's ear.

"Ugh, fine."

Mr. Floyd looked a little puzzled. "Yes, I suppose I am getting up there these days. Believe it or not, though, some of these weapons hanging on the walls surpass even me in years."

"You don't say?" I said, trying to keep his attention off Dawn and Tara.

"Oh, heavens yes, young man. You'd be surprised."

"So people just don't like certain weapons, then?"

Mr. Floyd looked confused by my comment. "Huh? Oh! No,

no, that's not how weapon pairing works at all. You see, the weapon will choose the runic."

Now I was the one looking confused.

"You see," Mr. Floyd went on as Tara and Dawn walked back over to us, "every weapon in the Rune Realm is made from the natural materials within this world. And because of that, rune technically resides within them. This causes each weapon to almost have a mind of its own, reacting uniquely to the runic who wields it, some possibly *never* choosing a wielder, even."

"Ah," I said. "So some of these guys are just stubborn bastards, then?" I joked, looking around at the wide range of different "bastards" hung up along the walls.

Mr. Floyd let out a wheezy chuckle. "Yes, I suppose you *could* put it that way. But as a sorcerer, you won't need to worry about *those* guys." He gestured to the swords and axes directly above our heads. "No, you and your pretty friend, there," I could practically hear Tara biting her tongue behind me, "will be using *these*." He hobbled his way back to the counter opposite the small shop, with the rest of us trying our best to remain patient as we slowly followed behind him.

When we finally made it to the counter, he gestured up to the many staves on display on the back wall; there were at least fifty of them, all different shapes and sizes, some made of wood while others a type of shiny steel. They were all way more beautiful than I'd imagined them to be, and I suddenly wasn't so bummed about not getting a sword to wield.

"Wow," was all I could get out.

"They're beautiful," Tara whispered.

"They sure are," the old man agreed, "though I've always been partial to a good bow myself. Now, let's see." He hobbled behind the counter and gazed up at the staves, pondering them. "Let's try this one out for size." He pulled a chair up and cautiously reached up to grab a metal staff (for a second, I thought he was going down, and that we'd have to call for help).

He handed the metal staff over to me. It was a nice silvery-blue that caught the lights shining down from above in an entrancing sort of way.

"Go ahead, hold it straight out," he said.

As I did, nothing happened.

"Feel anything?" he asked.

"I don't think so. But how would I really know—?"

Mr. Floyd shook his head and snatched the pretty staff from my hands. "This won't do, then," he mumbled to himself.

He went back to considering the staves on the wall before pulling down a gray one made of wood. "How about this one?"

I took it from him and held it straight out. Not a second later, the staff began to violently shake, even thrashing back towards my head, as if it were trying to beat me to a pulp.

"What the hell!" I yelled out, holding the staff out as far as I could from my face while it continued to flail about like a pissed off cat that didn't want to be picked up.

Mr. Floyd managed to snatch it from me. As he did so, the staff seemed to "calm down," allowing him to hang it back up on the wall.

"That one must have heard you call it a bastard," he chuckled, looking a little embarrassed. "I ought to start having customers sign a waiver before coming inside the shop. Sorry about that!"

He continued tossing me staff after staff, all of them doing weird things which seemed to prove that they weren't the correct weapon for me. One staff even launched from my hand, shot across the store, and broke through the display glass before continuing to sail away through town.

"Dear me," Mr. Floyd broke the silence, "we may not be getting that one back. Don't worry about the glass, we can have it fixed up easily later."

Feeling horribly guilty over damaging Mr. Floyd's shop, and also growing concerned that there may not be a staff in here for me, Mr. Floyd decided that my predicament called for drastic measures, and hobbled his way into the back section of the store.

"Very difficult case, yes, very difficult," he muttered from the other side of the wall as various staves flung past the opening of the doorway. "Not that one, no, definitely not you."

Tara was leaning up against me, rubbing my shoulder. "Don't worry, Nate. Your staff is in here somewhere, I just know it."

"Right, definitely." I tried to act like it wasn't starting to worry me.

"Yeah, no sweat," Dawn added. "There's never been a runic who didn't have a weapon call to them before. Mr. Floyd will find it back there for sure." She was clearly trying to comfort me, but even she seemed to have a hint of concern in her tone for once.

"Not to worry," Mr. Floyd's voice rang out again from the back room, "we will get you—oh—could it be? No, it would be inconceivable, and yet. . ."

Mr. Floyd came strolling out from the back room holding what was perhaps the most beautiful thing in the store (other than Tara and Dawn). In his arms, he carried a long, wooden staff, shining bright gold, it seemed endowed with a certain level of dignity beyond anything I've ever been able to display. I couldn't help thinking that Mr. Floyd was way off the mark with this one.

"Give it a try?" He gazed up at me, still carefully holding the staff.

I figured I had nothing to lose at this point (though I couldn't say the same for Mr. Floyd's shop), so I gently grabbed the gold staff and held it out.

To my utter amazement, I felt a comforting, warm sensation originate from the staff itself. Then the sensation traveled down my arm, eventually flooding throughout my entire body. It was strange. I felt safe, at peace with everything around me. It just felt right.

"Unbelievable!" Mr. Floyd gasped.

"Is that the one?" Tara eagerly asked.

"How's it feel, Nate?" Dawn questioned.

"It feels . . . good." I smiled brightly, taking in the beautiful golden staff. It had a slight bend to it in the center, which made it feel very natural in my grip. And it came to a twist at the top. "Really good!"

"Oh, I'm sure it does!" Mr. Floyd blurted out. "This is no doubt your staff, it always has been. But I just can't believe it to be so. If I may?" He slowly reached for it, inspecting it closely again as he held it up to the light. "This staff, young man, has been in this shop even longer than I have. I believe it to be older than me, much older."

"You're kidding," I said, feeling amazed but also kind of grateful that the staff apparently waited ages for me to come along. It was kind of neat to think of, and already made me a little fond of it.

"Not kidding at all. And as you can see, the wood itself shines a bright gold. While I have aged and withered since my first day on the job here, all those years ago, this staff has never dulled, never lost its luster, not even a bit. It's remarkable, really."

"What's that thing even made of, for it to be that resilient?" Dawn asked.

"That's the most amazing part of all," Mr. Floyd began, "the type of wood cannot be identified, it never could. I'm not entirely sure where it came from, nor were my predecessors before me. I was starting to consider that it was just a prop, or faulty. This is truly a marvelous occasion. Young man, you take care of this staff. I'm sure it will do the same for you." He handed it back to me.

"Thanks, Mr. Floyd. I will," I said, still in awe over its beauty.

Mr. Floyd cleared his throat. "Now, that will be one thousand givets." He held out his hand.

"A give-whata?" I blurted out.

When buying our books earlier, the store accepted cash without question, so I figured that currency worked the same here as it did back home. Regardless, one thousand of anything seemed like a lot of dough.

"Uh—you take visa?" I asked.

Dawn laughed and stepped forward. "Here you go, Mr. Floyd." She pulled out a thin wallet from her tight pants and dumped out ten small golden coins. "Courtesy of Dean Celestine and the Academy. Students have to buy the books themselves. Weapons can be a bit pricier, so they come included. One of the many perks of attending Magic Rune Academy."

"Wow! Not many schools back home are that generous. I'll take it, though!" I happily said. "But should I be worried that I don't have any of those givey things you just used to pay for?"

"You're a silly boy, aren't you?" Mr. Floyd spoke up. "I just prefer givets."

"Ah, I see," I muttered.

"Givets are one of a few forms of currency that are accepted in the Rune Realm," Dawn added. "It's really the primary and universal form of currency, but cash is also accepted as the human form of currency. Orcs and elves have their own forms of currency, too."

"Makes sense," I said. "So, Mr. Floyd," I addressed the old timer, "you're clearly human, you don't prefer cash?"

He gave me an ornery look and gestured for me to come closer, and when I did, he whispered, "I like my money like I like my girls, boy . . . *foreign.*"

I lowered my brow, silently staring at the horny geezer. "Right, *I'm* the silly one."

We left Clean Sheathes about fifteen minutes after that. Tara had found her staff, a white one, made of steel with a half-moon design on the top, on just her second try, which she was very relieved about (if anything because it meant less time around Mr. Floyd).

We were now walking down Hilt Street with our individual staves, Dawn right behind us in her tight shifter clothes. Back home, we would have stood out like a sore thumb. But here? We were just starting to finally blend in a little.

Our next stop was at the clothing and armory store, Iron Guild, where we picked up a few different sets of robes and cloaks. Tara's were primarily white and yellow, as healers apparently wore lighter and warmer colors to differentiate themselves from sorcerers. My personal favorite of hers was a white robe that hugged her curves in a way that could kill on sight, ironic for someone who was meant to heal instead of fight, but I wasn't complaining.

On the other hand, my robes were primarily darker, cooler colors. I had a couple light blue robes I picked out, many navy-blue, and even a black one that Dawn said made me look like an "ominous snack," whatever that meant. I took it as a good sign, though, because she gave me one of her classic winks after saying it.

It was a little after three in the afternoon when we finally finished up the checklist, now venturing through Hearthvale with our staves, books, and bags of clothes. I figured it was about time to head back, but Dawn had other plans, as she suddenly led us down an alleyway between a couple of shops, toward the beach.

"Come on, Nate, don't be a party-pooper, now!" Dawn shouted out, turning back to grin at us as she pulled me and Tara through a tight alleyway between two shops. "It's our last stop, I promise. Nothing beats the beach after a long day of shopping, right, Tara?"

"Uh, yeah, I guess, but it's a little cool out for the beach, isn't it?" she said, not so enthusiastically. Tara was always more of a pool girl, if anything.

"Oh, just wait. It'll be fine, trust me!" Dawn replied.

I could see the clean white sand on the other side of the alley from here. And when we made it back out on the other side of the buildings, the whole view really opened up to us. The coastline was part of a very large cove, gradually coming to a bend way off in the distance. The water was like glass, appearing to be even clearer and bluer now that I was up close. And the sand was so white, so clean, that it actually could have been mistaken for freshly powdered snow if you didn't know any better.

"Just when I think this place can't get any prettier," Tara whispered to herself.

"You guys will love this!" Dawn blurted out. "Come on!"

We took our shoes off and swiftly followed Dawn down the concrete ramp, taking our first steps onto the soft sand. It was surprisingly warm, like my feet were getting a comfy hug, and it somehow didn't appear to be sticking, instead slipping off my feet with each step before immediately settling back into place, leaving no trace of my footsteps behind. By the time we made it to the middle of the beach, my feet were still spotless, as if we hadn't even touched the sand at all.

"The sand here is different from anything back home," Dawn said, noticing the perplexed expression on my face.

"No kidding," Tara bent down to grab some, but it almost instantly fell right through her fingers, leaving her hands squeaky clean. "I guess there aren't any sandcastles being built in the Rune Realm."

"It's kind of nice, though, right?" I expressed. "I personally hate having to clean myself off after going to the beach."

"Yeah, and that's why the sand here stays so clean and looks unscathed. It only reacts to disturbances for a moment before sliding and settling back into place. That way we keep our dirt and germs to our own bodies, and the sand sticks to itself. It's a mutual agreement, a win-win." Dawn said, softly laughing.

I looked around, noticing that even though there were many other students and townies who were already occupying the white beach, the sand remained neatly settled, like nobody had ever stepped on it.

"It's so warm, too!" Tara stated, plopping down on it. With no concern over getting any sand on my clothes, I joined her.

"Yep!" Dawn agreed, also taking a seat. "Some would consider it to be alive, even, since there are small amounts of rune within each individual grain!"

Tara instantly seemed a little less comfortable upon hearing this (she had been doing sand-angels, but immediately stopped and sat back up).

"It's . . . alive?" she asked.

"In a way, yes. But don't think of it as being alive in a sense that it has thoughts and feelings or whatever. It's more like how trees and plants are technically alive."

"Ah, I see," Tara said, gently brushing the sandy surface with the back of her hand and looking a little relieved.

"But yeah," Dawn continued, "that's why it feels so warm, it adjusts its temperature based on the weather conditions. The hotter it is, the cooler the sand becomes. And on colder days, it heats up."

"I see," I said, "so it has a way of regulating its own temperature, then. Probably a way of sustaining itself, like a defense mechanism, even. How neat!"

We continued to lie in the warm sand for what felt like ten or twenty minutes. It had a way of relieving any tension in the body. I could easily see why this would be such a popular spot for stressed students to let some tension out.

Different groups of people were partaking in various activities around us. An orc to our left was sunbathing, a few elves were passing an oddly shaped ball around to each other, knee deep in the water up ahead, two humans behind us were lounging about in a couple beach chairs, and three girls to our right were tossing a frisbee to each other, catching it in their mouths and occasionally running on all fours to gain speed when needed. I assumed they were shifters of some kind.

"Werewolves," Dawn muttered, a look of disgust on her face.

"Werewolves?!" Tara repeated.

"Yeah, but not like the kind you see in horror movies. They're a type of shifter, and have complete control when in their primal forms. Although, that doesn't help most of them from still acting like animals."

"Don't like werewolves?" I assumed.

"They're not all bad, but most seem to just have a natural tendency to be rude or aggressive, for some reason. I try not to be prejudiced, though."

"And it has nothing to do with the fact that you're a cat shifter?" I asked, an ornery, knowing look on my face.

Dawn smirked. "That could be part of it. But nah, plenty of others would agree with me."

We continued bathing in the sun for a few minutes when a thought hit me.

"There's something I've still been trying to wrap my head around," I said.

Dawn propped herself up, looking curiously over at me.

"It's the whole mytosome and rune thing," I continued. You said this sand is technically alive because it has rune in it. And the weapons in the store had small amounts of rune in them, too. And *those* certainly seemed alive." I thought back to the gray staff that tried beating me up. "So, what makes something alive here? Is it the rune or the mytosomes?"

"That's a good question. I mean, what makes any of us alive, really," Dawn began, grimacing over at the werewolves as they gradually moved closer and closer to us. "So mytosomes only reside in runics and beasts in the Realm; they exist within intelligent life-forms, as part of us, like cells. But rune is more of a form of energy. It gets produced by all things in the realm, living and non-living. And it exists in all forms of matter in the Realm. It's in this sand, the air around us, the water down there, even raw materials.

"So one begs the question if everything in this world is technically alive, really," she continued. "Even the air itself. That's kind of what I meant with the sand. I mean, if something can't think, yet produces energy, then does that make it alive?"

"I think so, maybe . . ." I said.

"Well, there you go, then." Dawn smiled.

"So, is there rune in us?" Tara asked, "Since we or our ancestors technically come from this world, too?"

"There is! And we refer to it as interior rune," explained Dawn. "Think of interior rune as the energy within a runic's body, whereas exterior rune is technically any rune that doesn't exist within your own body. And then we also have the mytosomes in our bodies, which react with and can manipulate both the rune inside us and outside in the Realm, depending on what class you are. That's what Lackers would define as magic: being able to manipulate the rune to do *magical* things. So just remember," Dawn added after noticing the puzzled expression on my face, "mytosomes are like cells and rune is like energy. It's said that the greatest runics are the ones who have mastered the connection between their mytosomes and rune—"

Dawn had lost her train of thought as a frisbee came flying past us, almost hitting Tara in the face. One of the werewolf girls came jogging over, a tall slender one with thick, wild dark hair. She appeared to be in her hybrid form; her eyes a deep red, and four large canines popping out from her gums. "Sorry about that!" For some reason, she was looking at me, when she should have been apologizing to Tara.

The other two werewolves came running over after their friend, one being a short, pudgy girl with a pink pixie cut, the other of average height, and having long blonde dreadlocks.

"Yeah, sorry," the girl with the pixie cut said, also looking at me with a smile.

"It was just a mistake, but you should really apologize to my friend here," I said. "It almost hit her."

"Oh, that's strange," the first girl started, sneering. "I didn't even notice she was here." She sniffed dramatically. "Could barely smell the mytosomes on this one. Is she even a runic?"

The two girls behind her chuckled.

I quickly shot a glance at Tara to see that she was gazing down at the sand, turning a shade of pink. Already knowing how insecure she was about being a D-tier, the remark really pissed me off.

"*You*, on the other hand," the first werewolf dawdled closer to me, "I could smell your mytosomes from across the beach." She smiled seductively. "What's your story? Haven't seen you around campus before."

"My name's Nate, and I think it'd be best if you ladies took your frisbee and went somewhere else."

The werewolf girl turned to her friends behind her. "Oooo, you hear that, girls? We're his *ladies*, now."

"Interesting," the girl with the pixie cut said. "Don't think Chuck would like that, though. Perhaps we should let him know." She bit on her lip with one of her canines.

I didn't know who Chuck was, but he sounded like he was connected to these girls in some manner. And if I could take my anger out on anyone, I'd much rather it be him than these three, even if they *were* the ones instigating things.

"Come on, girls, this one's no fun," the first girl said before turning around to leave. But as she walked past Tara, she scuffed up some sand in her face. "Especially if he's hanging out with a wannabe runic like her. What a freak."

This was all it took. I started striding over to them, but before I could do anything else, I felt a hand on my shoulder, and then I turned to see Dawn.

"I'll talk to them," Dawn calmly said, smiling kindly at me.

I took a few deep breaths and nodded. "You sure?"

"Mhm," she said in a sweet tone. And then began smoothly walking over to the werewolves, her hips swinging about.

I bent down closer to Tara. "Don't listen to them, okay? Dawn was right, I guess werewolves can be a disgusting bunch."

Tara looked up at me with a somber expression. "I know, you're right. I just—" Her eyes went wide as she looked past me.

I turned around just in time to see Dawn, in her hybrid form, slap the girl with the wild hair across the face. She left three long red slash marks on the werewolf, causing her to stumble backward while holding her cheek.

"AND IF YOU BITCHES EVER TALK TO MY FRIEND LIKE THAT AGAIN, I'LL HUNT YOU

MUTTS DOWN AND TURN YOU INTO PUPPY CHOW!" Dawn blurted out.

Tara and I were dumbfounded.

"How dare you!" the girl with the pixie cut spoke out. "We'll be getting Chuck to deal with you! Better watch your back!" And the three girls stumbled away from Dawn, their tails literally tucked between their legs.

"Yeah, yeah! Tell Chuck to come find me! I'll kick his furry little ass, too!" she yelled after them before turning around to stomp back to us.

We remained frozen, silently staring at Dawn. It was a side of her we had yet to see, but I was happy to see it, and proud to call her a friend.

"They said sorry," Dawn calmly said as she sat back down beside us, looking out toward the clear blue water and smiling.

"Th-thank you, Dawn," Tara said, looking astonished and genuinely grateful.

Dawn turned to her and waved a hand. "Ah, it was nothing."

At that moment, I wasn't entirely sure what was going through Tara's mind, but based on her expression and her quiet demeanor the rest of the time on the beach, I could have taken a pretty good guess. Before now, she was never quite sold on Dawn, keeping her distance and almost going out of her way not to warm up to her, which she seemed to now be regretting, possibly even feeling a little guilty over it. Regardless, that would soon become a thing of the past. From that day forward, Dawn and Tara would become great friends.

I guess certain actions from people just have a way of changing how you feel about them, slapping a werewolf in the face on your behalf, being one of them.

Chapter Six

THE DAY that I was eagerly waiting for had finally arrived: my first day of classes at Magic Rune Academy. But where I was excited and hopeful, Tara appeared to be a little bundle of stress, though I could tell she didn't want to admit it.

"Books, staff, cloak . . ." she ran through her list of things to remember for about the third time as we walked through the campus quad, our new cloaks blowing behind us in the morning breeze and our individual staves at our sides.

Dawn couldn't escort us to our first classes as she was already in a class of her own, so Tara and I were left to venture through campus by ourselves for the first time since arriving. Luckily, there were plenty of other students strolling (and to my great surprise, some even flying) through campus, if needed.

I pulled my schedule out and ran through it again, still swiftly walking to keep up with Tara. "At least we're in the same building for our first class. We both have Intro to Classes in the General Studies building, right?" I asked.

Tara flung her own schedule out and scanned it over. "Correct! I think I remember seeing the General Studies building to the right of the quad last time we were here," she said, shoving it back inside her white robe and continuing onward. "It seems a little pointless, though, doesn't it? *Intro to Classes*? Like, why do we need a class to introduce us to other classes?"

I chuckled. "I think it's a course to go over the *classes* that exist in the realm. You know, like the healer class, sorcerer class, shifters . . . not a course that reviews other school courses."

Tara stopped in her stride and smacked her forehead. "Nate, I don't know if I'm ready for this. I'm going to suck. I just know it!"

"You're not going to—"

"I couldn't even put together that this class is about the *runic* classes! I don't belong here."

"Tara, that's ridiculous. You're a healer." I gently placed my hand on her shoulder. "You got placed by the Reader and everything. And you're going to be an amazing healer, to boot. Trust me. You and I, we're in this together, no matter what."

Her nervous frown lightened a little.

"Besides, it's a confusing name for a course, anyway," I scoffed. "It's not just you, I thought the same thing at first."

We reached the small plaza in the center of the quad with the large statue that looked like a combination of a butterfly and a woman before veering right, and from here, I could see our destination. It was a modern-looking, circular building. A monumental sign made of fancy stone that read *Generic Studies* was posted on the neatly trimmed lawn leading up to it.

"Think that's it?" I sarcastically asked, pointing to the conspicuous sign.

"At least they make it idiot-proof for us!" Tara said, smiling with relief.

Upon entering the building, the first thing I noticed was the distinct structure of it. The entire interior was made up of two big circular floors, with classrooms stationed along the outer walls of both floors. There also seemed to be a large auditorium at the heart of the inner walls. It was as modern and bright on the inside as it was on the out, with its white walls and shiny white marble floors.

"Okay," Tara's shaky voice echoed out, "I'm in classroom 114 with Professor Hucklebee. And you're ... ?"

"Classroom 119, with Professor Morran. I'll meet you out here afterward?"

"Yeah," she smiled nervously, "good luck. I know you've got this!"

"And so do you. You'll do great!" I said, and gave her a kiss on the lips.

When I pulled away, she looked a little surprised, but then quickly beamed, her cheeks beginning to flush pink. Clearly flustered, she turned around to head into her classroom, occasionally glancing back at me a few times and waving, a big smile still painted all over her face.

Now that she was inside, I dropped the confident smile. Truth be told, I was a little nervous myself, but seeing Tara so apprehensive gave me a sort of selfless strength that helped keep me calm. But she was gone now, and I was still standing out in the hallway alone, the other students already in their classes.

I took a deep breath and walked a little way down the circular hallway before stopping just outside of room 119. I could see Professor Moran through the small window in the door as the reddish elf with long blue hair was getting some notes organized at her desk.

"Ah, hello there," she kindly said as I entered the room. "Welcome to Intro to Classes." She gestured for me to take a seat. I wasn't sure if she was simply acting like she hadn't just met me two days ago for the sake of the other students, but she *had* to remember me. The look on her face when she saw the Reader said it all.

"Thanks, Professor," I replied. "Glad to be here."

As I strolled down the occupied rows of chairs, I could almost feel all the eyes in the class peering at me, and I don't think it was just because I was showing up a week into the semester. I caught pieces of whispers throughout the room as I walked, and it would seem that the word had already gotten out about there being another S-tier runic on campus.

I ended up taking an empty seat toward the back of the room (all the seats closer to the front had already been taken), which gave me a view of the many students in front of me. There appeared to be students of all different classes in the room, based on their attire. From a stocky orc dude wearing plate armor in the front row to a slender elf girl wearing a navy-blue robe similar to my own, there was no shortage of variety in this class.

Professor Morran got up from her desk, holding her neat stack of notes. Even though she was my professor, I couldn't help noticing how sexy she looked. I wasn't quite sure what her class was exactly, but she was wearing a green and brown leather tunic. Her blue hair was flowing down past her hips, and her purple eyes were glowing brightly, even in daylight. I wondered again about her age. She couldn't have been much older than me.

"Okay, class," she started, "we shall resume where we left off last week, going into further detail on exactly how the classes differ regarding rune sensing and manipulation."

At that point, something happened that already took my attention off of the lesson. I felt a very light tap on the back of my shoulder, so I turned around and was pleased to see a very cute girl with pink hair bashfully looking at me. Somehow, she looked familiar. Her hair was fashioned in a long braid, which finally gave it away.

"Sakura?" I whispered. "From the Bronze Dragon, right?" Between having the extra attention on me while walking in and her now being in her base form, I had barely noticed her when I sat down.

She silently nodded.

"Small world! How are you?"

"Hi," she softly said, smiling and glancing down at her desk. "I'm surprised you recognized me." She fiddled with her fingers.

I casually waved a hand. "Nah, other than your eyes being blue now instead of green and not having your fox ears, you look the same to me." I smiled. Even in her base form, she was still cute as ever.

Sakura blushed hard. "You—you remember the color of my eyes?"

"Of course! I've never seen green eyes like yours before. I wouldn't forget them."

Her current blue eyes remained glued down to her desk as she continued fiddling with her fingers. It looked as if she was holding back a big smile.

"Th-thank you. That's really nice of you."

"Yeah, no problem. So, are you just starting school here then, too?"

"Mhm." She nodded. "It's my first year here. It's been really nice so far."

"Yeah, this place is awesome. I'm technically a sophomore, but it's my first year here too. Actually, this is my first cla—"

"Mr. Gannon," Professor Morran's voice rang out, pulling me back around to the front of the room (I *knew* she remembered me), "would you be able to?" she asked.

It was definitely not how I wanted to start my first class at Magic Rune Academy, but I had no other choice but to give myself up and ask, "Could you repeat the question?"

Professor Morran's expression lowered. "The primary difference, Mr. Gannon," she began, her tone drier than before, "on how a sorcerer interacts with rune compared to that of a shifter. Do you know the answer?"

"Uh, well," I figured I'd give it my best try here, "you see, a sorcerer, they cast spells, and well, a shifter . . . shifts."

A few snickers broke out from my fellow classmates. But Professor Morran looked disappointed, which, for some reason, really bothered me. "Well," she began, "you're not wrong, but perhaps Miss Redd could give us a more elaborate response? I assume you two were brainstorming ideas earlier, correct?"

A nervous squeak squeezed out from behind me. "Y-yes, ma'am," Sakura's soft, high-pitched voice spoke out. "Um, it has to do with internal and external rune. Shifters specialize in manipulating the rune inside their own bodies. Sorcerers can't do that, they can only manipulate the rune around them—external rune."

Professor Morran smiled. "Very good. What Miss Redd says is correct." She raised her voice, addressing the whole class now as she resumed pacing back and forth up front. "Shifters and rune-knights are limited to working with the rune inside their own bodies, otherwise known as internal rune. Meanwhile, sorcerers can only interact with external rune. Now, where does that leave healers?"

"Healers use both external and internal rune," said an elf guy wearing a white cloak in the front row.

"Yes," Professor Morran replied, "to a degree, at least. While it is true that healers *do* have the ability to manipulate internal and external rune, they are very limited when it comes to external rune compared to a sorcerer. In fact, the only external rune they can manipulate is the rune within others' bodies—replenishing it and using it to heal the wounds of that individual. This, of course, is how they interact with internal rune as well, when healing themselves."

"But wait," I found myself blurting out as a thought hit me, "I thought the rune within someone's body was considered internal rune?"

"A very reasonable assumption," replied Professor Morran, "and a common misinterpretation of rune. But it's rather simple, really. The rune within your *own* body is considered *your* internal rune, while the rune within another's body would be external rune, to you, while being internal rune to that other individual."

"So, internal rune can also be external rune?" I slowly asked.

"It's all about perspective, Mr. Gannon," replied Professor Morran. "For example, you as a sorcerer could manipulate the rune within another person's body, since that would be considered external rune to you, but you cannot manipulate the rune within your own body, since that is your internal rune."

"Well, maybe if I try really hard, I could manipulate my own internal rune, too. Can't be too much different than manipulating someone else's internal rune, right?" I genuinely asked, but some more chuckles emerged from my classmates (and now some flirtatious glances from some of the girls, too). I think they all thought I was trying to be funny, but really, I was just genuinely curious.

"Well, you'd be the first sorcerer to do it, Mr. Gannon," said Professor Morran, with a hint of sarcasm in her voice, "so good luck with that. Now," she continued, addressing the class as a whole, "if you'd all please turn to page 27 in your textbooks, we'll review the different origins for each class."

From there, we read through the origins of each individual class, which all revolved around certain individuals from the earliest days of the Realm. All of them learned how to harness the rune in the unique ways that were still used today by people from each of the class groups. I found myself being so interested in it that the rest of the class seemed to fly by, so much so that when Professor Morran dismissed us, I thought she was joking.

As I made my way through the crowd of students and outside into the hall, the same light tap on my shoulder that I had experienced earlier caught my attention again. I turned around to see Sakura.

This was the first time I was actually standing next to her, and I hadn't realized just how short she really was. She must have had to stand on her tiptoes just to reach the back of my shoulder. She was maybe five feet tall at best. But what she lacked in height, she made up for in her curvy hips and massive chest. She was wearing some form of what looked to be a shifter outfit— a tight white tank with a silky, loose pink skirt made of a light material that hung down just above her knees. It sort of looked like a cute tennis outfit.

"Hey, Sakura." I smiled.

"Hi, um," she stammered, looking upset about something. "I just wanted to say sorry for earlier."

"Sorry? Oh! You mean about Professor Morran calling me out?"

She silently nodded her head, looking down at the shiny white floor.

"You don't have to worry about that, really! She was just testing out the new guy . . . I think," I chuckled. "Besides, it was worth it. I'm glad I got to talk to you again. To be honest, I was starting to think I'd have to go back every day for a runic beer just to get the chance."

She tried to hide her smile and started to blush again, a usual occurrence with her, it seemed. "You wanted to see me again?" she asked with that soft voice of hers.

"Yeah, definitely! Is that all right?" I asked.

She blushed harder, still looking down at the floor. "Uhm, yes, yes, of course." She was beaming as she quickly glanced up at me, her eyes meeting mine for what felt like the first time.

"Awesome, well—" I started, but before I knew it, she spun around and took off in the opposite direction.

"It was really nice seeing you again!" she squeaked out without turning around.

"Yeah, same here," I muttered to myself, waving at her back as she darted around the bend of the hallway and out of sight.

As I approached Tara's classroom, I noticed she was already there waiting for me.

"Hey!" she hollered out, waving to me with a big smile on her face. "I just saw our waitress from the Bronze Dragon the other day run past here. Why do I feel like you're behind that again?"

"She's in my class, believe it or not. I think she's a freshman here."

"That's great! Just try not to put too much of that Nate charm on her at one time," she said with a grin. "I think she'd pass out on you, that one. So, how was your class?" she asked as we began walking out of the building.

"It went really well! Way more interesting than anything we learned back home. I was actually engaged the entire time for a change."

"Oh my gosh, right? I love it so far! My professor was a sweet old lady, kind of boring, but the material itself makes up for it! How was Professor Morran?"

"She seemed nice," I said, choosing to leave out a few of the details, like when she had called me out. "A little strict and by the book, maybe, but nice."

I was relieved to hear that Tara had a great first session as well. And having that first one out of the way made for a much less stressful walk over to our next class, which we would have together in a building on the opposite side of the quad called the Bailey History Hall.

The building had a museum feel to it, with different artifacts and exhibits on display in the large open lobby that greeted us when we walked in. The lobby gave way to a huge auditorium where our next class, Basic of History of the Realm, was to take place.

It was dark in the auditorium, which already made me kind of sleepy. But it was nice, in a way, because it gave us the opportunity to sit together and blend in with the large crowd of first-year students.

The course was taught by an ancient-looking elf named Professor Brookes. His skin was a faded pale-blue, and he was so tall and thin that I could have sworn he disappeared when he turned sideways. He had a monotone and drawling voice which, between that and the dimmed lights, caused me to drift off halfway through the lecture.

Tara, however, was still somehow on the edge of her seat, taking notes and enthusiastically absorbing everything having to do with the lesson, which revolved around the creation of the Academy's name.

"I still cannot believe that's how the name Magic Rune Academy came to be!" she blurted out as we left the building (I was more than thankful to be back out in daylight). "I mean seriously, humans and elves couldn't decide on what to call rune at the time? Was it magic or was it rune? And then they just split the difference and never looked back," she giggled. "Funny how things like that can happen."

"Yeah," I said in an unenthused tone, similar to the one used by Professor Brookes. "Makes sense that the humans wanted to call it magic. But I just don't get why they didn't change the name to Rune Academy over time. It seems like rune is what stuck, right?"

"Definitely!" Tara replied. "Guess they didn't want to bother with the paperwork or something."

"Well," I yawned, "I guess if it isn't broke . . ."

We ended up meeting Dawn for lunch at the campus dining hall after that, where we caught her up on our morning.

"Yeah, no one really knows why they never changed the name. That's a good thought, though!" she encouragingly replied to Tara, who was still passionately going on about it.

"Oh, I ran into our waitress from the other day again," I said. "She sits behind me in Intro to Classes."

"Oh yeah? The shy, pink-haired girl?" Dawn asked with an intriguing expression.

"Yeah, Sakura. She seems nice. Kind of weird, but in a good way, you know?"

"Hmm, 'weird, but in a good way.'" Dawn pursed her lips. "Sounds like she'd fit in perfectly with our little gang here!"

"You're saying we're weird?! Speak for yourself, Dawn." Tara blurted out, pretending to look offended.

"Tara," Dawn started, "you just went on for the past ten minutes telling me all about the *fascinating* origin of our school's name."

Tara's face went blank, as if she just realized something. "Shit . . . maybe you're right."

I took a bite out of my burger and practically melted on the spot, my eyes rolling back. "Okay," I mumbled, "why the hell is all the food here so damn good?!"

"Careful, don't have an orgasm over there now." Dawn winked.

"I think Tara already beat me to it during History," I said with a smirk. "You should have seen the look on her face when old Professor Brookes was going on about the Academy first getting accredited by the Magical Board of Higher Education back in 1697."

"Hey now," Tara began in a dignified tone, trying to hold back a laugh, "you can't fault a girl for appreciating a good old-fashioned history lesson." She pushed her glasses up the bridge of her nose. "And it was 1692."

I had one final class left for the day, which happened to also be the one I was looking forward to the most: Rune Sensing and Manipulation. It was my first class that was specifically designed for sorcerers, taught by Dean Celestine herself. This would be the true start of fulfilling my S-tier ambitions, to be the most powerful sorcerer that I could possibly be. Just the thought alone filled me with excitement.

I had to really book it across campus from the dining hall to the Cathedral of Tranquility, and when I finally made it through the fancy courtyard, up the stone steps, and into the marble-floored lobby, I was practically sweating through my robe. My class was in room 139, which, of course, had to be the last room on the right wing of the building, so I never had a chance to even catch my breath before finally entering the classroom.

I guess I shouldn't have been surprised, though, upon entering and noticing that Dean Celestine wasn't even there yet herself.

Showing up on the later side again, I was left with an empty desk closer to the back of the room, so I made my way through the conversing students and took my seat.

As I surveyed the room, I noticed that this time every student was dressed similarly. With this being a sorcerer specific course, the chain mail, plates of armor, and shifter clothes were no longer present, instead giving way to the many cloth robes worn by every student in the class. It was kind of nice having a sense of belonging.

"Where is she?" a surprisingly skinny orc muttered to my right. He must have been the nerdiest-looking orc in the Realm, with his circular glasses, buck teeth, and thin black hair.

"Can't believe she's late again. Kind of strange for a dean to be consistently late," said a slender elf with dark red skin sitting a couple rows in front of me.

"Oh, give it a rest," another elf, a girl, muttered back. "You said it yourself, she's the dean. I'm sure she's plenty busy as it is."

I couldn't help but smirk. Based on my initial encounter with Dean Celestine, I could probably take an educated guess as to the reason for the delay, and it had nothing to do with her dean duties.

"Hey, you're new, aren't you?" The skinny orc noticed me. He had a nasally voice. "Nice gold staff! The name's Dak Driftwood. Pleasure to meet you."

"Nate—Nate Gannon." I smiled and shook his hand.

"Nice to meet you, Nate! You're a transfer?"

"Yeah, sort of."

"Well, let me know if you have any questions," he went on. "I've been studying rune manipulation for years."

"Thanks, Dak. Appreciate it. All of this is still pretty new to me, if I'm being honest. I'm an outsider. Just got recruited this year."

He looked surprised. "You don't say?! Are you nervous? I got categorized into the sorcerer class when I was fifteen and lived in the Realm my whole life. I can't imagine discovering the Realm and then being thrown into the Academy shortly after."

"It was definitely a lot to take in," I admitted. "But now I'm just enjoying the ride, really. Do all runics from the Realm get categorized into their classes at fifteen or something?"

"Just depends," he began. "Most runics don't start showing signs of what class they are until they're old enough to start manipulating rune, usually around puberty."

"I must have been a late bloomer," I replied. "I didn't start until, well, about a week ago." I thought back to what Dawn told me before I had even arrived in the Rune Realm, and how I wouldn't show any signs of rune manipulation until I physically resided in the Realm.

"Yeah, that's because you were an outsider. You can't show signs of rune manipulation if there's no rune to manipulate, after all," he snorted with laughter. "Well, I guess if you were in another class there would be a chance, though. But we're sorcerers. We need exterior rune to work with."

"Yeah, that's what I've been hearing." At that point, I pretended to get my notes together. Nothing against Dak, he seemed all right, but also kind of like a know-it-all.

And as luck would have it, Dean Celestine had finally entered the room with a dramatic entrance. She warped into the front of the class, almost unraveling herself out of thin air. She was wearing a long robe that was royal purple and had glimmering silver streaks running vertically through it.

"All right, class," she began, looking around the room, "how are we all doing today? Wow, you're a bunch of early birds, aren't you?"

"Actually, Dean Celestine," the elf with dark red skin blurted out, "you're late again."

"Quiet, Charles," Dean Celestine brushed off.

"That's not even my name—!"

"So, where did we leave off?" she said, before doing a double take at me. "Oh! And how could I forget? Everyone, we have an addition to our ranks, Mr. Nate Gannon."

I smiled, quietly hoping she would quickly proceed onward with the lecture as all the eyes fixated on me. Nothing against having attention on me, but I just didn't want to come off as a cocky S-tier on the first day. But, of course, she did not.

"And a *special* addition to our ranks, of all things. You may have already heard, but Mr. Gannon here is an S-tier runic."

Any remaining eyes in the class that may have been lingering elsewhere in the room now darted back to me. You could have heard a pin drop.

"Uh, hey, everyone," I muttered to all the stares and noticed again that many of the female sorcerers were shooting looks of sexual thirst in my direction.

"Now, don't think this means that you shall receive any extra leeway from me, though, understood?"

"Yes, Professor," was all I could say, remembering the guaranteed A that she said she'd be giving me the last time we had met.

"Very good. Now . . ."

As she continued on with the lecture, Dak whispered over to me. "You're an S-tier?" he hissed. "I was over here offering you help, and you're an S-tier?" he had an incredulous look on his face.

"Yeah," I replied, looking a bit sheepish. "I can't do jack shit right now, though. Really, I'm a total noob," I added, figuring it best to keep expectations low until I actually started learning some spells.

"Before actually *manipulating* rune, the first step is to always master the art of *sensing* rune."

She waved a hand, summoning a large jar on her desk the size of a five-gallon bucket; it had a strange yellowish jelly substance in it. "This here will help assist all of you with learning to sense rune. Can anyone tell me what this is?"

Dak raised his hand to my right.

"Yes, Dirk?"

"It's Dak, ma'am. But that appears to be jam from a surveybee, used to help with sensing rune, I believe?"

"Correct, my young friend. You see, class, surveybees are unrivaled when it comes to sensing rune. It's said that they can even pinpoint and identify someone's interior rune from miles away.

"This here," she gestured to the jar, "is the jam that they produce in their hives. It will help guide you all in sensing rune. One of the most difficult things for beginner sorcerers to grasp is learning what it's supposed to feel like to sense exterior rune. Whether that be rune within the natural elements of the world, like in the air or in plants, or rune within another person's body. As long as it's not within your own body, that's all considered exterior rune, and in turn can be manipulated by the sorcerer."

I thought back to my comment in Professor Morran's class about me manipulating my own interior rune by "trying harder" and felt dumber by the minute.

"By coating yourselves in the surveybee jam," Dean Celestine went on, "you'll be able to sense exterior rune much easier. And once you know what it feels like to sense rune using the jam, you'll have the hardest part out of the way. As you continue to develop your skills in rune sensing, you'll eventually be able to sense it without the need for the jam. Now, if you would all be so kind as to form a single file line, we'll get you coated up with some surveybee jam."

One by one, the people in front of me dipped their hands and arms in the thick, yellow jam, some even going so far as to lather up their faces and legs with it. When it was finally my turn to dip my hands in the jar, Dean Celestine held her hand out.

"You know," she muttered quietly to me and grinned. "If you have any doubts about where to put this stuff, I can always help you out. I tend to know the best spots to coat on a person for the most *optimum* results."

Once again, she had left me speechless, not entirely sure whether she was joking or not. "I—I think I'll be good. Thanks, though." I smiled anxiously.

"Of course you are!" she blurted out, her tone becoming professional again. "I'm just messing with you, Nate. You know that by now." She laughed. "Now go on and dive in."

I walked up to the jar of jam and stuck my hands in. It felt like a warm jello. As I pulled out, I had enough of it coated over my hands that it was dripping down my arms.

On my way back to my desk, I heard Dak blurt out to Dean Celestine, "Could you help coat it on me, Dean Celestine? If you think it would give me an advantage, then I'd really appreciate it!"

"Take the damn jam and go back to your seat, Derrik."

I was sitting at my desk, my hands held up to make sure that none of it dripped down on me, when I started to feel kind of strange, almost like some intrusive thoughts were slowly forcing themselves upon me. At first, I thought that I was maybe just imagining it, but they slowly became more apparent to the point where I could no longer deny them. It was like I suddenly had two different brains with two different sets of thoughts. There was the mind inside my own head, which I was obviously very familiar with, but then also a mind outside in the room somewhere. And I was connected to it, somehow.

"Well, class, how are we feeling?" Dean Celestine asked after a few minutes of quiet observance.

As I looked around, I could tell that most people weren't feeling a thing, still fixated on the weird jam coated on their bodies. But then, somehow, I knew a few others were feeling what I was feeling. And it wasn't just the weird, trippy expressions on their faces that gave it away. No, somehow, I just knew. But to make things even stranger, I also felt that they knew I was feeling something as well. Could I have been reading their minds? Were they reading my mind? It was as if I was linked with everything in the room: the air, the desks and books, even the people themselves.

"Ah, I can feel that some of you are already beginning to sense the rune around you," Dean Celestine said.

"You can feel it?" A girl on the other side of the room asked.

"Indeed, I can. I can sense plenty in all your minds right now, and I could explore your thoughts even further, if I wanted to," Dean Celestine explained. "It's one of the many advantages that comes with being able to sense rune within another person's body and mind."

Her saying this made me feel a bit uncomfortable. Was she able to read my mind when I was noticing how good she looked for her age back when I had first met her?

At that moment, her eyes darted toward my own. Her gaze lingered on me for a few uneasy seconds, all but confirming that she was, at the very least, reading my thoughts at *this* moment.

I quickly tried to let my mind go blank. Maybe there was a way to protect yourself against having another sorcerer sift through your thoughts and emotions like some sort of gemologist searching for diamonds. After all, though it seemed I was picking up traces of thoughts and feelings from other students in the room, Dean Celestine was still a blank canvas, like some invisible force was barricading her mind.

"Now," she went on, "some of you may be wondering why you're not picking anything up from yours truly."

Guess I did a poor job of letting my mind go blank.

"A skilled sorcerer will manipulate the rune around themselves to form a defensive barrier, preventing another sorcerer from reading their thoughts and emotions. That would be the reason why a few of you, I won't mention any names, are failing miserably at picking up my own thoughts, though I applaud you for your efforts."

I felt myself go a little red in the face.

"The more skilled you become with rune manipulation, the stronger you'll be at both penetrating another's thoughts, and protecting your own from being breached. Even members of other classes can protect their thoughts from being read by a sorcerer if they master their own interior rune. But no need to concern yourselves with that for the time being.

"All that being said," she proceeded, "mind-reading is clearly not the only weapon sorcerers have in their arsenal. Being able to manipulate exterior rune brings with it many powerful advantages, advantages runics from other classes could only dream of having. As you gain more confidence in rune manipulation, you'll be able to use the surrounding rune to guide you when the need to make quick decisions and actions arises. Let's say, in battle, for example. At times, exterior rune can provide you with the best course of action, one that perhaps your unguided mind would fail to realize on its own. Yes, learn to trust the exterior rune around you, and it could become a sixth sense for a sorcerer, your strongest sense, even."

My classmates seemed just as amazed as I was, their baffled faces matching the thoughts and emotions that seemed to be projecting into the room, practically bouncing off the walls and into my mind.

"In addition to that," Dean Celestine proceeded, "exterior rune can provide plenty more to the sorcerer who wields it. From casting spells, to bending the elements, and even," at that moment, Dean Celestine rose up a few feet in the air, effortlessly levitating in place, "flying."

Gasps around the room sounded out. Even though I had already seen some people flying through campus earlier, witnessing Dean Celestine up close hovering above the ground seemed to have an entirely different level of amazement to it.

"This world is literally within your grasp, my young sorcerers," she said as she gently landed back on the floor. "It's up to you to reach out and grab it."

"Are you going to teach us how to fly today?!" someone in the front row eagerly blurted out.

"What, are you kidding?" Dean Celestine replied incredulously. "You kids barely know how to sense rune, even with the jam. If I tried to show you how to fly now, some of you may take off and never come back down—or worse, you *will* come back down. It takes quite a level of control with manipulating exterior rune in order to have it guide you through the air. No, today we'll start with something much easier, and safer—the Telekinesis Spell."

Some mumbles from the other students broke out. I heard Dak mutter next to me, "The ability to move stuff with our minds. How exhilarating!"

"Yes," Dean Celestine continued, "we'll start with this—" At that moment, a shuffling from the shelf in the back of the room sounded out, and then a book instantly shot past my head, only coming to a halt after reaching Dean Celestine's extended hand. She then placed the book on her desk at the front of the class.

"Now," she directed, "I would like everyone to again form a line. You shall take turns attempting to gently pull the book to you, using the external rune residing between you and the book. The jam from the surveybees will help you in sensing out the rune. However, I'd also recommend you each to be holding your staff while attempting this. They aren't just for show. Think of your staff as a magical pillar for yourself. They help further empower a sorcerer, and strengthen the sorcerer's connection with rune.

"But I must warn you to really concentrate. Focus on your connection with the rune. If you're not connected, the rune will respond accordingly. However, if you are, then it will be as easy and natural as if you were to pick the book up with your own arms. I'm afraid that is all the direction I can give you. This is one of those things that can only be learned through action and feeling."

We all grabbed our staves and formed a line going down the center of the room. Student after student took their turn at trying to mentally bring the book into their grasp as they stood a few feet away from it, holding a sticky arm out.

Plenty of my classmates failed miserably, the book not even budging, which kind of helped put my nerves at ease, at least.

"Classic case of never establishing the connection," Dak muttered from behind me in his nasal voice. "I've been reading all about rune manipulation for years, and it always starts with establishing the connection."

One student had gotten the book to levitate up off the desk, catching Dean Celestine's attention until it then floated off toward the exit door to our far right, not even close to its caller, and then repeatedly banged at the door in a way that made it appear like it desperately wanted to escape the room.

A few others ended up making the book flop off the desk, which seemed to at least indicate better-than-average results.

Before I knew it, my turn had come, and even though most of the other students didn't fare very well, I still felt the pressure as Dean Celestine seemed to now perk up with interest

(I guess pressure was just something I'd have to get used to with my S-tier status).

With nothing to lose, and not much to go off, I reached my sticky right hand out to the book on the desk, while tightly gripping my shiny gold staff in my left. At first, nothing happened at all. I chalked it up to nerves, as it was hard to think straight with everyone watching me.

I quickly glanced over at Dean Celestine, who smiled and gestured for me to breathe. And so I did, attempting to clear my mind and focus on all that I had experienced since dipping my hand in that jam. I focused on the sensations it had brought with it, the feeling that the air around me even had a mind, or a conscience of its own. The air around me had felt alive.

That was when I realized it, I had been thinking about this the wrong way. I had assumed that the caller had to call on the book for it to be moved, but that wasn't right at all. I had to call upon the rune in the surrounding air to move the book for me, essentially manipulating the air itself! Telekinesis was a misleading term. This was more along the lines of controlling the elements.

Upon realizing this, almost immediately, the book lifted up off the desk. Dean Celestine moved closer, and the class became eerily silent with attention. The book continued to rise until I focused on making it pause in mid-air. Surely enough, it slowed to a halt. I was in complete control, complete connection with the rune in the air around me, which I somehow knew was there, patiently waiting for my every command. The two minds I had sensed earlier, my own mind and the other one that seemed to exist outside of me, had become one; I felt in control of both.

And now, realizing that the other mind belonged to the exterior rune, there was nothing that prevented it from working with me, as it smoothly guided the book directly into my sticky hand, exactly how I intended it to.

"Wonderful!" Dean Celestine shouted out, clapping her hands together. "That, class, is exactly what to aim for. Fantastic job, Nate."

The whole room applauded me, and I had to admit that it felt pretty good, to the point where I had a huge smile plastered on my face. As I spun around to thank my classmates for the generous applause, I couldn't help noticing most of the girls in the room had that thirsty look for me in their eyes again.

I raised my sticky hand in thanks and started my way back to my seat. However, before I even had the chance to sit down, a loud yelping noise screeched out from the front of the room. I turned around just in time to see the book whack Dak square in the nose, so hard that it took him clear off his feet.

The class made a loud "ooo" noise and fell silent.

"And that, class," Dean Celestine said as she walked over to Dak, "is what happens when you confidently establish the connection, panic, and then lose the connection. You okay, Derrik?"

"It—it's Dak . . ." a quiet mumble from the floor broke out.

"Yeah, he's bleeding. All right, class," Dean Celestine addressed, "that will be all for today. I'll have to take this one up to the medical building. Great job, everyone! We'll pick up where we left off on Thursday. Class dismissed."

As Dean Celestine floated a barely conscious Dak up off the floor and telekinetically carried him from the room, I couldn't help wondering that maybe book-smarts only get you so far in *this* world, too.

Chapter Seven

WITH MY FIRST day of classes at Magic Rune Academy in the books, feelings of excitement and a sense of belonging overwhelmed me. I truly felt like I was a runic now and was happy to be a part of this amazing world.

The rest of my week was filled with more of the same excitement that my first day had offered, with every class offering a new lesson and every day presenting a new adventure. It was as if I was experiencing life from the eyes of my youth all over again. The Rune Realm offered new discoveries everywhere you looked, from the courses at the academy to the creatures which inhabited the grounds.

Once our first week was completed, Tara and I took a quick trip back to our old university to grab our remaining things. I had to admit, after being in the Realm for a week, coming back home just didn't feel . . . well, like home. It never seemed to be more bland, grayer, and just all around dull. It was like I had nothing else to gain from being in that universe any longer, like my chapters there were finalized. So it really wasn't a huge deal when I officially withdrew from Boltan University and texted some of my closer friends (who were more like acquaintances in recent years) that I'd be moving across the country.

Tara's situation was a little different from my own, as she still had a family there. But even she seemed to be more lively and happier while in the Realm.

After once again stepping through the portal at the bottom cavern of the Magic Gateway to head back to the Rune Realm, I even went as far as to wondering if it would be the last time I would be doing so. And when we emerged through the back door of Glendor's and out onto the streets of Hearthvale, the place somehow seemed even more welcoming than it had during my first arrival. The sky appeared to shimmer brighter than it had before, the air smelled even cleaner, and the grass looked greener (well, greenish-bluer).

From there, the weeks seemed to meld together, rolling onward with there being no thoughts of my old *home* crossing my mind, not even once. And before I had even realized it, the temperature dipped, the clouds in the sky looked heavier and painted with a glossy gray, and the leaves on the trees around the grounds went from their blue-green to magnificent shades of oranges, yellows, and reds, even bright purples. October had made its abrupt debut in the Realm.

For some reason, Halloween seemed to be an even bigger deal in the Rune Realm than back on Earth. Maybe it was because creatures like werewolves and witches actually did exist here, but people really seemed to be getting into it. The town of Hearthvale was decorated to its fullest, with pumpkins and jack-o'-lanterns placed outside all the shops, their windows filled with decorations of ghosts and ghouls and witches. Even the tunes played by the groups of musicians throughout town seemed to have spookier vibes to them.

And it didn't stop at Hearthvale, the Academy went all out, too. The fountain with the four creatures in it outside of the North Gate was surrounded with glowing purple candles, there were two large jack-o'-lanterns on each side of the entrance gates into campus, and the big, abstract statue in the center of the quad was wearing a witch hat. And I don't know if this was intended or just a coincidence, but I could have sworn I was seeing bats soaring above the grounds more frequently than earlier in the year.

Of course, though, the decorations were only one aspect of Halloween festivities, and I was reminded of the other by Dawn at lunch one Friday afternoon in the middle of October.

"Guess what, guys!" she happily blurted out as she joined me and Tara at a table by the window in the dining hall. "Big party tonight! A costume party, too! You both have to come with me. A friend of mine is hosting it with her sorority. You guys will love her. She's a blast! And the parties at this place are always the best ones of the year!"

Tara looked over at me with an uneasy expression. She was never too big on the whole party scene. Her ideas of fun were more laid back and secluded, like playing Kingdom Monsters or even just going to a park on a weekend, which I didn't mind myself, really.

"Oh, come on, guys!" Dawn desperately said. "You can't let me go to this by myself. I'll only know Zula there, but she'll be plenty busy keeping everyone else entertained. I need you guys. Come on, pleeeaaasseee." She had her hands clasped together and was practically on her knees on the other side of the table.

"It could be fun!" I shrugged my shoulders. Dawn's face lit up. "What do you think, Tara?" I added, wanting to make sure she was okay with going.

"Well . . . I *suppose* it couldn't hurt to branch out a little . . ." Tara began, but before she could finish, Dawn had leapt across the table to give her a hug.

"Thank you, thank you, thank you, Tara! You guys are the best!"

"But we don't even have costumes, though," she squeezed out, struggling to catch her breath in Dawn's tight embrace.

"Oh, you just let me handle that! I have to run to my next class, but I'll be over your place tonight at seven sharp! Nate, I've got you covered, too. Don't you worry." She winked at me and then took off, practically running out of the dining hall.

There were a few moments of silence between us before Tara finally said something, smirking. "A Halloween party, but with actual werewolves, orcs, and magic. What could possibly go wrong?"

At around six-thirty that evening, I hopped in my luxurious shower to quickly get ready for the night out. I figured I didn't need to worry about dressing up, since apparently Dawn had that taken care of, so I just threw on a loose gray shirt and a pair of sweats before leaving my room and heading down the hallway to Tara's room.

When I knocked on the door, I heard Dawn's voice ring out from the other side. "Come on in! Door's open!"

To say that I was not ready for what I was about to see was an understatement.

The first thing I noticed was Dawn doing Tara's make up for her on the couch, which I thought was nice of her, but then I picked up on what they were both wearing and almost became as hard as a rock right there on the spot.

They were each sporting skin-tight crop tops, Dawn's purple, Tara's a light brown, with purple and brown leather skirts, purple and brown fishnet stockings, and matching high heels. It was like entering a colorful dream. I'd maybe expect this sort of thing from Dawn (it looked like a more sexualized version of her shifter clothes), but I'd never imagine to see Tara in something like this, not in a million years.

"Uh," I cleared my throat, trying to get a hold of myself, "what exactly are you two supposed to be?"

"We're peanut butter and jelly!" Dawn happily blurted out. I noticed the word *Jelly* printed in white letters on her purple crop top when she turned to face me.

"Please . . . help me," Tara muttered to me, trying to keep her face still so that Dawn wouldn't mess up her makeup.

"You're peanut butter and jelly?" I repeated her, trying to hold back a bit of laughter.

"Damn right we are!" said Dawn. "And you're going to be our thick slice of bread!" She giggled.

My laughter stopped and my face went blank. That was when I noticed a huge slice of bread propped up in the corner of the room. It had holes for arms and legs to stick out of, as well as a hole on top for the head.

"Nooooo, no, no!" I blurted out. "We gotta think of a new idea."

"Oh, don't worry," Dawn casually said, "we only spread ourselves for you," she purred and playfully swiped her hand at the air toward me.

"It's not you two that's the problem. You both look stunning. It's that ridiculous slice of bread. I'd look like an idiot with that thing on!"

Dawn pursed her lips and put her hands on her hips. "Well, too damn bad. It was last-minute, so they didn't have anything else left for threes at the shop in Hearthvale."

"We couldn't have gone as like, ghosts wearing bed sheets or something?"

"Nah, that's lame," she waved off. "And we are leaving in like, ten minutes. So hurry up and get dressed, Nate—all done!"

Tara slowly stood up, giving me a very apprehensive expression. "Well, how do I look?"

I couldn't find the words. Again, both girls looked absolutely stunning, but seeing Tara like this just completely took me off guard. Her silvery-blonde hair was up in the messy bun, her glasses were still on, but this outfit . . . her breasts were pushed up to their limits in that tight crop top, and she was showing more skin than I had ever seen from her. The heels only further highlighted her curves. She had heavy eyeliner on, too, which transformed her usual cute face to an even sexier one.

And then there was Dawn, already in her hybrid form and now standing right beside Tara. The outfit only accentuated everything about her: her cute black ears which currently poked through her jet-black hair with the maroon highlights running through it, choppy and coming down just above her shoulders; her paler complexion contrasting perfectly with her dark lipstick; her bangs, which covered one of her yellow cat eyes; and her tight, toned body with that cheeky ass practically popping through the tight skirt. Her tail was happily wiggling about from behind her through a hole that looked to be carefully cut out by her doing.

This was heaven.

"I'll put on the bread," I said with a grin.

If there was ever a sight to see, this would have been it: the three of us walking through campus on a Friday night— Dawn and Tara dressed as the sexiest peanut butter and jelly ever known to the Realm, and me, the idiot bread waddling through the grounds. At least it wasn't too cold out, considering the girls weren't wearing much in terms of warmth.

Fortunately, all the other students strolling through campus were dressed up in all sorts of costumes, some as silly as a toilet and toilet brush, others monstrous as zombies and vampires.

"So where *is* the party at, anyway?" Tara asked as we headed closer to the North Gate entrance.

"Oh, did I not tell you guys?" Dawn asked. "It's just outside of town, actually. There are rows of houses up on the hillside just before you head up the mountain to the Academy. You actually pass the street every time you ride to and from town."

As we made our way through the North Gate and out to the front plaza, I noticed a predicament up ahead.

"Shit," Dawn muttered, "all the axe beaks have already been claimed."

"They have?" Tara asked. "But there are usually hundreds of them in the stables."

"Yeah, it happens, especially on weekends. The students who left for town earlier already took them all. Guess we got here a bit too late," Dawn concluded.

"Darn . . . guess we just have to go back to the room," said Tara unconvincingly.

Now that we were closer to the stables, it really did seem to be entirely vacant.

"Damn, if only I could fly . . ." I said.

Tara giggled.

"What's so funny? I asked.

"Just picturing a flying slice of bread, is all."

My expression lowered as I fought to hold back a smirk.

"Well, guess we'll just have to walk! Oh, don't worry," Dawn quickly added after seeing the looks on mine and Tara's faces, "students walk through the mountain to town all the time. There will be students walking through there even now. The whole path is lit with lanterns through the mountain at night—it's actually really pretty. Just sucks that it'll add about a half hour to our arrival time. But all good!"

At that moment, I heard a scuffle from deep within the stables. "No way!" I excitedly let out. "Looks like we'll be making it there right on time. Check him out!" I was pointing to an axe beak, a scrawny purple one, happily trotting toward me like it was already an old friend of mine.

"Hey, buddy. Good old reliable! Did nobody want to pick you again?" He lowered his head to me, and I gave him a gentle pat. I was surprised that he seemed to recognize me, even in this costume.

"Um, Nate, can he carry all three of us, though?" Tara asked with an expression of genuine concern. "To be honest, he looks like he's barely built for one passenger."

"Nonsense!" I blurted out. "You can hack it, can't you, Clyde?"

He vigorously shook his head about and snorted.

"I'd take that as a resounding yes!" I said.

"You named him Clyde?" giggled Dawn.

"Yeah, he just looks like a Clyde, don't you think?" I replied, then hopped on Clyde, Tara right behind me, with Dawn taking up the rear. It was a good thing that the girls were both small, because the three of us just barely fit on the back of the axe beak.

I yelled out "Zapzap!" and tapped Clyde's side twice with my foot.

The axe beak took off (surprisingly still fast as ever) toward the mountainside.

The cool night air was soothing against my face. And as we ascended the mountain, I took in the marvelous sky, looking just as amazing as it always did in the Realm, with its streaks of purple and pink running through it, like the northern lights on Earth, but brighter and more colorful. The big white moon, along with its two "little brothers," illuminated the wild terrain around us, and the stars were in no short supply, marvelously glistening about.

The sides of the path were lit, not with any old lanterns, but jack-o'-lanterns.

"I forgot!" Dawn hollered out from behind. "They swap the lanterns with pumpkins during this time of year!"

"I love that!" shouted Tara.

Dawn was right about all the students who walked to town, we must have passed about a dozen groups of people as we swiftly walked up and then back down the mountain.

Hearthvale looked even more peaceful at night. Most of the shops and restaurants were still open, their many windows glowing yellow with the warm light emanating from their insides.

Clyde came to a halt at his stable, this one much more crowded than the one back on campus.

"Nice work, bud!" I gave him another pat as the three of us hopped off the axe beak. "Knew you could pull it off. We'll be back in a few hours or so, if you're still here."

For the first time, instead of heading further into town after leaving the stables, we took a turn back up the hillside, passing a few different streets with houses and apartments along them, eventually coming to a street sign that read *High Street*.

"This is it!" Dawn pointed out before leading us down the street.

Many older-looking houses were closely spaced apart as we strolled down High Street, and plenty of other runics were walking down the sidewalk, all seemingly flocking to the same place. I was surprised to see, though, that all the houses looked to be unoccupied, at least at the moment.

"Are these houses vacant or something?" I asked Dawn.

"Nah," she replied, "actually, this entire street is usually booming with different house parties. Most upperclassmen live off campus, and High Street is very much a high demand area."

"Doesn't really seem like it," I said.

"That's because literally *everyone* comes to this party every year," said Dawn. "It's in a big sorority house around the bend here at the end of the street. Just wait until you see it. . ."

And she wasn't joking, I didn't need her to point it out to me. As it came into view, perched on a hill in the distance, it stuck out like a sore thumb, almost appearing to be scrutinizing the smaller old houses below which lined the street leading up to it.

"That's . . . that's not a big house, Dawn," Tara began in awe. "That's a whole ass mansion!"

"Well, I didn't want to oversell it," said Dawn, grinning widely.

As we followed the crowd of students through a fancy black entrance gate and up the long driveway leading to the big white mansion, I could hear the music blasting inside from here. Even the vast, sloping lawn was crowded with students, all of them dressed up in their different costumes and conversing amongst one another while holding red plastic cups.

We walked up a small flight of stone steps and entered through the large wooden front door. We were greeted by a crowded sea of orcs, humans, and elves, all in various costumes as they stood packed tightly together in the large, luxurious foyer. There must have been at least half of the university here.

The two-story entryway was nothing short of magnificent: A glass chandelier shimmered about from the top of the high ceiling, the floor was made of a bright tile, and two big wrought iron staircases placed on the far ends of the large foyer rounded toward each other, coming together on the upper landing, where many more runics congregated together.

"Follow me!" Dawn shouted out to us over the loud music and started forcing her way through the crowd, with Tara and me (I had to do my best to squeeze around people in this obnoxious bread costume) following close behind her.

Even dressed as bread, I couldn't help noticing plenty of flirtatious stares coming from the women I passed. A small group of orcs to our right were taking turns bonging runic ales. "That's a new personal best for Throk!" one of them yelled out as we weaved through them and into the kitchen, where the music wasn't quite as loud and you could actually freely move around.

"No way!" an orc girl yelled out from the other side of the kitchen. She had been talking to a few other girls, but immediately stormed over to us after we had entered the room. "Dawn! You made it!" The orc girl embraced her in a tight hug.

"I did, we did—" Dawn rasped, seemingly unable to catch her breath in her friend's grasp. "Don't break me, please—"

"Oh, sorry about it," the girl instantly let go, looking a bit embarrassed. "My dad put me on a new training program over the summer. It's been promising so far, I think!"

"I'd have to agree!" said Dawn as she rubbed her shoulders tenderly. "Can't argue with results like that. Guys, this is my friend, Zula—she's a freshman this year, but we met in town last year. Zula, these are my friends, Nate and Tara."

Now that I had a closer look at Zula, I couldn't deny the surprising feelings and thoughts popping up in my head, feelings that, if I'm being totally honest, I never anticipated having for an orc.

Not that I'm sure they didn't exist, but I had yet to meet an orc that I'd consider attractive (at least by typical human standards). Zula, however, broke the mold. She had a gorgeous face, the kind of face that could win beauty pageants back on Earth. Her skin was flawless and glowing green; it actually really complimented her long, thick, wavy black hair. Her two lower *tusks*, which were more like two small fangs, still protruded from her mouth, but just barely. As for her body, her arms were very toned, even muscular, but by no means would I consider them to be bulky. And her legs were thick and toned as well.

She appeared to be dressed up as a cheerleader, but her eyeliner was done in a dramatic way that made it look like it was running down her face.

"Oh my gosh!" Zula blurted out in a shrill tone. "I freaking love your costumes! Oh my . . ." She took a sudden look at me, hungrily eyeing me like I was a piece of steak instead of a slice of bread.

"Hi," I began with a smile, "nice to—"

Before I could even comprehend what was happening, she had me pinned up against the wall, her fiery red eyes just inches from my own. They looked a bit chaotic and crazy as they contrasted with the heavy mascara painted around them.

"Well now, what do we have here?" she whispered in a smooth, low tone that sounded completely different from her previous voice. "I bet you're the tastiest slice of bread in the Realm. I tend to cut out my carbs, but I'd cheat for you." She slid her hand down the bread and stopped it just above the waistline of the black sweats I had on. Her tits, which were an impressive size for as toned as she was, were firmly pressed up against where the bottom of my chest would be as she was maybe just a couple inches shorter than me.

"Nice to meet you, too," I said, glancing back at Tara, who looked scared for me, and Dawn, who looked to be holding back laughter.

"Nice? But you haven't even *really* met me yet. I promise, there's nothing *nice* about me." She was practically whispering in my ear at this point.

"Okay, there Zula," Dawn gently pulled her away from me, chuckling. "Still haven't gotten a handle on those *urges* of yours, have you?"

Zula blinked a few times. "Wait—shit, did it happen again?" she asked Dawn, her voice high and innocent once more. She had a guilty expression on her face. "But I've had such a good hold on it lately! That hasn't happened in forever."

"Yeah, well, this one," Dawn gestured to me, "may pose a bit more of a challenge for your *other* side. He's the S-tier I told you about."

Zula's eyes went wide. "He's the S-tier? I didn't know you were friends with him. Oh, I'm so sorry, but no wonder that happened. You should have warned me, Dawn!"

"And avoid missing *that*?" Dawn laughed. "No way in hell."

Zula scowled. "Not funny."

"Um," I muttered, finally peeling my sore back away from the wall, "I feel like I might be missing something here."

"Some orcs have a sort of . . . battle frenzy that can trigger during combat," explained Dawn.

"Combat?" I asked incredulously. "All I did was introduce myself!"

"I hate the term 'frenzy.' I wish us orcs could just agree to stop using it," Zula groaned. "But, yeah . . . I'm sorry, Nate. It's a pretty rare gene among my people, but it's incredibly helpful for fighting. Plenty of orcs actually *wish* they had it. If only they knew . . ." she muttered. "It's something inside me that just takes over, and when it triggers, it's almost like I black out and turn into an entirely different person."

"But . . . I don't think Nate was trying to fight you," Tara hesitantly piped up.

Dawn and Zula exchanged ornery looks. "It also happens when—" Dawn began, but was interrupted by a pair of green hands covering her mouth.

"So! Like I was saying, absolutely love the costumes!" said Zula, leaving me quite perplexed.

"Thanks!" Tara replied. "I'm guessing you're a cheerleader, then?"

"Yes! Well, technically I'm a psychotic, murdering cheerleader. I gave myself a whole backstory and everything!" She clapped her hands together excitedly. "I'm a cheerleader, and my boyfriend was a star MVP Quester who cheated on me. So I chopped the fucker's slimy hands right off, and now I hang them around my neck like this!" She pulled out a necklace from underneath her top, and to my surprise, there were two small green hands fashioned to the bottom of it.

Tara and I stared at her blankly. "Um . . . those are . . . ?" Tara began.

"Oh my gosh!" Zula gave a startled look. "They aren't real, of course!" she cackled. "I bought these at Stop and Prop, in town!"

"Oh . . . yeah . . . of course," Tara carefully said with a skeptical look.

"So," said Zula, "you guys down for some keg stands, or what?"

"Keg stand?" Tara asked innocently.

"You don't know what a keg stand is?!" Zula blurted out before grabbing hold of Tara's arm and pulling her away. "Girl, we are gonna get you wasted! Come on!"

Tara desperately looked back at me and mouthed "help me" as she was practically dragged out of the kitchen.

Dawn was chuckling to my left, holding two red cups filled with runic ale.

"Should I be concerned?" I asked her.

"The drinks? Don't worry, if I wanted to roofie you, I would have done it by now." She smirked.

I grinned, taking the cup of beer. "I meant about Tara getting dragged away by the bipolar orc cheerleader with severed hands around her neck. . ."

Dawn giggled. "Zula? Nah," she brushed off, "she's perfectly harmless. Well, unless you're her opponent in a Questing Games match, then you're totally fucked. But otherwise? She's just really fun! Trust me, Tara is in for a great ass night."

"Guess I'll just have to take your word for it," I said. "So these Questing Games, I've heard you mention them before. Zula competes in them?"

"Yep!" Dawn confirmed, gesturing for me to follow her out of the kitchen through an exit leading to the backyard. "It's a big tournament that students in the Quester program can compete in. It takes place throughout the school year. Technically, Zula isn't officially in the program yet, being a freshman, but she got a recommendation from her father, who was apparently a pretty good Quester back in his day. He's been training her since she was little, so she'll do great. That whole frenzy gene she has makes her a force to be reckoned with."

The fresh air felt amazing after being inside the stuffy house, and even though there were still a bunch of people hanging out back here, the yard was big enough to offer plenty of space to breathe.

"So, about that whole frenzy thing," I began as we headed over to a relatively private bench off the side of the house. A glowing purple butterfly quickly fluttered away when we sat down, but Dawn didn't seem to notice.

"What about it?" chuckled Dawn.

I gave her a knowing look. "You were about to say something before Zula stopped you. So what was the deal with her jumping me like that? I mean, for a second, I thought she was going to reach down and grab my cock right in front of everyone!"

Dawn laughed, her hybrid eyes illuminated in the night. "I'm almost shocked that she didn't, really!"

As she sat there at my side, laughing and gazing at me with those penetrating eyes, I was hit with the sudden realization that this was the first time we really had some one-on-one time together since I had first met her. From the start of the semester, I had been primarily hanging out with Tara, and Dawn would happily sprinkle herself in here and there.

"But yeah," Dawn continued, "it's probably not my place to be telling you this, but as an S-tier, there's something *you* should at least be aware of regarding that frenzied state certain orcs like Zula have—just something to keep in mind."

"I'm all ears."

"Well, like Zula said, it's a very rare gene that some orcs can get, and it makes them amazing in battle, especially if they're a class that primarily relies on physical strength. Zula's a rune-knight, so it works out perfect for her when she's in combat. And she'll one day thrive as a Quester because of it, too."

"That all sounds great to me, but to be honest, it didn't seem like combat was on her mind when she had me pinned against that wall."

"And that's the drawback, and the side of it that Zula tries to fight against—she gets pretty embarrassed about it. . ."

"It can trigger with *other* situations, can't it?" I concluded, finally connecting the dots.

Dawn smiled guiltily and nodded. "It's a dominant gene, designed in a way that ensures it continues to get passed down among the strongest of orcs, by means of . . . reproducing."

"Ah," I said, "that would explain the sexual forwardness."

"Exactly," said Dawn, "*that* side of the frenzy tends to surface when the holder interacts with people who have higher mytosome counts."

"Which is why you felt I should know about it, since I'm an S-tier . . ." I said slowly.

"You got it!" replied Dawn.

"You know, sometimes the whole S-tier thing is a lot to deal with," I sighed.

Dawn's yellow eyes widened. "What do you mean?"

"I don't know. I mean having all the potential is great, don't get me wrong. But I'm quickly learning that there's also a lot of pressure that comes with that potential. To be honest, it's something I'm not entirely used to."

"Yeah, I get that," said Dawn. "But trust me, Nate, I think you'll grow to love it. You'll have a stronger connection with rune than anyone else, not to mention your choice of just about any girl—or *girls*."

"Yeah, and that's just it. I mean, not to sound ungrateful or like a whiny bitch about it or whatever, because I know I should be ecstatic about a bunch of girls wanting me, but how do I even know who's into me, well, for me, instead of someone who's just subconsciously attracted to my mytosomes."

Dawn went silent for a few seconds, and I didn't make eye contact with her. The thought had crossed my mind a couple of times before, that maybe even Dawn had only been hanging around me because of that same subconscious pull most girls in the Realm seem to feel when I'm around them.

"Well, that could be true," she admitted. "I mean, you never really know for sure, I suppose. Even so, I wouldn't over-think it, you know? Just relish in it!"

And there it was again, the other thing that had been on my mind when it came to Dawn: her acting so casually over me being with other girls. And I was again left to wonder whether she was actually into me or just a friend.

"Dawn," I carefully began, figuring now was as good a time

as ever to finally put my wondering to rest, "there's something I've been meaning to ask you."

"You can only taste me if you ask nicely," she joked, tugging at her purple jelly costume.

"I appreciate that," I laughed. "But for real, though . . ."

Dawn leaned closer to me. "Ooo, we're getting deep now, are we?"

"Maybe," I replied. "It's just, I've gotta be honest here, I've been having a hard time getting a read on you—since I first met you, even. Sometimes, it feels like you're putting out some pretty damn clear signs. But then other times, I'm left to think that I was far off the mark in assuming you're into me in any way that's more than just friendly. I just wouldn't want to mistake the flirting for something else and then make a move and have it go wrong with you."

"Ah," she casually let out, "well, maybe that's how I like it. Perhaps I like to keep you on your toes." She gave me one of her signature Dawn winks.

"Really?" I smirked. "Well, I was thinking maybe you were just all talk."

She gasped loudly and put on an overdramatic, offended look. "Are you calling me a *tease*?"

"Well, I wouldn't go that far," I playfully said, "but . . ."

Dawn smiled and slapped me on the shoulder (well, more like slapped the corner crust of my bread). I couldn't help noticing how she smoothly deflected the question, and maybe even a potentially awkward conversation, with humor. It was something I was starting to realize she often did.

But then she suddenly put down the rest of her drink, abruptly stood up, and reached her hand out. "Come on."

"Oh. Yeah, sure," I obliged.

She practically dragged me back inside the kitchen of the mansion and out into the large, crowded foyer again.

"We should probably try to find Tara!" I hollered out to her over the loud music and hundreds of chatting people.

Almost immediately after I said that, chants of "CHUG! CHUG! CHUG!" broke out to my far right.

A group of people were huddled around some sort of event that was transpiring. Dawn and I inched forward to get a better view, and I almost couldn't believe my eyes when I saw Tara doing a handstand over a keg. Zula was holding her up by her legs shouting "CHUG!" along with the others.

"I think she's doing just fine!" Dawn yelled into my ear and grabbed my arm to pull me up one of the big stairways leading to the second floor.

"I'm the fucking shit!" Tara's voice blurted out from below as the crowd cheered for her.

When we reached the second-floor landing, Dawn urgently squeezed us through the crowd of people and down the hallway.

"Where exactly are we going?" I asked, still a bit confused as she silently walked past the many closed doors off the long hallway, towing me behind her.

Finally, she stopped at a door about halfway down the hall and knocked on it a few times. She pressed her ear against the door. "Okay, I think we're good." She quickly opened it and then shoved me into the cozy, vacant bedroom before shutting the door behind me, enclosing us in the room together.

She locked the door and spun around on her heel to face me, grinning devilishly.

"You're going to pay for that 'tease' comment."

Chapter Eight

"I THINK you were technically the one who said teas—"

Before I even realized what was happening, Dawn had quickly embraced me, wrapping her arms around my neck and passionately sinking her soft lips into my own.

I said nothing, but instead firmly grabbed her waist and pulled her closer into me. At that moment, I couldn't care less about seeking further explanation, nor the fact that I was still dressed as bread.

She ran her hands through my hair as she continued attacking my face, and it was a minute or so of this before she finally pulled away. Her eyes remained closed as she breathed against my face, and she whispered, "Still need further confirmation?" Her lips curved into a grin.

I kissed her harder. She responded with moans of pleasure as she pulled me in tighter. Her dark lipstick offered subtle hints of grape and strawberry.

As things continued to escalate, I decided to inch our way over to the large bed placed up against the back wall of the room. The bedspread was a light blue and neatly made, at least for now.

"Mmm," Dawn let out as I ushered us over to the foot of the bed, still going at her face like it was the last night of our lives. "Take this stupid thing off," she chuckled, helping me hastily squeeze my way out of the bread costume.

Finally, I tossed her petite body over the bed. She lay there on her back, beaming up at me with those bright yellow eyes, her pupils like black slits. She blew up at her messy bangs in an attempt to get them out of her eyes, but I loved the way she looked when they covered half her face like that.

With her cat ears popping through her black hair, her tail eagerly wiggling from underneath her, and that skin-tight purple jelly outfit, she was a forbidden fruit (almost literally). I knew how strange this might be by *normal* standards, but I was no longer normal—maybe I never was. And something inside me called for this little cat girl. Her ears, her tail, those eyes, they all just turned me on even further.

My pants tightened as my cock swelled with excitement. Unable to resist her for a second longer, I collapsed over her small frame, where we continued going at each other's lips for a few minutes, our tongues intensely dancing together.

I felt her cat ear twitch as I brushed her hair back with one of my hands and began to kiss her pale neck.

"Oh, yeah, that's perfect . . ." she groaned as she clawed at my back, her tail beginning to lightly thump against the bed.

As I lowered my kisses down her neck and toward the top of her perky chest, her tail thudded a little faster. I couldn't help chuckling at the repetitive sound it was making off the bed.

"Is my tail funny to you?" Dawn whispered, giggling back.

"Just a little," I admitted. "I mean, I love it—it's so fucking cute. It's just, I think it's kind of funny how it's basically projecting your inner feelings right now. Let's just say I don't think you'd be the best poker player."

Dawn grinned. "Well, once you see the things I can do with it, my thoughts won't be the only thing in this room getting *projected*." She slid out from underneath me and then shoved me down on the bed, biting her bottom lip with anticipation.

"I think I like where this is going," I said.

"Oh, you have no idea," she smoothly purred, straddling my legs. She then gestured for me to come closer, so I sat up, allowing her to slowly lift my shirt off before gently pressing me back down on the bed.

And now it was her turn to go at my neck, sucking and play-fully nibbling away at it, she sent chills down my spine. I threw my hands around her tight waist and slid them down to her cheeky ass before giving it a firm squeeze; the purple leather skirt was so tight that it may have well been her bare skin.

Her tail fluttered back and forth as I felt her kisses trail down my neck, my bare chest, stomach, and finally ending just above the waistline of my pants.

She looked up at me with her yellow eyes and gave me a smile before caressing the waistbands of both my pants and underwear, and then gently pulled them down my legs.

My engorged cock, tortured with anticipation, flung up as it was finally freed from the resistance of my briefs, and it nearly smacked her in the face.

"Oh, my . . ." She failed to hold back her smile, her eyes as wide as I'd ever seen them. "I guess your mytosome count isn't the only thing about you that's huge. S-tiered and packing—you literally might just have it all!" She beamed up at me before pulling my drawers entirely off my legs.

I chuckled and laid my head back. Her small hand felt cool against my warm shaft as she gently grasped it.

"Now, you just relax while I . . . prove myself to you."

The next thing I felt was the inside of her warm, soft mouth sliding down the head of my penis. She twisted her tongue around the tip in a teasing way that practically drove me mad, while simultaneously writhing the bottom of my shaft with her hand.

"Oh, fuck, Dawn. That feels amazing," I let out.

She responded by finally lowering her mouth further down my shaft. I lifted my head to take in the sight. To my surprise, she made it about halfway before letting out a gurgling noise and coming back up for air.

"This is one hell of a cock you have," she breathed, smiling up at me while still jerking me off, the subtle sound of smacking lips filled the otherwise quiet room as she continued sliding and twisting her hands around my now lubed up cock.

"Thanks," I groaned, "I eat my greens."

It was a stupid thing to say, but Dawn let out a laugh and didn't miss a beat. "I bet you do." And she went down again for another swig, this time reaching a little past halfway. From there, she continued sliding her hot mouth up and down my shaft, and it seemed to only get warmer and wetter as she let her saliva build up.

As she slurped away, it started to feel so good that I couldn't restrain myself—I reached down and placed my hands on the top of her head, forcing her further along. Her cat ears perked up while she did her best to take it all, but started to gag a little and had to come up for air again around three quarters of the way down.

"Fuck, I love it," she gasped. "You taste fucking amazing."

I smiled at her. "You *feel* amazing."

"Yeah?" she whispered, working her way back up my body until she was straddling my stomach. Her tail waved excitedly. "Let me know how *this* feels," she said, bending down and kissing me on the lips. As she did so, I felt what can only be described as a soft, furry towel wrap itself around the base of my cock. It was then that I knew she had my penis gripped firmly with her tail.

I felt her lips curve into a grin as she continued passionately exploring the inside of my mouth with her tongue.

I pulled away for just a second. "Is that what I think it is?" I whispered.

"Not so funny now, is it?" she smoothly said, and then I felt her tail start to slide up and down my still wet shaft.

"Holy fuck, Dawn," I let out, gently pulling her closer to me. We resumed passionately making out as her tail continued to fondle my penis.

I threw my hands around her cat ears and gently rubbed them. "Mmm," Dawn moaned into my mouth.

I was pleasantly surprised by the amount of control she had with her tail. It was like she knew exactly the right pressure to use. The entire idea of it had me turned on to new heights, and before I knew it, I started to feel close to the edge.

As I groaned into her, she seemed to pick up on exactly what was about to happen, and her grin widened.

Dawn's tail wrapped tighter around the base of my cock, and it rapidly pumped away, almost begging for my orgasm.

"Yeah, you like that?" whispered Dawn.

"Fuck yeah," I replied, grabbing hold of her ass in that tight leather skirt.

"Does master want to cum for his little kitty?"

Holy fuck, this was hot.

"Come on, I want it, baby. I want that fucking cum all in me," begged Dawn. "I want to know what you taste like. I've been wondering since I first met you. Now give it to me! Please!"

Her tail pumped even faster as I edged closer.

"Fuck, Dawn, fuck yeah, I'm gonna cum!"

She immediately spun around on me and forced her mouth down my cock again, firmly pumping the base of it with her hand.

She made it just in time as I exploded into her hot mouth, deep down in her throat. Dawn wasn't fazed though as she continued rapidly sliding her head up and down my cock, slurping and gurgling away.

I looked up to see her thick ass just inches away from my face and her tail happily wiggling about, so I tightly squeezed it while shooting my final jets of semen into her.

When it came to its end, my head fell back against the pillow. Dawn didn't cease in her slurping until she knew for a fact that I was entirely emptied.

She wiped her mouth and turned around to inch her way back up to me. "That clear up any remaining doubts about how I feel about you?" she smoothly asked, sitting up against the headboard next to me.

"I think whatever doubts were left just got launched down your throat," I breathed.

"Well, those *doubts* tasted pretty damn good," she chuckled.

"Felt good, I know that. Easily the best BJ I've ever had."

"Bet it was the first TJ you've ever had, too," Dawn added.

I laughed at her play on words. "I don't have much of a sample size to go off with receiving *tail jobs*, but that thing can be categorized as a sex toy. I just can't believe you have so much control over it."

Dawn grinned. "What can I say? I've been putting it to use on myself for years."

My eyes widened, and I turned to look at her.

"What?" she asked. "You even said it yourself, makes for a great sex toy."

I was left struggling to find my words as I stared blankly at the white ceiling, the fascinating image of Dawn using her tail to please herself popping into my mind.

"Well," Dawn finally said, smoothly swinging her legs over the side of the bed, "guess we should head back out to the party. Don't want Zula barging into her room and asking if we need a third hand. Or do we?" She winked.

"This is Zula's room?!" I blurted out.

"Well, yeah . . . come on, Nate, I'm not gonna give you a blowy in a stranger's room—I'm not an animal."

"I guess I just wasn't expecting it to be so . . ."

"Girly? Believe it or not, Zula's pretty feminine—well, her usual side is, at least. But don't let that fool you. Even when she's not frenzied, Zula can be a bit . . . eccentric. Take a look." Dawn pointed over to the computer desk in the corner of the room. Placed on a lower shelf of the desk was what appeared to be a very wild, erotic-looking vibrator. It had three uniquely shaped heads to it, each one the size of my forearm.

"Holy fuck," I muttered, "maybe we should go check on Tara. . ."

"I'm not even tha drunk, I promish," Tara mumbled into my ear as I continued treading toward our dorm building, bent forward underneath Tara's arm to support her limp body with her feet dragging along the ground behind us.

"No, you're not drunk at all! Sober as a baby, Tara!" Dawn hollered out from behind us, her voice cracking with laughter.

"Thas what I sayin'!"

"You're good," I reassured her, "it's not much further ahead."

"You know," said Tara, "I really like tha' Zoooola, she's such a nice orc. We should hang out with her more offen. That girl knows how to haff a fun time."

I could hear Dawn struggling to keep herself from laughing harder.

Seeing her condition now, I had no idea how we managed to get her back to campus from the party. It seemed to only hit her harder as we rode back from town on the axe beaks (I made sure she rode with me on Clyde).

I was met with a wave of relief when we finally reached our dorm building, and once inside, I tossed her entirely over my shoulder and swiftly stormed back to her room, Dawn following close behind.

"I can wait out here," Dawn said from Tara's living room. "Oh, make sure she falls asleep on her side, okay?"

"Right," I muttered, and carried her into her bedroom, softly closing the door behind us.

I gently laid Tara down on her bed. Her eyes were still closed and there was a blissful smile printed on her face. "That was so fun, Nate," mumbled Tara dreamily. "I'm soooo good at keg stands, who woulda thunk?" she giggled.

"Yeah," I laughed, genuinely appreciating the fact that she had a good time tonight, "you really showed 'em who's boss."

"I did, didn' I?"

Suddenly, her smile vanished, and I began frantically looking around the room for a bucket. To my surprise, though, that wasn't the cause for her sudden look of apprehension.

"Nate," she slowly began, "I saw you and Dawn go upstairs to the bedrooms . . ."

"Oh . . . Tara, I—"

"No, no . . . iss okay, really. I swear, I swear." She was waving her arms above her body, her eyes still tightly shut. "Wow! This room is spinny!"

I smiled softly. "Tara, are you sure you're okay with it? Because if not, I can—"

"No, no, no," she repeated in a whisper, "I mean it, Nate. Iss like I said last month, I was only jealous because I didn't want to be left out. I know you are an X-tier and I know what that means, and iss okay, rurrly. And I rurrrly like Dawn, like a lot. Sheesh so nice and thoughtful. Iss like we got our own club going—the Fuck Nate club!"

"You know," I chuckled, "that can be taken in a way that makes it seem like you both hate me."

"Hmmm, yeah, guess you're right. Dammit! I'll leave the naming 'sponsibilities to Dawn."

"Well, regardless," I began, still guiltily amused, "I'm really glad you've grown to like her. I do, too. I like both of you, a lot. And you'll never get left behind. Promise. I'll wait—however long it takes for you, Tara."

Her smile widened. "Thasss so sweet. I'm so sorry that you have to wait for me, though. Iss just," another anxious look on her face appeared, "I never did it before, Nate . . . so iss just kinda a big deal for me, you know?"

I paused to take that in. She had her hands covering her eyes.

That was the first time she admitted it to me, not that I was entirely surprised about it. It wasn't a matter of her appearance or anything (she was clearly stunning enough to pull just about any guy she wanted to at this point), it was just that I figured she was a virgin because she was always around me, never even entertaining the idea of being around another guy. Even while I was with my ex, she had always remained by my side, supporting me no matter what.

"Are you still there?" She waved a hand, still lying flat on her back with her eyes closed.

"Yeah, yeah, of course," I urgently replied. "But Tara, there's nothing to be embarrassed about. I actually love that you're a virgin. You're just being patient about it—that's how it should be. It's a big deal, your first time."

"Yeah, I sippose that it is. I just need a little more time, is all. I promise."

"That's completely understandable. Like I said, I'll wait for however long until you're comfortable with it."

"Thanks, Nate . . ."

There was a brief moment of silence where I thought she might have fallen asleep.

"Okay!" she blurted out. "I'm ready now. Less do it." She waved her hands, gesturing for me to come to her.

I burst into laughter. "I think sober you would be just a little bit pissed if you couldn't remember your first time, Tara."

"Ugh," she groaned, "guess you're probably right. . ."

I remained sitting at her bedside for a few more minutes of silence before assuming she had finally fallen asleep, and then went to gently roll her over on her side. As I stood up to head out of her room and tell Dawn that everything seemed good, she piped up again from underneath her covers.

"Oh, and Nate?" she asked.

I paused in my stride and turned to her. "Yeah?" I patiently replied.

"I think Zula should join the Fuck Nate club, too! She'd be a fun addition to our little group."

I smiled. "I'll keep it in mind."

Dawn was sitting on the couch when I came back out to the living room.

"All good in there?" she asked as she quickly stood up.

"Yeah," I said, "she may not be good tomorrow morning, but for now, I think she'll be all right. I'll probably sleep here for the night, just to play it safe."

"That's good to hear," Dawn replied, rubbing her shoulders and glancing up at me kind of awkwardly. "Well, I should probably get going, then."

"You sure?" I asked. "I mean, we can chill on the couch. Tara won't mind at all."

"Oh! Um, I'm just one of those people who likes their own bed, you know?" she stammered.

"Yeah, I guess I get that . . ."

"I'll catch you guys on Monday, though? We can grab lunch," she happily added.

"Sure, that works. We'll see you Monday, then."

She waved anxiously and then swiftly made her exit, leaving me standing alone in the living room, feeling a bit perplexed.

I couldn't help noticing that this was now the second time where I offered her to stay the night, with both occasions ending in her politely shutting me down. Perhaps there was a deeper side to Dawn than what she let on—a mask of her own, plenty thicker than any of the ones worn at the party tonight.

Chapter Nine

"THAT'S IT, Nate. Yes . . . just like that . . . you're so close . . . fantastic!" Dean Celestine cheered.

I had finally managed to levitate the book directly into my hand, without the assistance of any surveybee jam.

"That's exactly how it's done, class! Notice how the book never faltered off its trajectory once Nate initially established the connection—oh, well done, Nate, bravo!" She enthusiastically clapped her hands and the rest of the class joined in with her.

I casually raised a hand in thanks, trying my best to not come off as cocky even though I had been excelling with telekinesis more than any other student in the class. But I had to admit, it *did* feel pretty good to be naturally good at this.

It was only a couple months into the semester now, and Dean Celestine's Rune Sensing and Manipulation had easily become my favorite class. With my other classes, I was average at best (which was pretty typical of me regarding schoolwork), but it was like anything having to do with being a sorcerer just came naturally to me. I was the first person in the class to successfully use telekinesis without the surveybee jam, whereas plenty of students still struggled to even lift the book off the desk without the jam. Poor Dak still couldn't seem to find a way around hitting himself in the face with various objects.

"Well, if everyone could please return to your seats," Dean Celestine began, standing up from behind her desk, "I'd like to take the rest of the class to introduce you all to another very useful technique."

I looked around and noticed quite a few dubious expressions on the faces of my classmates.

"Now, now," said Dean Celestine as she paced back and forth in the front of the room, her elegant, long red robe swaying behind her, "I understand that all of you are still working on mastering telekinesis, but I *must* make sure we stay on track with the curriculum. And the only way to do that is to force all of you to push yourselves! Besides, every sorcerer takes differently to each technique—some may excel at telekinesis, while others at flying or spell casting. The only way you'll discover what you are good at is by trying different things. The best sorcerers are well rounded, capable of casting many different spells.

"And so, our next lesson shall be revolving around the Cloning Spell—manipulating the exterior rune around you to replicate another version of yourself."

I was far from an expert on understanding how the rune works in this world, but having said that, even I could tell that this would be a much more difficult task than pulling objects to me.

"The key to successful cloning, and the reason it's so different from an ability like telekinesis," Dean Celestine continued, "is that *this* ability relies heavily on knowing your own mytosome count and structure like the back of your hand."

I leaned forward, her words sparking my interest. Since I first arrived in the Rune Realm, I've too often heard from others about my high mytosome count, but I've never really dived much further into the topic.

"Knowing this information is vital to successfully pulling off the Cloning Spell because you'll essentially be creating a copy of yourself by first copying your own mytosomes, using them as the foundation."

"So, how do we use rune to familiarize ourselves with our own mytosomes?" asked Dak. "I thought classes that specialize in manipulating interior rune—like shifters and rune-knights—were the only classes who can manipulate their mytosomes."

"And this is true," Dean Celestine replied, "which leaves us to do it the good old-fashioned way—through meditation."

The room was silent with skepticism, something as normal as meditating somehow seemed abnormal in the Realm.

"As our Dak so kindly pointed out, class, and as you all know very well by now, sorcerers are limited to using only external rune. However, manipulating your own mytosomes can only be done through controlling the rune in one's body. But that's just it—to do the Cloning Spell, we don't need to *manipulate* our mytosomes. We just need to familiarize ourselves with them, with their structure. We need to learn what they look like, how many there are within us. And then, using that knowledge and the external rune around you, you'll eventually be able to manipulate the rune into a copy—or even copies—of yourself, originated from your very own mytosome structure."

With that, Dean Celestine had us all sit in the center of the room, Indian style (she had mentally pushed all the desks and chairs back against the walls of the room), and focus on our breathing for the rest of the class. Even I had to admit that this was by far the most boring of all her classes yet, but if it would eventually result in being able to clone myself, then I figured it'd be worth it.

"Fantastic start, everyone!" Dean Celestine proclaimed after we all returned to our desks. "I know it seems tedious, but learning to clone oneself is only the start of the Cloning Spell. Eventually, I'll be teaching you how to take it to the next step—sensing the rune and mytosomes inside another person to familiarize yourself with *that* person's own mytosome count, thus learning how to transform your own clones into clones of other individuals. A very useful tactic for things like gaining intel and causing diversions."

Mumbles of excitement broke out from my classmates.

"By then," said Dean Celestine, "it'll actually be much easier than you might be thinking. Again, sorcerers excel at sensing and manipulating exterior rune, that includes the interior rune of other runics apart from the sorcerer. The hardest part is first learning to copy yourself."

"I'm going to make fantastic use out of that!" Dak blurted out with an ornery look on his face.

"The clones aren't solid," a female elf said in front of him with a flat tone, "so don't get any ideas, weirdo. If I see you trying to clone me, you'll wish you hadn't."

"I knew that . . . I was clearly joking!" he retorted.

"And lastly," added Dean Celestine, "I must advise that you all start seriously considering what profession you would like to pursue. By now, I hope you all know that at the end of the semester, you'll be asked to enroll in a major.

My eyes shot open. Somehow, this was the first I was hearing of this, and I couldn't help feeling that I probably should have actually looked at my syllabus earlier in the year.

"It's a very important decision in a runic's life," Dean Celestine continued, "and so, I am inclined to suggest not taking it lightly. Whichever program you choose to enroll in—whether it be the Guard program, Quester program, Business program, or various others—you'll be expected to complete a final project specifically catered to the program at the very end of the school year. I know right now that may seem too far down the road to care, but I highly suggest you start thinking of it sooner rather than later. It will be here before you know it."

"I really didn't tell you guys that you need to pick a major?" asked Dawn as she pursed her lips over her runic ale across the table.

Tara, Dawn, and I had all agreed to meet for drinks and food at the Bronze Dragon, considering it was a Thursday evening, close enough to the weekend.

"No, you didn't!" Tara blurted out. "Kind of important information to let slip your mind, don't you think?"

"Hey, I was your guide into the Realm. I got you here. There are technically no requirements for members of the Guard to be advisors for their recruits through all of school," Dawn replied, casually shrugging her shoulders. "Besides, I definitely mentioned the Quester profession to you guys on your first day here. I remember that much."

"Yes," sighed Tara, "but you never mentioned anything about having to pick a major by the end of term!"

"Regardless," I decided to step in, "it needs to be done. So we may as well start considering our options."

"Well, there's always the Guard!" said Dawn, hopefully.

"I don't know if that'd be the right fit for a healer." Tara frowned.

"You could always join the Nursing program," Dawn added.

"Yeah, maybe . . ." Tara still had an unconvinced tone.

"Maybe I should just join the Business program or something," I joked, trying to hold back a smirk.

Tara scoffed, as she knew very well that I was never any good at math or really anything business related back on Earth.

But Dawn gave me an incredulous look. "Nate," she slowly began, "you are an S-tiered sorcerer. I am not about to let you waste your talents on doing other runics' taxes!"

At that moment, Sakura came by to give us our food (she just happened to be assigned as our waitress again.)

"Here's the chicken salad," she softly said, handing it to Tara, "the burger," she passed it to Dawn, "and the Reuben sandwich." The corners of her lips curved in a smile as her eyes quickly met mine. I couldn't help noticing that the picks on the bread of my sandwich were carefully aligned to form a smiley face.

"Thanks, Sakura. You're the best!" I said, giving her a bright smile of my own.

"Thanks . . . I mean, you're welcome. You're the . . ." She stopped herself, her face gone blank. It was almost as if she realized what she was about to say wouldn't make any sense. "Enjoy your meal!" she peeped up and then swiftly walked away.

"Well, I'd say that's progress," said Tara. "At least she didn't sprint away this time."

"She's getting there," I replied, chuckling. "I try to talk to her as much as I can during Intro to Classes. Professor Morran's one tough cookie, though, I have to admit; she has eyes and ears like a hawk."

"You seem pretty interested," Dawn pointed out. "So is she going to be the newest addition to our little group?" She grinned.

"I'm just trying to get to know her," I said. "She's interesting, you have to admit."

"Yes, 'interesting,'" Tara began with a knowing look as she picked at her salad. "It has nothing to do with that huge rack and those thick hips?"

Dawn and I remained silent, gazing at each other with shock. Tara hadn't seemed to notice, as she was still fondling with her salad.

"Tara!" Dawn gasped.

Tara finally looked up from her food. "What? I have eyes! For such a little thing, the girl is built like a—"

"Yes, but coming from you!" Dawn interrupted, holding back a laugh. "Just didn't expect it. Besides, you're one to talk over there!" Her eyes fell to Tara's chest. "If I had boobs like those, I'd have to change my shifter form to something with a much sturdier back!"

"All right!" I blurted out as Tara blushed and pulled her shirt up a couple of inches. "Not that I'm not enjoying this, but what are we going to do about the whole major thing?"

"Well," Tara slowly said, "it's not like we have to decide anything today . . . but how about the Quester program?"

Dawn gave her another incredulous look. "Okay, who are you and what did you do with sweet, overzealous, Kingdom Monster-playing Tara?!"

Tara scoffed with a smile. "Listen, I have Drakthor now. I'll gladly still take either of you on in Kingdom Monsters. But seriously, it would beat being stuck in an office or wiping asses as a nurse. Plus, it's not like we'd *have* to take the real dangerous missions. From my understanding, the more dangerous missions compensate the group higher upon completion. But it's not mandatory, you know? I think it could be fun, actually!"

Dawn glanced over at me. "It *would* suit an S-tiered sorcerer, much better than being an accountant would."

I had to admit, the Quester program was going to be my first choice. It seemed by far the most interesting and challenging program to choose from, something I could see myself thriving in compared to being a number cruncher in an office or something.

But even *I* was a little surprised that Tara had brought it up. If anything, I was concerned about *her* being a Quester, more so than myself; it wasn't exactly the safest profession, from what I picked up on so far during my time in the Realm. She had a point, though—we would never be obligated to take on extremely dangerous missions. Questers in the Realm work for the government and complete tasks initiated by civilians, but they get to select which tasks to complete, so we could simply do lower-level tasks, like helping with escort missions or even just finding someone's lost dog. It wouldn't be as exciting as fighting a dragon or some shit like that, but it would ensure her safety.

"It may not be a bad idea," I admitted.

"Well, if you want to get an idea of what it could be like being a Quester, then you should come check out the first round of the Questing Games!" said Dawn excitedly. "They happen to be this weekend, always the first weekend of November. Zula will be participating in them, so I was planning on going anyway. Most of the school goes to watch, actually. It's like going to a big school football game or something back on Earth."

"Sounds like it could be fun!" said Tara. "But I don't think I'd ever want to compete in the Games. And as far as missions go, I'd probably rather avoid combat."

This confirmed my suspicions that even though Tara wanted to be a Quester, she didn't have quite the same ambitions I had.

"That's fine!" Dawn replied. "There are plenty of Questers who don't participate in the Games. And like you said, you could be a Quester and never fight a day in your life. But I always hear the final project to officially get into the Quester program at the end of the year is similar to the Games, so it'd be good for you both to see what it's all about. You in?"

Tara and I exchanged looks and then nodded in agreement.

"Sounds like a good time to me!" I admitted excitedly. "It'd be cool to see Zula in action, too. That frenzy state of hers is nothing to play around with."

"You would know, wouldn't you?" Dawn asked with a gleam in her eyes.

Tara giggled as she went back to her salad.

The energy in the air that following Saturday had a lively feel to it as the three of us strolled through campus after a hearty breakfast at the dining hall. There were more people out walking the grounds for a Saturday morning than usual. It seemed that Dawn was right, the Questing Games were a pretty big deal at Magic Rune Academy.

"Wait 'til you guys see the inside of Reddick Stadium, it's way bigger than anything back on Earth," said Dawn as we followed the crowd of people ahead of us along the pearly white path through the grounds. The stadium was on the North side of campus, the same side as the dorms. It was wide and tall enough to where it could be seen almost anywhere on campus, but I had yet to go inside.

The stone pathway widened as we got closer to Reddick Stadium, offering more space for the surrounding crowd to disperse. Small trees, all of them showcasing bright orange leaves, were evenly spaced apart on the sides of the pathway leading up to the stadium entrance. Now that I was closer to it, the massive, oval-shaped building somehow looked bigger than ever, towering over the many students dawdling below it.

Some older looking runics in front of the impressive entrance were checking peoples' bags and tickets before waving them through.

"Students get in for free," Dawn assured us, and we scanned our thumbs at the gate after the runics running security had us empty our pockets and checked the girls' bags.

"Enjoy the show!" replied one of the guards, an older elf with wild white hair and a long white beard.

"So people who don't attend the Academy come to this, too?" asked Tara as she eagerly took in our surroundings.

Upon entering the stadium underneath the bleachers, we were greeted with what must have been hundreds of concession stands and vendors, selling anything from different types of delicious looking food (some of which I had never seen before, but smelled amazing), to various bobble-heads, shirts, and hats, all of which sported what looked to be the colors and logos of the various teams competing today. I even noticed some of the bobble heads looked exceptionally similar to Dean Celestine.

"Oh, yeah," replied Dawn. "Alumni come, of course, but also runics from across the Realm attend the Games here! It's a really big deal. Other schools host their own games as well, but Magic Rune Academy's games have always been the most highly respected and easily bring in the largest crowds. The school is renowned for its Quester program."

"I see that," I agreed, unable to deny the packed crowd of people (and this was only underneath the bleachers).

"Follow me," said Dawn, "I like to sit pretty high up to get a good view."

As we headed toward a tall escalator that spiraled upward, I noticed huge banners of different people posted along the high walls around us.

"Are they all runics who compete in the Games or something?" I asked.

"Competed!" Dawn corrected. "They were all some of the best to do it. You only get on the wall if you win all four years that you attend the Academy."

"Hey, look!" Tara pointed out. "It's Dean Celestine!"

I looked to my left and there she was, a seemingly younger Dean Celestine, wielding a slender black staff and looking fierce. I wasn't surprised to see that she was even better looking back in the day. Her body was somehow even tighter, as she sported a skin-tight purple robe with a gleaming black cloak over the top. Her hair was black instead of silver, but short and choppy textured—similar to how she wore it today. She didn't have glasses on back then, but her eyes were just as blue as ever.

"You got that right!" Dawn blurted out. "Dean Celestine is a legend. She got her reputation from competing in the Games years ago. Won every year by a landslide."

"No kidding!" I said, having a newfound level of respect for her.

The spiral escalator continued escorting the three of us up the stadium, higher and higher. Upon arriving on each floor, the railing opened up and the escalators briefly came to a halt, so that runics could get off at their desired level, before enclosing again and resuming its ascension.

"You know," Tara began. "I find it amazing how some aspects of the Rune Realm are quaint and older, like all of Hearthvale, and then you have things like this and other buildings around campus that are more advanced than anything back home."

"You'll never get bored or too comfortable in the Realm, that's for sure!" Dawn happily agreed.

The crowd thinned out the higher up we went, and it wasn't until I could see the top of the stadium and the bright blue sky before Dawn finally said, "This is us!" and hopped out of the escalator.

Tara and I followed her out. To my amazement, there were still plenty of vendors and food stands on this level, even.

We continued walking around the large stadium until Dawn seemed to find a section that was in line with what she wanted. And as we made our way out from underneath the stadium ceiling and into the fresh, outside air, the rest of it opened up to me.

Most of the runics appeared to have already made it to their seats, as the majority of the bleachers were already filled around the enormous oval stadium. Way below us was a massive grass field, although it wasn't square in shape, like how a football field would be. Instead, it was circular, with a wider radius than anything I'd seen before; it must have been a few hundred yards long and wide. Two magnificent Big-screens were on opposite sides of the stadium.

"There has to be over a hundred thousand people here!" Tara yelled over the sounds of the conversing crowd.

"Easily!" replied Dawn. "Probably a couple hundred thousand, to be honest."

I had to admit, this was bigger than *anything* I had expected. To the point where I felt like a loser for not planning to come, originally. This was clearly a *huge* deal—not only for the Academy, but maybe even the entire realm.

We staggered our way down some rows to an area that had a few open seats and sat down, Tara and Dawn on either side of me.

"So how do the Games even work?" I finally asked, now more intrigued than ever before.

"Oh, man, where do I begin?" said Dawn. Tara leaned forward with interest in her seat to my right. "Well, for starters, there are two big competitions throughout the school year. This is the first one, of course, that's held every November, the preliminary rounds. The championship match is in May, at the end of the school year. For the preliminaries, there are four rounds that go on all day long. Four teams of five people simultaneously compete against one another per round, with the winners of each round getting to move on to compete in one final match—the championship round in May."

"Neat! So we'll get to come back in May to watch again," Tara concluded.

"Definitely! The preliminaries are fun because they last longer, with there being four rounds instead of just one. But damn, that championship round is always nuts!"

"How do the rules work?" I asked.

"Well, technically, the rules change with every tournament," Dawn explained. "The objective for this year's preliminaries will be different from last year's, and even the championship round later this year. And the objective is always a surprise, even for the competitors."

"How do they prepare for it, then?" I asked.

"There's really no way to be entirely prepared, but one thing is almost always guaranteed in the Games—and that's that there will be combat involved in some way."

"And how does that work?" asked Tara, looking a bit anxious after hearing that.

"Luckily, the combat is never *actual* combat. I mean—it is, but it's also not. The players' weapons are covered with a strong rubber material that dulls the blows, and they all have to wear suppressors around their wrists, which limit the power that can be put out, like from sorcerers' spells, for example."

"Damn," I muttered, "guess I'd be handicapped, then!"

"Well," Dawn chuckled, "the suppressors and rubber coating over weapons only do so much. So, the stronger the runic, the more advantage they still have. Also, each player wears a specialized suit that registers damage—it basically measures the impact or blow delivered by an opponent. If a player takes a big enough hit to the arm by a weapon or a spell, the suit will tighten up, preventing the player from moving that arm. If they take a serious enough hit to the chest, head, or any vital organs, they'll be eliminated by means of 'KO,' and be forced to leave the field."

"Wow, must be some pretty high-tech gear," I said.

"Yeah, I think the suits are somehow digitally connected to the suppressors, too. Without the suppressors, the suits wouldn't register damage and tighten on impact."

"Pretty cool stuff!" Tara hollered out. "Are there any healers in the Games?"

"Oh, of course!" said Dawn. "it's almost essential for each squad to have at least one. They can use their healing spells to heal themselves or their teammates, and the suits respond to their healing the same way they respond to damage. So in that arm example I gave you, they can heal it and the suit would eventually unfasten around the 'injured' player."

"Nice!" shouted Tara excitedly. "It feels kind of cool to be important—"

"WELCOME, LADIES AND GENTLEMEN!!!" a loud, deep voice of a man boomed out from the speakers placed around the stadium, making Tara jump. The stadium erupted into cheers. "Welcome back to another highly antic-ipated season of the Questing Games!" the voice went on. "Today, sixteen squads will participate in a particular quest, but only four shall move on! Four exciting rounds of action, spanning over the next four hours! The stage is soon to be set, the teams are as prepared as they can possibly be, I hope, so with that, LET US INTRODUCE THIS YEAR'S PRELIMINARY QUEST!!"

Suddenly, a rumble erupted from the field below, vibrating even our own chairs all the way up where we sat. For a second, I feared that there was an earthquake, and that the stadium was in jeopardy of crumbling down. But then I noticed different sections of the turf on the field opening up, slowly revealing many concrete walls of various sizes, which crept up from beneath the surface. They continued rising, some connecting with others, some over twenty or thirty feet high, others short and twisting about. The walls appeared to be forming an enormous labyrinth.

The crowd's cheering grew louder as the walls continued to rise, they must have figured it out, too.

"THAT'S RIGHT, FANS!!!" the voice boomed out again. "This year's preliminaries will feature the Maze Finder

Quest! Each of the four teams will enter the maze from a different side of the field. As they come into contact with each other, they have the option to fight or flee! A large crystal has been placed toward the center of the maze—the objective is for each team to venture deep into the maze, retrieve the crystal, and return it to the entrance they had started at! With the quest now set, let's not keep you all waiting a second longer! Bring out the teams for the first match!"

The crowd exploded with anticipation as four different groups of five emerged from opposite tunnels around the stadium. I looked up at the massive Big-screens, both of them now split into four images showing close-ups of each team. They were all wearing the same tight material (they looked like full body suits), but in different colors and sporting different logos. The suits went up to their necks, but I noticed they didn't have any headgear on.

"What happens if they take a hit to the head?" I hollered over the cheers.

"The impact will still be suppressed, but a hit to the head almost always means elimination of the person who took the hit. Notice how the suits come up to their necks? It's designed that way so that it still registers hits to the head without actually covering their faces—"

At that moment, Dawn abruptly stood up to cheer. I looked over at the screen and saw Zula waving enthusiastically to the crowd. She was hoisting a very large double-sided battle axe over her shoulder, with the blades covered by a thick, black rubber material. The axe looked to be almost as tall as she was, and I couldn't help wondering just how heavy the damn thing was.

"There's our girl!" Dawn let out a loud whistle. "You got this, Zula!"

Tara and I joined Dawn in standing up to cheer for her.

"That's one hell of a weapon she has!" I shouted out.

"Yep!" shouted Dawn. "Rune-knights like Zula all use fierce weapons. It's their defining trait, sort of like how you have your staff. Some rune-knights have animals that call to them too, though. Take a look at that one!" She pointed to the far lower section of the screen, where a large man holding a mace was walking out with what looked to be a massive saber-toothed tiger at his side.

"How the hell are they supposed to fight off a tiger!" Tara blurted out.

"Take a look at what's around its neck!" replied Dawn.

The tiger appeared to be wearing a large silver necklace made of some sort of metal material, a purple gem at the center of it. That was when I also noticed similar bracelets around all the other competitors' wrists.

"Are those the suppressors? They even suppress the power of the animals?" I assumed.

"Exactly! It's the only way to ensure safety for everyone. After all, the beasts don't know how to hold back. Not in their nature!"

Each of the teams had a different color on. Zula's team was wearing yellow suits, with a logo of a boar on them. The names for each team popped up on their respective four corners of the screen.

"The Boarhounds?" asked Tara curiously, referring to Zula's team. "Like the dog?"

"Not quite!" replied Dawn. "A boarhound in the Realm is an animal that is basically a hybrid between a boar and a wolf. LET'S GO ZULA!!!"

A countdown had begun in the middle of the screen: 10, 9, 8, 7 (I noticed a slight change in Zula's demeanor, one that I recognized all too well and told me her frenzy form was starting to overtake her), 6, 5, 4, 3, 2, 1 . . .

A loud horn erupted around the stadium. "AND THEY'RE OFF!"

Each team sprinted into the massive maze, all entering from their designated spots around the field. For the first few minutes, the crowd was relatively quiet as the squads of five forced their ways further into the center of the field, carefully navigating around each bend and surveying their surroundings for any potential opponents. The advantage of being in the crowd, though, was that we could see when a collision was getting close. And the cheering began to slowly intensify as two teams on the far end, further away from where we sat, drew closer to one another.

They both turned the corner and paused with the realization that they had finally encountered an opposing team. For a second, they stared each other down with consideration, most likely trying to decide whether to flee or fight.

I wasn't entirely surprised when they both chose the latter.

It started with the large, human rune-knight sending his tiger after the other team's apparent leader, an elf who I assumed to be either a sorcerer or a healer (he was holding a bright red staff). The elf launched some sort of laser beam out of the staff, confirming to me that he was, in fact, a sorcerer. The beam shot directly at the tiger, but the large cat quickly dodged it, and then pounced from a surprisingly far distance away onto the poor elf.

Screams of terror filled the stadium, amplified by an apparent microphone coming from one of the cameras floating near the action. "OH! That's gotta hurt!!!" boomed the announcer as cheers roared around us.

I was shocked to see the rest of the elf's team immediately abandon him, retreating back in the opposite direction while the tiger continued to claw at the sorcerer, at times even biting at its victim's head.

"Is he going to be okay?!" asked Tara, her hands pressed over her mouth as she forced herself to watch in horror.

"Yeah, he'll be fine," Dawn casually waved off. "This stuff happens all the time. That big suppressor around its neck has its work cut out for it, but it's doing just fine. Take a closer look." She pointed at the screen.

She was right, even though the Saber-tooth looked to be holding nothing back, its strikes and bites were unable to penetrate the elf's skin. At that moment, a large red X popped up on the sorcerer's tight green suit, and the rune-knight whistled for his cat to return to him. As it did so, the announcer yelled out, "And we have our first KO of the tournament, folks!"

The elf then casually stood up, holding his shoulder a bit tenderly, but otherwise looking to be fine. He walked over to the rune-knight, and they quickly shook hands before parting ways.

"This is just wild to me," I scoffed unbelievably.

"Pretty intense, huh?" Dawn muttered back, keeping her eyes focused on the show.

"Player One of the Grasshoppers, if you are capable of doing so, please escort yourself from the maze at this time," the announcer kindly suggested.

"The Grasshoppers?" Tara chuckled. "With a name like that, I'm not surprised his team left him to die."

"Will he be all right to leave the maze?" I asked. "I mean, what if he gets attacked again?"

"I'm pretty sure that the red 'X' on his suit remains until he leaves the maze. Nobody can attack a fallen player like that, otherwise their team forfeits the match," said Dawn.

From there, I noticed that two teams seemed to be getting closer to the center of the maze: Zula's team and the rune-knight's team with the saber-toothed tiger (unironically called the Saber-tooths). The other two teams were in complete dismay, though. The four remaining members of the Grasshoppers were retreating even further away from the center, while the fourth team called the Brass Nuggets were still struggling to navigate themselves out of the corner they had started in.

"They made it!" Dawn blurted out as Zula's team finally arrived at the center of the maze—an open circular section with a large crystal diamond, about the size of a small dog, perched upon a pedestal on a small platform at the very center of it all.

The Boarhounds wasted no time, immediately sprinting toward the center of the ring. But just as they made it to the pedestal, the Saber-tooths had arrived, sporting their white and purple outfits.

"Ladies and gentleman . . ." said the announcer suspensefully, "I hope none of you left your seats, because it looks like things are about to HEAT UP!"

Immediately, the Saber-tooths darted toward the center.

"Alice!" Zula called out to one of her teammates, an elf holding a blue staff. Her voice, which was slightly deeper and raspier than normal, was being amplified by the microphone of a camera floating around her team. The crowd quieted down, eagerly listening to the conversation taking place on the screen. "Take the crystal and get to the exit. All of you. I'll stay here." Zula had a fiery grin on her face.

"Are you out of your mind—?"

"Just do it! I got this . . ."

Another one of her teammates, an orc who looked to be a shifter of some sort in his hybrid form (he had a long reptilian tail), spoke out, "Let's listen to her, Alice. It's not a bad plan. Even if she *does* get eliminated, she'll hold them off long enough for us to get this crystal back to our exit. We'll win this, and all move on."

Alice quickly contemplated the situation as the Saber-tooths closed in on them. "Okay, fine. Do your thing, Zula!" she hollered out, lifting the crystal from the pedestal and sprinting off back through the maze, the rest of her team following close behind.

"After them, Kaelan!" The rune-knight on the other team hollered out to one of his teammates. Immediately, Kaelan, an elf seemingly in their hybrid form with a yellow tail, sprinted past his teammates while shifting into a slender cheetah.

The camera zoomed in on Zula's face, whose grin broadened into a wicked, blood-thirsty smile. "HERE, KITTY!" She leaped at Kaelan, her axe still fastened on her back. Before I had even fully registered their movements, she tackled the shifter, rolled over with him in her grips, and then brutally threw him into the solid pedestal.

The cat's back seemed to bend around the pedestal from the impact, and he let out a gruesome yelp. Immediately, he shifted back, appearing to be unconscious, with a red X showing on his chest.

Without a further moment's hesitation, the rune-knight sent his saber-toothed tiger after her.

"Oh, no!" Tara squeaked beside me, looking terrified for Zula.

"Guess I'm slaying all kinds of pussy today!" Zula's frenzied voice blared out of the screen.

She grabbed her axe off her back and swung it at the cat. With one blow, the tiger was knocked backwards about twenty feet, struggling to get back to its feet. The opposing rune-knight now looked concerned, but still charged Zula.

He took a swing with his mace at her, but Zula quickly slid past him. She had noticed that their healer was trying to help the tiger. The healer never had a chance, though. Zula tossed her axe at the poor girl, knocking her backward into a surrounding concrete wall. The healer was helplessly trying to catch her breath as a red X popped up on her chest.

At that point, the remaining three players on the Saber-tooths banded together. All three of them were human. The large rune-knight with his mace, an apparent sorcerer, and the third, who I assumed to be another rune-knight (he was shakily pointing a crossbow at Zula).

The runic wielding the crossbow launched an arrow directly at her. What happened next brought me to my feet, along with everyone else in the stadium: Zula somehow caught the arrow with her bare hand.

That was all it took for the shooter to bail, as he cowardly sprinted off back through the maze.

"Some teammate you got there!" Zula rasped.

The sorcerer on the opposing team immediately launched a laser beam from his staff, which actually made contact with Zula's left arm.

"Shit," she muttered, her arm becoming stiff.

"Oh, no!" gasped Dawn, a hint of concern in her voice for the first time today. "That attack did some damage. Her suit registered it, and it looks like it tightened up around her left arm. She won't be able to move it without a healer to help!"

"Who needs it," Zula mumbled to herself.

Suddenly, the sorcerer did something else that surprised me. He raised his hands up, as if he was lifting something heavy, and the ground beneath Zula's feet seemed to respond, shifting up and forming clasps around her ankles. She was trapped.

The rune-knight let out a loud laugh. "Nice work, Reggie. Go on ahead and try to catch up to the rest of her team. I have unfinished business with this one."

The sorcerer named Reggie then took to the air, swiftly flying off through the maze (though he stayed only a few feet off the ground, leading me to believe that maybe there was some sort of invisible barrier preventing a sorcerer like that to fly high above the maze and locate the crystal from above).

"You're a skilled rune-knight, I'll give you that," her opponent began. "But you've pissed me off. Nobody hurts Sky," he gestured to his limp tiger, "and gets away with it."

To my surprise, Zula looked finished; she wasn't even trying to break free from the earth clamping down around her ankles, her head lowered in defeat.

"Now, be gone with you!" The rune-knight raised his large mace to send it down on Zula.

But suddenly, Zula's gaze shifted up to her opponent, that wicked grin on her face. She abruptly swung one of her legs upward, breaking it free from the earth-clamp, and brutally kicked the rune-knight directly in the balls.

The man's eyes shot open wide as he let out a nasty groan. His mace slid from his grip, and he fell to his knees with a large red X printed across his crotch, gasping helplessly for air.

The crowd erupted with sounds of groans, laughter, and

cheers. "OOOOO" The announcer let out. "I think even I felt that one, folks . . ."

"Can she do that?!" Tara asked, cringing.

"Well, there are no rules against it, technically," said Dawn, with a subtle look of sympathy for the man.

Zula broke free from her other clamp, hoisted her axe over her shoulder, and waved to the crowd with an innocent smile.

A horn sounded out from the stadium. Reggie hadn't reached the remaining Boarhounds in time, as they all were celebrating and embracing each other at their original entrance, Alice holding the crystal.

"WE HAVE OUR FIRST TEAM MOVING ON, LADIES AND GENTS! CONGRATULATIONS TO THE BOARHOUNDS!"

Chants of "Zula!" erupted around the stadium, and I was left feeling amazed, excited to enter the Quester program (maybe even the Questing Games), and also a little grateful for the fact that I had gotten away with only a sore back during the Halloween party, when Zula had me pinned to that wall.

Chapter Ten

AFTER THE PRELIMINARIES for the Questing Games, the rest of the semester primarily revolved around hunkering down and preparing for the midterms. With each passing week, the chill in the air became more noticeable, and the students of Magic Rune Academy traded in their time spent outside on the grounds for evenings in their dorms or the library.

It wasn't long before the first week of December had arrived, as well as the first snowfall, and midterms shortly after that.

By far, my easiest midterm was in Dean Celestine's Rune Sensing and Manipulation class. The test consisted of having to use telekinesis to pull a book into our hands. However, the twist was that we were to be blindfolded and couldn't use the surveybee jam.

I ended up effortlessly pulling the book directly into my hand on my first try, warranting perhaps the easiest A of my life. Most of my fellow students were able to at least pull the book within their general vicinity at this point, which meant for a passing grade. Even Dak launched the book toward himself (though it drilled him in the face yet again).

In regards to the classes that I shared with Tara, specifically Basic History of the Realm, the only reason I passed was because of her suggested study sessions, which we had in the library together during evenings leading up to midterm week. It amazed me how even studying seemed to be enjoyable, as long as I was doing something with my nerdy blonde bombshell of a girlfriend.

Without question, my most difficult midterm came from Professor Morran's Intro to Classes course. It would seem that I was trying a little *too* hard to sneak conversations in with Sakura all term long, to the point where it had interfered with my learning about the other runic classes.

Professor Morran had pulled me aside after class to review my test results with me (which I thought was a little strange, as she didn't do this with anyone else), and to say that she seemed unenthused as she scanned through my results was an understatement.

"You've barely passed, Nate," she muttered, slamming my test paper on her desk.

"I did pass, though?" I asked.

"Well, yes, but this is not what I had hoped to see from you. You are an S-tiered runic, Nate. Don't you expect more from yourself than just *barely* passing?" She looked up at me with those big purple eyes. Her mane of silky blue hair was forced up into an amazingly long ponytail, showcasing her cute, pointy ears.

"I—uh . . ." I swallowed, trying to regain myself after being drawn into her gaze. "Well, yeah, I suppose so," I lied.

The truth was, just passing was good enough for me, at least for this class. S-tier or not, I was still human. I mean, I was already crushing my sorcerer class with Dean Celestine, which was my primary focus. All this other stuff was almost background music in comparison.

"You suppose?'" Professor Morran repeated.

"Yes, Professor," was all I could think to say at the moment.

She gave me a long, intrigued stare, and for a second, I thought maybe she was secretly a sorcerer trying to read my mind.

"Very well, then." She raised her brow in disapproval and threw her hands down on her desk. "Well, you passed." She then stood up and practically walked through me, but not before shoving my test paper into my hands, a little too aggressively.

"Oh, and Mr. Gannon!" She stopped at her door, not even turning around to face me. "Don't think I haven't noticed your fixation with Miss Redd. Unsurprised as I may be, given your tier rank, I expect more from you next semester. I know you're an adult, but if I must, I will treat you like a child and give you an assigned seat."

I left Professor Morran's class feeling perplexed and filled with mixed emotions. On one hand, I had passed my last midterm, meaning that I had the next month to kick back and enjoy the fruits of the Rune Realm and Magic Rune Academy. But on the other, Professor Morran seemed more than just a little disappointed in me, and for some reason, that really irked me as I strolled back to my dorm through the snow dusted grounds, replaying her words back in my mind.

The way she had handled it was a little strange, too. She didn't just come off as a professor disappointed in her student, she seemed to almost take it personally—like she really cared about my success. Kind of strange, considering that before today, that was the longest conversation I had had with her. The whole thing just caught me off guard.

Regardless, my first semester at Magic Rune Academy came to an end, and overall, I'd say it was a successful one. Tara and I had passed all our midterms, and after making sure Tara was still okay with it after watching the Games, we submitted our request to enter into the Quester program. We wouldn't officially be allowed into the program until passing the final project, but that wouldn't come until the end of the school year in May. Now was the time to kick back and relax for a bit.

"Are you sure you don't want to come back with me for winter break?" asked Tara, standing outside the entrance of Glendor's. Large snowflakes were slowly falling all around us as she stood bundled up in a thick winter coat, sweats, gloves, and a hat.

"Yeah, I just don't see a point in heading back yet if I don't have to, you know?" I replied.

"No, I understand," said Tara, clearly forcing a smile. "To be honest, I'm kind of bummed that I decided to go back. The parents would disown me, though, if I didn't visit them for the holidays," she groaned.

"Don't worry, I'll make sure she gets back okay!" Dawn brightly said. She was wearing a winter version of her shifter clothes, which surprisingly was made of the same thin, flexible material of her summer outfit. The main difference was that she ditched the sports bra and short skirts for long sleeves and tight pants. She was also wearing black gloves and a black winter hat that had two holes in it for her cat ears to poke through when needed.

"Guess I'll be seeing you in a few weeks, then," sighed Tara.

"Yeah, I'm sorry, Tara. It's just . . ."

"No, I get it. I promise," she genuinely said before giving me a kiss goodbye.

"Awe, that's sweet," Dawn joked.

From there, I watched as she and Dawn made their way into Glendor's, leaving me standing outside in the snow, wondering if I was making the best decision to stay in the Rune Realm for winter break instead of going back with Tara.

The truth is, if I didn't *have* to go back to Earth, then I'd prefer not to. I no longer even had my own place to stay back there since dropping out of my old college (and when my grandpa passed, his house was left to me, but I ended up selling it before starting my second year of school so I'd have a solid cushion in my savings). On top of that, just being on Earth for the holidays would remind me of times with my grandparents, spending Christmas with both of them for so many years. So it was just easier this way. Somehow, being in the Realm made those memories feel like they were from another lifetime, and maybe that wasn't necessarily a bad thing.

Tara seemed to know exactly how I felt about it all, without me having to say it out loud, which I was grateful for.

I made my way through Hearthvale toward the Bronze Dragon (Dawn had agreed to meet me there for a late lunch once she came back through the Magic Gateway), the town now decked out with Christmas lights and Christmas decorations. Wreaths hung on all the shop windows and doors, and a big Christmas tree was put up in the town center, with lights of all colors running through it and a big bright gold star perched on its peak.

As I entered the Bronze Dragon, I was pleased to be almost immediately greeted by Sakura.

"Hi, Nate," she quietly said, beaming at me.

"Sakura! Hey! You're still working, even on winter break?" I asked.

"Yes, but I don't mind. I like the holidays in town," she replied, escorting me over to a small table.

"I get it. It really is nice here. They do a great job with decorating the town and everything."

"It really is magical, isn't it?" she agreed.

"You have a minute to sit?" I asked, gesturing to the seat across from me.

"Oh!" Her big blue eyes widened. "What about your friends? I—I just don't want to interrupt."

"You won't be! Dawn will be here soon, and I'm just killing time until then, really."

"Um," she fiddled with her thumbs, pondering over it. "Maybe next time, I should really get back to work. I'm sorry. . ."

"No worries. I'll be right here if things slow down!" I said, figuring the best idea would be not to push. By now, she was just starting to come out of her shell a little. But that was just around me. I had noticed that she was still plenty shy around other people.

"Sounds good," she giggled. "The Reuben?"

"With the picks in it, shaped like a smiley face?" I chuckled. "You know me so well!"

She let out another cute giggle before quickly stopping herself from laughing too hard. "I hope you didn't think that was childish. . ."

"Nope! Not at all! Actually, now I expect it. If I don't get it, I may return it and ask to speak with your manager," I joked.

She tried to hold in another snicker with her hand. "Oh, gosh. One smiley Reuben coming up!"

I was happy to notice that she seemed calmer than ever talking to me today. It could have been because the place was pretty abandoned, given half the students were away on break, or the fact that it was just me and her talking. But either way, I was pleased to see her showing brief streaks of her natural personality.

At that point, Dawn had arrived, and I waved her over to my table.

"Did she make it back all right?" I asked.

"Good as gold! So," she winked at me, "just you and little me for the next few weeks, huh?"

"Your wish is my command," I replied with a smirk. "You don't have anything going on?"

"Nah," she waved off. "I've never been too big on the holidays, really. And the Guard gave me off the next few weeks, so I'm all yours."

"All mine, huh?"

"*All* yours," she purred.

I tried my best not to think about *all* of Dawn just yet, considering we were still out in public.

After finishing up with our meals, we went for a leisurely walk around town, eventually making a pit-stop at a quaint novelty shop called Whimsical Wonders. Apparently, it was one of Dawn's favorite places to stop at during her free time. She enthusiastically strode up and down the aisles, pointing out all kinds of unique looking collectibles and trinkets (she was particularly fond of a silver necklace with a little cat charm at the end of it, which was happily holding a gem with its paws). I had to admit, it was nice seeing her show so much passion for something, even if it was over a bunch of used, half-broken stuff. Actually, that just made it even more adorable.

With it being December now, night was already quickly approaching once we finally left the shop, and with the snow still steadily falling, we agreed to head back before it got too dark out.

We hopped on the axe beaks and made our quick trip through the snowy mountains back to campus, which was so decked out with Christmas lights that you could see the entire valley below glimmering about from the mountain peak.

"I'm kind of surprised that Christmas is really big in the Realm," I said to Dawn as we made our way back down the mountain and through the North Gate entrance. "I mean, I kind of get Halloween, given the nature of the Realm and the people here, but Christmas just seems so . . . Earth-like."

"Yeah, I used to think the same thing!" replied Dawn, treading by my side through the thick snow covering the campus grounds. "But that's what I love about the Realm. Humans bring their traditions and holidays, orcs have theirs, and elves, too, and then they all share them with each other. It means for plenty of good times in the Realm, really. Although, ages ago it was unanimously agreed upon by all the races to adopt the Earth yearly calendar here.

"Makes it easier for us at least, right? Hey, where are you going?" I hollered out to her as she veered off the snow-covered path into the thicker, unscathed snowy terrain.

"Just come on! You want all of me, right? Well, let's have some fun!"

For perhaps a lack of better judgment, I followed her lead, treading off the path and shuffling through the thick snow, which was further piling up with every passing minute.

"Come on, slowpoke! We're almost there" she waved onward from in front of me, scooting along closer to one of the campus ponds, which was entirely frozen over.

The first thing I noticed was that there was no coating of snow blanketed over the pond. Instead, it remained solid and clear, smooth as glass. But way more interestingly, an odd and fascinating phenomenon seemed to be occurring, one that I'd never even imagine witnessing back home. A neon blue aura was emanating from the pond, lighting up the night air around it. The closer we got, it became evident that the "aura" was a result of thousands of individual bright blue specks periodically and briefly illuminating along the dark, frozen surface of the pond.

"The snowflakes are . . ."

"The surface of the pond is cooler than the snow," Dawn whispered, staring mesmerized at the scene. "I love when this happens."

I looked down at her, the blue light casting against her fair skin, which currently had just a touch of pink in it from the cold. She looked exactly how she did the day I had first met her, as she was currently in her human form. It was amazing how she could look beautiful in both her human and hybrid forms.

Almost reluctantly, I pulled my gaze away to rejoin her in taking in the marvelous occurrence in front of us.

"But how?" I asked curiously.

"It's the noctillia," she softly said, slowly striding closer to the edge of the pond.

"Come again?"

"They're tiny, single-celled organisms that inhabit the waters in the Realm. Harmless little guys, but beautiful as ever! You'll see them at night, more often during the warmer months. They glow blue when they're moved or touched. In the winter, though, they freeze at the surface. And when anything warmer comes into contact with them, they briefly glow like that. In this case, the snowflakes are warmer, so when they fall to the surface of the pond . . ."

"You get a winter light show," I softly added.

"And that's not all—" Dawn quickly ditched her boots, exposing her bare feet to the snow and gasping.

"Dawn! What are you—?!"

"Come on!" she hollered back to me. "We're going ice-skating!"

"But we don't have any skates! Don't be ridiculous, your feet will freeze!"

"Who needs skates! Just get over here, Nate!"

I let out a long sigh and prepared for the worst. Then I slid my shoes off my feet and discarded my socks.

"Holy piss, this sucks!" I blurted out.

"Hurry up!" Dawn laughed. "I promise, it'll get better."

"Gonna have—to disagree with you—" I shivered.

"Just take my hand," she said, beaming up at me.

It was hard to argue with her, so I grabbed her hand, and together we took a step out onto the frozen surface.

A bright neon blue light suddenly glowed from beneath my foot, followed by a soothing warmth. I almost took a step back on land, out of fear that the ice would quickly melt. But Dawn's laughter made me pause.

"It won't melt. Trust me. The noctillia don't just glow, they briefly warm up when touched, too. But the weirdest part of all? They only exchange their heat between themselves and whatever touches them, bypassing anything else around them, like this ice!"

"You've gotta be kidding me. That defies any and all laws of your basic thermodynamics!" I exclaimed in astonishment.

Dawn giggled. "Yeah, sure, why not!" She then proceeded to glide along the ice, barefoot, leaving a brief trail of blue glowing in her wake. "I'd call it magic!" she hollered back to me. "But would that be too cliché?!"

I followed her lead. It was like running my feet across warm sand on a hot, sunny day. "This is something else . . ." I muttered to myself, marveling at the blue path I was leaving on the ice behind me, and then trying to draw various shapes before the trail vanished.

Meanwhile, Dawn was doing what I would perhaps call "light-angels" in the center of the pond.

"Are you sure this won't break on us?!" I yelled out to her. "I swear if I have to dive in and save you . . ."

Dawn waved a hand, still lying flat on the ice. "Nah, we're fine!"

A little skeptical of her overconfidence, I slid my way closer to her, just to be safe.

"Pretty amazing, huh?" she breathed dreamily, gazing at the sky above us with a content smile.

I carefully laid down beside her, letting the warmth over-whelm my entire body. The sky was as clear as the glassy pond beneath us, showcasing its usual streams of pink and purple.

"It's stunning," I muttered. "It's all stunning. . ."

I looked over at her, unable to deny her beauty. She was still in awe, smiling at the sky and taking it all in. The glow from beneath her illuminated her body, making her look other-worldly—like an angel or even a goddess.

"*You're* stunning, Dawn," I added.

She drew her attention away from the sky to look at me. Her black eyes, shaded blue from the light, were beaming at me. "You're just saying that," she whispered.

I slowly shook my head.

A big smile started to break across her face, but then she quickly turned to face the sky again.

We continued lying there like that for a few minutes before Dawn finally made her way back up to her feet again. "I'll race you to the other side!" she shouted out and started gliding across the pond again.

Before I could even make it back up to my feet, though, I felt an abrupt and icy impact on the side of my face.

"Did you just—? Was that a snowball?!" I yelled out to Dawn, who was bent over laughing.

"Sorry! I kind of figured your sorcerer skills would just take over there and you'd sense it coming!"

"We haven't gotten to sensing incoming threats yet in my Rune Sensing class!" I mumbled back.

"Oh! So now I'm a threat? Little cat girl is a threat to the big bad S-tier spellcaster?" She taunted.

"Oh, now you did it!" I laughed, gliding over to the bank and quickly building a snowball of my own. I then chucked it at Dawn, who was bent over trying to quickly build another one. It hit her right in the ass, making her shriek and jump forward a couple of feet.

"That's it! Now you're fucked!" She grinned and then darted her snowball right at my head.

I figured I'd be a good sport and take it to the face. That turned out to be a mistake, though, as the chunk of ice slammed into my forehead, knocking me down onto the snowy bank.

"Ow! Shit!" I groaned, rubbing my head.

"Oh, no, no, no! I'm so sorry, Nate!" Dawn glided over to me. "I thought that was all snow! I promise. Fuck, I'm such an idiot!"

"No, no! It's okay, really." I muttered, still rubbing my forehead.

"Are you sure?" she asked with a look of genuine concern in her eyes.

"Yeah, I'll be fine." I looked up at her and tried to give a reassuring smile. "See? All good!"

Dawn cringed a little. "Oh, Nate . . . I think it's already starting to swell. Maybe we should go somewhere inside where we can get a better look at it. Ugh, I'm so sorry!"

"Really, Dawn," I groaned, making my way to my feet. "I promise, no big deal! Though, it *does* feel like it's getting even colder by the second, and this snow doesn't seem to be letting up at all, so getting indoors feels like a pretty good move to me."

"Yeah, of course! I know a good place. . ."

We put our socks and shoes back on and frigidly shuffled back to the pathway. Then Dawn led the way a little further through campus to the Student Union, which sat on the North side, just before reaching the quad.

The warmth and smell of fresh coffee hit me like a truck as we entered the lobby of the building. The few students who were inside were lounging about, quietly keeping to themselves at their own tables while sipping on some hot beverages.

Dawn and I immediately went to order a couple hot drinks of our own to warm up (I got a coffee, black, while she ordered a hot chocolate). We found a small table by a tall window and watched the snow's peaceful descent through the thick glass. Dawn was still apologizing and analyzing my head when I noticed that Christmas music from back home was quietly playing from the speakers in the ceiling above us. A fire was lit below a tall mantel in the center of the lobby, which offered a 360-degree view for the few students sitting in lounge chairs around it.

To say it was a peaceful scene was an understatement, and sharing it with Dawn made for a special and memorable evening (even with the bump on my head). It was so serene, in fact, that I took an extra-long time finishing my coffee, and found myself sharing old Christmas stories with Dawn.

As it would turn out, she was an amazing listener. She simply sat with her hands under her face, seemingly basking in my stories. If I hadn't known any better, I'd say there was even a subtle look of envy on her face when I talked about a particular year when my grandparents took me ice fishing on their pond and we got snowed in, forcing us to spend the entire Christmas day together in my grandpa's truck.

". . . it was also when I first learned how to play the harmonica," I continued. "My grandpa was a natural at it! I remember, he pulled an old one out from the glove box and played Christmas tunes on it to pass the time. He even managed to teach me a few easy songs before someone finally found us! It should have been a scary situation for a kid to be in. Instead, he managed to make it a good memory for me."

By the time I had finally finished with my coffee, I noticed Dawn was just getting toward the end of her hot chocolate as well. I took this as a sign that she was also enjoying our time together. So, with a fervent urge to keep the night going, I decided to ask her to come back to my dorm and watch a movie. To say the least, I was both relieved and pleased when she happily obliged.

"It's the least I can do after drilling you in the face with a ball of ice!" she laughed, still displaying inklings of guilt over her genuine smile.

About twenty cold, wet minutes later, we finally reached my dormitory, coated in snow from head to foot. It seemed like it was coming down even harder now, maybe even turning into a snowstorm. But it just made my room feel that much warmer and more welcoming.

Dawn shuddered, practically running toward my living room couch inside my dorm room, but then she paused.

"All good?" I asked.

"Well," she slowly pondered, pursing her lips, "it's just . . . my shifter clothes are all wet, and I didn't bring a spare pair."

"Before I knew it, my pants started to tighten a bit with the realization of where this seemed to be going.

"Oh, well, I have plenty of shirts and stuff, if you want," I played dumb for now. "They might be a little big on you, but . . ."

She started stalking her way closer to me. "I may still have that pesky chill, though," said Dawn innocently. Even though her eyes were currently a different color than the night of the Halloween party, they had that same deter-mined look in them. "You know, one of those chills that only a shower seems to fix." Her lips curled into a smile.

"Yeah?" I quietly asked as she moved even closer, now just inches away from my face.

"Yeah," she whispered, closing her eyes and wrapping her arms around my neck before gently kissing me on the lips.

That was all I needed for my crotch to swell up against my pants. I leaned further into her, passionately kissing her back. It dawned on me that this was actually the first time

I had felt her soft lips since a couple months back (we had been so busy studying for midterms, and Dawn working almost nightly with the Guard, that time just escaped us), yet they tasted exactly as I had remembered them, her dark lipstick having those same hints of strawberry and grape.

I wasted no time at all. Forcing our way into my bedroom, we remained clung to each other before practically bursting through my bathroom door.

Things were heating up quickly, aggressively, and passionately; a result of having waited so long for this very moment to present itself again. I pinned her up against the bathroom wall, her arms still wrapped around my neck, all while remaining glued to each other's faces. It was one of those confirming moments where you just know it's ending in sex. Nothing could ruin it for us. No interruptions could be had. Things were too hot to cool down, the only solution being my cock deep inside of her.

I pulled myself away just long enough to open the glass shower door and turn the shower head on. When I turned around, Dawn was already swiftly attempting to throw her shifter top off. But with it being wet and hugging her damp body, it fought against her wishes and made it appear as if she was not so gracefully trying to wrestle herself.

I couldn't help but laugh. "You need an extra hand there?" I asked.

"Yes, please!" she politely sighed, her head trapped underneath her tight, black, long-sleeved top.

I slowly tugged at her snug top until it was completely off, realizing that this was the first time I was looking at Dawn's tits. I took a grateful moment to admire them. They were perky and perfectly shaped, and an absolute fit for her petite frame.

She looked up at me through her bangs with those black eyes and smiled. "I hope you like what you see. . ."

"Fucking love it." I gently caressed one of her tits and bent over to start sucking on her small nipples, making sure that I paid equal attention to each one.

"Oh, mmm . . ." she moaned as they firmed up in my mouth.

The steam in the room was growing thicker, so I took that as a sign to hop in. As I threw my shirt over my head, I felt a small pair of hands grab at my pants and force them down. My cock then sprung upward as Dawn discarded my briefs.

"Oh, I missed you," muttered Dawn with a grin.

I smiled and then grabbed hold of her waistband before tugging her tight pants down. She had to help me out a little when I reached her thick ass, wiggling her hips as I jerked them past her luscious cheeks.

When I finally got them off, I took another quick moment to bask in my view. Her pussy was picture-perfect, tight and petite, like the rest of her. The hair above her otherwise smooth mound was shaved into a cute little black landing strip that trailed down the center.

"You're fucking beautiful," I said, eyeing her tight body up and down, my cock fully sprung and pointing directly at her.

She smiled happily and flung her cool, damp body into my arms again, going at my lips even harder yet.

My shower was spacious enough for the two of us to freely move around (really, it was big enough for three people). The steam was thick, but felt amazing after being outside in the cold.

I couldn't help myself—I immediately pinned Dawn against the tiled wall of my shower. It didn't phase her at all, though, as she started sucking on my neck. With my engorged cock pressed tightly against her flat stomach, I reached down and firmly grabbed two large handfuls of her thick cheeks, squeezing tightly.

"Ohhh, fuck," she let up off my neck and grinned into my eyes. Gazing up at me from underneath her soaked black bangs, she whispered, "I want you inside me. I can't wait any longer, baby."

Hearing her say that sent chills of erotic excitement down my spine. I had been waiting for this moment since the day I first met her, unsure, at times, that I would ever actually get here. Yet here I was, with nothing to stop me from finally claiming my sexy little cat girl.

She reached down and gently caressed my cock. I bent lower to get a good angle before she started gently and slowly rubbing my head in a circular motion around her opening.

"Oh, fuck, Dawn," I breathed.

"That feel nice?" I saw her lips curl into another grin.

"Fuck, yeah," I groaned.

It was the torturous type of "nice." And as she continued rubbing it around her lips, I felt her becoming wetter by the second.

"Mmm," she moaned as she bit at her mouth.

I couldn't take anymore of it, and I was just about to start edging in, when she took the liberty for me, grabbing my hips and pushing me ever so slightly forward.

"Mmm!" she let out again, as the tip of my head finally entered her hot sex, just barely.

She threw both her arms around my neck again and grinned up at me before kissing me fiercely again.

As she did so, I continued gently edging my hips forward, gradually inching my way more and more into her.

She felt amazing—her tight, hot pussy squeezing around my shaft. I had managed to edge myself about halfway inside her when she pulled her lips away from mine, her mouth hanging open in a mesmerized sort of way.

"Oh, shit . . ." she gasped. "You're so fucking big. I'm too little for this!" She breathed a shallow laugh.

"I can slow down a—"

"No!" she interrupted, "whatever you do, don't do that."

We looked into each other's eyes and chuckled.

"Sounds good to me," I said and resumed gently thrusting while kissing her neck.

"Ohhh, mmmm, yes . . ." she gasped as I furthered my way into her now with each passing plunge. I slowly repeated this, with her further warming up to me by the minute.

Her pussy was the wettest it had been, and at last, able to take most of my cock. Now practically pressed against her mound, I could smoothly drive each long thrust into her and back out again.

"Oh, my—oh, my . . ." she stuttered into my ear while clawing at my back hard enough to where I thought she may have been transforming into her hybrid form on me without realizing it.

"Fuck, you're so big," she gasped and swallowed. "I don't know how you're inside of me right now. I can practically feel you in my stomach. Keep—keep going! Please!"

Her eyes were closed tight, a begging desire written all over her face, which told me that I was in the clear to speed things up. So unable to resist any longer, I grabbed hold of her ass again, squeezing tightly, and then sped up the pace, thrusting faster and harder with every lunge forward.

"Oh! Oh! Oh, yeah!" she yelled out, responding with deeper breaths and louder moans of pure sexual pleasure. "Fuck, yes, baby! Keep pounding! Just like that!" she shrieked.

I was now thrusting into her so hard that I was practically drilling her through the wall. I then lifted her up by her ass so that she was at eye-level with me, her arms still wrapped around my neck.

A dominant sensation overtook me as I roughly pounded her against the wall, my cock plummeting in and out of her sex as she wailed away into the night. "Yes! Yes! YES! I love it, baby! You're so fucking good! Holy shit! Mmm! Oh! Oh! Oh, yeah!" she moaned with each drive forward. I was somehow still managing to further myself into her tight pussy as it stretched for me, desperately adapting to my penis.

She opened her eyes—to my surprise, they were now yellow. A second later, her black cat ears sprung up from her hair, and a tail squeezed out from between her and the wall.

"I just couldn't help it, Nate!" she quickly yelled out while I continued thrusting into her. A dazed smile was plastered on her face as her yellow eyes rolled back ever so slightly. "You just feel so *fucking* good! I can't help it. Keep pounding me. I need it!" she gasped.

"I want it like this," I muttered. "I want all of you! You're so fucking hot."

Her breathing picked up. She clawed further into my back, her cheeks rosy with sexual ecstasy. "I'm gonna—I'm gonna cum! Don't stop! Please, don't stop!"

Still having her lifted a foot off the floor, tightly pinned up against the wall, I kept my same exact rhythm going into her tight, hot sex.

"Oooohhh! It's happening!"

Her inner walls seemed to be pulsating tighter around my shaft. And with that, I drove my way even harder into her, the urge to cum quickly arriving for me now, too.

"Oh, fuck, Dawn. *I'm* gonna cum!"

"Ye—yes! Cum inside me! Just—just keep going!"

"Oh, shit!" I groaned as I edged even closer, with no intention of stopping or slowing down.

"Give it to me! I want to feel you shoot inside of me, baby! Oh! Oooohhhh, YES!"

She clawed harder into my back as her insides quivered from her orgasm, causing her to go mute, other than the occasional desperate gasps for air.

I got her there just in time, right before my own orgasm erupted, bringing on an automatic need to ram my hips faster yet, and at last, launching several jets of my thick seed deep inside of her. Dawn was so tight that I knew she could feel every stream of my cum bursting into her. I continued thrusting for a few more moments after the last shot of semen, ensuring that I had emptied myself entirely.

"Holy fuck . . ." she panted, beaming up at me with her yellow eyes as I slowly pulled out of her. "That was amazing."

We were both breathing heavy, the shower still as hot and steamy as ever.

"I'll say," I agreed. "A perfect end to an amazing day, really."

"Yes, definitely."

Seeing her genuinely satisfied and happy like this was enough to bring a smile to my face, especially considering how cool and casual she always liked to play things off. It was as if I unlocked an entirely new side of her tonight, witnessing her offer herself to me in such a vulnerable way like that. It was so rewarding, and more than worth the wait.

Upon stepping out of the shower a few minutes later, a thought occurred to me, though. "Just curious," I said, grabbing a towel to dry myself off, "are you on the pill?"

Dawn laughed, shaking herself out dry, ironically like a wet dog. "I don't need anything like that." She waved off, and for a second, my stomach dropped a little. "I've learned to control my internal rune to prevent *that* from happening."

"What?" I asked with a baffled smile.

"Yep! It's something us classes who can control their own interior rune can learn to do, like shifters and rune-knights. Even healers can learn to do it. But sorcerers? Sorry!" she taunted.

I scoffed. "Well, that's good to know! And also, good enough reason to want to be any other class besides a sorcerer."

"Oh, sure," Dawn sarcastically began, "trade being able to bend the elements and read minds for a free form of birth control," she giggled.

After drying ourselves off, we put on some fresh, warm clothes (Dawn slipped into one of my shirts, which was basically a dress on her) and chilled on my living room couch for around thirty minutes or so, happily watching television while the snow continued falling outside my window.

"Well," Dawn began, standing up.

"Dawn, no way," I interjected.

"What?" she laughed. "I have to get back."

"Dawn!" I repeated. "There's like two feet of snow out there, and it's still coming down. You can stay here for the night, really."

"Awe, that's sweet. You gonna miss me?" she teased.

"I'm serious. It's bad out there."

"I'll be fine, don't worry," she casually said, throwing my shirt off and squeezing back into her damp shifter clothes. "Are you forgetting that I can turn into a full-blown panther? I'll be back at my place in no time at all. Plus, the fur keeps me warm!"

"You're a panther, not a snow leopard!"

She giggled. "I'll be fine. This was fun, Nate, really. See you tomorrow?"

Against my better judgment (and after coming up with plenty more excuses to get her to stay, all of which she had an answer for), I finally agreed to let her go. It seemed like there was just no changing her mind on this.

It was an abrupt ending to an otherwise amazing day, as I was left to watch a large black panther dart past my window, leaving her massive tracks through the fresh white snow.

Chapter Eleven

I woke up early Christmas morning to the sound of loud rapping on the other side of my door.

"Merry Christmas!" Dawn exclaimed after I groggily opened the door for her.

It may have been the first time I saw her in something besides her various shifter outfits. She was bundled up in a thick black winter jacket, scarf, hat, boots, and fuzzy mittens, though the material of her pants was still very shifter-like, a charcoal-gray.

"I thought you weren't big on the holidays?" I gave her a tired smile, letting her in my dorm room.

"Well, maybe I found my Christmas spirit for once!" She walked over to the living room window and took the liberty of sliding open the curtains. Bright rays of sunlight beamed through the room.

"It's too early for that," I mumbled, squinting at her.

"Too early!" she replied brightly. "We've got the whole day to enjoy together." She plopped down on the couch, her oversized, puffy jacket riding up underneath her chin as she did so. "So I was thinking, first we can get some breakfast at the dining hall—they're doing a Christmas feast for every meal today—then we can take a stroll through campus, maybe do some sled riding, and then get dinner in town tonight. Then after that . . ." She winked and made a sexual gesture, sticking one of her fingers through a hole she made with her others.

I couldn't help but laugh over her enthusiasm for the day. "Sounds like an amazing Christmas to me. I'll go get dressed."

"Oh!" Dawn blurted out, jumping up from the couch. "I almost forgot." She bit her lip excitedly and ravaged through her coat pockets.

"Dawn . . ." I started, pleasantly surprised by her gesture.

"I told myself that I'd wait, but who am I kidding—"

She pulled out a small box. The wrapping was messy and crinkled, barely kept together with many pieces of scotch tape, but the bow was neatly placed on top.

"*Merry Christmas!*" she sang out, excitedly holding it out to me. "Wrapped it myself!'

I beamed at her. "You really didn't have to," I said.

"I know, I know. Just open it!" She eagerly shoved it into my hands.

Not wanting to keep her waiting any longer, I quickly unraveled the crinkly wrapping, which revealed a small, sleek black box. I carefully pried it open and was shocked to see a shiny black harmonica sitting inside of it.

I swallowed. "Dawn . . . you really didn't have to. . ."

"Do you love it?!"

"Love it? This is one of the best gifts I've . . . thank you, Dawn."

"And don't worry, it's brand new! I got it at a shop in town—not from Whimsical Wonders! Wouldn't want you blowing on a used one!"

"Seriously, Dawn, thanks so much. You have no idea how much this means."

"Ah, it was nothing, really," she tried to coolly wave it off, but her subtle blushing gave her true feelings away.

"Well," I began, "speaking of Whimsical Wonders . . ." I swiftly walked into my bedroom and grabbed her gift out of the top drawer of my wardrobe before returning to her in the living room, holding it behind my back.

Dawn's mouth hung open in shock. "Nate, you got me . . . ?"

"Merry Christmas, Dawn," I said, handing her a small gift bag.

As I handed it to her, she had a confused expression on her face.

"It's under the wrapping. You know, you have to dig through it to get to the good part," I joked.

She blinked a few times, coming to. "I know!" she scoffed with a grin. "I just . . . I never . . ." She didn't finish her sentence, but instead dived into the bag excitedly, carelessly tossing the pieces of tissue paper over her shoulder.

Seconds later, she was holding the small box in her hands. She opened it and pulled out the necklace of a cat holding a gem in its paws—the one that she was eyeing up a few weeks ago during the start of winter break, at Whimsical Wonders.

She held it up at eye level, marveling at it as it glimmered from the rays of sunlight shining in the room. "Nate, you . . . how'd you know?"

I chuckled. "Please, you couldn't take your eyes off it at the store! Even someone as oblivious as me could have—"

She practically ran into my arms, embracing me tightly. When she finally pulled away, she whispered, "I love it. Thank you, Nate," before giving me a kiss and instantly fastening it around her neck.

"How's it look?"

I gazed at her, fascinated by her beauty as she stood in the sunlight poking through the window behind her.

"Absolutely stunning."

Even though the sky was glistening a clear blue and the sun was shining brightly, the snow from prior weeks had accumulated enough to where there was still at least a foot piled up off the sides of the stone pathway, which Dawn and I walked along swiftly to the dining hall for breakfast.

For the remaining students who actually stayed on campus for the holidays, a feast of a holiday breakfast was prepared. It was almost overwhelming, even for me—a buffet of many different foods including pancakes, sausage, eggs, layers of French toast, homemade cinnamon rolls, bacon, and those were just a few of the ones that I could recognize.

Dawn had a bewildered look on her face as she witnessed me finish two large cinnamon rolls that were flooded with a sugary coating of vanilla icing on top.

"I'm starting to see Tara's point about your eating habits, Nate," she said from across the table, a half-finished bowl of cereal placed in front of her.

"Oh, don't you start now, too," I retorted with a smirk.

After breakfast, we took a walk over to the large sheet of snow that was now the quad. At the gathering area in the center of it, the big abstract statue had been temporarily replaced by an enormous Christmas tree, banded with strings of warm white lights and silver garland. Ironically, perched on the peak of the tree, was a similar abstract object to the statue it had replaced: a large golden ornament, shaped like something between a butterfly and a woman.

We sat down on a nearby bench and huddled up together, gazing up at the tree while the occasional student strolled on by. It was already turning out to be a Christmas for the books.

"You know what?" Dawn gazed up at me with her black eyes, her bangs slipping down through the front of her hat. "It's getting a little chilly out here. You want to go back to your place and . . . warm up a bit?" She grinned, telling me all that I needed to know.

"Yes, definitely! *Warming up* sounds good to me," I quickly agreed, and then grabbed hold of her hand to lead the way back to my dormitory, making record time.

When we arrived, Dawn immediately unzipped her coat and threw it off, revealing her shifter outfit underneath: a tight, dark gray long-sleeved shirt that matched her charcoal-colored pants she had on.

"I'll meet ya in the bedroom!" she sang out before excitedly running into the room.

I smiled and followed her in.

When I had entered through the door, I had half expected her to already be throwing off her clothes, but instead, she was standing over the bed, looking curiously at my yoga mat in the corner of the room.

"What's with the mat?" she turned to me, giggling.

"Oh, that? It's nothing," I brushed it off. "Just something stupid."

I was a little embarrassed to admit that it was for my poor attempts at meditation, something I had been trying to work on since Dean Celestine first introduced the Cloning Spell in my Rune Sensing and Manipulation class.

"You do yoga? I don't think that's stupid!" She smiled.

"It's not yoga," I added, walking over to the mat. "Actually, it's for meditating," I admitted.

"Really?" She had a shocked look on her face. "Are you stressed or something?"

"No, it's just a thing we were working on in my Rune Sensing class." I sat down on the edge of my bed. "It's for the Cloning Spell. Apparently, I need to get in touch with my inner mytosomes in order to perform the spell. And since sorcerers can't manipulate internal rune, the best way to do that is through meditation."

"Really? That's kind of cool! Any luck?"

"Nah," I muttered, waving a hand, "I haven't gotten anywhere with it. Guess I just suck at meditating."

Dawn pursed her lips. "Well, if it's getting in touch with your mytosomes, maybe I could help!"

"What? Like, right now?" I chuckled. "I thought we were going to . . ."

"Oh, we have all day for that!" She bent over to pick the yoga mat up and enthusiastically carried it off to the living room yelling, "Come on, this could be fun!"

A little disappointed, I followed her back out to find her already sitting Indian style on the mat.

"So, I don't know much about meditating, but I'm plenty familiar with getting in touch with my mytosomes! Shifters thrive on knowing our mytosomes, as well as manipulating them. That's how we transform ourselves into animals, after all! We basically transform our *own* mytosome structure so that it mimics that of whatever animal we shift into."

"Yes," I slowly said, unconvinced, "but you do that by manipulating your own internal rune. I can't do that."

"Yeah, but sorcerers can read minds, right? Maybe you can read mine to get a better understanding of what it feels like to manipulate the mytosomes. That makes sense, right?"

"I don't know . . ." I said slowly. I had mixed feelings about even trying to read the minds of others. It just felt so invasive.

"Just try it! You have my permission." She looked up at me innocently.

"Well, we actually weren't taught how to read minds yet, either. I only did it once, accidentally, and it was only because I had the surveybee jam coated over me."

"Hmmm," she pondered, tapping her chin repeatedly, "but you *did* do it?"

"Yeah, kind of—I was able to start sensing people's emotions and stuff. Really, I don't know about this. I wouldn't even know how to control—"

"It'll be fine. Come, come!" she waved for me to sit down next to her.

A little reluctantly and very unsure of myself, I sat across from her, mirroring her position.

"Okay," she started, "they say that reading someone's mind is easier if you make physical contact with them." She grabbed my hands. "Now, just try to remember how it felt back when you had the jam on you. How'd it feel when you started reading the emotions of others in your class? Close your eyes and try to focus on that. I'll bend my internal rune in a way that leaves my thoughts open to you. That should help, too."

For about ten minutes, we sat in silence as I tried to think back to my first day of Rune Sensing, and how it felt to feel the emotions and thoughts of the other students in the room back then. I then spent another five or ten minutes trying to recollect that feeling and bring it to the surface before finally focusing all my attention on Dawn. Her touch, her breathing, her general existence.

Suddenly, I started to feel the presence of another mind, just as it had felt back then. There were two separate minds, each with their own memories and thoughts, sharing one head, my head.

I tried to remain calm as her mind further opened up to me. It must have been because she was using her internal rune to basically welcome me into her, but now that I had essentially *located* her mind, the rest came relatively easy. It was as if the two minds were slowly joining and becoming one.

It wasn't long before I realized that I was now feeling her current emotions. She was happy, excited, and genuinely cared about helping me in this moment, as she focused on her own mytosomes and the time she first learned to manipulate them.

The further I dived in, the clearer things became, clear enough to the point where I was now seeing a strange image manifest within my mind. A visual of what could only be described as her mytosomes—tiny cellular looking things that were just ever so slightly vibrating about.

Shortly after that, the image in my mind changed to one of Dawn, sitting in a classroom. It was of a slightly younger version of herself, maybe even just from a year ago or so.

This must have been one of her memories she wanted to show me.

As I observed her in the flashback, I began to feel how she felt during this moment, and think her thoughts, too. She was trying to focus on her mytosomes at the time, and on using her internal rune to alter them. Her thoughts from back then confirmed that this was her in one of her first shifter classes at the Academy.

It was a fascinating, wonderful thing, to be able to not only see this memory of her, but also feel the things she felt back then, think the thoughts she had at that time. I had never felt closer to her.

And yet . . . I still didn't fully know her. There were still certain things about her I had been wondering about. . .

Suddenly, with no intent or control, the reel of her memory blurred and morphed around me. I was completely baffled, not having the slightest clue as to what was happening. It was like a ride that I suddenly could not get off of, and before I knew it, I was in a different room than before, staring at a little, very frail-looking girl.

The girl couldn't have been much older than maybe five or six. She was wearing a raggedy old pair of pajamas with cats on them and was clinging to a black cat, even. Her hair was black as the night, unkempt and tousled. Two little cat ears were popping through it. And that was when I realized that this little girl was Dawn. I was surprised to see her already in her hybrid form at such a young age.

Distracted by that thought, it took me a minute to realize that she looked distraught, trembling as she gently stroked her cat for comfort.

I looked around, noticing all the drawings and pictures of cats. Even her old and dingy bed sheets had cats on them. This was clearly Dawn's childhood bedroom.

A voice of a man was muffled from the other side of her room, but it became clearer as Dawn cracked open her bedroom door to peek through. I walked over to stand behind the little girl, looking through, too.

". . . I don't care what paperwork needs to be completed, get over here immediately and take this thing away!" he yelled over the phone.

Dawn whimpered from behind the door, trembling harder. Her yellow eyes were wide with fear, and her thin black tail was slumped to the floor. I was starting to actually feel her emotions now at this moment: fear, confusion, sadness.

". . . she just turned into the creature! Right before my eyes. I'm telling you, I'm not crazy!" the man continued angrily.

Starting to understand the situation now, I became furious. If it were up to me, I would have run over to the man and wailed on him right then and there, but I was limited to Dawn's own memory, not actually existing in this scene.

"Daddy . . ." Dawn's voice quivered as she pushed the door open, still bravely holding her cat. "Daddy, I'm scared. What's—what's wrong with me?" she squeaked. I could feel from her confusion that this must have been the first time she had shifted, and it wasn't intentional.

The man pulled away from the phone to face Dawn. His hair was as black as his daughter's, and he had fair skin like her, too. But that was where the similarities stopped. His face was stern and rough, whereas Dawn's was always cute, warm, and welcoming, even with the darker makeup she liked to wear now that she was grown.

"Go back in your room, Dawn!" the man blurted out.

"But . . . but, Daddy, I—" she started, tears running down her cheeks as she gasped and shook about in her doorway.

"I said, back in your room! Now!" He stormed over to her and slammed the door in her face.

Dawn's tears turned to sobs, but even so, she still bravely cracked the door open again.

"For the last time, come now and just take her away. I don't care! You can say 'she's my daughter,' but there's absolutely no way that, whatever she is, came from me! I refuse to believe it. Not to mention, she's the reason that my—my wife . . ." His voice cracked, and for the first time, it had a hint of sincerity in it. "It's no wonder she died giving birth to this—this monstrosity!" He took a deep breath. "Look . . . just come and take it away. I've had it. If you don't, I'll find a way to get rid of it myself."

The scene blurred and morphed again to a new one.

Whether intentional or not, I wasn't sure, but Dawn had managed to change back to her human form since the prior memory. And to my complete horror, I watched helplessly as she was getting pulled along by a man and woman. Dawn was crying hysterically and reaching out for her father, who had just closed the front door without even looking back at her.

"DADDY!! DADDY!!! NO! I DON'T WANT TO GO WITH THEM! PLEASE, DADDY! I'll BE GOOD. I PROMISE! I'M SORRY!! DADDY! COME BACK! HELP ME!" she shrieked toward her small shack of a house, but nobody came.

The two caseworkers from Child Protective Services had packed most of Dawn's things in a little suitcase, but her cat remained at the house, staring back at her from the upstairs window while Dawn was forced into the strange vehicle. She pounded against the car window, crying up to her cat as they drove off.

The scene morphed once more, and now I was standing in a small, fenced-in yard. It appeared to be a playground area in the back of a large building that looked to be a combination of a house and a school. Dawn's thoughts confirmed my suspicions that this was an orphanage.

At that moment, a large group of kids came running out to the yard. I could spot Dawn from here. She was quite a bit older from the previous memory, and healthier looking, too, now maybe around the age of twelve or thirteen. Her hair was more well-kept than before, and actually longer than I had ever seen it, cascading down to about the middle of her back. She didn't have her signature maroon highlights in it yet, though, and she had no makeup on at all.

The kids separated into smaller groups as they broke apart into different activities among their respective friends. Dawn went with a group of about a dozen girls to play a game of soccer.

I followed her as she stuck close to one particular girl, a blonde with short hair (her feelings expressed to me that this girl had been her closest friend since coming to the orphanage as young girls).

"Just make sure I'm on your team, okay, Chrissy?" Dawn whispered to her.

"Don't worry! I'll pick you first if I'm captain!" her friend happily said.

Surely enough, Chrissy was voted as captain, and just as she had promised, she picked Dawn first to ensure they were on the same team.

The girls all began playing their game of soccer, and I was happy to see that Dawn was easily the best among them as the game progressed, scoring most of her team's goals.

It seemed everything was going well, until a larger girl on the other team took a slide into Dawn's friend's knees. Chrissy got up, limping, and yelled, "You did that on purpose!"

"So what if I did? Did I mess up your hair? Little bitch . . . bet Jake won't like you anymore if you end up in a wheelchair."

That seemed to be all it took for the girls to start going at it, and unfortunately the other girl had such a size-advantage over Chrissy that it didn't take long for her to overpower her.

Seeing this, Dawn didn't hesitate. She leaped into action, wrapping her arms around the big girl and trying to pull her off of Chrissy. The girl was too big, though, easily flinging Dawn off of her before continuing to slap Chrissy in the face.

Then it happened: Dawn came back at the girl, but this time in her hybrid form.

Sensing Dawn's thoughts, I knew that she hadn't even realized she had transformed again, it must have been brought on by the urgent desire of trying to help her friend in need.

Dawn grabbed the girl again, this time a little stronger than before, and threw her off of Chrissy. She then went to slap the girl, but her claws had protruded from her fingers, causing her to leave three bloody slash marks across her opponent's face.

Everyone on the playground seemed to have stopped what they were doing to take in the sight of Dawn, standing there with black cat ears popping through her hair, yellow eyes, a thin black tail, and claws sticking out from her fingers.

"Wh—what the heck are you?" said the large girl, still holding her face with wide eyes. "You're some kind of freak!"

231

All the remaining girls on both teams quickly scattered and scurried away from Dawn, with murmurs and whispers of fear. The rest of the kids around the yard had even run back to the building, too.

Dawn, still blissfully unaware that she had even shifted, turned around to reach a hand out to her friend, Chrissy, who was still lying flat on the ground. Dawn's claws had receded back, now that there was no threat.

Chrissy didn't reach back, though. She had a look of terror on her face as well, as she gazed into the yellow eyes before her.

"You okay, Chriss?" asked Dawn.

"Stay away!" Chrissy shrieked. "Who are you? What happened to Dawn?"

"What?" Dawn had a perplexed look on her face, but then looked down and noticed her tail wiggling about. She took a step back. "Oh, no . . . no, not again. . ." she muttered to herself with her hands over her mouth, looking just as shocked and terrified as everyone else had. "Chrissy, this—I can explain!"

But Chrissy jumped to her feet. "No! Don't talk to me! What the heck are you, some kind of animal? You . . . you really are a *freak!*" she screamed, running back to the building, leaving Dawn standing in the yard by herself.

As her feelings poured out to me, I sensed that most of Dawn's remaining days in the orphanage left her secluded, standing alone in the yard like this, while all the other children kept their distance.

The scene morphed yet again, but this time I felt myself being desperately ripped from Dawn's mind, and it wasn't long before the two minds, hers and mine, had become separate again.

I was now back in my living room, Dawn's present self still sitting across from me on the mat as she held my hands. She had a look of horror and confusion on her face, her black eyes, which were becoming glassier by the second, stared back at me widely.

"How—how did you—?" she quietly stammered.

"I don't know. Dawn, I didn't mean to. I'm sorry. It just happened!"

"You saw it all, didn't you? You saw . . ."

I sat there, staring blankly at her. The silence, which seemed to stretch us further apart by the second, all but confirmed her suspicions.

She ripped her hands away from me and stood up. "I have to go." Her voice cracked.

"Dawn, wait!" But before I had even gotten up to my feet, my door slammed, and she was gone.

Dawn clearly had not planned on showing me those memories. They were memories that she most likely had buried deep down, with no intentions of ever bringing them back up.

Only later did I realize how I had managed to do it. I had always felt that Dawn had a deeper side to her, one that she was keeping from me. And unfortunately, my curiosity had gotten the best of me during a time where I should have kept it in check. My single desire to learn more about Dawn—like why she disliked Lackers, as she called them, and why she kept me at a certain distance, never wanting to spend the night or open up much to me—sprung up while I was reading her thoughts. Somehow, without her having any control over it, her mind responded to my will, causing me to breach her memories during a time where she had left herself open.

I didn't do it on purpose. I hadn't even realized *how* I was doing it at the time. But it was still an invasion of her privacy.

I felt terrible. It was like I had lost all of her trust I'd been slowly gaining, trust that she clearly was hesitant on giving away to begin with. And now I knew why. Unintentionally, I had finally obtained the answers to my questions, as gut-wrenching as they were to witness.

Chapter Twelve

The remainder of my winter break consisted of me trying to get in touch with Dawn. I had texted and called her every day since Christmas, but my calls went straight to her voicemail, and my texts were all left on *read*. It also became painfully clear to me at that point that Dawn had never shown me where she lived on campus, so it wasn't like I could just go knock on her door, either.

Instead, I spent many hours strolling through the grounds, hanging out at the dining hall or the Student Union, just hoping to run into her. It was getting to where I was becoming increasingly concerned that I may have messed things up beyond repair.

Needless to say, the weeks dragged by, and when winter break had come to its end. The only glimmer of light I had to look forward to was finally seeing Tara again.

I was talking with Glendor about the newest Kingdom Monster cards when Tara finally emerged from the back room, a huge smile on her face and her big green eyes beaming at me.

"Nate!" she ran into my arms, and it felt amazing just to

235

touch her again. "I missed you so much," she muttered into my shoulder.

"Hey there, Tara. Taking good care of that Drakthor?" asked Glendor, smiling at us both through his thick white beard.

"Hi, Glenny!" she blurted out. "Sure am! It's my most prized possession."

"I knew you were the right choice to give that one to!" He gave a hearty laugh. "You kids have a good day now!"

"Ugh, I missed it here so much!" Tara breathed in the fresh air as we walked down the streets of Hearthvale again, now more bustling than they had been in weeks.

"Well, I sure missed you, Tara. It feels like it's been forever!" I smiled at her.

She blushed. "You have no idea. I missed you every freaking day! I had to deal with listening to the same fishing stories from my dad every evening. Not to mention my mom always telling me to brush my hair." She rolled her eyes and ran her hands through her messy bun before glancing around at her surroundings. "Hey, where's Dawn, by the way? I expected her to be at the Magic Gateway, but it was some older woman from the Guard today, instead."

My stomach dropped a bit. "Oh— uh—she's . . . well, it's a long story, to be honest. I can tell you about it later, but let's catch up just the two of us for now." I just didn't want to ruin the mood already.

Tara gave me a questionable look. "Oh, okay. Well, we'll have to meet up with her for lunch tomorrow or something. It wasn't anything too serious, was it?"

"Maybe," I admitted.

Tara's smile went flat.

"Let's catch up for now, okay? And then I'll fill you in."

After she got herself settled back into her place, Tara came over to my dorm room later that evening, where we spent the rest of the night watching a movie and simply enjoying each other's company like we always did so easily. I knew I missed her, but as we lay together cuddling on my couch, it became blatantly clear to me that I didn't want to be separated from her like that again.

But I still wasn't ready to bring up Dawn, and Tara must have realized this, because she didn't mention it either. We ended up falling asleep together in my living room, almost forgetting that classes were due to start back up in the morning.

Unlike most colleges, where you'd take different courses per semester, the classes ran yearly for most students at Magic Rune Academy, with them having to take the same courses all year long (Tara and I were more the exception than the norm, being second-year transfer students who had some extra classes packed on for the second semester, to allow us to catch up).

Regardless though, my spring term started much the same as the fall term, almost like déjà vu. My Intro to Classes course picked right back up where it left off in the General Studies building—the modern, circular building that was placed just to the right of the quad.

Professor Morran had resumed her lectures as usual, and it was like our last interaction had never even happened. I was happy to see Sakura again, not having talked to her since our brief conversation at the Bronze Dragon a month prior. Even though Professor Morran had threatened to separate us, I still couldn't help muttering the occasional joke back to her just for the sake of hearing her cute giggles.

Basic History of the Realm with Professor Brookes was as dry and boring as ever, with its only redeeming quality being that I got to share it with Tara, as I sat next to her in the big, dark auditorium.

It wasn't until lunch in the dining hall where Tara finally brought up Dawn again.

"Still no Dawn?" she asked as we sat down at our usual booth by a window. "It's not like her to not join us for lunch."

"Yeah, well . . ." I started.

"Nate, what happened with you two over break?" she asked anxiously.

I figured there was no point in putting it off any longer, so I drew out a long sigh and spilled mostly everything. I left out the details about what exactly I had seen, as those were Dawn's personal memories, which she obviously didn't want people knowing about. But I still got the point across, explaining to Tara that I had basically breached some personal information of Dawn's, leading to her not speaking to me for weeks now.

"Well, you better fix it!" she finally said, when I had finished explaining it all.

Her reaction had me staring blankly at her with my mouth hung slightly open in amazement.

"I mean, I'm trying," I replied, "but she's not answering my calls or anything. I haven't even been able to find her since then."

"Well, then *I'm* texting her! We finally found a cool and fun addition to our group. She's perfect for us," she began, pulling out her phone, "we can't just let her go like that."

Seeing Tara act this way about the whole situation brought a smile to my face, especially when thinking back to how she initially acted toward Dawn.

"Thanks, Tara. I'll keep trying too," I said.

As I made my long hike across campus to the Cathedral of Tranquility for my Rune Sensing and Manipulation class, I was filled with a bit of anxiety knowing that my afternoons for this term were going to be busier than last term's; Dean Celestine had scheduled me and Tara in a way that would essentially make up for the fact that we joined the Academy as "transfer students." But that just meant a more difficult second semester, now that we were settled in.

A perfect example of this was my upcoming afternoon classes. A day like today would usually end after Dean Celestine's class, but now I had a course called Weapon Guidance after that, which I thought was a bit strange for me to take, unless you considered my staff a weapon. Regardless, though, it meant for longer days ahead, which I wasn't exactly thrilled about.

The first half of Dean Celestine's class also resumed where it had left off, with us once again focusing on meditating for the Cloning Spell. This was a disappointingly boring start to my favorite class.

But the second half took a more exciting turn as Dean Celestine started teaching us a defensive technique called the Shield Spell, to prevent our own internal rune from being manipulated, basically using external rune as a shield to stop another sorcerer from doing things like reading your mind or even controlling your body (which I didn't even know a sorcerer was capable of until now). Not only that, but it apparently could also protect your mytosomes from being sensed, or sniffed out, too.

"Dean Celestine, why should we bother learning how to defend against these spells before learning how to actually cast them ourselves?" asked one of my classmates, Harold.

"A fair question, Hank," replied Dean Celestine, "and you may find the answer to be relatively straightforward. The Shield Spell is easier to learn than most spells that it counters, like the Mind-reading Spell or the Penetration Spell. But also, it's vital to build our spell kit with the proper foundations first. Learning how to defend yourselves against some of the more advanced offensive spells will only help you better understand those offensive spells when the time comes for you to learn them. That said, it's also just vital knowledge. Defensive abilities are absolutely crucial for people to know. Even the other classes can defend themselves against your spells by manipulating their internal rune, if they are talented enough to do so."

We spent the remainder of the class focusing on bending the exterior rune around us in a way that formed an invisible bubble, so to speak, and placing the bubble around our bodies. It was a complicated task, considering you really had no way of knowing for sure if you were getting close to succeeding, other than having someone actually try to cast one of those offensive spells against you. But I felt a little reassured by the end of class, when I had finally sensed a sort of warmth overcome my body, like a literal security blanket.

By far the most notable class of my first day back happened to be the last one of the day—Weapon Guidance, taught by Professor Kravitz, the tall, bulky human with the big beard who I had only met once before during my Reading.

I got the feeling back then that he hadn't liked me for some reason—he was very quiet, and only really acknowledged my presence after I received my S-tier rank from the Reader.

Even then, though, his *acknowledgment* appeared cold and bitter.

As it would turn out, after taking just one of his classes, my suspicions that he hadn't liked me were not only confirmed, but perhaps even underestimated. It seemed that he didn't just dislike me, but, for some reason, despised me.

"Good morning, everyone," Professor Kravitz started. His voice was surprisingly quiet for such a large, burly man, and yet, it somehow still commanded the attention of everyone in the room. Nobody dared make a peep or look away from him. "I'd like to first start today by introducing a new student."

I perked up in my seat.

"His tardy enrollment to our class is due to him being in the accelerated program, as he comes to us as a transfer sophomore from another realm; a rare situation, though it does occur at times, as you all know very well. What *doesn't* occur often, however, and the true *special* circumstances with this one," he continued, now sounding sarcastic and a bit overdramatic, "is his tier ranking. Isn't that right, Mr. Gannon . . . ?"

I sat quietly in the middle of the room, feeling the gazes of my fellow students burn against my skin. I stared right back at Professor Kravitz, who remained silent for a few more seconds before adding, "Well?"

"Oh, I thought that was rhetorical, sir—I mean; Professor," I replied, my voice practically echoing in the small, still room.

"It was not," he calmly and quietly added, remaining seated in his chair behind his desk, which looked way too small for him. "Well, go ahead, tell everyone your tier rank, Mr. Gannon."

"I, uh," I stammered, taken back by this weird interaction, "Professor, I'm not entirely sure why that's really needed, if I'm—"

"It is necessary because I deem it to be." He stared blankly at me with those cold black eyes, creating a tight sensation in my throat. I think I would have rather had him glaring at me, so I'd at least be able to get a clear read on the guy. Not only that, but his face was practically hidden behind that black beard, which was even burlier than it had been when I first met him months ago.

The silence stretched for a few more awkward moments before I finally obliged: "I'm an S-tier."

He abruptly stood up, towering over his students, "An S-tier sorcerer! You don't say? Very impressive," he began in that same sarcastic tone. "Although you really shouldn't brag about it, Gannon. Nobody likes a cocky sorcerer."

There were a few snickers from my fellow students. As I glanced around, I was hit with the sudden realization that I was one of the few students in this class wearing a robe and having a staff. Most of the other students were wearing plate armor and had their axes, swords, or bows at their sides. Although, a few students *did* appear to be shifters, with even a couple healers sprinkled in, judging from their attire.

"Well, now," Professor Kravitz continued, and my heart sank further as he took a few large strides closer to my desk, "an S-tier sorcerer like yourself should easily know why you're in my Weapon Guidance course, correct? That was *not* rhetorical, Gannon."

"I assume, to learn about weapons, Professor."

A couple more snickers from my classmates sneaked out but were quickly silenced by just one glance from Professor Kravitz.

"'To learn about weapons,'" he quietly mocked, smirking. "Well, you *are* quite the observant sorcerer, I'll give you that. However, I'm sure you were under the misguided assumption that, being a sorcerer with your staff, there, that you wouldn't need a basic knowledge of weapons—"

"I wasn't—"

"But you were most definitely mistaken, as even that pretty, gold stick of yours could be considered a *weapon*, by some. In the hands of a *proper* sorcerer, even something as feeble as a wooden rod could provide such a sorcerer the opportunity to thrive in close combat. Now, surely someone of *your* stature would know the reason why and how?"

I was starting to get irritated now, as he continued to press me further into a corner. "No, sir, I don't." I glared at him, but his stare remained blank and unwavering. "But why don't you ask one of the other people in class wearing a cloak? After all, they've been here longer. Probably smarter than I am, too."

"They are healers, Gannon. Don't be a fool," he casually said, his voice still calm as ever. "And the answer lies in a sorcerer's uncanny ability to manipulate external rune. You create a barrier with the external rune and form it around your staff to essentially *harden* it, similar to how you'd create the Shield Spell around *yourself*. Or are you not even capable of doing that yet?"

A couple more snickers snuck out of some plate-wearing orcs sitting in the front row.

"Oh, I'm sure he was just being tough on you because he expects a lot out of you, Nate. Try not to take it personal, okay?" said Tara encouragingly, as we walked through the quad together after our final classes of the day had ended.

"Tara, there's 'tough on you,' and then there's just being a dick. Trust me, this guy is the latter. I don't know what the hell his problem is, but it's just immature. He's a professor teaching grown ass adults, not some teacher who can bully kids. Professor Morran is tough on me, but she's fair, at least. This guy is just ridiculous!"

"Is it really that bad?" She looked up at me with her green eyes, which went perfectly with her bright white robe and gold cloak, which was rippling in the bitter, winter wind.

"He singled me out right away and called me things like a 'fool' and 'cocky.' And he even forced me to tell everyone I was an S-tier runic." I pondered over it all, replaying parts of it back in my mind. "I'm not sure if he has an issue with S-tiers or just sorcerers in general. I mean, I *was* the only sorcerer in his class. That's a red flag in itself, I think."

"He really said those things?" asked Tara with an incredulous expression.

"I almost wish I was lying about it, believe me."

"Maybe you should go to Dean Celestine about this," advised Tara. "I bet she could get you switched. She seems to like you a lot and has way more pull than he would, of course."

"I thought of that," I muttered, "but then it'd be like I'm just running away, which is what I think he wants. I don't want to give this guy the satisfaction."

As we continued walking through the snow-dusted quad, I was left thinking that my day couldn't get much worse. I, unfortunately, was quickly proven wrong.

"That's them!" a voice rang out from behind us, just as we were about to leave the quad; I recognized it from somewhere, from a little while ago. "Knew we'd see you again sooner or later! That's them, Chuck!" That name struck a sort of familiar nerve with me, and then it all came back. I knew who it was before even turning around to face the group of werewolves.

They were currently all in their base forms, so they looked a little different from the last time I had seen them, but still close enough: the girl who seemed to be the leader back on the beach, tall and slender with her wild, dark hair, flanked by her two friends, the short one with the pink pixie cut (which was now orange), and the blonde with the dreadlocks.

However, they had a few additions to their all-human pack of werewolves this time around. Three other guys, and I could take a good guess which one was the alpha known as Chuck—a tall, blonde, athletic-looking guy, who had *bro-vibes* written all over him. He was wearing what looked like a leather jacket, and leather pants, but something told me it wasn't actually leather, instead the same material that all the shifters wore. The girls were certainly all wearing tight shifter outfits, showing quite a bit of skin for it being such a brisk winter day.

"So, you're the punk who threatened my betas back on the beach last semester?" said Chuck, popping his collar as he strutted his way over to me.

"Get his ass, Chuck," taunted one of his beta males, a skinny, pasty-skinned dude with long black hair.

I couldn't help but let a smirk escape. These dogs were as cheesy and cliché as it gets, and their leader was king of the cheese.

"Are you doing that on purpose?" I asked, leaving Chuck with a dumbfounded expression on his face. "Sorry," I added, "just didn't think people like you actually existed in real life, is all."

Tara nudged at my side with her elbow. "Let's just go, Nate," she quietly muttered.

"Oh, no!" Chuck blurted out. "You two aren't going anywhere. Not until you get on your knees and beg for forgiveness."

Chuck's yelling was starting to draw a crowd in around us.

I gripped my staff a little harder. "Get on my knees?" I laughed. "Listen, man, I don't know what your trio of lassies told you back then, but they started that whole thing. Also, that was like four damn months ago! How about we just let bygones be bygones? Come on, Tara." I put a hand on her shoulder and turned around to start walking away, but then I heard loud footsteps closing in.

I spun around but was too late. Before I even had a chance to react, Chuck had tackled me to the frozen, hard ground, breaking me apart from not only Tara, but also my staff. He was already in his hybrid form, bearing his fangs and glaring over me with red eyes.

"Nate!" I heard Tara scream shrilly over the chaos.

"Nobody turns their back on me!" rasped Chuck.

"Tara, stay there!" I yelled out to her as I wrestled with Chuck, doing all I could to prevent him from slashing down at my face.

The last thing I wanted right now was to get into a fight with a werewolf. I hadn't learned nearly enough in my classes yet to put up a decent fight against a seasoned alpha, S-tier or not.

The crowd of people around us was quickly accumulating as bystanders walking through the quad stopped to take in the scene.

I tried to push the werewolf off of me, but it was no use. In his hybrid form, Chuck now had a significant size advantage over me. Then I remembered that I was a sorcerer, not a rune-knight who relied on physical strength alone.

I glanced over at my gold staff lying on the snowy ground about ten feet away from me, and reached for it, focusing on the rune in the air between it and myself.

Immediately, the staff flung into my hand. Then the thought hit me. It was so obvious, yet I hadn't even considered it until now. If I could pull things toward me, I could also push them away.

I had to focus a little harder, Chuck being much heavier than my staff, but now having it in my hands, I felt a surge of power and connection with the rune around me that I didn't have a second ago. And just before the werewolf sent a swipe down at my face, I mentally flung him off me, launching him twenty feet in the air. His body tumbled and twirled about before crashing back to the surface, all the while the surrounding crowd was looking on.

"Nate! Are you hurt? I can try to hea—"

"Stay there, Tara!" I made it back to my feet, holding my hand out to signal her not to come any closer yet. "I don't think that was enough to end this."

And sure enough, Chuck leaped back to his feet just a moment later. I was shocked to see that his five betas weren't getting involved yet, and wondered if this was some sort of werewolf, alpha type thing going on with them—like maybe they weren't helping him out of pride or respect.

"You sure seem to care about that blonde bitch of yours!" Chuck hollered out, stalking closer to me. As he did, he rolled out his shoulders and craned his neck. More hair was sprouting along his face as he started to hunch further over with his spine curving in an unnatural sort of way. It became clear to me that he was finished playing around, now slowly transforming into his primal form, becoming a full-on wolf. "It would be a shame if something happened to her!" he growled, his voice growing deeper by the second, his ears and nose elongating as he slumped on all fours.

Meanwhile, I was feeling some sort of transformation manifesting within *myself*. Maybe not as obvious as Chuck's, but it was certainly noticeable to me. I was feeling emotions that were foreign enough to make my hair stand on ends: anger, darkness, even an overwhelming sense of hatred. And they were growing stronger by the second. Chuck's words, his threats, they had no impact on me until now—until he brought Tara into this.

"I think, once I'm finished with you, I'll take *her* for a spin! Show her what it's like to be with a real animal." Those were the last words he got out before finishing his transformation. And now I was staring at a huge gray timber wolf, like a giant beast dragged straight out of Canada. It had eyes as red as rubies and was salivating with hunger as it stalked closer to me.

The stalking turned to a charge, but his last words had etched themselves into my brain, leaving me filled with an anger unlike anything I had ever experienced before.

I held my arm straight out at the wolf, manipulating the external rune between us in a way that would repel it away from me. I felt more connected with the rune than I had ever felt before, yet something about it seemed different.

I didn't care, though. I marched closer to the wolf, who was now struggling to run at me, fighting against the force of the rune between us. And that's when it called to me, the rune all around me, begging to be manipulated by my will, even the rune within my opponent.

He deserved it. He needed it. He needed to know.

It was as easy and as natural as reaching for a drink. I grabbed hold of the rune inside the wolf and squeezed. Immediately, the pathetic dog yelped and cried a shrill howl as it crumbled to the ground, curling into itself.

I had complete control over its body. I could make the mutt dance, if I wanted to.

"Nate!" a distant yell sounded out. "Nate, that's enough! Come on!"

The wolf phased back into Chuck, who was now screaming at the top of his lungs in pain and agony, but I still clenched at his insides, reveling in it without a care in the world.

"Nate!!!" Tara's desperate screams grew louder in my head. "Nate, you might kill him! Stop!!!" I felt her hand on my shoulder as she pulled me back, and it was like waking up from a dream. I immediately realized what I was doing, what I was about to do, and let go of Chuck's internal rune, leaving him lying on the ground, helplessly and pathetically groaning and gasping for air.

The surrounding students watched in silence, with looks of terror and horror on their faces. Chuck's group of betas ran over to him, all of them looking at me with expressions of fear painted clear on their faces. They didn't dare say a thing.

To make matters even worse, the situation seemed to draw enough attention that some of the professors came darting out from some buildings around the quad, and to my utmost displeasure, Professor Kravitz was the first one to reach us.

He slowed to a walk as he approached the werewolf lying in pain on the ground. He bent down to quickly assess the damage done to Chuck, and then slowly looked up at me with wide eyes.

"You are to report to Dean Celestine's office. Immediately," Professor Kravitz muttered. "You will tell her everything that happened here. And I mean, *everything*. She'll deal with you accordingly."

I figured it best not to argue with a man who already seemed to hate me, even *before* this moment, so I swiftly strode back through the quad, Tara following close behind as the crowd of students remained standing, immobilized with shock and probably fear over what they had just witnessed.

It wasn't until we made it to the courtyard of the Cathedral that Tara found her voice again. "Nate, are you okay?" she asked, but I kept trotting forward. "Nate, talk to me, it's okay!" I felt a hand on my shoulder and came to a halt, turning to face her. "Are you okay?" she quietly repeated, her big green eyes filled with concern.

"I don't know—I—I think so. I just need to talk to Dean Celestine right now, though. Okay? I'll be right back, I promise."

"Yeah, okay," she softly agreed with a nod. "I'll be out here waiting."

"Thanks, Tara, really."

As I walked up the big marble stairs of the Cathedral, I felt a little bad about how I brushed Tara off. She was clearly concerned and just wanted to help. But to be honest, I was concerned for me as well, and was in dire need of answers, answers that maybe only Dean Celestine would have. But as I knocked on the big wooden door to her office, no one came, so I slowly opened it and peered inside, but nobody was in there.

I hesitantly entered, and as I did so, I heard some noises from the back room again—sounds of giggling and even a few moans.

Rolling my eyes, I stomped over to the back door and knocked. The giggling stopped for a second.

"Were you expecting someone?" a man's muffled voice sounded out from the other side of the door.

"Dean Celestine," I said firmly, knocking louder, "Dean Celestine, it's Nate. I need to speak to you. It's importa—"

Suddenly, a warping noise sounded out from behind me, and I turned to see Dean Celestine standing there, fully dressed in a wrinkled purple robe and propping her silver hair in a flustered sort of way.

"Ah, Nate—" she cleared her throat before taking a seat behind her desk, "my finest student—how can I be of assistance?"

I beckoned my head at her back door. "Really?" I quietly asked.

She gave a sheepish smile and bit at her nail innocently. "What can I say? I have a weakness for thirty-something-year-old men . . . I *think* he's in his thirties," she muttered that last part to herself, tapping her finger to her chin and pondering in silence for a second before bringing herself back to me. "Neither here nor there! Young Nate, I sense you didn't come here just to scorn me over my guilty pleasures."

"No, Professor," I quickly started, "something just happened to me out in the quad, something that I'm not even entirely sure on how to explain, but—"

She held up a hand. "No need."

"No need? But—?"

"You've already told me everything I need to know." She tapped the side of her head a few times. "Starting to see why learning that Shield Spell is so crucial? Your mind is my book, and it's one of my *favorite* reads." She winked and made a clicking noise with her tongue and the roof of her mouth.

Ignoring that little gesture, I pressed on. "So you saw everything that happened between me and Chuck, then?"

She nodded slowly.

"Then can you please explain to me," I desperately began, "what the hell that was all about? I think back to it even now, and it's like I'm watching someone else's thoughts in my head. That wasn't me back there. It couldn't have been! I've never felt like that before, Professor. Those types of emotions, and the genuine desire to . . ."

"It was you, Nathan, and it's okay," she calmly said.

"It's not though! Nothing about that was 'okay!'" I breathed.

"You didn't kill the dog," she started, standing up to walk over to a window and gazing out of it, "so I'd consider that to be 'okay,' in this case. Was quite the blessing that your friend was there, however."

"Yeah—but—what was happening to me back there? Why'd I feel . . . ? Is that . . . normal for a sorcerer?"

Dean Celestine scoffed. "Nothing about you is normal, Nate. You're an S-tier, and with that, comes many amazing things, things you will only continue to uncover as your studies progress."

"I don't think anything about this was amazing."

"Oh, it is." She turned from the window to face me. "While the abilities and consequences tied to being an S-tier runic may be debated as good or bad, them being *amazing* results in nothing less than absolute certitude, Nathan."

"Well . . . I'd say that this was the bad type of amazing, then."

"And I'd probably have to agree with you."

"So what caused it? So I can make sure I never let it happen to me again?"

Dean Celestine had a careful expression on her face. "Years ago, when I first received my S-tier reading, in this very same room," she began, "I was ecstatic. Eager to master my powers, capabilities, and the rune around me, which was readily available for me to be bent to my will, ready to *guide me to greatness*. I was a fool."

My eyes widened upon hearing her say that.

"I was ignorant of the very thing I wanted to wield, like a child who's been prematurely gifted a gun for Christmas. My goal was to study and learn every spell that I could possibly cast, using the rune as my accomplice. And I'd say I nearly achieved that goal, too. The issue was, that I gained that knowledge and those powers, without first under-standing the ins and outs of the very thing that made those spells all possible: rune itself."

She paused for a moment, pursing her lips in thought as she considered me closely.

"Sound familiar, Nate?"

I stared blankly at her, thinking back to how I took to her Rune Sensing and Manipulation course so quickly, while overlooking my other, less exciting classes. She was the same as me.

"You're ambitious, no doubt, when it comes to your sorcerer course. But how are your others going? You see, I tell you this, because perhaps if I had been a more well-rounded student from the start, and also focused more on the basic foundations of rune, well, I would have fewer regrets in this life."

"I'm sorry, Professor, but I don't quite understand where . . ."

She smiled warmly at me. "I see greatness in you, Nate. Whether you openly invite it into your life or not, greatness shall come. It's one of the inevitable traits tied with being an S-tier. Unfortunately, though, hardship and opposition are also tied to being an S-tier. You found that out today, didn't you?"

I had a feeling that she wasn't just talking about my encounter with Chuck, but maybe even my interaction with Professor Kravitz, too.

"Yes, it is indeed a thin line that us S-tiers walk," she sighed, "teetering between 'good' and 'bad,' if there really is such a thing. I believe the more appropriate terms should be positive and negative. I'm sure you're wondering where all my rambling here today is getting at."

I wasn't certain if she was just assuming, or that she had read my mind again, but that was exactly what I was thinking.

"What you experienced today, Nate, during your scuffle with Charlie, or whatever, was what we call the negative side of the rune."

"Negative?"

"It's not all sparkles and butterflies, the rune, is it, Nate? I know how it made you feel. And I know that you now fear your abilities because of it. And I'd be inclined to tell you that you should instead fear the rune itself, but that would be poor advice as well. Because, just like all energy in this universe and the next, rune has a pure and a corrupt nature to it. The positive side, which up until today, was all that you had known, and then the negative side.

"As I said before, amazing can be both good and bad. Clearly, by now, you have realized that rune allows us to do such amazing things. It's a fascinating gift and an incredible weapon. But just like any incredible weapon, it can be used for both right and wrong. So with that, I must advise you not to fear rune, but rather, respect it. It's your most powerful tool, being an S-tiered sorcerer."

"So what happened earlier with Chuck, I used the negative side of rune?"

"Yes."

"But I didn't even realize what I was doing! I didn't try to use it! It just . . ."

"Called to you, I know," she concluded. "Under certain circumstances, the negative side of rune can be easily tapped into, especially for an S-tiered runic. In fact, most situations where it gets wielded are unintentional. The risk of accidentally using it is much greater for individuals with higher mytosome counts, though. That's where someone like you needs to be careful. When in conflict, it'll be vital for you to remember to keep your emotions in check. You must learn to harness them to a point where you feel indifferent to what's taking place around you during those crucial times." She paused momentarily before continuing.

"And I say this, because the negative side of rune thrives on darker emotions and thoughts, even heightening those emotions. This results in a give-and-take type of relationship between the rune and its wielder, creating a vicious cycle that, if abused, can engulf even the noblest of runics, sending them down a spiraling path of darkness filled with nothing but pain and agony.

"When that wolf threatened your friend, you felt the hatred, didn't you? A hatred like you've never experienced before. It magnified the rage you felt in that moment. And then you used the rune to perform a spell you hadn't even learned yet, the Penetration Spell—reaching inside a runic and bending their internal rune in a way that lets you control them, even crushing them from the inside, if you so desire. And you performed it quite impressively, too, not to my surprise.

Even if the werewolf was smart enough to manifest his internal rune defensively, essentially creating a Shield Spell from within, I still don't believe it would have made a lick of difference."

"Why was it so easy, though? I was never taught that spell, but it was like I've known how to do it my whole life," I asked.

"Part of it is because you're an S-tier. The other is because of how negative rune works. It's designed to be easier, and maybe even more powerful than positive rune. I believe it's built that way so that it can continue to thrive and essentially 'exist' in the Realm. Because without those advantages, why would any runic bother with the side effects of using it?"

"So, the negative side is more powerful?"

"Perhaps, although I feel it to just be an easier, quicker way to power. I still prefer to believe that the positive side, when mastered and its potential fully realized, trumps its darker counterpoint. But to get to that point takes years of hard work and determination, not to mention a certain level of natural skill, as well."

My thoughts then shifted to something that had been bothering me the most about the whole thing, even more than the actual outcome of the fight. It had been weighing on my mind the entire way over to the Cathedral.

"Professor," I hesitantly began, "there's something about all of this that—that has me really concerned."

"I assume that you are referring to your fear over the fact that it felt good, what you did to the wolf earlier. After all, he was trying to hurt you, and even worse, threatened your friend right in front of you."

"I . . . but what does that make of me? Because to be honest, I think—I think I *did* enjoy it, at least at the time."

Dean Celestine once more pondered me intensely, making me think she was, again, reading "her favorite book," as she put it.

"Let me ask you this, and think hard on it, Nate. Would you say that you enjoyed the pain you delivered upon that boy? Or was it, rather, the feeling of not caring at all, for once, of the consequences of your actions, that you enjoyed so much?"

I quietly took in her words, astounded. Could she know me even better than I know myself? But how?

"I know it felt good, Nate, being free of life's burdens for once, free of your own burdens. It was an escape. But what matters most is that you returned from such an escape. You are a good person, Mr. Gannon. The fact that you have these concerns is concrete proof of such. Cling tight to those burdens, they are exactly what separates you from those who are truly lost."

She strode back over to peer out of her window, the view overlooking most of the campus grounds.

"Also," she broke through the silence, "don't think I didn't notice that you happened to dabble with the negative side of the rune on the same day you had your first class with Professor Kravitz." She turned to me, a clever smirk on her face. "I know he can be an ass, that one, and being as rune-knight as they come, he's never been able to get over his misguided bias against sorcerers. But his knowledge of weapon combat is, without a doubt, unrivaled. And if I didn't think you could take it, I wouldn't have put you in his class."

Her words of encouragement had a way of somehow already lessening the weight in my chest.

"Thanks, Professor." I gave a subtle smile back at her.

"Of course," she calmly replied. "Now, I shouldn't keep my —uh—guest waiting. It would be a bit rude, wouldn't you agree?"

I chuckled.

"Oh!" she added, stopping in front of her back door. "And neither should you. I believe you have two young ladies outside, both of whom are very eager to see if you are okay."

"Two?" I asked, feeling even lighter yet.

Chapter Thirteen

"DAWN!" I yelled out from the front doorway of the Cathedral.

She was pacing back and forth next to Tara, out by the fountain on the front lawn. When she turned to see me for the first time in weeks, she sprinted at me and didn't stop until she was tight in my arms.

She gazed up at me with her dark eyes, which looked glassy and tired. "I'm so sorry, Nate. This happened all because of me. Because I had to lash out at those girls back then! And then I left, and I shouldn't have. It was my idea in the first place to have you read my mind. I practically forced you to do it. I know you didn't mean to see what you saw. I'm just so sorry! I am—"

"Hey, hey . . ." I gently rubbed her back. She looked as if she'd seen better days, with her hair a little ragged, her makeup smeared around her eyes, and even some dry dirt marks on her cheeks. Her tight shifter clothes were ripped along the elbows and knees. But even so, I still found her more adorable than ever. "It's okay, really. I'm just glad you're back, Dawn. But are *you* okay? You look, well, drained."

"I'm fine," she muttered, her face buried in my chest. "Just been in my primal form the past few weeks."

"'Few weeks?!'"

"Yeah," she looked up at me again, smiling guiltily. "It's sort of . . . how I cope. When I'm in that form, I don't *feel* as much."

My heart sank. "Dawn . . . I'm so sorry."

"No." She shook her head vigorously. "Don't you apologize. This is all on me."

"How'd you find out about everything that happened with the werewolves?" I asked.

"It was Tara," replied Dawn. "She texted me and told me everything. I came back to campus earlier this morning because my internship with the Guard is to start back up tonight, but when I got her text, I freaked and took off to come over here. Oh, I'm so sorry, guys. This was all my fault, really!"

"It's not your fault, Dawn," said Tara, giving her a warm smile. "Even back then, you were only sticking up for me. We're just glad to have you back! It hasn't been the same without you."

As Dawn buried her head back into my chest, fighting back her glossy eyes, I mouthed over to Tara, "Thank you," and she happily nodded back to me.

"Besides," Tara continued, "if anything, I'd say we should apologize to Chuck, if he wasn't such a dick. But honestly, he deserved it. How are you doing, Nate? Everything go alright with Dean Celestine?"

"Yeah, I think everything will be okay now. She explained everything to me, and it's just something I'll need to be careful of moving forward. Something I need to be aware of as a sorcerer," I said reassuringly, leaving it at that. I figured it best not to let Tara know that I temporarily dipped my hand into a darker side of the rune. I just didn't want to worry her, and as long as I was careful, hopefully it would never happen again.

When the three of us left the Cathedral of Tranquility, Tara suggested we head back to her place so that Dawn could get cleaned up and into some warm, clean clothes. Dawn shut that idea down immediately, though.

"Nope! No way! This girl needs some food! I've been living off frozen berries and sketchy-looking plants the last few weeks. I could really go for a pizza!"

"Dawn," I began, amused, "your primal form is a giant panther. You could've hunted down an elk if you wanted to."

"And kill a cute, furry animal? Absolutely not!" She shook her head back and forth.

"I think you're the kindest panther I've ever met!" Tara laughed.

We ended up making a pit stop at the dining hall, where we filled ourselves with a nice, hearty dinner, and Dawn's was even bigger than my own, for once.

And then something happened for the first time, which surprised me a bit: Dawn invited us back to her dorm, so that she could get a shower and change before we'd head over to Tara's so that she and I could also change out of our robes and cloaks for the day.

Dawn's dormitory happened to be on the west side of campus, and even though her dormitory building looked similar to ours, her room was quite different. First, it was on the third floor of her building, where ours was on the first. So after scanning us through the building and into the elevator, she guided us down the hallway, finally stopping at a door that was decorated with all kinds of interesting art on it.

"Wow, did you do these yourself?" asked Tara.

"Sure did!" said Dawn proudly.

I took in the many drawings and paintings of various landscapes and animals pinned to her door, and couldn't help remembering the drawings of cats she had on her wall as a little girl. It became clear to me that Dawn had always had a knack for art, and I also realized, when walking inside her room, why she was hesitant to invite people over. It was almost like a glimpse into Dawn herself. And for someone who doesn't let just anyone close to her, it made sense for her to want to keep people away.

She must have painted her walls at some point, as they were purple instead of the standard off-white color that mine and Tara's were, and her king-sized bed had a purple bedspread neatly placed over it, along with black drapes that formed a canopy around it. A few floating shelves above her bed held all sorts of interesting trinkets she most likely had bought from Whimsical Wonders, while more of her drawings were pinned all around the rest of the room.

"It's not much," said Dawn. "The dorms on the west side of campus are a bit older than the ones on the north side, so I don't get the living room and bedroom like you guys have. But I don't mind. It's my little happy place."

"It's cozy!" Tara added.

"I'll say," I agreed.

Dawn's lips curled to a smile and her eyes showed a glimpse of relief.

"I'll be quick," she said. "Then we can head back to your guys' dorm."

"Take your time," I said, as Tara and I took a seat on the corner of her neatly done bed.

As I sat there, taking in her room, I couldn't help smiling. I wasn't sure if Tara realized it, but from what I knew about Dawn, this was a huge step for her. She was basically opening up to both of us, officially welcoming us into her personal life without actually saying anything. I was sure that it wasn't an easy thing for her to do, so I didn't take it lightly.

Later that evening, the three of us went back to Tara's room after I had changed into some more relaxing clothes, where we sat around the living room TV, exchanging stories of experiences we'd had over winter break. Tara told Dawn all about her mom nagging her about her hair, while Dawn shared an experience she had in the mountains, where she had encountered an injured squirrel and watched over it while it recovered. I couldn't help making a joke about it. Just picturing a big panther nursing a little squirrel back to health in the woods was enough to make us laugh.

The hours flew by, and before I had even realized it, my eyes had grown heavy, my head nodding off. I pulled out my phone and was shocked to see that it was already past twelve. Tara had been fighting against falling asleep for the better half the last hour, but it seemed to finally get the best of her, as she snoozed away on her couch, her mouth slightly open and a little dribble of drool running down the corner of her lips. She wasn't the most graceful sleeper, yet she still looked cute as ever.

Not wanting to wake her, Dawn and I quietly snuck out, gently shutting her door behind us.

We meandered down the hallway, and when we arrived at the lobby, I prepared to say goodnight to Dawn. Again, to my surprise, though, she asked to come back to my place. I more than happily agreed.

Dawn looked a little uncomfortable, to say the least, as she stood a bit rigid and awkward in my living room, rubbing her shoulders anxiously.

"Dawn," I softly started, making sure that I sounded as empathetic as possible, "you can head back to your place if you want to. Really, it won't hurt my feelings. I understand."

"No," she quickly said. "I want to be here. I don't—I don't want to leave tonight."

A warm sensation filled my chest. "Are you sure?"

She nodded, clearly trying to force a smile. "I want to get past this—this quirk of mine. And there's also . . . I owe you an explanation . . . you deserve to know everything revolving around what you saw that day inside my head."

"Dawn, I really appreciate that. I promise, though, you don't need to revisit those memories just for me."

She shook her head. "No, I want you to know. I want to willingly tell you everything."

I raised my brow in amazement and smiled softly.

"Okay," Dawn started, practically hyperventilating. "You know what? I think it'll be easier if we do it in the bed, actually."

"Oh! Uh—yeah, okay," I stammered.

"I know, I'm weird! I promise this isn't my way of getting you in the sack, either," she said, grabbing my hand and leading us into my bedroom.

"I don't think I'd really complain about it if it was, to be honest," I chuckled.

I turned on the bedroom television for some background noise (my attempt at making things a little less awkward for her), and we got into my bed together. I then wrapped an arm around her petite frame to try to make her feel as comfortable as possible. But she remained a bit rigid and stiff. It was obvious that this was foreign territory for her, but I still genuinely appreciated her for just making the attempt.

We continued laying in my bed for a few minutes, as I stared blankly at some random documentary channel on my tv, the minutes rolling by to the point where I thought she could have actually fallen asleep.

"My mom," she softly muttered, grabbing my attention, "she . . . she had died giving birth to me. The man you saw in those flashbacks, that was my father, of course. But he barely raised me. My grandma, my mother's mom . . . she took care of me for most of my childhood. She was the best, and really, the reason I had anything as a kid—clothes, food, everything. And she loved cats, which led to me loving cats too, of course. She even bought me the cat I was holding, Shadow."

I stared up at the ceiling, remembering her vision as clearly as if I saw it only a second ago. I continued listening closely as she went on, quietly saying, "It was only later, after she had passed, that I discovered my grandma, too, was a runic— a shifter with a cat form of her own. She had even gotten Shadow from the Rune Realm. That was why I had shifted so early. I loved Shadow so much that I found myself wanting to be like her, wanting to talk to her, I remember. And that somehow allowed me to subconsciously transform my mytosomes to mimic hers, causing me to shift.

"The scene you saw—with me in my bedroom, my grandma had died only a couple of months before that, leaving me at the mercy of my father. He was a man who loved my mom dearly, but could never get over the fact that I had been the reason for her dying. He refused to care for me, and after seeing me shift, he was terrified. They sent me away after that, as you saw. I don't know what ended up happening to Shadow."

I swallowed loudly, my eyes still fixated on the ceiling; I figured it best to just keep listening, if she was still willing to go on.

"So fast forward to my little mishap at the orphanage. I hadn't shifted since the day they brought me in. I was starting to even think that it had just been a bad nightmare or something. But then that big butch of a girl started that whole thing with someone who I thought was my friend, Chrissy. We were best friends at the time, having started at the orphanage at the same age. It was the first time I had had someone close in my life since my grandma and Shadow. We were friends for years, until the moment she saw me for who I really was—'a freak,' as she called me. She never even bothered to talk to me again after that, none of the kids at the orphanage did.

"By the time I went back inside, I'd shifted back without realizing, most likely because the adrenaline had gone away by then. The caretakers didn't believe the kids, nor had they believed my father when he tried to tell them years before. I remained at the orphanage for five years after that. Five years of never having anyone to speak with, eat meals with, or share my thoughts with. There were times where I just wanted it all to end. I did my best to stay strong, though, and after finally turning eighteen, I was more than ready to leave the place. Luckily, just after my eighteenth birthday, two people from the Guard came to recruit me into the Realm, and they brought me straight to Dean Celestine. They saved me. Saved me from that place, that world, even myself. Looking back, that's probably why I wanted to join the Guard to begin with."

I waited a few more moments in silence before deciding to finally say something, anything, really.

"Dawn, you have no idea how sorry I am to hear you say all of that. When I first witnessed it for myself, I hurt for you.

And it was all I could think about after you left. I couldn't get the image of that little girl with the cat pajamas out of my head. To be honest, all I wanted to do was reach out and hold her, and it killed me that I couldn't." I hugged her a little tighter. "But . . . I can now. I promise, I'll do whatever it takes to make sure you don't have to feel that pain ever again."

"It's just difficult still, you know?" she said. "The only few people I've gotten close to, well, they left shortly after, some of their own choosing, others not. I was starting to think that maybe—maybe I was cursed or something."

"I think I understand, at least a little," I admitted, rubbing her shoulder and meeting her gaze for the first time in minutes. "When I was a kid, and found out that my parents had died before I could even remember who they were, I didn't know what to feel. I was sad and confused. I always felt like I was missing someone. But how can you miss someone who you never even knew? I had pictures and videos, sure, but that only goes so far. Eventually, I became angry, angry over the fact that I didn't have any parents, while other kids did. I remember thinking how unlucky I was, and that maybe I was cursed. So hearing you say that, it just . . . well, I just want you to know that I'm with you on this. I'll always be with you, no matter what. If by some chance we really are cursed, then we'll just be cursed together."

She smiled faintly up at me, her bangs covering her eyes, which were narrowing further out of exhaustion. "This may sound crazy," she whispered tiredly, "but when I heard what had happened to you, I had this aching in my chest, far more painful than anything I'd ever felt for myself, even back during those tough times. I had to come back, because, well, I'm not really sure I know what . . . love is, but . . . I think that aching feeling might have been . . ."

Her breaths turned to snoozes as her eyes closed shut. She had a peaceful smile on her face, one that I never wanted to see her lose again. I thought back to the little girl, alone and secluded, and was just grateful that she now trusted someone enough to open up again, enough to fall asleep in that person's arms.

"Yeah," I whispered, "I also think that aching feeling is it, Dawn. And I ache for you, too."

Chapter Fourteen

I⊤'s funny how the second semester always seems to go by faster than the first. My classes practically blurred together, along with the days, and then even weeks. Before I had even realized it, the frozen, snow-dusted terrain was replaced with a wet, muddy one, the bluish-green grass revealing itself once again (though it still had yet to flourish quite as brightly as it had at the beginning of the fall term), and the consistent silvery-gray skies were starting to regain their shimmering blue more and more frequently. Even some of the streams of water, which would always peacefully and consistently flow down a few of the surrounding mountains, had thawed and returned to life after being dormant for months.

March had arrived, and with it came the festivities and perks of early springtime, some typical and familiar, others not so much. I'd say the most interesting of them was an elvish holiday called Ehtele'mele—an entire week dedicated to romance and song, which had the town of Hearthvale alive with ambient music, most of which was played with flutes and harps.

In addition to the music, the town and even the grounds on campus were lavishly decorated with royal blue, pink, and indigo flowers. Many runics were walking around town and through campus sporting flower crowns of the same colors, too, cheerfully shouting "Ehtele'mele, friend!" to one another as they crossed paths.

It was the first big holiday event of the school year that wasn't based around humans, and I was all about it, not so much because of the flowers and stuff, but because of the fact that we got an entire week of classes off for it (basically Magic Rune Academy's version of spring break).

"Ehtele'mele!" I blithely shouted to Tara and Dawn as I sat down next to them at our window seat in the dining hall, my tray filled with a few sandwiches, fries, and a couple of cookies.

"Ehtele'mele, Nate!" they both said before taking in my bountiful lunch with expressions of bewilderment on their faces.

"I have to say, I'm loving this holiday," I said between bites of my first sandwich. "An entire week off with nothing to do but chill out with the two of you? I'm all for it."

"Sounds good to me, too!" Tara smiled in agreement after finishing a sip of her drink.

"Actually," Dawn slowly began with an ambivalent look, "I'll be busy with the Guard all week. They're short staffed at the Magic Gateway, so I got called in almost every day."

"Wait, really?" I asked, hoping she wasn't serious.

"Yeah, sorry guys."

"That's a total bummer," said Tara. "We finally get a week to ourselves, and you have to work?"

"I know, it sucks something serious," said Dawn, fiddling with something in her pockets. "But," she slowly added, "I have a little surprise for the two of you."

Tara and I exchanged looks of curious confusion.

"Ta-da!" She held out two tickets to us, biting her lip to suppress an eager smile. "A little Ehtele'mele gift from yours truly!"

Tara let out a small gasp.

My eyes went wide with astonishment. "Dawn . . ." I began, "what—what is this?"

"Two flight tickets for my best friends, that's what!" she exclaimed. "To Kharador!"

"You booked us a trip for Spring Break?" asked Tara incredulously.

"Yep! Well, just the weekend was all I could afford, but it's all covered. Consider it a gift from the Guard." She smiled, passing the tickets across the table to us.

"Dawn . . . are you—? I don't know what to say . . ." breathed Tara, marveling at the tickets in front of her.

"You really didn't have to," I said. "This is probably the nicest thing anyone has ever done for either of us."

"It definitely is!" Tara agreed. "You sure there's not a catch or something?" She grinned.

"The only catch is that you both agree to have an amazing weekend!" Dawn happily said. "And that should be easy! Kharador is a top tourist destination in the Rune Realm. I don't want to spoil anything, but once you're there, you'll see why! *And* it's the week of Ehtele'mele! Ugh, I'm actually jealous, to be honest! But so excited for you both!"

"I think . . ." said Tara with a hint of reluctance, "I really think you should go with Nate, Dawn. It's only right. You bought these tickets. You shouldn't have to work over the break."

"Nope!" Dawn quickly shut her down. "Not an option, Tara! I bought these specifically for the two of you. And that's exactly who will be going. If you don't accept, all you'll do is hurt my feelings."

Tara gave a guilty smile. "Seriously, Dawn. Thank you so much!"

After we finished our meals and started making our way out of the dining hall, I quickly pulled Dawn aside.

"Dawn, this seriously was so nice of you. But really, though, what's the reason for it?" I muttered.

Dawn grinned devilishly.

"I knew it!" I almost shouted.

"Oh, come on, Nate," she started, playfully rolling her eyes, "you both deserve this, and you know it. You've been close with Tara way longer than you've been with me, and I know you two haven't gone all the way yet. This is the perfect opportunity! Kharador is so romantic, and with it being the week of Ehtele'mele, it's the perfect time for a girl's *first* time."

"She told you?!"

"Well, duh! Girls talk, you know?" She winked.

I scoffed, amazed. "I can't believe this. You're like my wing woman right now!"

She let out an innocent laugh. "Look, Nate. We've been getting closer these past few months. And I *love* that! But you and Tara both deserve to take it to the next level now. Call it guilt or whatever, but I had to step in and pull a bit of *Dawn Magic*."

"I—I've only been waiting out of respect for Tara, for your information."

"I know, I know," she threw her hands up in a way that proclaimed her innocence, "and that was very nice of you. But it's time."

A thought occurred to me. "Are you even working this week?!"

She smiled, pursing her lips. "I am, though I may have exaggerated when I said I had to work *every* day."

I shook my head, grinning.

Dawn's words echoed in my mind as we continued our way out of the dining hall. Maybe she had a point after all. She wasn't wrong when she said that she and I had gotten closer the past couple of months, both emotionally and physically. It wasn't an entirely rare occasion anymore where she'd come back to my place and fall asleep in my arms (often having some rather intense sexual encounters beforehand).

After she had finally opened up to me that night a couple months prior, our relationship just took off, never really looking back. And now, saying that things have heated up between us would be putting it lightly, really.

Tara was different, though. She wanted to play things slow. And I appreciated her for that. I wanted to respect her wishes. But had I somehow neglected her a little recently? If I had, she never brought it up to me.

The more I thought about it, the more this trip *did* seem like a good idea, and I was extremely grateful to Dawn for putting everything together for us, not to mention covering for the whole thing with her hard-earned money at her internship with the Guard.

"Okay!" Dawn announced after we left the dining hall and stepped out into the cool, damp air to head to our last afternoon classes of the week. "Your flights leave at ten tomorrow morning.

I'd recommend getting to the flightport around nine though. Oh, and don't worry about packing any of your cloaks and robes or anything like that. People usually dress in their homeland clothes when traveling by griffin. Just be sure to pack plenty of lighter clothes and some bathing suits, though! I'll come over later tonight to give you guys the information on the resort."

"Resort?" I asked, baffled.

"Did you say, 'griffin?'" asked Tara nervously. "We fly by griffin?"

"Of course! What, you haven't noticed by now that there haven't been any airplanes flying through the sky here?" Dawn giggled.

"No," said Tara hesitantly. "But I kind of just figured we weren't close to an airport. Not to mention I haven't seen any griffins flying around, either!"

"That's a good point." Dawn pursed her lips. "There must not be any flight paths that go over campus. Not to mention the flightport is about an hour east of here by axe beak."

"Ugh," I groaned, doing the math. "So we'll have to wake up before, like, eight o'clock tomorrow? But it's a Saturday."

"Oh, come on!" Dawn blurted out with disbelief, hitting me playfully on the shoulder. "I got you a weekend in Kharador and you're bitching about waking up early?"

"True, true. Sorry." I smiled sheepishly back at her.

I met Tara in our dormitory lobby the next morning and was practically immobilized by the sight of her. Tara always had a way of drawing me into her, especially in recent years. But that was with her usual, more casual outfits—like her over-sized hoodies and yoga pants, or more recently, her healer robes. It had been a while since I'd seen her dressed in anything showing off her most luscious physical traits, probably since Halloween, actually.

So when I saw her that morning, it was like being hit by a truck. She was wearing a navy blue, long-sleeved top, with a low-cut neckline that plunged its way down just above her bountiful breasts, highlighting them in such a way that I'd never seen before. Her blue top was paired with a white skirt that hugged her curvy hips just tight enough to see the outline of her amazing shape underneath.

If not for her standard glasses and usual messy bun, with the two strands of bangs cascading down the side of her face, I may not have even recognized her. I couldn't help thinking that Dawn was behind this new suggestion of clothes for Tara, not that I was complaining.

She was more than ready for the trip, with her suitcase placed by her side and a smaller leather bag strapped around one of her shoulders, which, knowing Tara, was meant for some light studying over the break.

The one thing that seemed most unusual for her, even more so than the outfit, was the fact she was wearing jewelry—a pair of blue, diamond-shaped earrings and a necklace with a green, diamond-shaped pendant at the bottom of it, resting just above her cleavage. It matched her eyes almost perfectly.

"Hey, Tara! All ready?"

"Hey! Sure am!" she said, looking nervous and excited at the same time.

"Nice jewelry, by the way! Very fancy." I smiled, gently flicking the green pendant.

She blushed subtly. "Thanks. It's stupid, really. Just something that some healers wear for certain reasons. I doubt that

I'll actually get anything out of wearing them, though," she muttered, looking down at the ground.

"Hey now!" I gently lifted her chin for her so that she was looking right at me. "Don't even go there. If this jewelry allows for stronger healing powers or something like that, then you'll get it out of them. You can do anything the other healers can do. I know it!"

"Thanks," she smiled innocently, brushing a strand of hair out of her face.

It was a cool and dewy morning as we strolled through campus toward the North Gate, wheeling our suitcases along behind us.

"Kind of a bummer that Dawn had to work so early this morning!" said Tara, as we walked through the gate, leaving the campus grounds behind us.

"Yeah, it would have been nice to see her one more time before we left. I still can't believe she did this for us."

"Right?" replied Tara. "I can't help wondering why. I mean, besides the fact that she's like, the nicest person ever."

I remained mute, feeling it best not to tell Tara of Dawn's *expectations* for us.

Once reaching the axe beak stables, we hopped on two of the ostrich-looking mounts after hoisting our baggage onto the back of their saddles. Per usual, my trusty purple steed, Clyde, was eagerly awaiting my arrival.

"Dawn said just to wave our flight tickets in front of their eyes, right?" Tara's voice rang out from the stall next to Clyde's. "Then they should know to take us to the flightport?"

"I guess so," I said, digging into my pockets for the ticket. "Apparently, they're really intelligent, these axe beaks.

Guess they have certain routes memorized." I gave Clyde a couple pats on his back. "But I already knew you were a smart guy, aren't you, bud?!"

He shook his head about in agreement and made some snorting sounds.

I heard a laugh bust out from the stall next to me. "I just can't with you and that axe beak of yours," said Tara.

"Don't be hating on our bond," I joked, finally pulling the ticket out and slowly holding it up to Clyde's left eye. "Got it, bud?" I asked, to which he seemed to nod.

Taking that as a hopeful "yes," I tapped Clyde on the side twice and hollered out, "zapzap!"

My ticket almost flew out of my grip as Clyde darted off. "Race ya there!" I managed to shout out to Tara as I zoomed past her stall.

Clyde continued striding along, and I was reassured that the ticket-method had worked when instead of striding up the mountain (the usual path that the axe-beaks took to Hearth-vale), Clyde veered right, darting off the stone path and running parallel to the base of the mountain, treading his way through the damp grass.

I glanced to my right to see the wall that surrounded the north side of campus in the distance, which extended throughout the entire valley. I then turned over my shoulder to check on Tara, who was about fifty yards behind me and looking excited as ever to be going a different route from usual.

After a few minutes of riding, we reached the far east side of the large valley which Magic Rune Academy resided in, and were now presented with the base of another large mountain. There was a narrow pass between this mountain and the one north of campus, though, and Clyde shot through it without missing a beat.

With Tara close behind, the axe beaks voyaged their way through the narrow pass, and it wasn't long before we made it to the other side. As we did, it was like a whole new world opened up to us.

A massive open field of wet grass was now all I could see in front of me. To my far right, the field stretched out for what looked like forever. But to my left, the land eventually sloped downward. Past it, way off on the distant horizon, a huge body of water extended for as far as I could see.

With it being so early in the year still, the blue grass was short and still coming in, the field wet and muddy. But I could tell just from looking around that by mid-summer this field becomes a vast prairie, abundant with life.

We continued treading through the flat terrain for what felt like ten or fifteen minutes, and with not much to offer as a barrier, the steady morning breeze was starting to sting a little against my face. Fortunately, soon after this thought, Clyde veered left down the subtle slope toward the large body of water.

Clyde carefully meandered his way down the hill, and then we continued heading east, but now riding along a secluded dirt path that ran parallel to the white sandy beach, which preceded the impressive ocean after it. I glanced back to see the village of Hearthvale and the cove that surrounded it, looking smaller than it ever had, way off in the distance.

We rode further and further along the coast for what felt like almost an hour, passing a couple of small villages along the way, their inhabitants surely still inside as they were probably just waking up to enjoy their sleepy Saturday mornings.

The minutes continued to roll by, and I was starting to fear that maybe Clyde wasn't taking us to the right destination, when I saw it in the distant inland: a large city, abundant with tall buildings of all shapes and sizes. As we rode closer, I could make out more of the details of the buildings. Many were tall and thin, peaking with spires and turrets which practically touched the clouds in the sky, while others were stout and wide, some dome shaped and topped with cupolas.

My suspicion of this being our destination was confirmed after coming to a crossroads on the old dirt path. Clyde made an abrupt right turn toward inland, following the path that led to the impressive city, which seemed to get taller and more intimidating the closer we got to it.

The thin dirt path eventually evolved into a wide stone one, and I could see a big sign in front of a long, wide stone bridge leading into the city from here, which read *Welcome to Dreoon, City of Stars and Moon*.

We passed the sign and proceeded across the long bridge, which rose maybe twenty feet above a low stream bordering the city. Tall black streetlights and stone statues of various elves and humans were evenly spaced apart, perched on top of the short outer wall on the perimeter of the bridge.

I got a view of the surrounding land as we made our way across. It seemed that Dreoon had been built smack dab in the middle of the giant prairie, most likely the same vast prairie that we were riding through earlier.

When we made it to the other side of the bridge, Clyde led us through a short little stone underpass and slowed to a light trot as we emerged into the narrow, cobbled streets of Dreoon. Luckily, as it was a Saturday morning, it wasn't entirely too crowded (although we still passed plenty of different looking runics as we made our way further into the city).

As it would turn out, the flightport happened to be located at the complete opposite side of the city, which took us around ten minutes to navigate through. I didn't really mind, though, as it allowed me plenty of time to take in the fascinating, older-looking architecture—the tall skyscrapers towering over us with their spires and dome tops, mixed in with plenty of smaller buildings, most of them made of a fancy white marble and having red clay tiled roofs.

Finally, after weaving our way through the tight streets of Dreoon, the city had opened up. No longer surrounded by the tall buildings, I felt as if I could breathe in some fresh air again, and I could see what had to be the flightport from here—a long red-bricked building with multiple tall red doors to enter it. Glass windows were placed above each of those doors, and an enormous clock was installed in the center of the building. A gold flag with a red griffin on it was erected at the highest point of the building. Perhaps the most interesting feature of the building, though, was the fifty or so huge chimneys sprouting from the roof, all of them equally tall and wide.

Clyde brought me all the way to the plaza area directly in front of the building before finally coming to a halt. I nearly fell to the brick pavement, my stiff legs almost giving out after unseating myself from Clyde's saddle.

"Great job, buddy," I breathed to the axe beak after pulling my luggage off his saddle. "If I'm this beat from the trip, I can't imagine how you must feel."

But he doesn't seem fazed by the journey, even happy, as I gave him a pat on his head and watched him trot off with Tara's axe beak, back through the city.

"Are you ready to head in?" I asked Tara, grabbing her suit-case for her.

She gave me an awkward smile.

"Are you okay?"

"Yeah," she panted. "I just . . . I don't know, flying on a plane is fine. But a griffin? I'm kind of nervous, is all."

I walked over to her and put a hand on her shoulder. "I'll be right there with you."

"I know, thanks, Nate," she tried to smile back.

"Besides," I blurted out, "if you fall off, I bet I can pull you back with my Telekinesis Spell! I've gotten pretty good at it, after all!" I winked, earning a chuckle and a playful slap on the shoulder.

We entered the flightport, and the first thing I noticed were the people: humans, orcs, and elves all dressed up in their clothes from their homelands. The humans, I noticed, were mostly dressed in business casual outfits, to which Tara and I blended in quite well.

Surprisingly, there were also quite a few students around our age walking around with their backpacks strapped around their shoulders, most likely traveling back to their homes in the Realm for the break.

A few ushers, wearing their fancy suits and hats, were readily available to help any runics with questions and directions.

Overall, the station was relatively crowded due to it being the week of Ehtele'mele, the sounds of chattering people and the wheels of luggage swiftly clicking along the marble tiled floors echoed throughout the vast building.

I was still marveling at the shiny flooring and stone pillars, which extended all the way up to the high, curved vault ceilings, when Tara noticed I was dragging behind.

"Earth to Nate! Are you coming?" her voice rang out.

I looked down to see her practically glowing underneath the lights hanging down from the ceiling above. Her smile was contagious. Out of all the beauty this place had to offer, she was by far the star of the show.

"Yeah, sorry," I replied. "Got lost in the wonder of it all . . ."

"It really is something, isn't it?" she agreed as we resumed our stroll through the flightport, passing pictures of various griffins hung on the walls.

To our far left and right, were multiple lines of people, each of them leading toward what looked to be the enormous chimney chutes I had noticed earlier. Above the lines of people hung wooden signs with a specific number on them.

I pulled out my ticket and noticed we were to board our griffin on *Chute* 17 (we were currently standing under *Chute* 7). So we continued pacing down the station as I dragged both our suitcases behind me.

It seemed we arrived at Chute 17 just in time; a large clock above us showed that it was now 9:54 in the morning, six minutes before our flight was to leave. Luckily, there were only about half a dozen people standing in line in front of us, and everyone was moving pretty quickly through the velvet rope stanchions.

As we got closer to the chute entrance, I was able to get a better look at them—maybe a dozen griffins, all about the size of a car, were lying happily inside the roomy chute, which was layered thick with loads of hay. As one of the griffins flew up the chute, carrying away a young elf couple, another one came down with an orc on its back.

"Nate!" Tara tapped me hard on the shoulder. "That's Stormchaser!" she pointed a shaky finger at a particular griffin towards the back of the chute, peacefully lying on its thick nest of hay.

"Kingdom Monsters?" I assumed.

"Do you even have to ask?" she squeaked. "He's been a high-end card for years now. Not on Drakthor's level, of course. But he's still impressive!"

He looked impressive, too—half eagle, half lion, the griffin had black feathers streaked with yellow. Its eyes were a fierce bronze, and its beak black as its feathers.

"Hey, maybe we'll get lucky and get to ride him!" I said excitedly.

"Oh gosh," muttered Tara, "I don't know if I'd want to . . . he might be really fast."

"Next up? Step on up! All aboard a trip to Kharador!" shouted an older orc lady. She was wearing a fancy usher suit and standing in front of the entrance to the chute. "Having a fun getaway weekend, are we?" she happily asked us as we walked up to her.

"That's the goal!" I smiled politely, which she returned before scanning our tickets.

At that moment, sure enough, the griffin named Stormchaser slowly stood up, stretching out its wings in a confident manner.

"Well, can't go wrong with Kharador, that's for sure! Looks like you guys will be taking griffin 58, here," said the usher, gesturing to Stormchaser. At that point, I noticed the number 58 was carved into its thick leather saddle.

As our usher bent down to pull something out of the compartment to her right, Tara muttered behind me, "Can you believe it? She refers to a legend like Stormchaser as 'griffin 58.' I mean, where's the respect?!"

"I know, right? The audacity," I said with a smirk, failing to hide my sarcasm.

"All right, then," said our usher, returning from scavenging through the compartment and now holding a pair of thick goggles in each hand. "You'll be needing these, of course, especially with *that* guy. Make sure you put them on tight, now," she said with a smile, stepping aside to let us into the big, red-bricked chute.

We walked through the hay-covered floor. Some of the griffins were peacefully snoozing away, taking advantage of their intermissions before their next flights, where others appeared to be enjoying the company of their chute-mates, playfully snapping their beaks at one another.

Stormchaser met us halfway in the middle of the chute, looking excited for another flight.

"Uh—hi, there, buddy," Tara nervously said from behind my shoulder.

Stormchaser let out a happy squawking noise and flared out his wings.

"I think he likes you, Tara!" I said encouragingly.

"Yeah . . ." She let out a nervous laugh and gave him a gentle pat on the head. "You're a good boy, aren't you?"

"I'll take those for you," said our usher, grabbing our bags and hoisting them into a compartment fastened to the back of Stormchaser's saddle. "Up you go, now," she kindly gestured for us to mount the griffin.

"Would it make you feel better if you sit in the front?" I quickly murmured to Tara.

"No, that's okay," replied Tara, with a slight quiver in her voice. "I'd rather you not see me freaking out."

I made my way up onto the large griffin, helping Tara up once I was secured in my seat. The saddle was big enough for multiple people, so we had plenty of room.

"Okay, now—there you go . . . very snug, just how we like it . . ." Our usher was swiftly walking around me and Tara, fastening us tightly into the saddle with the attached harness. "All right, then! Should be all set. Have a nice flight, you two. And enjoy your trip!"

She had barely finished her sentence when the large griffin stretched its wide wings out and began to flap them powerfully. Hay was being blown everywhere throughout the chute as we slowly lifted off the ground. The griffins below looked up at Stormchaser with what seemed like a subtle hint of envy in their eyes.

I felt Tara wrap her arms tightly around my chest as we continued ascending higher up the tall chute. Above us, the gray, cloudy sky shimmered through the wide, square opening at the top of the chute, becoming closer by the second until we emerged into the bright morning light, leaving the chute entirely.

It was like the entire world revealed itself to us. Floating above the flightport roof, we were already up pretty high. I felt the cool hair gently licking my face. I could see the various, uniquely shaped skyscrapers of Dreoon to my right, with its tiny residents below it, all swiftly walking to their individual destinations. And I marveled at the vast prairie, which extended way off to my left, seemingly going on forever.

Now that the griffin was free from the restraints of the chute, it flapped its wings harder, faster, and as we slowly ascended higher into the air, I felt us start to tilt upward, so that we were facing the cloudy heavens above.

"Holy shit!" I heard Tara blurt out from behind me as we abruptly took off further into the sky, closing the gap between us and the clouds with every passing second.

"Holy shit! Holy shit! Holy shit!" shouted Tara shrilly over the rushing wind in my ears, and now I understood, better than ever, the need for the goggles.

I dared to look down, and saw the flat ground below quickly losing its detail as the griffin proceeded to further separate Tara and me from it, the towering city no longer towering at all, its buildings looking like a child's play set.

We had already touched some of the lower clouds when the griffin flattened its body out a little, its wings no longer flapping, instead stretched outright as it glided smoothly through the occasional passing cloud.

This gave me the opportunity to really take in my surroundings below. As someone who had never even flown on a plane before, this was exhilarating, to say the least. Being this high up provided me with a sense of detachment from the reality below—like any issues and stress that I may have had back on the ground remained there while I soared away from them. Surely, this was the best way to travel.

Feeling the wind rushing through my hair, I took a page out of Stormchaser's book and stretched both my arms out, bellowing out a loud scream of joy.

"Don't do that!" shouted Tara as she immediately pushed my hands back down. "You're making me even more nervous!"

I let out a laugh as the griffin flapped its wings again, bringing us even higher through the thick clouds until we poked above them.

And now everything seemed even more peaceful. Looking down, I could no longer see the ground, only the fluffy clouds below. To our left and right I saw nothing but clear blue, and the sun felt a bit hotter up here, too.

We continued soaring peacefully like this through the air for almost an hour before the clouds below began to open, and the sun swelled hotter. Tara seemed to be calming down a little now too, finding her griffin wings, so to speak.

As I peered through the now scattered, thin clouds below, I could see the terrain changing from the blue-green to more of a dry yellowish-brown. All the while, the temperature continued to rise.

"Man . . . feels like summer all of a sudden!" I hollered back to Tara, who was still clinging pretty tightly to me.

The initial euphoria from the flight had kind of lost its luster, as I was now starting to sweat, and my legs were even cramping up, too. According to our tickets, our flight time was to be around two hours, and I was just about to holler back to Tara to ask her how long she thought it had been, when the griffin dipped down beneath the few remaining clouds.

I could see, way off on the distant horizon, a massive body of pristine-blue water that was unmistakably a beautiful ocean.

"Did Dawn say anything about this place being an island, by chance?" I shouted back to Tara.

"No, I don't think so!" squeaked Tara. "Maybe she wanted it all to be a surprise!"

We continued slowly descending over the massive body of water, confirming my suspicions that our destination was an island off somewhere in the distance, when Stormchaser took a sudden nosedive toward the bright blue water.

Tara clung to me tightly and let out a loud, piercing scream again, and even I was starting to think that Stormchaser had lost his mind and decided to take the easy way out when he quickly flattened out again, just feet above the splashing waves.

We were now swiftly gliding along the water, the occasional spray of salty water brushing against our faces, which, after being so high up and close to the sun, felt pretty good.

A large strip of white sandy land slowly came into view way off in the distance.

"That must be it!" I pointed.

Stormchaser flapped his wings eagerly, signaling that he, too, was looking forward to reaching land for a quick breather.

The closer we got, the clearer the details of the island became, with its over-water bungalows branching off from its white beaches in every direction and strips of small buildings along various boardwalks preceding them. I even saw a tall Ferris wheel and a small park at the end of one of the boardwalks. The center of the island looked rather natural, though, relatively wild and yet to be touched by runic hands.

As we reached the island, Stormchaser circled its perimeter until the flightport came into sight—a building of similar appearance to the red-bricked one in Dreoon, but a little smaller and appearing to be made entirely of some sort of modern white clay.

Stormchaser paused in mid-air, hovering directly above one of the chutes on the flightport's roof before gradually descending us into it. I felt Tara's grip finally loosen around my chest as we slowly lowered through the chute.

She let out a long, deep breath. "That wasn't too bad," she said.

I had to suppress a chuckle.

We finally returned to the solid, hay-covered surface at the bottom of the chute, where there were a few other griffins around us, all of them taking a nice snooze.

As we hopped off our griffin, another usher came rushing over to us, this one being a male elf, but wearing a very similar outfit to the orc usher back in Dreoon.

"I'll get those for you," he said, happily pulling our luggage out of the back compartment of Stormchaser's saddle and handing them to us.

Before leaving the chute, Tara and I gave the griffin a pat on the head and said our thanks.

"Hope you enjoy your stay at Kharador!" shouted the usher enthusiastically as we stepped out onto the bright tile flooring of the Kharador flightport, more than ready to enjoy the start of a well-earned Spring Break.

Chapter Fifteen

AFTER LEAVING the flightport and stepping outside into the balmy weather of Kharador, we took a couple of axe beaks to our resort. By simply waving our resort information in front of their eyes, they transported us around the perimeter of the large island until we arrived at a quaint strip of restaurants and shops that ran parallel to the white sandy beach and bungalows to our left. At the very end of the strip, way off in the distance, stood the tall Ferris wheel.

We strolled down the white concrete path, which stretched along the entire boardwalk before arriving at the first building—a small establishment with a bright blue exterior. Several white columns around the front entrance extended upward toward the awning above and a large wooden sign that read *Welcome Center* in big white letters hung between the middle two columns in front of the entrance door.

Once inside, we were greeted by a young girl behind the front desk, a human who looked to be a shifter in her hybrid form; she had green scales along her body, yellowish-green eyes with slits for the irises, a reptilian-like tail, and when she spoke, her long tongue flailed about. She was wearing a flower crown and purple flowers around her neck for the holiday.

"Ehtele'mele, friends!" she said from behind her desk, beaming happily at us.

"Ehtele'mele!" Tara and I replied as we handed our resort information to the girl.

"Welcome to the Northwest Resort of Kharador!" she said, walking to the back wall and pulling a pair of keys off the shelf, which held many. "You two will be in Suite 17. This whole strip—all the way down to the park—is yours to explore. And of course all the restaurants, along with the food and drinks they offer, come included with your package," Tara and I exchanged quick glances of amazement, "while you enjoy your stay at Kharador. Here are your flower crowns," she slowly added while sliding two crowns of purple, pink, and blue flowers across the desk to us. "Have to get into the holiday spirit, right?!" she giggled.

"Oh, *definitely*!" said Tara enthusiastically, taking one of the crowns and immediately jamming it on my head. "It's a perfect fit!" She grinned at me while I gave her an unamused look.

The girl behind the desk chortled away. "You look pretty cute with that!" she said, her scaly cheeks turning from green to red as her yellow eyes fluttered at me.

"He does, doesn't he?!" agreed Tara, with a little too much enthusiasm before turning and giving me an ornery look."

"Yeah, yeah, laugh it up," I muttered and then gently placed the crown of flowers on top of Tara's platinum, blonde hair.

No matter how "cute" I may have looked, it was certainly nothing compared to how the flowers made Tara pop, accentuating the green in her eyes.

"Here are your keys. The bungalows are out past the beach in front of us. But I'm sure you saw them already on your way over here," said the girl, sliding the keys over to us. "And if you guys need anything at all, please do not hesitate to come and ask," her eyes lingered on me for a second longer than what I'd say is normal, "I'm more than happy to help!"

We left the Welcome Center and immediately discarded our shoes and socks before heading straight across the white beach toward the over-water bungalows, yearning to see our place.

The sand felt amazing under my feet, cool and refreshing, and I remembered how Dawn told us earlier in the year how the sand in the Rune Realm regulates temperature. Back then, it was cooler out, so the sand had warmed up. But now, with it being hotter here, it had clearly cooled itself down to adapt, acting like the cool side of a pillow for my feet.

Not only that, but I was abruptly reminded of how the sand doesn't stick to things here, as it slid off my bare feet, keeping them clean and dry. This also allowed us to conveniently wheel our luggage through the beach without too much friction, and no concerns of getting sand in the wheels.

The walkway holding the bungalows, which was made of a clean, light gray wood, stretched out into the water for about a hundred yards.

Twisting and turning about, we followed it, passing bungalow after bungalow, all of them topped with straw thatched roofs and boarded with wooden sidings. But what I was most excited about, was the fact that every bungalow seemed to have its own little back deck, with a small pool and steps that led down into the clear blue water of the surrounding ocean.

"I *cannot* believe this place, Nate!" Tara finally blurted out after she finished swerving her head around, captivated with every bungalow we had passed.

"Neither can I . . ." I was practically at a loss for words. It felt way too fancy for us, almost like we were intruders attempting to live false lives for a weekend. "Long way from Maine, aren't we?" I laughed.

"Just a little!" Tara giggled excitedly. "We *definitely* need to do something nice for Dawn when we get back!" she added.

"I agree! Though something tells me that she probably wouldn't accept it even if we forced it on her."

After several minutes of wheeling our suitcases along the wooden walkway, passing maybe twenty or so bungalows, we finally reached Suite 17. It was a suite just as fancy as the rest, even better, really, as it happened to be located at the very end of the walkway, in the back of what acted like a sort of cul-de-sac for the *neighborhood* of bungalows.

"Oh, wow!" Tara gasped almost immediately upon entering our bungalow, darting straight into the living room. "Nate, look! You can see the ocean through the floor here!" She bent down, nearly pressing her face against the underwater window in the middle of the living room floor.

"See any fish?" I asked, now standing over it myself.

"No, no fish," she muttered into the floor, "the water is beautiful, though!"

We took a quick stroll through the place. It really was beautiful, coming with all the necessities and more. The central room was composed of the living room and kitchen area, with the master bedroom branching off from it. A glass sliding door led to the back deck where the small pool was.

"Nate . . ." Tara emerged from the bedroom, letting out a deep breath of amazement. "This place . . . it's just so romantic, don't you think?"

"I'll say! Couldn't ask for a better setup," I replied, still taking in the surroundings, when I felt Tara run into my arms.

Pleasantly surprised by her sudden offer of affection, I gazed down at her green eyes and gave her a deep kiss. Her lips were so soft and thick that they could have kept me there forever. And I was starting to feel the pressure around my pants build up when she finally managed to tear herself away from me, a subtle expression of thirst on her flushed face.

"This is going to be a fun little trip," she whispered, slowly stepping away from me, but not before rubbing a finger down my chest in a teasing kind of way.

She held her stare for a few seconds, smirking, before heading back toward the master bedroom. It was such a confident move that it had me slightly baffled, and I couldn't help wondering if she'd been getting tips from Dawn on the art of seduction recently. "I'm going to change real quick," she added. "Be right back!"

"Change?" I asked, curiously.

About a minute later, she returned, now wearing a black two-piece bikini, which made my mouth almost drop to the floor. Her thick curves (and especially her massive tits) were now more apparent than ever. In all the years I'd known Tara, I had yet to see her quite this exposed.

"What ya think?" she asked innocently, her hands locked behind her back in a way that forced her chest forward.

She knew exactly what she was doing right now.

"I think," I managed to find my words, "that they can kick you out of here for looking that good. . ."

"Oh, darn," she sighed sarcastically. "Better get everything we can out of this place before that happens then." She meandered over to the glass sliding door and walked out onto the back deck.

I didn't even bother changing into my suit, not wanting to waste another second. Instead, I hastily threw my pants and shirt off and darted outside, wearing nothing but my boxers.

Tara was already gracefully treading water off the deck, a pair of snorkeling goggles strapped to her face. "Come on in!" she hollered. "Grab a pair over by the chair, there!"

I grabbed the goggles, fastened them over my head, and took a dive into the clear blue water, which felt invigorating, exactly the perfect temperature. And with the goggles, I could see for miles in every direction.

Tara and I swam together like a pair of dolphin shifters, occasionally diving below to take in the amazing view beneath the surface, which was a realm of its own. Plenty of interesting fish swam by, some were blue and purple, some gold and red, others zebra striped. There were even some fish that I'd never seen before, having two tails, or leaving streaks of bright fluorescent colors behind them as they darted by. The blue-green seaweed swayed peacefully on the ocean floor below, which surely held plenty of other sea creatures within it.

We remained in the water for what must have been at least over an hour, enjoying every individual second to the fullest until we both agreed to listen to our stomachs and head back to our bungalow to get ready for dinner on the strip.

But when Tara stepped out of the water and climbed up the ladder to our back deck, her soaking wet body glistened in the sun, and I had to fight the sudden urge to hold off on dinner and instead further pursue my blonde bombshell of a girlfriend. But when my stomach let out an obnoxious growl while drying off, Tara burst into laughter and urged me to get dressed before I became the first person to "die of hunger at an all-you-can-eat resort."

And so, we finished drying off and got ourselves dressed up for an evening out (I felt the tight sensation around my pants again as Tara came out of the master bedroom sporting her flower crown, a white belly shirt that was tied off just below her breasts, and a tight jean skirt).

By the time we made it back to the boardwalk, the late-afternoon sun was finally starting to cool down, making for the start of a very comfortable evening along the beach. The now familiar sounding Ehtele'mele music was being played all throughout the boardwalk, its ambient vibes having a way of making everything feel even more peaceful than it already was.

The long strip of restaurants and shops was busier than earlier, overflowing with positive energy as many runics strolled along it, wearing their crowns of flowers.

We decided to stop at an intriguing restaurant that sat right on the beach. It had a pavilion with a bar under it, which was bordered with warm, overhanging lights and tiki torches. Behind the bar, closer to the water, were about fifty small tables for two, all aligned in rows. Each table had their own pair of tiki torches, creating a very romantic atmosphere for any couples wishing to dine on the sandy beach.

"Welcome to The Sandset Eatery," a middle-aged elf-woman greeted us from behind the Hostess Stand, which was placed in front of the pavilion. "Table for two?"

"You bet!" I happily said, and we followed her back through the pavilion and toward the waterside tables (many of which were already occupied by other runic couples) until we were seated at a small table of our own in a row closest to the water.

"Wow . . . this is perfect. Thank you!" said Tara to the hostess before taking our seats across from one another.

"Of course! Enjoy your meal," she politely replied.

Tara immediately snatched a menu, eagerly reading through it and muttering things like "Oooo, that sounds good" and "Oh, we are def getting that," to herself.

I couldn't help but grin as I took in the view across from me, and an overwhelming sense of gratitude and euphoria set in.

I mean, how could it not? Between the deep orange sun, which was now setting halfway below the watery horizon, the soft sand at our feet, and the tiki torches, which not only provided the perfect amount of warmth but also further illuminated Tara's beauty, it was like I was in a masterful painting.

At that moment, our waiter came by, so we each ordered a drink. Tara decided on trying a fruity-looking beverage that came in a large coconut, while I stuck with my favorite—a runic ale, with its blue-green tint and subtle fruitiness as well.

"I just realized this," I began, after taking another sip of my ale, "but I don't think I ever asked you *exactly* what the purpose of the jewelry was," I had noticed her fiddling with the necklace, "I think I just assumed that it heightened your healing capabilities, but we were in a rush earlier, so I didn't ask."

"Yeah, no worries," she said, blushing a little. "To be honest, it's kind of dumb anyway. I don't want to bore you with the details of it all."

"Oh, come on. Try me!"

"Well, all right." She let out a little sigh. "The jewelry basically acts like a container for rune. A skilled healer can apparently channel some of their internal rune into it, so that they can pull from it at a later time, if ever needed—mainly in case of emergency. I guess it can give a temporary healing boost, even self-sustaining energy, when we finally use it. A battery is probably a better analogy than a container. You can pull from the internal rune you've stored up in the jewelry when casting your healing spells, so that way you don't lose any energy when healing. At least, that's what's supposed to happen."

"Really? That sounds awesome, though! Why'd you say it's dumb?"

"It's not the concept that's dumb," she hesitantly began, fiddling with her fingers while a gentle breeze off the water lightly flicked away at her side bangs. "It's just . . . I don't know, a part of me thinks that for me to even attempt the technique is dumb. It's a high-level healing skill. And I'm . . . well, needless to say, I haven't gotten anywhere with it."

"That's okay, Tara," I encouraged, taking another sip of my ale. "There are spells that I'm still struggling with, too. Just keep at it! I know you can do it—"

"Yeah, but Nate, it's not just this," Tara sighed. "*All* spells are a struggle for me. I hate to keep playing the D-tier card, but I'm starting to think it really *does* make a big difference. Every spell we've been taught in my healing class, I'm always one of the last ones to learn it. I *just* now started getting a grasp on the basic Healing Spell—a spell that we were taught during my first month here.

"And since then, most of the other students have even mastered the Invisibility Spell. I've only been able to pull that off once, and it was barely for a second. So me just *considering* something as difficult as the Regeneration Spell with this jewelry—it just seems like I'm kidding myself."

"Wait . . . healers can turn invisible?" I said, becoming blatantly aware that I still hadn't been paying enough attention in Professor Morran's Intro to Classes course.

"Yeah, it's a way to protect ourselves from being sitting ducks, since we don't have many defensive or offensive spells. But that's beside the point . . ."

"Right, sorry," I shook my head about, "just my brain getting sidetracked. But Tara, you *did* learn the basic Healing Spell, right?"

"Well, yeah, but—"

"I guess that's what I'm trying to say. Sure, it takes you a little bit longer to learn the spells, but you power through. You learned it, even as a D-tier, through nothing but hard work and plenty of studying. That's who you are. You're a fighter."

Tara paused and gave me a guilty smile. "Nate, I appreciate what you're saying, I really do. But to be honest, I know that even *you* have your doubts about my capabilities."

"What?!" I asked incredulously. "Tara, that's not true at all. I *know* you can do anything you set your mind to."

Tara sighed. "I really hate to even go here, because I don't want to put a damper on this amazing evening."

"No, really. Talk to me," I pushed.

"I just . . ." she carefully began. "Look, I know you may believe your words—I'm not saying you're lying to me intentionally. And I do appreciate them. But . . . actions speak louder than words, Nate."

"What do you mean?"

"It was back during your fight with that asshole Chuck," Tara softly began. "I wanted to help you. I think I could have, but you told me to stay out of it. And yeah, I know you were just trying to protect me, and I appreciate you so much for that," she quickly added before I could retort, "but I should be the one to protect you and keep you safe. I'm the healer. And more importantly, that's what I want to do. I just think . . . that if you really trusted me and my abilities, you would have been confident enough to let me help you back then."

I pondered over her words, thinking back to my tussle with the werewolf. At the time, all I was concerned with was her safety. I wanted to make sure she stayed out of the fight, away from any danger. But if I really did believe in her, then . . .

Maybe she had a point. Perhaps, if I *was* more confident in her, I would have let her help me back then.

"Tara, I . . ."

"It's okay, Nate, really. I understand."

"No," I shook my head. "It's not okay. I think you're right. I *should* have let you help me back then. I didn't even realize it at the time, but I did treat you like some sort of helpless kid."

She tried to force a smile of understanding.

"But that's not who you are. Tara, you're a healer. And when we pass this final project in a couple months and officially get into the Quester program, you'll be *my* healer. I wouldn't want anyone else having my back, and I mean that!"

"You do?" she asked with a glimmer of hope now came back to her eyes.

"Of course! And they're not just empty words. I'll prove it to you, I promise."

"Nate . . ." she breathed gratefully. "Thank you. I just . . . I hope I don't hold you back, or let you down."

"Not possible! Honestly, I think if I would have let you help me back then, I would have never had my accidental run-in with the negative side of rune."

"Negative side?!" she abruptly asked, her soft tone immediately a thing of the past.

301

I then remembered how I never gave Tara the details of it all, out of fear of her being worried about me. But if this conversation had taught me anything, it was that hiding things from her wasn't going to push us forward, neither in skill nor in our relationship, so I gave her the rundown of everything that Dean Celestine had told me that day regarding the negative side of rune and the risks with using it, especially for an S-tier.

"Wow," said Tara, after I'd finally finished explaining. "I had a feeling something was up with you. You had this look in your eyes. I'd never seen it from you before."

"Yep! All the rune's doing. At least it makes me feel a little better if I tell myself that."

"No, I know you, Nate. It *definitely* was the negative rune."

"Thanks," I replied, feeling lighter about it, "that makes me feel better, knowing you agree. Wouldn't want you thinking I'm some sort of blood-thirsty, murdering mage."

Tara scoffed with a devilish grin. "Well," she said slowly, tapping her chin and pursing her lips, "I guess you never really *do* know a person."

"Haa-haa," I sarcastically muttered, as we let out some genuine laughs after that.

"I guess we're *both* still trying to figure this world out, huh?" Tara asked a few moments later.

"That's the beauty of it, isn't it?" I smiled warmly at her, to which she happily nodded in agreement.

A couple of things seemed to blur together around the same time after that. First, our food came (I had ordered a steak with mashed potatoes, and Tara, the honey garlic glazed salmon), and then, shortly after our initial, savory bites, we simultaneously noticed a bright neon blue light coming from the water, illuminating the dusky evening.

"Oh, wow!" Tara gasped.

"It's the noctillia . . ." I muttered in awe.

"The noc-what-a?" asked Tara.

"Dawn was telling me about them over Winter Break," I chuckled. "They're these tiny, single-celled organisms that live in the waters of the Realm. They become active at night, glowing this bright blue color when moved around or disturbed. Guess they even glow just from the motion of the waves! They're perfectly harmless. Just designed to put on a show for everyone, I suppose. Oh, and they heat up when they glow too! Bet that water is like a jacuzzi right about now."

"That's amazing, this place never ceases to fascinate me," said Tara, gazing at the neon blue ocean before us, which reflected delicately off her glasses.

I managed to pull my stare away from her and take in the scene myself. Back during Christmas on the icy pond, they were idle, frozen just below the surface, so they only lit up sporadically when touched. But tonight, because of the constant motion of the waves, the entire ocean was illuminated at once, with the individual crests of the waves that washed ashore sparkling brightest.

For the remainder of dinner, we had the background show of the dancing neon blue water to further entertain us, while the faint glow of orange beneath the horizon disappeared entirely, engulfing us in the night.

It was a colorful collision of natural and (to us) almost unnatural beauty that kept us hanging around a bit, even after finishing our food, just to simply take in the view a little longer before finally getting up to head back to our bungalow.

Our entire walk along the wooden path was illuminated by the noctillia as we passed bungalow after bungalow, finally arriving at our own way out in the calm ocean. Even our living room area was actively lit with a glowing blue square through the underwater window when we entered our place.

We were barely inside for a minute when Tara swiftly trotted out onto the deck to sit down along the little pool. She had her feet dipped in the water when I walked out to join her.

"Care for a seat? It feels great!" she asked, patting the wooden floor beside her as a gesture.

"Don't have to ask me twice!" I replied. The water in the pool felt warm and soothing against my shins.

"What a beautiful place," whispered Tara, dreamily, as she gazed out at the glowing water, the bright blue contrasting heavily with the black sky. The ambient tunes of Ehtele'mele were peacefully humming away from the distant boardwalk.

She scooted closer to me and then rested her head on my shoulder.

"Sure is," I replied, laying a hand upon her thigh, goose-bumps appearing on her skin as I did it. "Cold?" I asked.

"No, it just feels good. I like your touch," she murmured before placing her hand on my leg as well.

I wasn't sure if it was from her words, her hand placement, the feel of her smooth thigh against my hand, or perhaps the sudden realization that something I'd been waiting and hoping for, for so long now, was possibly within my grasp, but whatever it was—it was causing that stir from underneath my shorts.

Given the romantic moment, I tried to hold it back for now, but it was helpless. And sure enough, Tara appeared to notice. But then, quite surprisingly, she started to inch her hand down my thigh, closer to my crotch.

"I like yours too," I whispered.

I could hear her breathing hasten a little as she hesitantly crept her hand closer to my cock, which had now swelled to its fullest with excitement as it pressed firmly against my shorts.

When she finally reached it, she gave a gentle squeeze and then rubbed her hand in a circular motion over it.

I was blatantly aware (and I'm sure she was, too) that this had been the furthest we'd gone yet. A decently big step, considering our history. And yet, it didn't feel weird at all. It felt *right*.

She proceeded to softly rub away, silently staring out at the water, until I could no longer resist. We had waited far too long and the time had finally come. I wrapped an arm around her lower waist, another around the back of her neck, and passionately kissed her on the lips.

Chapter Sixteen

Tara responded with light moans of consent before flinging her arms over my shoulders and pulling herself into me.

Barging our way back inside the bungalow, we remained intertwined in each other's grasps. It was as if we had waited so long now that we didn't want to waste another second apart, and I attempted to blindly lead us into the master bedroom while remaining glued to her soft, luscious lips.

When we finally stumbled our way into the bedroom, I placed her down on the bed. Her massive tits were on display for what they truly were—two beautiful, perfectly shaped mounds currently perked up by the white top she was wearing.

I pounced on her, picking up right where we left off. Things quickly heated up again, so I decided to make the first big move, knowing fully well that this was where events would officially reach levels of no return.

With that in mind, I still pressed on, grabbing the bottom of her top and gently tugging it upward. To my great satisfaction, she arched her back, silently granting me access to her amazing rack. As I reached the bottom of her tits, she stretched her arms upward, helping me the rest of the way.

I took in the magnificent sight, knowing that it was only about to get even more amazing. Reaching around to grab hold of the back of her white bra, I snapped it off with my thumb and middle finger. She looked impressed, chuckling as it shot off her body from trying to contain her melons.

I revered at the sight before me, goggling at her massive saucers, which almost seemed to be patiently waiting for me to bury my face in them. Her nipples were big, but not too big. They were perfectly shaped, and evenly proportional to the rest of her breasts.

Tara blushed a little, breathing a bit quickly, nervously. "What do you think?"

"I think we're long past being just friends now!"

She giggled cutely, looking calmer and more assured now.

"But seriously, Tara, those are the most beautiful-looking tits I've ever even imagined seeing. They're fucking perfect."

"Well," she began, grinning away at me, "they're all yours."

I gladly accepted her invitation, hastily throwing my shirt off before taking a nosedive into her ample bosom. I squeezed each breast together so that they were tightly smothering my face and sucked on her large nipples one at a time, making them equally hard. Tara gasped and moaned as I pulled and stretched them with my lips.

"Fuck, that's good," she whispered. "Mmm, I can't believe—I can't believe we are doing this. I love it."

I smiled up at her and moved to her lips again, sucking at them for a moment. My kisses trailed downward from there: first pecking at her neck again, then smothering her breasts before gently kissing her soft, toned stomach. When my lips reached just above the waistband of her jean shorts, she quivered slightly.

I grabbed her by her hips and pulled her closer to the edge of the bed. And when I tugged downward on her waistband, she once again silently granted me permission to further explore her body by arching her hips upward. She did a sort of shimmy with her hips as I pulled her tight pants over her thick, round ass.

She was wearing a sexy white thong underneath, which I decided to have a little fun with by pulling it off with my teeth. That ended up not going quite as smoothly as I thought it would, though (it snapped out of my mouth a few times, making Tara laugh, before I gave up and decided to just do it the old-fashioned way). As I grabbed them, she did another little hip thrust, and I slid them off her legs.

Tara was entirely naked now, and she was beautiful through and through, from her amazing tits to her perfect pussy.

I gently began kissing her shaved mound, inching closer to the hood of her clit.

"Nate?" she said suddenly.

I glanced up and noticed she looked nervous again with the realization that I was about to go down on her.

"It's okay, Tara. You're absolutely beautiful—everything about you is. I mean it." I smiled.

And I really did mean it, too; her pussy looked like a treat for me to indulge myself in.

Her looks of apprehension faded, and she nodded before laying her head back.

I proceeded to softly kiss down her smooth mound until finally pressing my lips against her hood, and as soon as I did, she let out a little gasp.

She was already quite wet, which was only turning me further on as I fondled her labia, occasionally lapping away at her clit. Each time my tongue grazed it, her body trembled slightly.

"Oooh . . . yes, just like that," she breathed, thrusting her hips toward my face as I slowly added more pressure to her clit, occasionally sucking on her lips as well.

"Shit . . . oh shit, yes . . . just like that—please don't stop. Fuuuuckkkk," she moaned and grabbed my hair. All apprehension had left her now as she attempted to force my face even further into her, squirming and writhing with bouts of pleasure.

Sensing that she was nearing an orgasm, I kept the same pace with my tongue. My cock was hard as a rock, throbbing against my shorts at the thought of her getting off.

"Oh—oh—ooohhh! It's hap—" she couldn't finish her sentence, instead going silent as she popped her hips up to the ceiling.

I continued lapping away at her sex while her entire body shook, sucking up her sweet nectar, which squeezed from her pussy as she came. A great sense of satisfaction overtook *me*, too, seeing someone who I cared about for so long now get off like this.

"Ohhhh god, yes!" she let out a big gasp, seemingly coming back from a quick trip above the clouds.

I licked her remaining juices and then crawled up the bed to lie with her, still fully hard. She rolled over and intensely kissed me on the lips.

"We should have started doing this ages ago," she whispered. "I'm so happy, Nate. It's not weird at all, right?" she quickly asked.

"Not weird at all," I chuckled at her brief moment of concern. "It's actually the total opposite. It feels right, you know? Like we should have been doing this for years."

Tara's eyes glimmered behind those cute, nerdy glasses she was still wearing. "I agree. I'm just so glad you feel the same." She had a huge grin painted across her face as she crawled down to the bottom of the bed. It was like her orgasm had soothed all her nerves, which were now replaced with an eager excitement.

She leaned over the edge to fiddle with something in the pocket of her shorts on the ground. From this angle, I got a wonderful view of her thick ass. When her head popped back up from over the bed, she was holding a small hair tie. Then she put her silvery-blonde hair back up in its usual messy bun.

"Time for me to go to work." She smirked.

I had a feeling where this was heading and was all for it.

I sat on the edge of the bed as Tara kneeled down, her head between my legs, and then she tugged repeatedly at my shorts and boxers. My penis flung out, and Tara's mouth dropped.

"Oh my . . ." she muttered in awe.

I tried not to smirk at the dazed expression on her face.

She quickly snapped out of whatever trance she was in, though, as she gently caressed me, her soft grip feeling nice and cool around my flushed penis.

"I had a feeling it was big when I felt it earlier," she said, "but I don't think my hands have ever looked so small before."

I glanced down and gave her a sheepish smile, which she returned in such a cute way.

From there, her gaze remained fixated on my own, as she slowly lowered her mouth to my cock, eventually encasing the head entirely in it.

She swirled her tongue around my head a few times, teasing me in an amazing, yet torturous kind of way before sliding her entire head further down my shaft. The warmth from her breath, the wetness from the inside of her mouth, it all felt amazing as she traveled further and further down my cock.

She made it about halfway before coming up, gasping for air.

"Wow, it really is big," she breathed, twisting her hand around my now lubed-up penis.

I laughed, not necessarily complaining about the morale-boost. "You know, for a virgin, you sure can handle it pretty well, though.

She smiled up at me. "It's probably because you taste amazing."

"I'm glad you like it," I groaned. "You don't have to take it all, though, I promise—"

"No, I got this," she said determinedly as she swallowed it again. This time the warmness of her mouth traveled all the way down my shaft, almost to the tip of my balls. It felt so good that I couldn't help myself from grabbing her messy bun and gently edging her head just a little further down.

She made a small gurgling noise and quickly came back up, once again gasping for air.

"Sorry," I quickly muttered. "Got a little carried away. You okay?"

"I'm great," she coughed, grinning as she jerked me off a little more. "Don't apologize. I love your cock, really."

She continued impressively slurping away at it, surprisingly making her way down lower and lower until she was practically sucking on my balls (the back of her throat felt absolutely amazing as she devoured me).

When she finally came up for air, her eyes lit up with another idea. "Just bear with me. We have a lot of catching up to do, and I want to do it all."

Seeing this side of Tara had me throbbing for her. It was like I was witnessing her transformation happen right in front of my eyes, from a slightly hesitant virgin to an adventurous and bold lover.

This thought had just passed when Tara heaved her tits up above my cock and then lowered them back down over it, immersing my penis entirely within the crevasse between her breasts. She then spit on it a few times before sliding her tits up and down repeatedly over my shaft.

"Holy fuck, Tara."

"Yeah, you like that?" she asked, grinning up at me.

"Fuck, yes."

She sped up the pace of her sliding, a look of hunger in her green eyes that told me she was thirsty for my cum. For a second, the tempting thought of exploding all over those sexy glasses of hers crossed my mind. But I didn't want to finish just yet, we hadn't gotten to the best part. I've been putting off sex with Tara for way too long now, and there was no way I was going to wait any longer. I wanted to officially claim her virginity.

"Tara," I breathed.

"Yeah?" she asked, stopping the amazing thing that she was doing and looking a little concerned.

"Oh—it's nothing wrong with what you were doing, trust me. Actually, that was incredible. But there's no way I can allow myself to cum before . . . the main event." I smiled.

Tara smiled back, but a bit nervously again. "I'd like that, too," she whispered, climbing over me.

I flipped her on her back before throwing myself over her, intensely kissing her neck again. I couldn't be more ready for it, but as I leaned my cock closer to her opening, I felt that her legs remained pressed together in a closed-off sort of way.

"Everything okay?" I asked.

"Yeah," she said. I noticed she was shaking a little.

"We don't have to, Tara, if—"

"No, no, I want to," she began. "I promise. It's just . . ."

"Nervous?" I concluded, to which she nodded.

I made the mistake of letting a slight chuckle slip out.

"What's so funny?!" she exclaimed softly.

"Nothing!" I quickly said, trying to immediately erase my grin. "Not funny at all, I promise. It's just . . . you were literally taking my cock down your throat like a champ. And you gave me the most amazing tit-job, of all things. So, I guess seeing you nervous about this—it kind of made me chuckle, because it seems like you're already a pro, to be honest. You're a natural!"

"Oh! Well, a girl can watch porn, you know! And I may have practiced with . . . things." She blushed, appearing as if she'd already regretted saying that.

I smirked. "I always had a feeling you had a kinky side."

She playfully rolled her eyes and gave me a sheepish look. "I hope that's not a problem?"

"No, not at all. I fucking love it. But I'll go slow. We can go at whatever pace you are comfortable with, okay?"

She beamed at me. "Yeah, okay." And then she opened her legs, offering herself up to me.

I slowly leaned my hips forward, gently pressing the tip of my penis against her opening. She was still soaking wet, but I knew it would be best to ease into things, so I reached around to grab my cock, and then slowly rubbed it in a small circular motion against her pussy. It was once again torturous fun, but Tara seemed to absolutely love it. Her face was practically drooling with an intense smile as her eyes occasionally rolled back a little.

I continued doing this for as long as I could bear it (which was maybe thirty seconds, max), before finally shifting myself inward, just slightly. The tip of my penis gently entered her, and she made a quiet, high-pitched noise. Her face was tight with tension as she clenched her jaw.

"Is this all right?" I checked.

She smiled and gulped, quickly nodding her head. "Yeah. Just go slow, okay?"

I nodded and smiled back, trying my best to comfort her at this moment. Making this night special and memorable for her was my primary concern, no matter what.

I carefully pressed my hips further into her, and she clutched tightly at the back of my shoulders. Even though her pussy felt ready for me, her mind still needed some time, so I continued to do some slow mini-thrusts for now, repeatedly and rhythmically entering her just past the head of my penis before sliding back out.

Tara's face eased up after a few minutes of this, and her smile returned. "I can't—believe—we are doing—this," she happily whispered over the quiet squishing sounds coming from each subtle thrust forward.

"I know," I replied, struggling with all my power to restrain myself from going any deeper for now, "not that I'm complaining."

"Me neither," she agreed, and then, to my pleasant surprise, threw her hands around my ass and pressed me a little further inward.

I took that as an encouraging sign and responded by easing in just a bit further with each thrust as I passionately kissed her on the lips. This seemed to open her further up, and she moaned into me, our tongues entwined.

With each passing second, she felt warmer, wetter. My thrusting drove deeper and deeper, until it wasn't long before I was practically fully inside her hot, snug sex.

When I finally took a break from her moist lips, I gazed at her and noticed that her cheeks were slightly flushed, her eyes closed shut, and she had the biggest smile on her face. It made me ecstatic to see her enjoying me, and she was handling my cock surprisingly well, so I picked up the pace a bit.

"Oh! Fuck, yes—" she moaned, clenching my upper back with her fingers.

"You like that?" I breathed.

"Yes—yes—yes!" she belted out as I continued to now hammer away at her. "You feel so fucking good! It's perfect. I love your big cock inside me!"

Hearing Tara talk dirty to me like that awoke something within me that I couldn't quite explain. I felt so unified with her at this moment, like I knew the exact pace and force to thrust away at her, in order to give her the absolute best experience I possibly could. It was like a sixth sense—sex instincts, or something.

"Shiiiitttt!" she let out, smiling away with her mouth half opened and her eyes rolling back. "How do you know exactly what I need—before I even do?!" she gasped.

We continued to go at it like this for quite some time, occasionally changing up our rhythm from slow to fast and back to slow again, as our hips danced the night away in unison. For a good while, the only sounds in the room were our heavy breathing, the squishing from her wet sex, and the intense moans bundled with the rapid clapping of our flesh smacking together when I'd speed things back up again.

It was during another slow, rhythmic session, though, where I noticed Tara's breathing really started to pick up, and she was clutching at my back again, even tighter than before.

"Nate—I think—I think it's . . . again! Oh, oh fuck!" As she heavily breathed away, I noticed her pussy somehow becoming even wetter than it had been.

I kept my motions the same, but whatever this "sex instinct" was that I was getting told me to speed up my pace. And it hadn't steered me wrong yet, so that's exactly what I did.

"Mmmm," she whimpered. "Oh! Oh, yes. Fucking hell!" she continued as I kept pounding away at her.

Seeing Tara like this started bringing me to my edge now, too.

"Fuck, Tara—I'm gonna cum," I blurted out, thrusting harder and faster, "gonna cum hard!" I slid my hands underneath her bountiful ass and grasped hold of each cheek before lifting her lower half up about an inch off the bed.

"Me too! Me too! Don't stop! Please, don't stop! Cum in me, Nate! I want all of you inside me!" Her soaking wet walls contracted tightly around my cock as she went mute with pleasure again.

Throwing caution to the wind, that was all I needed to take me to the finish line and further beyond. I gave a huge plunge forward as I shot what was quite possibly the largest load of my life into her. I could feel multiple jets of my seed launch out of my cock as I let out a satisfying groan before resuming my final thrusts.

Meanwhile, Tara's inner walls were still pulsing away, sucking up whatever was left over as she once again returned to reality, gasping heavily.

I slowly pulled out of her and rolled over on my back to lie down next to her. We remained like this for a minute or two, breathing heavily, and then I finally looked over to see her lying there with a tranquil expression on her face, her hands caressing her lower stomach.

"That was . . ." I began, still at a loss for words.

"Heavenly," she said, her eyes still shut behind those adorable glasses.

"I'll say," I agreed.

Tara rolled over to look at me. "You don't regret it now, do you?"

"Absolutely not," I said strongly. "I've wanted to do this for a while now, Tara. And if I would have known it'd be like that —well—I don't know if I would've been able to wait as long as we did."

Her lips curled to a grin. "Are you sure you don't regret anything else? Like one tiny, yet not so tiny, load?"

My eyes widened; I was so immersed in the moment that I'd almost forgotten I'd finished in Tara . . . a lot.

"Oh, shit!" I let out. "That was definitely *not* tiny, was it?"

"The load?" giggled Tara. "No, not tiny at all. In fact, I think I feel a couple of pounds heavier," she joked. "But the concern over getting me knocked up? I would say that's pretty small, and not to worry about it—I'm on the pill."

"Ah, okay—uh, not that I was worried, though, or anything."

I must have done a terrible job of sounding convincing, because Tara scoffed and rolled her eyes.

"Please, I know your 'Oh fuck' face by now, Nate," she chuckled. "Don't worry, I think we are good."

For the next hour or so, we simply stayed in bed, lying naked together. It was nice, and just felt so easy. Somehow, I was simultaneously feeling like nothing had really changed between us, but also everything had. I felt even closer to Tara than ever before. I'd known her for most of my life, but there was this whole other side of her that was hidden from me. And I was thankful that she finally revealed it as I replayed it all back in my mind, like a favorite scene out of my favorite movie.

Sure enough, just mentally replaying it seemed to spring life back into my cock as it rested up against one of Tara's ass cheeks (I was currently the big spoon). I was getting ready to ask her if she'd be up for another round when she spoke out.

"Nate," she softly began, still facing the wall. "Tonight really meant a lot to me."

I was a little taken aback by this, but more than happy to hear it.

"It meant a lot to me too, Tara," I replied, stroking the back of her blonde hair.

"This may sound kind of crazy. And please don't think I'm a weird virgin clinger or anything," she continued on, "but I love you, Nate. I've loved you for most of my life, to some degree, but now I don't know. It's just been, like, amplified or something."

I remained silent, a little shocked, but overwhelmed with joy. She had never said that to me before.

"Oh, hell!" she groaned, still staring at the wall. "You think I'm weird as fuck now, don't you?!"

"No, no!" I quickly spoke out. "I'm sorry, I just wasn't expecting that." I propped myself up over her so that my eyes met hers. "The truth is, I love you too. I mean, like you said, I kinda always have, really. But I know exactly what you mean—now it just feels like it's on a whole new level."

She gazed through me for a second, her eyes behind her glasses appearing to be a little glassy, even.

"Thank God that it's not just me," she breathed. "You have no idea how happy it makes me to hear that from you."

I gave her a comforting smile and kissed her softly on the lips before lying back down and holding her tightly, our naked bodies firmly locked together.

It was the perfect end to a monumental day, one that neither of us would ever forget.

Chapter Seventeen

I WOKE up the next morning with a smile forged on my face. It was one of those mornings where it takes the sleepy mind a minute to remember the details of the night before, and then when you do, you just hope that it all wasn't a dream. But this was one of those rare times where it actually was real.

I rolled over to see Tara still snoozing away. Usually, I'd be the one to sleep in, but I must have worked up an appetite the prior night because the rumbling of my stomach woke me up. So I crawled out of bed and quietly got dressed.

As I walked out onto our back deck, I noticed the weather had changed a bit compared to the day before. It was a cloudy gray morning, with a steady breeze blowing that made for some choppy water. But even though the water was more active today, the boardwalk along the distant shore was quiet and calm, no longer bustling with the energy the prior night had brought with it.

Pulling out my phone to check the time, it showed a little past eight. Most of the resort was probably still asleep, the perfect opportunity to head on the strip and beat the crowd for some breakfast.

"Tara," I whispered to my naked bombshell of a girlfriend. She was still lying in bed, her face buried in her pillow and her mane of tousled hair spread out everywhere.

"Ugh," she groaned into her pillow.

"You want to go get some food?" I asked.

"Ugh," she groaned again, this time waving her hand in a way that told me to go on without her (at least that's the way I took it), so I left the bedroom, found a pen and piece of paper in the kitchen, and left a note for her that read:

Went out to search for food. Be back in a bit! :)

P.S. Last night was amazing, also I really dig your sex hair.

It took me about ten minutes to get there, and when I arrived, I decided to meander to a donut shop that I had noticed the night before while walking to dinner, called Donutz Delightz.

A few other early bird runics were up and about, most of them cheerfully smiling while sporting their flowers and wishing me a happy Ehtele'mele, which I joyfully reciprocated.

It seemed that most of the runics who were already out had the same thing in mind, because the donut shop had a line running out the door.

And I quickly found out why. Upon entering the small shop, I was smacked in the face with the aroma of fresh baked goods, vanilla, and various spices, all of them making my stomach rumble with anticipation.

When it comes to donuts, I can never decide on which ones to get, so I just did the sensible thing and ordered two dozen, one of each, ranging from a blue frosted with sprinkles to a Long John with custard. There were even some purple frosted donuts in the shape of flowers for the holiday.

My original intention was to save them all for when I got back. That way Tara could try each one, too. As it turned out, though, I was just fooling myself. I ate four of them by the time I made it back to the bungalow.

"There you are! Ooo, are those donuts?" Tara bolted upright on the living room couch. She was wearing a pink cami top and pink shorts to go with it, looking like a tastier treat than any donut in the box.

"Only the finest!" I said.

We ended up eating the donuts outside on the back deck as the sun started to poke through some gaps in the thick clouds.

"For a second I thought you hit it and quit it on my ass!" said Tara, grinning as she took a bite out of one of the flower-shaped donuts.

"Yeah, I've known you my whole life, and *now* I decide to bail?" I said with sarcasm. "If anything, I would have left your ass after you accidentally punched me in the face back when we were twelve."

"Did I tell you that was an accident?" She smirked. "Yeah, let's go with that, then, sure!"

I chuckled and shook my head in amusement. "I tried to get you up this morning, but you were out cold. Did you read my note?"

"I did," Tara laughed. "I loved it. And I agree—last night was just, well, I thought I was waking up from an amazing dream this morning, I'll just say that."

"Me too. It was one of the best nights of my life, Tara."

She smiled amorously. "You know," she slowly began, "I wouldn't be totally against another round."

Almost instantly, the swelling feeling around my crotch ensued, causing the box of donuts resting on my lap to rise a few inches.

"Like, right now?" I asked for confirmation, to which she gave a slow and ornery nod. "Guess I need to come back with donuts more often!"

It was as if, now that the floodgates had opened, we simply couldn't get enough of each other. We wanted to make up for all the lost time by sexually exploring one another in every way possible, and so we eagerly scampered our way back into the bedroom, where we spent the next three hours doing exactly that.

It was a vigorous, passionate three hours of hot, sweaty sex, with plenty of spontaneous affairs during, ranging from me fucking Tara's bountiful tits (which I absolutely could not get enough of) to her riding me like a sex-deprived bunny. Needless to say, her apprehension about sex was now clearly a thing of the past.

But perhaps the most interesting part of it all was the fact that my *sex instinct* had once again taken over, confirming that I wasn't imagining things the night before. It was too much of a coincidence now. At first, I had boiled it down to me just paying close attention to Tara's body and her reactions. But it was more than that. It was like she said the night before—I seemed to know what she needed before *she* even did, somehow.

I mean, I don't like to toot my own horn, but I always felt like I was at least decent at sex. However, this was now on a whole new level. Tara's bouts of intense pleasure and sexual contractions around my cock told me she came around half a dozen times before I had finished once.

It was almost hard to believe, really. But I figured it was best not to question it. On the contrary, I was grateful for this extra instinct of mine—it allowed me to satisfy Tara in a way that made it look like her soul was being sucked out of her body.

And it took us about an hour of laying in bed, trying to rejuvenate, before we decided to get on with the rest of our day, mainly because my stomach let out a roar that made Tara laugh.

"I swear, your stomach is more vocal than your mouth. Work up an appetite again already?" she asked, rubbing her hand through my chest hair.

"How could I not?" I chuckled.

"I have to agree," she admitted. "I could really go for a fat, juicy burger right about now."

I fixated on her with subtle shock. "Now you're sounding like me!"

"What can I say?" She shrugged. "A girl can only cum so many times before she needs to refuel. After about the third orgasm, a salad was off the table for tonight."

"If my girl wants a burger," I chuckled, "a burger she shall get."

"Oh, Nate!" Tara blurted out later that afternoon as we strolled down the strip. "Let's hit up the carnival while we're here! We *have* to! I love them!" She was pointing at the Ferris wheel in the distance, bouncing up and down like an excited kid.

"Yeah, sure!" I cracked a smile seeing her giddy like that over a carnival. "And they'll have all kinds of food there, I'm sure. Sounds like a plan to me!"

So we made our way down the entire strip, which was getting busier again by the minute, before finally entering the fairgrounds at the end of it.

The smell of various fried foods filled the air, along with the chirping of carnival music. The grounds were packed with runics, from couples celebrating their nights out together to families with young children.

The first thing Tara and I did was hit up a small vendor selling hot dogs and burgers. I was stunned when we both decided to order the foot-long and burger with fries combo. Tara clearly wasn't joking when she alluded to working up an appetite earlier.

We ended up sitting down at a small table under a tent next to the vendor to enjoy our late lunch.

"I swear, I can never look at you eating a hot dog the same way, especially a foot-long," I joked, goggling at her from across the table.

"Don't be jealous now," she covered her mouth and muttered after taking another bite, "if you play your cards right, this can be you later." And she shoved about half the dog down her throat for a second bite, smiling innocently.

"You'll choke!" I shouted with genuine concern but couldn't keep a serious face.

After she finished chewing, she finally added, "I'm used to *that* by now."

I shook my head and scoffed in an amused manner.

We finished our food and then strolled around the fairgrounds, taking in the scene and all that it had to offer. There were plenty of rides and games to play, some that I knew from back home, like the squirt gun game and the one where you throw darts at the balloons. But then there were also some games I wasn't familiar with, most likely of orc or elf origin. One particularly interesting game revolved around chucking a spear through three rows of rotating hoops.

The prizes at the spear game happened to be the best, too—stuffed animals of various Kingdom Monsters. And sure enough, on the top row of the prizes sat an unmistakable red dragon with yellow eyes: Drakthor.

Tara was eyeing it discreetly as we dawdled past the game. It was obvious she wanted it but didn't want to be a bother by asking.

"That Drakthor is coming home with us tonight," I said determinedly, and Tara smiled brightly.

"You really think you can win him?!"

"Yeah, sure," I said casually and confidently, waving at the air.

"Step right up! Step right up!" yelled the carny in front of the game, a shady-looking, thin, pale orc, with his greasy black hair slicked back over his head. "Think you got what it takes to win big?" he smoothly asked me.

"Sure, maybe!" I replied. "What's it take to win Drakthor?"

"Ah, a good eye you got there. Not too hard, you'll have to throw the spear through three hoops in a row to get that guy. Care for a try?"

I glanced at Tara, who was eyeing the dragon hopefully, and then back at the rows of revolving hoops, rotating continuously like three wind turbines—three hoops to a row, and three different rows, but all the rows were revolving at different speeds, so the hoops in each row weren't lining up very frequently; I would have to time it out perfectly. That being said, they weren't revolving very fast, so as long as I was patient enough, it was very doable.

"I'll give it a try!" I decided. "How much?" I had noticed that the games were one of the few things on the entire resort that didn't come included with the package.

"Just five gems!" the carny said cheerfully.

I knew by now that gems were the form of currency that orcs used in their home world, and preferred to use in the Realm, it seemed. But I still was partial to paying for things with cash, if possible.

"Um—you take human money?" I asked.

"Eh, yeah, that'll do. Ten dollars is all."

I scoffed quietly, wide eyed. Ten dollars for one throw was not cheap, but Tara really wanted that dragon, so I paid the sketchy-looking carny, and he handed me a spear.

I was just starting to aim, carefully paying attention to the way the rows of rings were lining up, when they suddenly sped up to the point where they all blended together.

I lowered my spear and gave the carny a hardened look. "Really?" I asked, unamused.

He sneered and shrugged his shoulders.

All I could do was shake my head at the orc and try to regain my focus on the now rapidly spinning hoops. And when I finally took my throw, the spear barely made it through the first hoop before the wooden rim of the hoop knocked it off its course and down to the ground.

"Oh! So close!" blurted the carny with a slimy grin. "One hoop gets you a key chain, though!"

He pulled out a tiny, cheap-looking key chain shaped like a spear from underneath the front booth; it was chipped and made of plastic.

"This is nice, Nate!" said Tara, trying her best to force a smile. "Thank you!"

"I'll try again," I muttered, now more determined than ever (and also a little ticked off) after seeing how this carny liked to operate.

"Nate, no, it's expensive."

"I think I got this."

"Ten more dollars—thank you!" said the carny happily.

Sure enough, the rotating hoops sped up once again.

This time I was ready for it, though, and I had a strategy. If this carny was going to play things shady, then I would just have to stoop down to his level.

During the prior round, I had noticed the wooden rotors at the center of each propeller were what made the hoops spin. So, if I could somehow slow those down without this orc noticing...

I hadn't tried it yet, but I had a feeling it was possible. If I could pull things in and push things away using the Telekinesis Spell, then I could probably also control the movements of objects in other ways, like slowing the rotational speed of these rotors, for example.

It would be a challenging task, considering I didn't have my staff with me. And I'd also have to concentrate all my energy on slowing them down, while still somehow focusing on my aim and timing.

The rings spun away, almost taunting me, though, so I had to at least give it a try.

I focused on sensing the rune around the three rotors, eventually compressing it down upon them. To my great satisfaction and pleasant surprise, they began to slow, and so did the many individual rings.

"Wait a second," the shady orc mumbled to himself, seemingly catching on.

"Oh, what's that?" Tara's voice rang out curiously from behind me, pulling the carny's attention away from the rings for just a second.

This was my chance: I immediately chucked the spear (projecting it even faster than I could naturally throw it with a little extra telekinetic push), through a brief opening where the three rows of rings had aligned.

The greasy orc turned back around just in time to see my spear fly through the rings and wedge tightly into the back wall behind them.

"You did it!" Tara cheered. "We'll take the Drakthor, please!"

We swiftly departed the tent, Tara happily holding her Drakthor stuffed animal while the carny was left staring us down suspiciously.

"You know," Tara began, smirking up at me, "you didn't have to do that for me."

"Sure did! I saw you eyeing up that little Drakthor from a mile away."

"Was it that obvious? Well—just look at the little guy!" She held him out with straight arms, marveling at the little red dragon. "He's so cute! Thanks, Nate. I really do appreciate it . . . even if you did have to cheat to get him."

"You caught on, huh?" I said with a grin.

"Obviously!" she giggled.

"Well, what can I say?" I pleaded sheepishly. "He was more than happy to take my money before mentioning the rings would be speeding up like that. And technically, he never mentioned anything about not being able to use the rune for help."

"Hey, no qualms here!" She put on a high-pitched, adoring voice. "I'm just happy I got you, aren't I? Such a cute little guy!"

"Thanks, I try," I muttered, knowing very well that she was referring to the stuffed animal.

Tara rolled her eyes playfully and shrugged her shoulders. "You're not too bad yourself, I suppose!"

There were plenty of different rides and vendors throughout the large fairgrounds, and Tara and I spent the better part of the next couple of hours exploring as much of it as we could, from enjoying a little roller coaster, to relaxing on a peaceful swan boat ride that slowly took us around a bay which branched off from the fairgrounds, finally ending the evening with a funnel cake to split between us and a ride on the Ferris wheel.

We both basked in the magnificent view, nearly at the highest point of the Ferris wheel. We could see the entire island and the ocean that stretched out for miles beyond it, which was becoming darker with the onset of night.

It happened when I was looking down at the distant ground, taking a mental guess as to how high up we were. It was like someone suddenly pulled my arm up for me, causing me to catch something squishy in my bare hand just inches in front of Tara's head. To my surprise, she was just as caught off guard as I was—nobody had pulled my hand up for me.

The something I had caught turned out to be a deep-fried cookie, and the two troublemakers in the cart directly above us, a pair of young boys cackling away, quickly ducked down in their seats making it quite clear who had been the culprits to throw it.

Tara figured it out too, and was shouting up at them angrily, saying things like "that's very rude!" and "where are your parents!" Meanwhile, I was still struck dumbfounded, staring at the crumbling cookie in my hand and trying to figure out what the hell just happened.

It was like my body knew the cookie was coming at her and reacted before my mind had any clue as to what was going on. But how? Was this some sort of new sorcerer ability manifesting? Dean Celestine had mentioned before about being able to sense incoming danger, but we had yet to learn exactly how to do it in her class.

The two kids in the cart ahead of us managed to get out and escape before ours had reached the ground, which was probably a good thing, considering Tara was still fuming.

"I mean, honestly!" she belted out beside me as we left the grounds to head back to our place. "You try to enjoy a nice couple days off and almost get splattered in the face with a cookie!"

I was only half paying attention, though, muttering a couple of one-worded answers and nodding apathetically while still staring with wonder at my hand that had caught the cookie.

Could this be linked to my recent *sex instinct*? Was I starting to somehow subconsciously react to things in a way that guaranteed my success and safety?

About halfway back through the strip, the night clouds, which were highlighted by the largest of the three moons above them, grew thicker and darker over the ocean. Rain was surely coming, and we just barely managed to make it back to the bungalow before the light sprinkles turned to a heavy downpour.

"Phew!" Tara sighed, wiping her bangs out of her eyes. "Talk about a close one."

"Yeah, I'll say," I agreed, walking over to the glass sliding door. The raindrops were causing the noctillia to stir even more than usual, creating a vivid light show in the surrounding water.

I felt Tara's arm around my shoulder. "Sucks that we'll be leaving tomorrow. I feel like we just got here," she whispered into my ear.

"Same here. Back to reality, I guess."

"And finals before we know it," groaned Tara. "And then the final project for the Quester program, too, which we still don't even know all the details on, other than that it'll be similar to the Questing Games. Kinda has me a little nervous, to be honest."

"Ugh, I don't even want to think about all of that," I admitted. "This semester has *definitely* been tougher. Even in my Rune Sensing class—I still haven't figured out the damn Cloning Spell."

"That's the spell sorcerers can use to generate a copy of themselves, right?" asked Tara curiously.

"Yeah, and apparently you can use it to copy others, too." I muttered before plopping onto the living room couch. "But how can I do that when I can't even copy a version of myself?"

"You'll get it, Nate," Tara encouraged me as she sat down by my side. "I know you will."

"Thanks." I gave her a warm smile. "I think it has to do with the meditation crap. If it was just a matter of casting the spell, I think I'd be set. But the meditating thing is throwing me for a loop. Back when Dawn tried to help me, I was able to see what her mytosomes looked like, so I thought that'd help at least a little with trying to get a feel for my own mytosomes, but guess not. I think I just suck at meditating, really."

"Well, maybe I could help you there!" Tara brightly said, perking up on the couch.

"You think?"

"Yeah! We always meditate when trying to learn a new spell in my healing classes. But we do it to help with sensing our internal rune, instead of our mytosomes, like you're trying to do. It's probably the *one* thing I'm not the worst at in my class!"

"Tara, I'm sure you're not the worst at—"

But she had stopped me mid-sentence to stand up from the couch, pulling me with her.

"Come on! Have a seat next to me."

"Agh, I don't know," I began, remembering very well what happened the last time someone tried to help me with meditation.

"It'll be okay! We can do it together," she assured. "And it's not like I'm inviting you to read my mind. We'll both just be meditating. I'll show you how I do it. I actually need to meditate on my internal rune to help master the Invisibility Spell. Like I said yesterday, I've only been able to do it once before, and it was just for a blink of a second, not to mention half my body was still visible. So meditating together will be helping me, too!"

"Well," I pondered slowly, "if it's to help you, too, then I guess—"

"Great! Come!" She patted the ground next to her eagerly.

"Now," she softly began, closing her eyes while sitting Indian style next to me, "all I want you to do is focus on your breathing. Take deep, slow breaths, paying attention to nothing other than those breaths. This will help anchor your attention to the present moment. That's what meditation is all about, simply being present."

From there, she went mute, her breaths getting louder and slower as she breathed intentionally, with purpose.

I mimicked her to a T, trying to remain open-minded. But to be honest, I had attempted the breathing technique plenty of times by now and had gotten nowhere with it, so I wasn't entirely surprised when about ten minutes went by with no results; not even a single, split-second image of my mytosomes popped into my mind.

Meanwhile, Tara didn't seem to be faring much better. This may have been half the issue for me, but I kept occasionally opening an eye to sneak a peek over at her, hoping I'd instead see nothing where she sat. But there she remained, apparent and as beautiful as ever.

The minutes continued to roll by as we sat in silence, the only sound being the steady fall of rain against the roof of our bungalow. And I was just about to call it quits when a thought occurred.

The strange thing was that it didn't quite feel like *my* thought. But instead felt like someone else was trying to hand me *their* thoughts, revolving around the only other sound besides our breaths: the rain.

Was the rain going to be the key to both of our successes tonight? Was that weird extra sense thing occurring again? It certainly felt like a thought that wouldn't be typical of my own mind. Or maybe it was my thought, and now I was just losing it, unsure of what was coming from my own brain and what wasn't.

Regardless, it couldn't hurt to give it a try.

"Tara . . ." I quietly broke the silence.

"I'm *trying* to breathe," she softly murmured.

"Trying to—?" I stammered. "Look, I have another idea, if you're willing to give it a try."

She opened her eyes and rubbed them clear. "Sure! I'm all ears if you think you have an idea that could work."

"Well, no promises, but what if instead of listening to our breathing, we focused on the rain outside—like the sound of it against the roof?"

Tara pursed her lips in thought and then shrugged her shoulders. "Sure! Whatever you think might work for you! I'll give it a try, too. It *does* sound pretty soothing."

So we closed our eyes yet again, hoping for different results.

Minutes continued to melt away as I listened to the rain fall above us. Tara was right—it really was peaceful. It had a way of blending everything together, making everything else around us seem so distant, too, like we were encompassed in it, separated entirely from the world around us as we peacefully sat, mentally bathing in it.

I wasn't sure if I was imagining things, but an odd sensation began to occur—it was like the rain was becoming more and more immersive, while everything around me became fainter. Even Tara, to me, now seemed as if she was in a different world from my own rainy, peaceful container.

The realization hit me like a truck, that *this* must be what it feels like to be truly present.

Thinking to myself that maybe this was actually working, I then shifted my focus to my mytosomes, trying to feel them out and connect with them. I thought back to how they looked inside Dawn, when I had been reading her memories, and then tried to visualize that same image within my own body, the tiny cell-looking things, as they slightly vibrated about.

336

My suspicions that things were starting to actually work were finally confirmed a few minutes later, when images began to manifest within my mind.

At first, I thought it was all just my imagination, but as I focused harder, the images slowly came further into view, clear and vivid enough to remove any remaining doubt.

There they were, vibrating about in front of my closed eye view, almost as if they were right in front of me: little cellular things, very similar to Dawn's mytosomes. The main difference being that they seemed to be more condensed and were buzzing about in a more active way. I couldn't help wondering if this had to do with me having a higher mytosome count than Dawn.

My eyes snapped open with excitement. "Tara! I—"

But I was left at a loss for words at the sight before me (or rather, the lack of sight). It was as if I was suddenly the only person in the room.

"Tara! Holy shit—Tara! I think—I think you did it!" I hollered out to the air, baffled.

"Wait, really?" Tara's voice rang out next to me, and then a gasp. "Oh my gosh, you're right!"

"Holy hell, this is trippy!" I laughed, glancing aimlessly around the room.

"You're telling me! I'm looking down at my hands right now but can't see a thing! It feels so weird!"

"But how are you able to even make your clothes disappear, too?!"

"That's all part of it!" said her voice, excitedly. "I use the internal rune to first cloak myself in this layer of invisibility, but then I can expand it *just* enough to have it cover my clothes or anything else I'm wearing, like my jewelry!"

Out of nowhere, she reappeared right beside me, staring wildly down at her now visible hands, which she was holding out in front of her face.

"Aw, man!" sighed Tara, blowing her bangs out of her eyes. "I really thought I had it completely under control there for a second."

"Yeah, but still!" I quickly added. "That was definitely longer than just a blink!"

"That's true! And it's all because I focused on the rain this time instead! It was just so peaceful. I thought you said you weren't any good at meditating!"

"To be honest, I think it was just a hunch," I said, still unsure myself if it was actually just a hunch or something more.

"Well, how about you? Any luck?!" she asked.

"Actually, yeah! I think so!" I replied excitedly. "I'll say this much—it's the furthest I've gotten with it so far!"

"That's great, Nate!" She threw herself into my arms. "I knew you could do it."

I scoffed. "I couldn't have done it without you! It was all your idea, after all."

"Yeah, but I don't think we were getting anywhere until you brought up the rain." She looked at me suspiciously. "Are you sure you aren't secretly a meditation guru or something?"

I chuckled. "You've known me practically your whole life. Have you ever seen me sneak away to meditate?"

"Hmmm," she pondered, pursing her lips and tapping her cheek. "Good point, good point."

"I really think it was just a hunch," I repeated. "Maybe."

Tara was grinning at me, giving me a look, one of which I was quickly growing to love.

"Well," she slowly said, jumping to her feet and strutting toward the master bedroom. "I've got a 'hunch,' too. And I think there's only one way to satisfy it." She stopped right in front of the entrance to the bedroom and spun on her heel to look at me. Shooting me a seductive look, she gestured with her finger for me to follow her in.

It was an amazing way to conclude one of the best weekends of my life, as we spent the better part of the following couple of hours fucking the night away, without a care in the world. During which, I witnessed Tara climaxing another three or four times before I managed to finish deep inside her yet again.

But even besides the sex, it was still a fantastic weekend, one that brought mine and Tara's relationship to new heights, both physically and emotionally.

Perhaps one of the more underrated parts of the trip was the fact that we were able to help further one another's abilities. This was something that would surely benefit us both during the remainder of the semester, especially for the upcoming final project. But as I lay in bed, holding tightly to Tara's smooth, naked body, I tried to push those thoughts to the back of my head.

Maybe it was from the meditating, or just the fact that I felt truly content right now, but I wanted to bask in the remaining few hours I had with her here, simply being in the moment.

And that was exactly what I did.

Chapter Eighteen

OVER THE COURSE of the next few weeks, I continued having the random experiences of whatever this extra sense of mine was.

There was the time when Tara and I were flying back from Kharador, where our griffin flew directly into a flock of geese, and I somehow was able to sense the large birds coming beforehand and duck (no pun intended) us down before they flew right over our heads, preventing what would have been a very painful start to our flight home.

But then there were a few other occasions too, most of them being on the trivial side—like when I was walking to one of my classes on campus and somehow knew to take an alternative route, only later finding out that my usual route was blocked by a small group of runics protesting against something called Lenders, whatever that meant.

Maybe the most beneficial part of it all, though, was the fact that it was starting to help me in my classes. One of my favorite cases being a time where Professor Kravitz tried to purposely trick me with the way he worded a question on parrying attacks, which I answered correctly, leaving him dumbfounded and silent.

It was, without a doubt, becoming a very helpful tool of mine, and even though I still couldn't call upon it at will, it had occurred often enough now to where I became confident in knowing the difference between my own thoughts and whatever this extra sense was.

I considered bringing it up to Dean Celestine multiple times, just to be sure that it was nothing potentially harmful. But every time I got close to telling her, something held me back. Perhaps it was because I wanted to be absolutely sure that the thoughts weren't coming directly from my own mind (which, by now, I was pretty damn sure of it), or even the fear that Dean Celestine would tell me that it was dangerous and to stop listening to it.

Regardless, though, its increase in frequency and blatancy had reached the point where I felt the conversation could no longer be delayed. So, as I entered my Rune Sensing and Manipulation class one rainy Wednesday afternoon in late March, I had a whole speech planned for Dean Celestine, one that I hoped increased my odds of her approving my use of the extra instinct.

The class started the same way that it had been every day for the past two weeks, with all the students practicing the Cloning Spell, which thanks to both Tara and Dawn, I now had a pretty good grasp on.

Initially, I had struggled with it, but after finally mastering meditation and learning the basic structure of my mytosomes, I quickly excelled at using it.

And now, not one, but two identical copies of myself stood in front of me waving at each other. I even had a pretty good understanding of how to control them by now, as I made them have a basic conversation with each other while I sat idly by, still baffled by it all.

It was one of those things in the Realm that seemed strange to me, even amongst the strangest things I'd often encountered here. There was just something about seeing identical versions of yourself from all angles that I just couldn't get used to.

"Very impressive, Nate," Dean Celestine complimented as she walked by me. "I'd say you're about ready to learn how to clone another individual. We'll be covering that next week for the students who," she gave poor Dak, who could only make one, slightly mutated clone of himself, a disapproving look, "are ready."

She continued strolling around the classroom, reviewing my classmates and their various clones. Most of my fellow students were about on par with me, either generating one successful clone, or even the occasional two.

"Well done, class, well done, indeed," she addressed, making her way toward the front of the room. I knew her well enough by now to know that some sort of announcement was coming.

"Now," she began, somewhat dramatically, "we have reached the point in the year where it's time to plan for your final projects."

I perked up with interest. It was finally here.

As I glanced around the room, I noticed others were intrigued as well.

"As I mentioned earlier in the year," Dean Celestine began, "the project will vary depending on which program you decided to enroll in. I know most of you have submitted to join the Quester program, so I'll start there. The final project for future Questers will consist of an objective. It will be of a similar task to the Questing Games, and you will be expected to complete it in groups of three. You may choose your two partners if you wish, and you are not limited to choosing someone in this specific class. If you do not select your own partners, then be prepared to get randomly paired up. If I may, I suggest you pick partners you are familiar with, as proper team chemistry will surely be required for this."

She paused to look around the room before continuing. "Once you finalize your team information, you will submit it to me, and shortly after that, receive more information on the quest you will be tasked with."

For the remainder of the class, Dean Celestine reviewed the premises of the final projects for the other programs, like the Guard program and the Business program. I was too distracted trying to think of who my third group member would be, though, to pay much attention to her.

Apparently, the final projects were to take place during the last week of school, one week after our finals for our classes. And, if we didn't pass them, we would have to wait an additional semester before trying to get into the program, which would set us way behind, considering internships begin the semester after getting into a program.

These final projects were nothing to take lightly. And as of now, I only had one person in mind for a partner, which was Tara (Dawn was already in the Guard program, so she couldn't be our third).

I skimmed the class, trying to think of someone to add. And as I did, I noticed all of them eyeing me back, especially the other girls in the class. But really, I hadn't gotten to know them all that well, at least not enough to where I'd trust them to mesh with Tara and me while completing some sort of objective.

I guess there was always Dak, but . . . yeah, not Dak.

Before I'd even realized it, class was dismissed, and I realized I'd been so distracted over trying to think of a third teammate that I almost forgot my initial intentions: bringing up that extra instinct to Dean Celestine.

"Hi, Nate!" Dak cut me off on my way up to Dean Celestine's desk. "You wanna group up for the final project?!" he asked enthusiastically.

"Oh—uh . . ." I frantically racked my brain, trying to think of a polite way to turn him down. "Well, I already have somebody in mind, Dak. And I need to talk with them before taking in our third. But maybe ask some of the others for now. I'm sure they could use your . . . strategizing abilities."

Dak fiddled with his glasses proudly. "I *am* a pretty good strategist. Well, if anything changes, just let me know soon, all right? I may go off the market before you know it!"

"Yeah," I said, trying to make myself sound as genuine as possible, "I'm sure you will."

I waited for the rest of the class to funnel out, lingering behind before finally approaching Dean Celestine.

"Ah, young, Nate." Her gaze from behind those sophisticated glasses pierced through me yet again in a way that made me feel like my thoughts were being violated, "Penny for your thoughts?"

"Yes, Professor. Uh, well," I tried to think back to the speech I had prepared, but I suddenly was blanking.

"I was wondering when you'd come to me about it. Took you long enough," she concluded.

"I'm sorry, Professor?" I asked, knowing there was no point in playing dumb.

"The Shield Spell remains neglected in your practices. You still permit me to indulge in that favorite book of mine, I've noticed."

I tried to keep my emotions in check, as I was a little ticked at the realization of her still actively reading my mind. I mean, that had to be some sort of invasion of privacy thing.

"So, you know?" was all I could ask.

Dean Celestine grinned. "About your dwellings with the Sorcerer Sense?"

"Is that what it is?" I asked, feeling relieved that she didn't seem to be surprised or concerned about it.

"I personally like the term 'sex sense' better myself," she suggested, trying to hold back her smile while my face went hot, "but yes, it is more commonly referred to as the Sorcerer Sense—an ability which allows skilled sorcerers to detect incoming threats, or can even be used as a guide to help them in deciding the most optimal route to walk in life. It's a very powerful tool, when used correctly."

"I think I'm starting to see what makes the sorcerer class such a powerful one," I quietly replied.

"Precisely." She smiled subtly. "A sorcerer's close relationship with external rune is what separates them from the rest. External rune is an incredibly powerful and abundant tool in this world, Nate. I'm sure you have learned that by now, though."

I nodded.

"Not only," Dean Celestine continued, "does external rune reside within things like the elements around us, but it is also an entity of itself, existing separate from even the air."

"So," I said slowly, "external rune exists in the air, but also outside of air?"

"Indeed," she replied. "For example, when you use the Telekinesis Spell, you call upon the external rune within the air to pull and push things toward you. But the Shield Spell, for example, is not a layer of air that you are coating over yourself, it is the external rune itself that you are bending. And it is also the external rune *itself* that calls to you, in what we refer to as the Sorcerer's Sense."

"So these thoughts—the thoughts that feel like they're not mine—that's like, the external rune speaking to me?"

"That is exactly what it is," she replied. "I usually save this lecture about external rune being separate from the air for second year students, as well as the Sense. It seems trivial, but it can surprisingly set most novice sorcerers back at first, because it further complicates the nature of external rune. But you are quickly proving to me that you are not to be handled like most of my students. Yes, I should not be surprised that you have managed to figure out the Sense all on your own."

"Well, I wouldn't exactly say I've figured it out. But I think I'm starting to understand it a little better, maybe. It's not dangerous or anything, is it?"

"Anything can be *dangerous*, depending on how it is used. But harmful to the wielder? If it is, I have yet to experience it." She stood up to walk over to the window of the classroom, gazing out at it as she seemed to like to do so much. "No, I don't believe it to be harmful. And that is coming from someone like me, who uses it quite regularly."

"So, how do I learn to use it at will?"

"You remind me so much of myself," she said, amused. "So ambitious to further your abilities as a sorcerer. Or do you just really enjoy leaving Professor Kravitz dumbstruck?" She smiled.

"I was just curious, that's all." I shrugged, smiling back at her. "Seems like a really useful skill."

"Of course. Only natural to be curious. And it is very useful, indeed. But unfortunately, you will find that our use of external rune is often more of a mutual relationship than anything else. We never command the rune, only work with it. The Sorcerer Sense is a perfect example of this. I don't believe it to be possible to use at will. If it is, that would be news to even someone of my stature."

"Oh," I muttered, a little bummed to hear this.

"However," said Dean Celestine, "I've found that if you remain calm, without emotion, the Sense seems to occur more frequently. It is another reason for sorcerers to remain apathetic, specifically during combat."

I was sure that the other reason she was alluding to was the negative rune and how it thrives on darker emotions, like anger.

"Thank you, Professor. Honestly, I'm just glad to hear that it's not harmful."

She smiled at me. "No, I'd say you should be fine to continue using it as it comes about. And next year, you'll just be ahead of the curve, not that you aren't already."

As I was leaving the classroom, Dean Celestine stopped me in my tracks. "Oh, and Nate!" I turned to face her. "Whatever you end up doing, avoid grouping up with that Dak for your final project. I don't think even *you* would be capable of carrying an imbecile like that."

"What are we gonna do?" groaned Tara at lunch the following day, her voice muffled into the table. "The final project is in a month and neither of us can think of a third person for our group. If we fail, we'll be even further behind than we already were this year." She was biting at her finger-nails again.

"You guys really don't have any other friends except for me?" asked Dawn with a smirk. "I don't know whether to be flattered or sad."

Tara scowled at Dawn.

"It'll be okay," I calmly said, trying to soothe Tara's nerves. "We'll focus this week on finding our third, and that'll leave us with a little under a month to prepare for whatever this objective ends up being."

"Honestly, though, Nate, you shouldn't have any issues with finding a third," Dawn pointed out. "I'd imagine that plenty of people would want to be grouped up with the only S-tier on campus. I'd just pick the most talented sorcerer in your Rune Manipulation class and call it quits."

"I thought about it," I admitted, "but I'm thinking skill isn't the only factor here. If it's anything like the Questing Games, we want to make sure our trio gels. I want to be careful with who we pick."

"I get that, probably for the best," Dawn agreed. "Just don't be too picky, though. I'd hate to see you guys miss out on picking someone more talented and getting paired with a random dud."

The thought of us having a Dak as our third made me a little uneasy. But I made sure I didn't show it for Tara's sake.

"There's still plenty of time. We'll find someone. It shouldn't be too hard," I confidently assured them.

As it turned out, though, it ended up being much more diffi-cult than I initially thought. The weeks seemed to churn by as the temperature further warmed up, the grass regained its colorful blue-green hue, and the birds chirped gleefully with the arrival of spring. And yet, we were still just as much without a third person as we were a few weeks prior.

Before I had even realized it, the end of April was upon us, along with the upcoming Questing Games championship match, finals week, and after that, would be our final project.

To make things even worse, it seemed that Dawn was correct to worry about the top prospects being picked early; concerned that we were running out of time, I ended up asking quite a few of the more talented students in some of my classes if they wanted to join as my third. But most of them reluctantly shot me down for different reasons, like them already being in a group, or some of them, to my surprise, not being in the Quester program.

A couple of girls, though, told me that they'd happily bail on their groups to join me, and though tempting, I took that as a sign they couldn't be trusted enough. Not to mention I'd feel bad poaching them from their already established groups so close to the deadline.

To say that things were looking dim would have been an understatement, but worse yet, Dean Celestine pulled me aside after her class one Tuesday afternoon to deliver more bad news.

"So, Nate," she began, gazing her penetrative stare at me that she often did, causing me to quickly put up the Shield Spell around my mind, "I noticed you still haven't submitted your group info for the final project. Decide to take your chances on a couple of randoms, have you?"

"Not quite," I replied. "Well, I have a second. It's just the third that I'm kind of struggling with."

"Your time is hastily expiring, as I'm sure you are aware. May want to settle on one of those lassies who were willing to bail on their friends for you." She grinned, and my heart sunk with the realization that my Shield Spell still wasn't enough to keep someone of her skill out of my head.

"Not really my type, I guess." I shrugged.

"Fair enough," she concurred, standing up to walk over to the window. "I wish that was all I had to speak with you about. But I'm afraid there's more. It would seem that Professor Morran seeks your company this Saturday, for some *extra* lessons, before her final, next week."

"She thinks I need more help in preparing?" I asked, not entirely surprised. She had spoken to me at the end of the first semester about how I barely passed her midterm exam, mainly due to the fact that I had been distracted with trying to break through Sakura's shy wall. And to be honest, this recent semester wasn't much different in that regard.

"It would seem so. Entirely her idea, really. I had nothing to do with the final decision." She had a distinct look in her eye, and I found myself wishing that I could break through *her* Shield Spell at the moment and read her mind.

"But wait!" I blurted out with a sudden realization. "This Saturday is the Questing Games! I was hoping I could go with Dawn and Tara to watch. We have somebody we know who's competing!"

"I'm sorry, Nate," she began, and my heart felt like it dropped into my stomach, "but if any of your other professors are to believe that you need extra help, I should not be one to say otherwise. Everything happens for a reason, though." she added, noticing my not-so-subtle gloom. "At times, the solutions to our problems reside exactly where we don't want to go. . ."

And so, the following Saturday morning began with me very reluctantly parting ways with Dawn and Tara at the quad, as they made their way up to the stadium while I moped my way toward the modern, round, General Studies building.

As I walked through the quad, I passed many groups of my fellow students, all of whom were headed in the opposite direction, thrilled with energy over attending the big match. Some were wearing shirts and hats with their favorite competing teams' logos on them, others carrying signs of different competitors (many were of Zula, who seemed to have gained a pretty large fan base after her performance earlier in the year).

Seeing this only made the Intro to Classes books in my backpack feel heavier while I reluctantly meandered my way into the General Studies building and eventually into Professor Morran's classroom.

"Ah, Mr. Gannon," Professor Morran's familiar voice rang out, "nice of you to join us."

"Hi, Professor," I muttered, looking down at the floor, when it hit me that she said "us."

I glanced up with curiosity, and it was like everything suddenly became brighter. There she was, sitting in the front row next to Professor Morran's desk, with her pink hair in a long braid and current, human-form blue eyes: Sakura, the pink fox shifter.

She was wearing a type of shifter outfit, with the thin material, not quite as tight as Dawn liked to wear it, though. The top was a yellow blouse, and even though it was loose, the outlined shape of her massive breasts still managed to show. As for the bottom, it looked to be a long white skirt that came down to her knees.

I tried to straighten my abrupt smile upon noticing her, since Professor Morran was staring intensely at me in a way that told me she knew exactly how I'd feel about Sakura being here, too.

"Care for a seat?" asked Professor Morran. Her long, smooth light blue mane was practically down to the floor, which contrasted amazingly with her light red complexion as she gazed into me with those glowing purple eyes.

Suddenly, I felt like I got the better end of the deal, being confined to a small room all day with two gorgeous women.

"Uh—yeah, of course," I stammered and sat down at a desk next to Sakura, who shot me a quick, discreet smile and a small wave.

"I'm sure you both know why you're here on a nice, sunny Saturday like today?" Professor Morran asked.

Sakura remained quiet, gazing down at her desk, so I figured I'd do the talking "Yes, Professor," I replied.

"Both of your grades have been slipping this semester," she continued, "and to be frank, I'm almost certain of the reason behind it."

Sakura's cheeks reddened slightly as she continued to fiddle with her thumbs.

"I also know," said Professor Morran, "that you are *both* better than the work I've seen out of you. So, with a little review today, I am confident you two will still pass my final."

"Thanks, Professor," I said, earning a genuine smile out of her.

From there, Professor Morran began reviewing some of the various topics we covered over the term, like strengths and weaknesses of each class, favorable and unfavorable match-ups, I even was reminded of how rune-knights could some-times have animals that bond with them, something I had somehow already forgotten about.

Most of the questions Professor Morran asked, Sakura answered, and as the morning went on, it became blatantly clear how much I really did need this review.

Professor Morran was in the middle of explaining the basic fundamentals of shifting (something I actually did already know, thanks to Dawn) when she had to leave the room to take a call.

"I trust I can leave you two alone for ten minutes without losing your interest when I return?"

"Yes, Professor," we both replied, and as soon as she closed the door to leave, I turned to Sakura.

"I am *so* sorry that I got you dragged into this!" I pleaded.

Sakura had a puzzled, almost startled look on her face. "What?" she squeaked. "No, it's not your fault at all! Don't do that to yourself. I'm here from my own doing."

"Yeah, but *you're* smart, Sakura. And I've been the one always turning around to talk to you. If I hadn't been distracting you all semester, you'd be passing this course with flying colors!"

Sakura glanced down at her desk and blushed. "No, I—I'm glad you talk to me." She smiled innocently at her hands. "I'd trade that for a good grade any time, really. So, please don't stop?"

A bright smile forged across my face. "I won't," I replied, and her eyes beamed at the desk.

A few moments of silence went by as I feverishly racked my brain over something else to say during this short window we had before Professor Morran came back.

"So, how have you been? I feel like I haven't had the chance to talk to you outside of class in months! How's the Bronze Dragon treating you?" I finally asked.

"Oh, it's going very well," she replied, finally making brief eye contact with me. "You should stop by again sometime soon!" She stirred from just the thought of it, looking exhilarated and leaning closer to me. But then she quickly pulled herself back and regained her composure, turning pink in the cheeks again.

"I definitely will! Now that I'm thinking about it, it *has* been a few months."

"I'll make sure to shake the rust off my smiley-sandwich-making-skills." She was trying to hold in a laugh. "How—how have *you* been, though?"

"Agh," I threw my hands behind my head and leaned back in my chair, thinking of the final project that had been lingering over my head now for weeks, "not great lately, I guess."

"Oh?" Her eyes widened with sincerity.

"Yeah, it's just this annoying final project thing for the Quester program—that's the program I'm trying to get into—but I need a third person for my group. Haven't had any luck finding one, though. So it's looking like we'll be getting assigned a random person. Who knows, though," I continued, almost talking to myself now, "maybe that person will be decent, right?"

I turned to look at Sakura and noticed she was staring at me with a blank expression.

"Sorry," I quickly added, "I didn't mean to flood you with my problems. That was probably more than you needed to hear."

"I'm—" Sakura quietly stammered, "I'm in the Quester program."

I sat up in my chair. "Wait, you are?!" I did a terrible job at hiding my astonishment, but I couldn't help it—I would have never pegged Sakura for the Quester type.

"Mhm!" She nodded her head vigorously.

As the idea hit me, I felt a glimmer of hope, but tried to suppress it with the reminder of how last minute it was.

"Sakura? By any chance, are you in a group yet for the project?"

She shook her head hard, clearly trying to hold back a big smile. My chest suddenly felt pounds lighter.

"Would you like to join my group as our third person?!"

"Yes!" she quickly squeaked out before covering her mouth with her hands to halt herself from coming off as too excited.

I could have hugged her right there. "Really?! You will?!"

She nodded again, her hands still covering her mouth, and her eyes gleaming gratefully.

"That's great!" I almost had to cover my own mouth now to prevent myself from shouting. "Sakura, thank you! Seriously, you have no idea how much of a lifesaver you are right now for me and Tara!"

"No! Thank *you*! I was really stressed about having to work with strangers. I can't wait, Nate. Thank you!"

Professor Morran returned to the classroom shortly after that, where she resumed her lecture about shifters. We spent the next few hours reviewing everything that had been covered this past semester. I could tell that Sakura was more relaxed now because she was confidently answering most of Professor Morran's questions.

The remainder of the morning rolled into early afternoon before we were finally dismissed from the study session.

"Good job today, you two," said Professor Morran from behind her desk as we were leaving the classroom. "Just goes to show that you're both very capable students when you focus. I look forward to seeing your grades this coming week." She smiled genuinely and waved us off.

With the Games still wrapping up, the campus grounds were completely deserted, as Sakura and I made our way back through the quad. The distant chants and echoed voice of the announcer could be heard even from here.

"Probably won't make it up in time to see how it ends, huh?" I muttered down to Sakura. I still couldn't get over how little she was, barely coming up to my stomach as we strolled along.

"No, I don't think so."

"Well, how about we get some lunch? The dining hall will at least be open. I haven't eaten yet today, come to think of it."

Sakura giggled. "That sounds good to me!"

"Perfect! We can talk some strategy for the final project, too!"

As expected, the dining hall was totally empty, which was nice because it clearly made Sakura more comfortable. So comfortable, in fact, that she didn't seem to hold back her appetite. I was absolutely baffled when she sat down across from me with a plate of food that rivaled even my own. I couldn't help myself from glancing down at it, and she seemed to notice as her cheeks turned a shade of pink, matching her hair.

"Hey, no judging here!" I quickly said with a smile, trying to make her feel better after my slip up. "I love a girl who can eat! I'm just wondering where you put it!"

Sakura let out a long laugh, and I was glad to see she didn't bother trying to hinder herself from giggling away. "I'm sorry," she got out after a break in between breaths, "I just love food!"

"Hey," I pleaded, raising my hands to the air, "nothing wrong with that! You can certainly get away with it. I'm kind of jealous, to be honest."

I had to admit, it was great to finally have the opportunity to really talk one on one with Sakura outside of class. She seemed to always have this unique way of making me feel very comfortable, and myself.

I even learned a few new things about her, too, like how she was a B-tier shifter, lived in the Realm her whole life despite being human, and had been shifting since she was only nine years old.

As it turned out, she wasn't exactly a fox-shifter, as I had assumed. But instead, she was something called a kitsune. The main difference being that she didn't have a choice of which animal to shift to, like some shifters could (Dawn, for example, made the decision to shift into a panther as she got older, but originally shifted into a cat as a young girl). Were-wolves were another example of a type of shifter that didn't have the luxury of choosing which animal to transform into.

The other difference was that she had multiple tails, gaining a new one after certain big life events (or certain *tales*, so to speak). Apparently, with every new tail, a kitsune's shifting abilities improved dramatically.

Needless to say, she seemed like the perfect fit for our group. And when the people started to slowly pour into the dining hall, signaling that the Games had ended, I figured it was time to meet up with Dawn and Tara to tell them the news.

"Sakura? You're in the Quester program?" asked Tara, back in my dorm room after I reintroduced everyone and explained the new turn in events.

Sakura nodded shyly, glancing down at the floor.

"That's perfect!" replied Tara. "We could use a shifter in our group—"

"Hey!" Dawn blurted out.

"Oh, you're in the Guard, you don't count here," Tara brushed off and grinned at Dawn, while Sakura snickered.

Dawn rolled her eyes, trying to hold back a smirk herself.

"So, I figure we can start trying to prepare next week in the evenings, after our finals," I explained. "We can get to know a little more about each other and our capabilities. That should at least put us in a decent spot regarding teamwork. From there, we'll just have to wait to get more info on the objective after we submit our team."

As it turned out, though, we wouldn't have to wait very long. We submitted our team information via envelope that evening at the drop box outside the Cathedral of Tranquility. And the following day, I was chilling on my couch, enjoying a leisurely Sunday afternoon, when a knock on my door sounded out, followed by an envelope sliding underneath it.

When I opened the door, nobody was there, just a package of what looked to be clothes inside. The label on the package had my name on it, though, so I glanced down the empty hall and surreptitiously picked it up before darting back inside my room.

I then bent down to pick the brown envelope off my floor. The words *Final Project Criteria* were written over it in black cursive writing, and my heart leaped.

I quickly opened the package of clothes and pulled out a silver shirt, along with silver pants. They were made of a thin, cool material. Thinking back to it, they looked very similar to the types of outfits the competitors wore during the Questing Games.

Barely a second later, my phone vibrated in the pocket of my shorts. Pulling it out, I saw that Tara had sent a text to the group chat, which now consisted of her, Dawn, Sakura, and myself.

> Tara: *Did you guys get the envelope too?!*
> Me: *Yeah I did. Did you open it yet?*
> Sakura: *I got it too! I haven't opened mine*
> Me: *Let's meet up at my place. We can open them together*
> Sakura: *okay :)*
> Tara: *Sounds good!*
> Dawn: *What's a girl gotta do to take a nap around here!*
> Dawn: *Damn questers*
> Dawn: *I'm coming, too...be there in 5 ;)*

About ten minutes later, we were huddled around in my living room, nervously eyeing up the three envelopes in our hands. It seemed that the girls got packages of silvery clothes as well, which were currently stacked up next to my door.

"I can't do it!" Tara nervously exclaimed as she bit at her nails.

Sakura was fiddling with her fingers in silence.

"Well," I started, "I'll open—"

"I can do it!" Dawn interrupted me and eagerly snatched the envelope from my hand.

I chuckled and let her do her thing as she held it out in front of her and began to read:

"'Dear future Questers, we formally invite you to partake in the final project this end of term. It is our great privilege,' Blah, blah, blah," she continued, skimming over the initial portion now to get to the main parts. "Okay!" she blurted out. "This is good. It's your basic objective where you have to retrieve an object of some sort, pretty much in line with the final Quester projects of past years, from what I've heard."

She mumbled along to herself, silently skimming away while Tara, Sakura, and I watched her intently.

"Which means it's probably guarded by someone that you'll have to get through," she slowly muttered.

"Ooo! Here it is! Okay—looks like there will be three professors you'll have to get past to retrieve the object. Ready?" she asked us dramatically as we silently nodded.

"First, is Professor Morran. Second," she shot me a knowing glance before continuing, "Professor Kravitz. And third . . ." She paused, her smile instantly replaced with a look of dread.

"Who is it?" Tara broke the silence.

But Dawn remained quiet, instead turning the piece of paper around for us to read it for ourselves.

And there it was in tiny black font at the bottom of the page: Dean Celestine.

Chapter Nineteen

It took a few moments for the realization to settle in, but once it did, I found myself in a lesser state of shock than the others. After all, they were the three professors in the room that witnessed my initial Reading. Maybe they had this planned all along.

"We have to get through Dean Celestine?!" Tara finally broke the silence. "Like, we'll have to actually—actually f-fight her?"

Sakura plopped down on the couch, her hands pressed firmly against her forehead.

"Well," Dawn said, trying to sound as hopeful as possible, "I've heard of this happening before, and all of the professors will be wearing suppressors, like during the Games. So their powers will be restrained, to a degree."

"Yeah, but this is Dean Celestine we're talking about," I muttered. "Even with the suppressors . . ."

"We are so fucked!" Tara blurted out, throwing her hands over her face and collapsing on the other couch next to Sakura.

"Come on, guys!" Dawn tried to rally the room as she paced around us. "You can do this! I'm sure Dean Celestine wouldn't give you guys anything she felt you couldn't handle. I mean, if anything, it's kind of a compliment! It's just a reflection of your talent! Right? Right?!"

"More like a reflection of Nate's mytosome count," muttered Tara. "They clearly want to put him to the test. I'm sorry, Nate. You should have picked a better teammate. I'm only going to hold you—"

"The only people I'd want on my team are already in this room," I sharply said. "I wouldn't choose anyone else in the entire school. I mean that."

Tara gave me a small smile of pity, while Sakura's eyes glimmered.

"Look," I began, starting to regain some composure, "what's done is done. Dawn's right—they wouldn't assign us anything they thought we couldn't handle. We just stick to the plan. Our first priority is our finals. We'll get through those, and then in the evenings, we can come back here to try our best to prepare. We've got this, I promise!"

But I only wished I was as confident on the inside as I hoped I looked on the outside.

It was a good thing that my finals weren't too troublesome, because if I'm being honest, my thoughts were elsewhere at the start of the week.

Thanks to Professor Morran's study session, my Intro to Classes final was a surprising breeze. She even shot me a genuine and proud smile when I was one of the first people in the class to finish it.

Dean Celestine's practical exam was also a cinch now that I had the Cloning Spell down. As for my Shield Spell, well, I could never be entirely sure, but Dean Celestine's gaze seemed slightly less piercing than usual while she fixated on her "favorite book" at the end of my exam.

As I left her class, she congratulated me on a job well done before ominously wishing me luck on my final project, her lips curling into a smirk.

Regarding my other exams, they weren't too bad. I felt I did pretty average on the Basic History of the Realm final, mainly thanks to my occasional glances over at Tara's answers. And finally, even though I couldn't stand the guy, Professor Kravitz had a way of demanding my attention, which allowed me to get through his Weapon Guidance exam with little difficulty. It was the easiest and least stressful class of his yet.

All the while, Dawn, Tara, Sakura, and I stuck to the plan, getting together in my room every evening to converse about, well, anything, really. We'd always start the sessions reviewing our abilities and what we could and couldn't do, our strengths and weaknesses, things like that. But then the conversation usually progressed into talking about random things like our favorite foods and colors (Sakura's was surprisingly not pink, but instead a warm shade of orange).

Even though a part of me was fretting that we may have been wasting time, I mostly figured it was good for us to branch out and get to know one another (mainly Sakura, as she was still new to our group) better on a personal level, and not just what we could do in regard to combat. It was a rewarding time, mainly because it helped Sakura warm up to the other girls, and by the middle of the week, I was glad to see her conversing with them as comfortably as she would with me.

But while I was happy and carefree during our evenings together, the hours where I was by myself during the day only reminded me of the existential task that was looming ahead.

It was on a Thursday morning, just a day before the final project, where the stress and concern over not having any strategy of countering Dean Celestine became too much, and I had to go for a walk around campus to clear my head.

I was strolling aimlessly through campus, deep in thought and unaware of where I was going, when I bumped into someone.

"Oh—shit, sorry," I automatically muttered and looked up, only to be caught off guard by the sight of an eccentrically beautiful green woman. She was a familiar face, and perhaps the prettiest orc in the Realm, Zula.

"Oh! No need to be sorry—hey, I know you, don't I?" she brightly asked after meeting my gaze with those fiery eyes of hers.

"Yeah, kind of!" I explained. "I'm friends with Dawn. We met at your sorority's Halloween party."

Her eyes lit up excitedly. "That's right! The bread! I knew I couldn't forget you—" But she paused, and her expression lowered with the realization of something. "Oh, no, I totally had you pinned up against that wall."

"It was fine, really," I chortled. "No hard feelings."

But she still looked a little embarrassed. "You're too kind. Thanks for being understanding about it."

"Of course!" I replied. "Hey, I'm sorry to hear about the Questing Games."

Dawn and Tara had given me the rundown of how the championship match ended. Apparently, the championship objective revolved around each team battling on a thin plank fifty feet in the air. They were all in harnesses to catch their falls and sorcerers taking flight was prohibited (which apparently caused a bit of controversy). Nonetheless, they told me that Zula did an amazing job and was the last person standing on her team before getting overwhelmed in a 1v3.

"Ah, it's no biggie! I'm already over it." She waved off. "There's always next year. None of my teammates are seniors, thankfully, so I think we'll have a good shot next time!"

"Well, I heard you did amazing," I complimented. "I was bummed that I couldn't make the match. I got dragged into a study session for a final. But I caught your match back in November! You were seriously impressive."

Her green cheeks turned a slight shade of purple. "Thanks, that was nothing!"

"Didn't look like nothing to me. Actually, I could sure use a little 'nothing' tomorrow," I mumbled that last sentence underneath my breath.

"Something got you hot and bothered?" She looked concerned, and I was a little surprised by how she talked to me like she'd known me her whole life, not that I was complaining, it made it very easy to carry on a conversation with her.

"It's just this damn final project of mine," I sighed. "I have to battle against a few professors to capture an object they're guarding, or whatever."

"Oh! You're in the Quester program, too?!"

My eyes widened. Of course she would know—she had to be in the Quester program to compete in the Games. "Yeah! So you went through the same thing?"

"You know it! Had mine yesterday. Wasn't bad at all! I wouldn't stress too much about it."

I knew she was being sincere, but her telling me this didn't make me feel too much better about my situation. She was extremely skilled when it came to combat, something my group was lacking. Not to mention she had that frenzy state of hers as well.

"Yeah, well," I replied. "I probably wouldn't be stressing about it quite as much if I didn't have Dean Celestine as one of the professors to go up against."

"Oh, yikes!" she blurted. "Who are the other professors? I may be able to give you some insight."

"Yeah? That'd be great! The other two are Professor Kravitz and Professor Morran."

Zula cringed a little. "Mmm, yeah, that is *definitely* not an easy board." She pursed her thick lips and pondered thoughtfully. "Well, Professor Morran and Kravitz are both rune-knights . . ."

This was already intel I hadn't had before, as I had always wondered what Professor Morran's class was. For some reason, she kept that information close to the chest, and the armor she wore never shouted out "rune-knight" to me, as it was made of leather.

"Kravitz is a unique type of rune-knight—a berserker. He can temporarily amplify his internal rune to the point where he'll enrage and become even stronger than he already is," she continued. "You *absolutely* need to handle him with long range attacks. If you find yourself in the clutches of a berserker, you're already finished. I hear his internal rune is off the charts!"

Shivers traveled down my spine at the thought of an enraged Kravitz finally getting his large paws for hands on me.

I couldn't help feeling how it would have been useful to cover this berserker trait in Professor Morran's Intro to Classes course. But maybe that was to be saved for a more advanced course.

"The thing about berserkers, though," Zula pressed on, "is that they lose their heads when transformed, almost becoming mindless beasts. It's their biggest weakness, so try to use that to your advantage, if you can."

She paused for a minute before continuing. "Now Professor Morran is a different case, though. I heard she uses a bow, and has a pet that calls to her—I think it's some sort of bird. Anyway, it's always best to take out the pet first in those situations. If you can do that, you're already limiting what the rune-knight can do."

Again, I thought back to how Zula didn't hesitate to attack that one rune-knight's saber-toothed tiger during the first round of the Questing Games. It was nice to know that she was giving me genuine information, knowledge that she relied on herself.

"Taking mental notes down as you speak! Thanks, Zula," I admitted. "Honestly, it's already way more than I had to go off of."

"Of course!" She looked genuinely happy over hearing this.

"You wouldn't happen to have anything on Dean Celestine, would you?"

Her face contorted into a dubious expression. "Sorry, I got nothing for you there. She's the dean for a reason, I guess, right?"

"Yeah," I agreed, feeling heavy again, "I suppose you're right. To be honest, I don't know if she has *any* weaknesses."

"Well," Zula slowly said, pursing her lips again, "I wouldn't go *that* far. If there's one thing I've learned during my combat training over the years—it's that everyone has at least one weakness, it's just a matter of finding it."

I pondered in silence for a moment.

"You're a sorcerer, right?" asked Zula.

I was slightly startled that she knew that, considering I was currently in normal clothing, just a t-shirt and shorts instead of my robe and cloak. I supposed that being as experienced in combat as she was, you pick up on little details and patterns, though.

"So," she continued, "I'm sure you've had classes with Dean Celestine all year long?"

"Yeah, I have," I replied thoughtfully.

"Well, my advice would be to think back to your interactions with her, your conversations—there may be a certain something that's buried somewhere in the engagement." She raised a finger and smiled brightly. "If given the opportunity, it's always essential to study your opponents and pay close attention to the little details—like how they act or what they say when out of combat—to ensure success!" She said it like she was told that by someone else, maybe a mentor or something.

I gave her a genuine smile of gratitude. "Seriously, Zula, thanks. I'll think about it!"

"Don't mention it! I love talking about this kind of stuff! And hey, come around sometime next year! Bring Dawn and that blonde you were with—she was hilarious! I'd love to hang with all you guys."

"Will do!"

She shot me a confident smile and reassuring wave before continuing her way back to the north side of campus, leaving me to think hard about the tips she gave me.

Could Dean Celestine have a weakness?

I thought back to all my conversations and interactions with Dean Celestine.

For the most part, she was always just giving me guidance. And even though she seemed a little questionable in the morale department when I first met her, she always had my back throughout the year, especially when I really needed her.

Although she *was* usually late to show up, due to her *extracurricular activities* she loved in that back room of her office. Still, though, she'd always at least put that stuff on hold when I needed her.

"Holy shit," I muttered to myself.

That was it. That had to be it!

It was a crazy thought, a long shot, even. But it was all I had to go off of. How could I pull it off, though? I only had one day left to prepare, after all.

Not wasting another second, I stormed off toward the North Gate, to head into the town of Hearthvale.

The next morning brought with it a level of stress that I had yet to encounter, so much so that it actually woke me up an hour before my alarm went off. It was still dark outside, so I tried to fall back asleep, but my racing thoughts seemed bent on preventing that from happening.

So instead, I made the decision to prepare myself for the day as I crawled out of bed, forced down a granola bar and some toast (for once, I wasn't hungry), and groggily put on my silver clothes that came in the package.

They were surprisingly comfortable, and somehow even lighter than they looked. It almost felt like I wasn't wearing anything at all, which was sort of alarming at first, but I quickly got used to it. A sleek, tight fit, they hugged me soothingly, like the cool side of a pillow. I couldn't help feeling like they did me some justice, and if I wasn't so nervous, I'd be excited to see how these clothes looked on Tara and Sakura.

According to the envelope, the match was to start at 8:00 AM on the dot at Reddick Stadium, which I wasn't thrilled about initially, but as it turned out, wasn't an issue since I was already awake. Actually, I was now grateful for the final project being so early, as it meant I didn't have to nervously wait around all day.

I stood up from my couch and gazed out of the window. The stars were fading into daylight as an orange glow poked out from above the distant horizon. And when the purplish sky turned to a lighter blue, my phone vibrated with the group text.

We ended up agreeing to meet up at the quad before heading into the stadium, so I first met Tara in the lobby of our dorm building. She was holding her white staff, fiddling with the half-moon shape at the top of it. I noticed she had her healing jewelry on again, too.

Just as I figured she would, she was looking like a curvy treat in her tight silver outfit, which clung to her ass and thighs as if they were glued to her. Meanwhile, her breasts were firmly pressed up against the top, seemingly begging to pop out and greet me with a hearty "hello!" Her hair was up in the messy bun as her side bangs dangled down. I would have complimented her on how beautiful she looked if she didn't currently look like she was about to throw up.

"You ready?" I asked.

"I don't know, Nate," she breathed.

Somehow, seeing her this nervous calmed me. I had to be strong and remain levelheaded for her and Sakura.

"We got this, okay? We've been preparing all year for it. Like we've said before—we've come a long way from Maine."

She forced a faint smile for maybe a second and then gulped and nodded.

It wasn't until we were about halfway to the quad when Tara finally spoke out again, voicing something that had clearly been on her mind.

"I just don't know, Nate," she quickly blurted out. "I'm sure you're tired of hearing it—but I *really* think you should have picked a higher tiered healer. I mean, what if I . . ."

But I let her voice fade away for a moment as I took a mental dive into her internal rune. There was something I had been wondering about for a while, and now I could confirm it.

As I sensed out her rune, I let it guide me in seeing her mytosome count and structure. Not a moment later, her mytosomes appeared in my mind. They were significantly less dense than my own and vibrating much more passively. But compared to Dawn's and the people who I observed in Hearthvale yesterday, they were actually quite similar.

". . . there's also the fact that I can still only become invisible for a few seconds at a time—"

"Just as I figured," I interrupted her from anymore self-criticism.

She gave me an alarming look.

"I just sensed out your mytosome count, and it's barely different from that of the average runic, Tara."

She blinked wildly a few times. "Wh—what? When on Earth did you learn to do that?!"

"Nothing to do with Earth." I smiled and winked at her. "But, well, I've been able to sense the internal rune in people for a good while now—that's how I was able to treat Chuck the werewolf like a puppet back then. However, I learned how to use the internal rune in people to show me their mytosome counts—well—yesterday, I guess." My smile turned a little sheepish.

"Yesterday? You picked up on a new trick that fast?! See! I *knew* tiers make a difference. I could never!"

"Tara, really, don't use me as a comparison. I never realized just how different my mytosome count was until exploring others', I'll admit. That being said, though, everyone else seems to be pretty close with their counts! D-tier to A-tier, honestly, I can barely notice the difference!"

Her eyes glimmered and her lips curled into a small smile, but she still tried to fight it. "But, Nate . . ."

"I'm telling you, Tara," I looked her straight in the eyes, hoping she finally would get the message, "the biggest thing holding you back this year hasn't been your tier. It's your own doubt. Just don't listen to it today, okay? And we'll be just fine."

Dawn and Sakura were both waiting eagerly for us by the big statue of the butterfly-lady at the center of the quad.

I couldn't wrap my head around how these women could all look so damn good so early in the morning. Dawn was wearing a black, two-piece shifter outfit, currently in her hybrid form, as she usually preferred. And Sakura looked adorable in her tight silvery outfit. If Tara's tits were politely asking to come out and say "hi," Sakura's were practically demanding to bust out and yell "FREE ME NOW!" And that said quite a bit, because Tara was not lacking at all in that department herself.

Sakura had her pink hair fashioned in its usual long braid, and three tails popping out from behind her, which I thought was interesting because I could have sworn that she only had two when I last saw her in her hybrid form.

"Nice staves, you two!" Dawn called out to us. "Looking legit! Are you ready?" she asked as Sakura shot me and Tara a small smile and a quick wave.

I adored them both, one pair of yellow eyes staring confidently back at me, while the other, a bright green, fixated nervously on the ground.

"I'm glad Dean Celestine gave me permission to come watch!" Dawn continued. "They're usually so strict on keeping the final projects private."

The quick hike up to Reddick Stadium was a quiet one, with the only person occasionally breaking the uneasy silence being Dawn, who seemed more excited than nervous. And with it being so early in the morning on the last Friday of the year after a tough week of final exams, there was hardly anyone at all strolling through the grounds, which only created an eerie, even ominous effect.

I tried to take advantage of the silence, though, mentally tallying all of the abilities that I had at my disposal on the way over: *The Telekinesis Spell, I thought to myself, which is basically just manipulated the air between you and your opponent or object, thus moving the opponent or object; the Shield Spell, that forms an invisible barrier around someone or something, protecting against other spells; which brings me to my next spell, the Penetration Spell. I only used it once, and that was because of the negative rune—basically, controlling someone's body by reaching inside them and grabbing hold of their internal rune. I'd prefer not to even bother with that, though. It just left me feeling so . . . dark. Of course, there's the Sorcerer Sense, too. Powerful, but I can't necessarily rely on that to come about when I need it. And finally, the Cloning Spell, which . . .*

"Well, this is where we'll part ways, guys!" Dawn spoke out, turning to us and smiling a bit nervously as well now.

We were standing in front of the entrance to the stadium. There were no lines, no guards scanning tickets—just the gate where we'd all have to scan our thumbs to enter.

"When we get inside, I'll head up the escalator while you three head down the steps to the entrance tunnels." She then paused to consider something, before throwing caution to the wind and giving each of us a big, tight hug. "Good luck, you got this," she whispered in my ear when it was my turn for a hug.

I tried to force a confident smile and nodded to her with a silent "thanks" before we scanned our way into the stadium and parted ways.

As we made our way down the steps, eventually through the closest tunnel leading out to the field, I addressed Sakura and Tara.

"Hey guys?" I paused about halfway through the tunnel, causing them to both turn and look at me. Sakura's eyes glowed green in the dark tunnel. "I just wanted to say— thanks for teaming up with me. I absolutely *know* that we can do this."

Tara nodded silently, her lips thinner than usual, while Sakura smiled at me.

"No matter what happens out there, I'm just glad you two will be in the trenches with me, really."

"I'm glad, too," Sakura quietly said.

Tara's face loosened just a bit, enough to form a small smile. "I couldn't ask for a better team," she said, and the three of us embraced each other in a hug that I didn't want to end. All good things must, though, and when we finally broke apart, Tara let out a big breath and added, "Okay, let's do this," in a tone that told me she was finally ready for the inevitable.

We emerged onto the grassy field, and the entire stadium towered over us, making me feel smaller than I'd felt in a very long time. Other than Dawn, who was sitting in the lowest row closest to the field and cheering enthusiastically, the stadium bleachers were completely vacant. If anything, it just made the place look more massive. I tried to imagine it being filled to capacity, and could easily see how it could overwhelm even the most experienced competitor in the Games.

Squinting across the field, I noticed there were plenty of natural barriers set up—various mounds of elevated grass, which could offer protection or a hiding spot from our opponents, and even a small stream of water carved into the field as it flowed calmly through the vast terrain.

And finally, standing on the opposite end of the stadium, way off in the distance, were Professor Morran, Professor Kravitz, and Dean Celestine, all wearing similar uniforms to what we had on, but black instead of silver.

I couldn't help noticing how good both Professor Morran and Dean Celestine looked in those tight outfits (hopefully Dean Celestine couldn't read my mind from this distance). But Kravitz looked as if he could burst out of his uniform. I think I could see the dude's veins in his arms poking through the shirt from here as his body raised and lowered repeatedly with every angry breath.

Perched up behind them, magically levitating inches above a

small cement pedestal, was a large, red gem—an orb about the size of my hand, maybe.

"Welcome, future Questers!" Dean Celestine's voice unnaturally boomed throughout the stadium, like it was being magnified by a megaphone, yet there was nothing there. "Professor Kravitz, Professor Morran, and I, are all honored to be your opponents for your final project today. The objective is simple: You will have thirty minutes," she gestured to a large 30:00 that appeared on the huge screen way above them, "to obtain the crystal orb behind us, all while the three of us wear suppressors, to help in creating a fairer match."

I took note of the silver bracelets clasped around their wrists, the same bracelets that the competitors wore during the Games.

"If you have any questions, now will be the time to ask them. When that clock starts, we will no longer be your professors."

Sakura and Tara exchanged looks of uncomfortable hesitancy. I shrugged my shoulders.

"Very well," Dean Celestine's voice boomed. "The uniforms you currently wear will register damage, as will ours. They're made of the same design the competitors wear during the Questing Games, which means that if you take enough damage, an X will display on your suit, and you will be eliminated. If the three of you get eliminated, or you fail to retrieve the orb within the time limit, you will fail. *No* exceptions."

I gripped at my golden staff, preparing for what was surely soon to come.

"With that," Dean Celestine announced, "let the countdown begin!"

The large 30:00 on the screen changed into a 10, followed by a 9 . . .

My heart raced faster with each number that ticked away, as the realization hit me like a truck—the moment had finally arrived.

5

4

"Let's go, guys!!! You got this!!!!" Dawn's voice hollered out from the distance, which seemed like another world entirely.

3

We can do this.

2

We *must* do this.

1

BEGIN!

Chapter Twenty

"THE S-TIER IS MINE!!!" bellowed Kravitz from across the field, as his muscles seemed to grow even larger by the second, his stature heightening while his long, curly black hair spiked upward.

Before I even had the chance to think of a plan, he was leaping through the air.

At least twenty feet high and far, the large, bearded man leaped and leaped, quickly closing in on us like an angry bullfrog. By his third jump, he was directly above us, and I attempted to push him away using telekinesis.

The mad berserker was too strong and heavy, though, and he plowed down upon the three of us, breaking the ground beneath our feet. The sheer force of the blow was enough to send us flying, separating me from Sakura and Tara.

Zula wasn't kidding—his internal rune in this berserker state was higher than I could imagine, far outweighing anything I'd sensed up to this point.

I barely looked up in time to see it—a pink blur darting past me, weaving its way toward Kravitz. The burly man sheathed a huge two-handed sword out of his thick scabbard (so that was Kravitz's weapon of choice, then). It had one of those rubber guards on it to make it less lethal.

He swung it at the small pink blur that was Sakura in her fox form. But she was too quick and dodged it before circling around Kravitz and leaping on his back. As she did so, she instantly shifted back to her hybrid form and latched herself onto the man's thick shoulders, clawing at the back of his head like a rabid animal.

"Holy shit, this chick can *shift!*" I heard Dawn holler out from the stands.

"Get off of me you little—" Kravitz's deeply unnatural voice boomed as he blindly circled about with Sakura strapped to his back like a little monkey. He was slowly swinging at the air with his massive broadsword. It was obvious to me that those suppressors were slowing his movements dramatically.

"Nate!" shrilled Sakura. "Take Tara and get to the orb! I think I can take him! He's slow! It's a—perfect match for me!" She was struggling to hang on as Kravitz lurched and shrugged fiercely with the attempts at flinging the small girl off him.

The thought of leaving Sakura to fend for herself against an animal like Kravitz made my chest heavy, but I had to put my faith in her (she seemed unexpectedly sure of herself now that the battle commenced). So I gestured to Tara to follow my lead, and we sprinted along the large field toward Professor Morran and Dean Celestine.

It was as if they were waiting for us, though. At that moment, a large falcon swooped down from the sky, followed by Professor Morran pulling an arrow out of her quiver and notching it on her bow before letting out a whistle and gesturing toward us with her head.

Her falcon obeyed her command, whooshing past Professor

Morran and gliding toward Tara and me, a fierce look in its eyes.

Meanwhile, Dean Celestine was hovering above the orb, eyeing us carefully. Could she be guarding it?

"Nate! Look out!" Tara shrieked.

I turned just in time to duck out of the way. The hawk flew over my head like a feathery bullet. It then circled back in the air above us and dove back down at its prey.

Suddenly, my hand snatched something that was whizzing right for my head. It felt thin and wooden. I turned to see that I was holding an arrow. Wide-eyed, I glanced over at Professor Morran, who was still aiming down her bow and smiling at me. Luckily, the head of the arrow was also rubber and very dull, but it still would have hurt like a bitch, maybe even had knocked me out cold. One thing was for sure, it would have eliminated me from the competition.

Looks like the Sorcerer Sense saved my ass again, I thought to myself.

"Nate! AHHHH!" Tara's voice screeched out from behind me, mixed with a sort of feral squawking.

I spun around to see the falcon fiercely pecking and clawing away at Tara, who was pinned to the ground and wildly flailing her hands about, attempting to push the falcon away from her.

I hadn't quite learned how to strengthen my staff with external rune yet, like Professor Kravitz mentioned on the first day of his class, but I didn't really care. Instinct took over, and I wound up my staff and clubbed the falcon off Tara. It made a high-pitched squealing noise as it tumbled clumsily through the air.

Quickly glancing over my shoulder, I noticed Professor Morran had already notched another arrow and was aiming it right at me, so without thinking, I quickly picked Tara up off the ground and headed toward a small mound, where we could at least be shielded from any more arrows.

Just before reaching the mound of land, though, I felt a blunt impact on the back of my right shoulder that knocked me to the ground, causing me to drop Tara. Fortunately, we were at least close enough to the barrier that we could both crawl the rest of our ways behind it, though.

From here I could see Sakura still tangling with Kravitz on the other side of the field, making him look like a fool as she repeatedly shifted from fox to girl and back to fox again, dancing around her opponent's clumsy swings. I may have been imagining things, but Kravitz looked red in the face, even from here.

"Oh, no," Tara noticed, "Nate, you're hurt! Let me heal yo—"

"No, I'll be okay," I rasped, my face clenched.

Even though it hurt like a bitch, I've felt worse pain before. The real issue was the fact that my suit registered the damage, causing it to tighten around my right arm to the point where I could barely move it. But still, all of that was just a minor inconvenience compared to the scratches on Tara's face from that damn bird.

"But I can fix your arm!" she stated, with an apprehensive look from those green eyes, which were currently a little glassy.

"I know you can. But you're our healer," I breathed. "You're our most important asset right now. I need you to get yourself fixed up first, okay? Then you can worry about me."

There was a quick notion of defiance behind her glasses, but then she nodded and (reluctantly) pressed her glowing hands to her face. A swishing noise emanated from them as I watched the scratches on her cheeks turn to light scrapes, before finally fading away entirely.

The sudden fear that Professor Morran could be using this opportunity to close in on us hit me, so I poked my head out from above the mound to survey the area. As soon as I did it, though, another arrow buzzed right over my head. She was still keeping her distance, using her long-ranged attacks. Her weakness was clearly close-ranged combat, and I suddenly found myself wishing we had a fourth member, particularly a rune-knight, on our team.

To make things worse, it seemed her falcon had gotten over the whacking I gave it. It was now circling above the air, trying to seek us out from the sky.

I remembered Zula's advice about taking out a rune-knight's animal first.

"We've gotta do something about that fucking bird," I muttered, becoming painfully aware that the only offensive spell at my disposal was the Telekinesis Spell, which really wasn't all that offensive, actually.

If only Dean Celestine would have taught me that damn laser beam spell that I saw some of the upperclassmen sorcerers using back during the Questing Games. Most of my spells were either defensive or for distraction, like the Cloning Spell. With the clones not being solid mass, it wasn't like I could actually use them to attack.

Then an idea hit me.

"Keep healing yourself, okay?" I asked Tara. "I might have a plan."

Quickly taking in our surroundings, I noticed another small mound of land about twenty feet to our left.

That would have to do.

I grasped my golden staff with my left hand and held it out, manifesting a clone of myself to stand in front of the mound of grass. I then made my clone whistle at the large bird circling in the sky.

The falcon noticed and eagerly charged down toward my clone at lightning speed. And then, somehow just as I had planned, it flew right through my hollow clone and smashed into the mound of land behind it.

Now buried under a pile of rocks and dirt, the bird lay almost motionless. If it wasn't twitching its large talons just slightly, I would have been concerned that it was dead. But then a loud buzz echoed throughout the stadium, and I could just barely make out the red X on the bird's anklet from here.

"You did it, Nate! That was genius!" shouted Tara, as we basked in a moment of relief. But it was quickly squandered by the sight of a pink fox striding across the field, the behemoth Kravitz chasing after her tails.

She immediately shifted back into her hybrid form when she reached us. "Are you guys okay?"

"Been a little better!" said Tara. "If only I had a couple minutes to heal Nate's arm!"

"No time!" I said, noticing a raging Kravitz quickly closing in on us, leaving cracks in the ground behind him with every step he took.

"I can buy you some time!" shouted Sakura confidently.

"Are you sure?" I asked. "Kravitz is one thing, Sakura, but Professor Morran and Dean Celestine are right over there, too. They can end up teaming up against you and—"

"I can do it!" she piped up. "Just a couple minutes, right?"

Tara nodded determinedly. "Two minutes tops!"

"Be careful, Sakura . . ." I said, but she had already shifted back to a fox and was now charging back at Kravitz.

It seemed that her plan was to lure the berserker away, as she danced around him while gradually leading him over to Professor Morran and Dean Celestine.

I despised the thought of her having to fight off both Professor Morran and Kravitz, maybe even Dean Celestine, too. But I tried to push those doubts out of my head while Tara began healing my arm, focusing intently as her glowing hand pressed gently over my shoulder. The swishing noise sounded out, and it wasn't long before I could feel my suit register her heal, loosening up by the second so that I could move my arm again. Better yet, the pain had quickly dissipated, too.

"Okay, you're good to go!" She smiled at me.

"Thanks, Tara. You're the best."

I poked my head over the mound to see Sakura somehow dodging both Kravitz and Professor Morran's arrows as she smoothly and effortlessly shifted forms, like a skilled driver shifting gears.

"Professor Morran is making sure to keep her distance from Sakura even though they've got her outnumbered!" I relayed to Tara, who was looking at me with a puzzled expression. "That must mean she's seen what Sakura can do in close range situations and isn't confident in defending herself against it. If I can get Kravitz away from her, maybe Sakura can get in close to Professor Morran and take her down!"

"But, Nate—Kravitz is—"

"No time to hesitate, Tara. I *have* to go help her. How long can you stay invisible?"

"Um—only like, ten seconds tops, I'd say!" she stammered.

"Okay," I replied, making sure not to sound disappointed, "stay back here and keep an eye on us from afar. I'll try to come to you if I get in trouble again. Sound like a plan?"

She had a concerned expression painted all over her face, but still managed to offer a small nod.

"Nate!" she shouted out as I hopped over the mound to head over to the action. "Please, be careful."

I forced an assuring smile. "I will. But I'm not worried!" I replied. "I know you've got my back."

I then stormed off across the field, noticing that Dean Celestine was still hovering above the orb, surveying the field carefully while gripping her slick, black staff.

There was a small part of me that thought about trying to use telekinesis on the orb to pull it to me and end things quickly, but I was right to assume that would be way too easy. As I closed in on the orb, I could sense a massive amount of external rune that was encompassing it, acting as a barrier—a powerful Shield Spell conjured up by Dean Celestine.

Maybe *that* was the reason behind her not using any offensive abilities yet. It was possible she needed a certain level of focus to maintain a Shield Spell of that level, especially while wearing the suppressor.

It seemed like my arrival couldn't have come at a better time, Kravitz finally had Sakura backed into a corner.

"Hey, meathead!" I hollered out before spamming my Telekinesis Spell at him.

Perhaps it was because he was caught off guard, but my spell somehow knocked him down this time.

The enraged Kravitz made his way to his feet and spun around to stare me down. It was only now that I noticed the irises in his eyes were completely gone in this form, leaving only two white ovals glowering at me.

Interestingly though, he seemed slightly smaller than he was at the beginning of the match, so I quickly sensed out his internal rune. It felt only about half as powerful as it had earlier.

I supposed this berserker form had a relatively short time limit. Could this be the key to beating him? Even without his berserker form, though, Kravitz would still pose a significant threat. But if he were to deplete his rune levels, he'd be a much weaker, more exhausted target. And me being a sorcerer, I don't rely on my internal rune. External rune doesn't act the same way as internal rune, where the user runs out of energy, so to speak. This was the advantage I had over him. I just needed to bide my time.

"Sakura!" I yelled out to her, as she shifted back to her hybrid form. "I'm leaving Professor Morran to you! I have a feeling that if you can get in close to her, you'll have it! I'll deal with Kravitz!"

"Right!" she nodded and shifted back to her fox form before scampering along toward Professor Morran.

"You think I'll just let you walk right up to me like that?!" declared Professor Morran, as she quickly notched an arrow and aimed down her sight.

I didn't have time to see that through, though, as Kravitz was charging toward me like an angry bull.

"THE S-TIER! The S-tier is MINE!!" he bellowed, brandishing his large sword at me.

Not wasting another second, I used the Telekinesis Spell to push Kravitz back, and it worked yet again.

Dean Celestine appeared to have a small grin on her face as I took a quick second to scout her out. It was clear to me that she was enjoying the show, and something told me that if she really *did* want to end this whole thing, she could do so in an instant.

Kravitz rushed at me again, this time leaping over my next Telekinesis Spell and closing the gap between us.

It was just as Zula had said. If this guy were to get in close against me, it'd be all over, sword or no sword.

I spammed another Telekinesis Spell, and it managed to blow him back once more. It seemed the effort he was putting out just to reach me was depleting his rune levels further.

If I could just hold on a little longer.

That thought was quickly impeded, though, as what Kravitz did next took me completely off guard. He angrily smashed his two large hands into the ground, like a child throwing a temper tantrum, causing the land beneath my feet to crumble.

My legs gave out from underneath me, and I was now lying flat on my back, vulnerable and unaware of my surroundings.

The next thing I knew, Kravitz was falling out of the sky directly above me (he must have leaped in the air while I'd fallen), plummeting toward me while he wound up his sword to hammer down a final strike.

Without thinking, I cast another Telekinesis Spell at him, but his momentum was too much, and he broke through it.

I was totally helpless. This was it. All I could do was throw my hands over my body and hope for a miracle.

I closed my eyes, waiting for the impact . . . but it never came.

When I opened them again, I was struck dumbfounded: I was safely standing on my feet again, about twenty yards away from the baffled giant that was Kravitz.

What the hell just happened? Had someone somehow teleported me out of there? It was too good to be true.

"Well done, Nate!" Dean Celestine hollered out from above, a proud smirk on her face. "The Blink Spell is an advanced one that even second-year students fail to grasp. I'm amazed to see you've figured it out!"

The Blink Spell? But I didn't have a clue as to how I did it. I was only hoping for an escape. Could my desperation somehow have caused me to do *exactly* that?"

"It's a spell that allows you to teleport a short distance," she continued. "The sorcerer essentially senses out the external rune within their vicinity and surrenders themselves to it, porting themselves to the area they had sensed out."

"Was that what I did?!" I shouted back.

She let out a cackling laugh. "Extremely useful for evading, or even surprise attacks! I'm impressed that you're improving even as the match goes on, yet not entirely surprised!"

"What, are you my opponent or my mentor right now?!" I asked with a grin.

"Fair point! You may want to keep your eyes on what's in front of you, though!" She pointed to Kravitz, who was looking wildly around at where I blinked off to.

He was now even smaller yet (though still a large man by normal standards), and the black hair on his head was no longer raised; he was slowly but surely regressing back to his normal form.

Staring at the scattered rubble around him, a crazy thought ran through my head: If I could learn a spell like the Blink Spell on the fly, then maybe I could learn another one. I remembered how, back during the Questing Games, a sorcerer somehow bent the ground beneath Zula's feet, trapping her in what was essentially some sort of ground clasp.

And as I knew by now, the Telekinesis Spell was really just controlling the air between you and your opponent—air bending, so to speak. So all I could hope for was that manipulating the earth of the Realm worked the same way.

I put all my focus on the external rune that resided in the rubble at Kravitz's feet. A few seconds passed with nothing happening while Dean Celestine looked on curiously.

But now was not the time to give up. I concentrated harder, more desperately, as I held my staff firmly out at my opponent.

My heart skipped a beat upon seeing some rubble finally shift around. It was actually working! Just in time, too, because Kravitz had finally spotted me.

"Damn Sorcery!" he barked, and I couldn't help noticing how his voice was becoming less monstrous, more human-like. His internal rune was almost depleted, as he panted away, trying to catch his breath.

It was now or never—tightly gripping my staff, I raised both arms, just as I remembered that sorcerer from the Games had done.

Almost on command, the rubble around Kravitz's feet scurried upward before finally tightening around his ankles, just as I had desired.

The exhausted Kravitz tried to break free, but it was too late. I had his feet clasped by the very ground he stood on. And I didn't stop there. I continued controlling the dirt and rocks around him, binding him in a sort of coffin of earth, only stopping when my opponent was completely and tightly engulfed in layers of rubble, all the way up to his neck.

He wiggled about, trying to break free, but he clearly was out of internal rune, rendering him weak and almost helpless.

"You little—!" he yelled out, now coherent and back to his normal self again, looking grumpy and sad.

Even though I didn't eliminate him, he had been rendered useless, partly by his own doing, as that berserker form was a double-edged sword.

Dean Celestine let out a surprising cackle. "What's wrong, Ivan? Run out of steam?"

He shot her a look of disgust as he continued trying to break free. I had other concerns, though, as I drew my attention back to Sakura.

She was doing surprisingly well, managing to get within close range to Professor Morran, and was now slowly chipping at her opponent as she strategically shifted to her primal form when needed, and back to her hybrid form when the situation called for it, all the while dodging Professor Morran's strikes and clawing at her with no remorse.

I still couldn't get over how such a cute, bashful girl could turn on this combative side when needed.

But then, perhaps because she could see the tables starting to turn, Dean Celestine finally unleashed an offensive spell, a Telekinesis Spell directed at Sakura. She was in her hybrid form when it hit her. And maybe out of instinct, she managed to grab Professor Morran by her leather tunic as she flew past her, bringing her along for the ride.

I was utterly astounded by the sheer force that Dean Celestine launched the two women across the field, even with her suppressor on. And it was only when they both crashed into the stadium wall surrounding the field that they finally came to an abrupt halt.

"SAKURA!!!" I belted out.

Tara came running out from behind the mound of earth, while Dawn strode over from where she was sitting in the stands, calling out to her as well.

A loud buzzer sounded out around the stadium, and not one, but two uniforms were now showcasing red X's from across the field: both Professor Morran and Sakura had been eliminated by just one spell from Dean Celestine.

But I couldn't care less about the buzzer I barely heard, or the red X's I hardly noticed. All I cared about was Sakura, and if she was okay.

"Oh, dear!" Dean Celestine's voice sounded out from way behind me. "I seriously overestimated these suppressors."

I sprinted across the field to join the girls, hoping with every ounce of fiber in my soul that neither of them were severely injured, that the suppressor somehow did enough.

"Sakura! Professor Morran!" I yelled out as I approached them, and an unbelievably heavy weight lifted off my shoulders as I saw them both tenderly help each other up to their feet.

"I'm okay," clenched Sakura. "I'm sorry, guys, I—"

"Don't!" I stopped her. "Don't even think about apologizing. You were seriously amazing!"

"Yeah, Sakura. We would have been toast without you! We can't thank you enough," Tara added.

"I had no idea you could shift like that!" Dawn hollered out from the stands above us. "You'll have to give me some pointers some time!"

Sakura blushed and gazed down at the grass, trying to hide a smile. "Thank you, all of you," she whispered.

"I hate to ruin your guys' moment," Professor Morran interrupted, "but if I don't, *she* sure as hell will."

I spun around to see Dean Celestine, now standing firmly on the ground next to the orb, brandishing her staff. She had a fiery look in her blue eyes that I'd only seen once from her before, on the banner inside the stadium, back when she was a young competitor in the Questing Games.

"Well," she stated loudly, calmly, from across the field, "it's about damn time I get in on the action. I was starting to fear I'd be left hovering around that orb all morning."

Chapter Twenty-One

Sakura and Professor Morran slowly made their way up to the stands to take their seats next to Dawn, leaving Tara and me to deal with Dean Celestine. Professor Kravitz was still trapped in his earth prison, looking pouty, but still relatively subdued as he weakly and hopelessly tried to wiggle his way out.

The screen above us showed 12:17 and gave no signs of slowing as it ticked away. Time was slipping out of our fingers while we stood nervously waiting for Dean Celestine's first move.

And then, like lightning itself, it struck through the stillness. She extended her arm at us, clearly planning to blast us away with another Telekinesis Spell, so I hastily formed an urgent Shield Spell around me and Tara.

"Tara!" I called out, remembering something I had learned in Professor Kravitz's class. "Use all your strength to force your staff into the ground!" I wedged my golden staff into the loose turf. "We can use them as anchors to try and resist the blast! I put up a Shield Spell, too, but I'm not sure it will hold!"

At that moment, a blast of air took my breath away. Glancing over at Tara, I could see she was struggling to stay on her feet (she didn't have the chance to anchor her staff). But my Shield Spell was helping, at least a little. I could feel the impact of Dean Celestine's attack colliding with it as it mitigated the force.

I wasn't sure how long I could keep this up though, and if this shield were to break, or even weaken, Tara was a goner.

It was a risk I had to take. I dropped the portion of my invisible shield in front of me so that I could reinforce more of it over Tara. As soon as I did so, the push from Dean Celestine's spell felt twice as powerful, and I clenched tighter on my staff, which began digging backward, cracking its way through the ground . . . it wouldn't hold for much longer.

"Hold on!!!" I groaned out to Tara, who had a terrified look on her face as I rammed my staff further into the ground while still focusing on keeping the Shield Spell up for her.

Dean Celestine showed no signs of letting up, though, and next thing I knew, I was flying through the air, tumbling helplessly about.

"NATE!!" I heard Tara's voice ring out as my surroundings blurred. I had no clue as to what was ground and sky until finally landing abruptly on my back.

It was like all the air escaped from my lungs as I frantically attempted to fill them again. But with every breath, it felt like a dagger piercing my back.

There was no time to feel sorry for myself, as Dean Celestine took flight and was now soaring toward Tara.

"Looks like that little plan of yours worked, Nate! Glad to see you're not eliminated from the impact, at least. But it takes more than one person to complete quests in the real world! What good is having a healer who can't even cloak themselves properly with an Invisibility Spell?"

"Tara!" I coughed. "TAKE COVER!!!"

She vanished, and a brief second of relief hit me before Dean Celestine chuckled. "As if I'd be limited to mere sight," she hissed. "A true healer must learn to cloak, not only their physical bodies, but also their internal rune. I can sniff you out like a dog to drugs, girl!"

She shot a laser out from her staff down at what appeared to be nothing, but then my heart sank as a piercing scream screeched out, followed by Tara coming back into view as she tumbled backward along the hard ground.

"NO!!!" I hollered out and began running after her, but Dean Celestine noticed me before I could make it over to her.

"Oh, come now," she sneered, "I ensured the blast wouldn't be enough to eliminate your girlfriend, Mr. Gannon." Still hovering in the air, she waved her arms around as if she was doing some sort of elegant dance. And then, to my great trepidation, all the water from the surrounding stream rose into the air. "Where would the fun be in *already* eliminating your healer? But, I suppose if you really want to play," she manipulated the water, which was floating in the air, forming a sort of giant sphere with it, "I suppose I am game."

It happened in an instant—like my body was being pulled and contorted against my own will, manipulated by some invisible strings. And the next thing I knew, I was being pulled up through the air toward the giant globe of water.

"Deep breath now!" As she said it, I gasped for a big breath of air, but it wasn't of my doing—she had made me do it with her Penetration Spell, handling me like her own little puppet.

It was a dreadful, helpless feeling. And I now even felt more guilt over using it on Chuck the werewolf earlier in the year, as Dean Celestine dipped me into the giant aquatic prison, not letting up until I was deep within it.

"You know, Nate," her distorted voice echoed from outside the orb of water, "this is new for me. Usually, the men are the ones getting *me* wet."

Ignoring that comment, I frantically focused on my options. It seemed that I at least had control over my body again, but now the water was spiraling around me in a way that kept me from being able to swim out of it.

As I tried to rack my brain for ideas, I could feel myself running low on air and desperately needing to take a breath.

Would she really go as far as drowning me in here?

I had no other choice but to try to counter her spell. I quickly learned how to manipulate the earth, so maybe I could do the same with water.

The necessity of my situation seemed to provide me with a level of focus that I had yet to encounter in my life. My lungs were burning for air, driving me to connect with the external rune circling around me in the water.

I hadn't had much of a clue what I was doing, but I tried to mimic Dean Celestine's dancing arm movements from earlier. And an overwhelming sensation of gratification flowed through me like the spiraling water around me, as it appeared to be responding to my movements and slowing down.

Then, hoping for the best, I flung my arms out: the encompassing water broke apart, giving way to fresh air, which I gratefully sucked into my lungs as I crashed back down to the hard ground.

My adrenaline must have been wildly pumping because the fall from about ten feet in the air left me with no pain at all, it was like my body was numb.

I rubbed at my eyes to get a better view of my surroundings. Dean Celestine was hovering above me, a satisfied smirk on her face.

"Nate! Are you okay?" Tara's voice let out from behind me. "I'm sorry, I'm so sorry! I didn't know what to do."

But Dean Celestine was pointing her staff directly at us.

I grabbed hold of Tara and cast a Telekinesis Spell at nothing, pushing against the air hard enough to project us both backwards as we just barely dodged another laser attack.

We continued soaring back until colliding against another small mound of land.

"Get behind here!" I groaned and pulled Tara with me to take shelter behind the natural barrier.

"I'm sorry, Nate!" Tara repeated. "All I could do was watch!" Her voice cracked.

"It's okay," I gasped, before coughing up some water, "just try and—try and get yourself healed up from that beam attack earlier."

I poked my head over the barrier to see Dean Celestine back on the ground, standing a few feet away from the orb. The screen in the stadium reflected a time of 4:37.

"We're running out of time," I desperately panted. "I think I have a plan, but I'm gonna need you, Tara!"

"A plan?" She shot me an incredulous look as she finished healing herself up. "Nate, I don't think any plan will work against her!" she cried. "I thought you were going to drown in that water prison! And there wasn't a damn thing I could do about it but watch! She's just too powerful. It's like she

401

has zero weaknesses! I think—I think we should just cut our losses and hide. We can try again next year. Maybe we'll get a different board of professors—"

"Next year?!" I blurted out. "Do you hear yourself right now? That's not the Tara I know at all!"

"I know, but—"

"We knew this wouldn't be easy! But we're still here. It's just you and me, okay? Sakura did her part earlier, and she's counting on us. We're not gonna let her down, nor ourselves!"

"Ah, I love when my prey hides from me!" Dean Celestine's voice echoed throughout the stadium. "There's just something about the hunt that really gets me revved up!"

"Listen," I continued, gripping Tara's shoulders and gazing deep into those green eyes, "we're running out of time. The way I see it—we've got one shot left. It has to be now! Can you shield your internal rune in a way that prevents her from sensing you?"

"Well, I thought I could. But she's so powerful that I don't think it works against her—"

"Well, try again. You're the key part in this plan, but for it to work, I'm gonna need you to cloak yourself with the Invisibility Spell while also shielding off your internal rune at the same time. That way, she won't see or sense you."

"Nate, I don't know if I can do it!" she cried. "It didn't work last time! She saw right through me! And I can't even hold the Invisibility Spell for more than ten seconds, and that's *without* shielding my internal rune. It's— it's because of my tier! I'm just too weak!"

"Tara, you're just gonna have to believe in yourself the way I do! I can only say it so many times, but *you're* the one who has to finally believe it! You're more than capable of pulling off anything you put your mind to!"

She opened her mouth to say something back but couldn't find the words.

"Today," I continued, "you're gonna prove it to everyone, but most importantly, yourself, that a runic isn't bound by whatever stupid tier they are! You got that?"

I must have had a sort of fire in my eyes that had yet to be displayed, because she was now gaping at me as if she was meeting a stranger for the very first time. And then, finally, she gulped and nodded slowly before whispering, "Okay, I'll do my best."

I smiled with relief, casting a Shield Spell around us to hopefully prevent Dean Celestine from reading our thoughts. "All right, then! So here's the deal . . ."

"I suppose I can just wait you out!" blurted Dean Celestine. "Time is running short, you two!"

". . . she has a Shield Spell around that orb, so I can't pull it to myself using telekinesis. I have a theory, though, that if I can distract her, it might cause her to drop it. If that happens, then I might be able to pull it to me. But if all else fails, that's where you come in! That Shield Spell only blocks against other magical spells, not solid people! While I'm distracting her, you're going to cloak yourself with the Invisibility Spell and sneak up to grab that damn orb! And then we'll all celebrate later at the Bronze Dragon and call it a year! How's that sound?"

"Well, that all sounds good on paper," she admitted. "But how do you plan on distracting her?"

"Earlier, you said Dean Celestine didn't have a weakness, right?"

She nodded.

"Well," I muttered, "I'm gonna have to disagree . . . I think she has just one."

"You both know," hollered Dean Celestine from some distance beyond our barrier, "that I can simply bend that little mound of dirt you feel so protected behind, right?"

"Look," I quickly added, "don't worry about it. Just make sure, that no matter *what* you see, you keep your focus on that orb, okay?"

She pondered me thoughtfully before giving an anxious nod of understanding. "I—I'll do my best!"

I clapped my hands together encouragingly. "You got this, Tara! I know it! Now, go get that orb for us."

She nodded nervously, and then vanished out of sight.

This was it.

I popped up from behind the small mound of land, quickly noticing that we had barely over a minute left before running out of time.

"HEY, SELENE!!!" I shouted out to Dean Celestine, and she shot me a startled look.

Not wasting another second of precious time, I held out my staff to generate three clones at once. The only thing was, that my clones weren't copies of *me*. Just as planned, three copies of different men, all in their early to mid-thirties, happily flung themselves toward Dean Celestine. One of the men looked identical to Kevin the elf, from back when I first met Dean Celestine.

"My dear, Selene!" one clone dramatically declared. "I must have you, my love!"

"Let's go into the back room of your office, Professor," I made Kevin say. "I've been longing for your touch since that day."

"Sweet, sweet, Selene, I will do *anything* for you!"

". . . WHAT THE HECK—?!" I heard Dawn holler out from the stands.

But Dean Celestine was struck in awe by the sight of the three men ogling over her.

"Oh, *my* . . ." she said dreamily, blushing slightly.

Everything seemed to be going as planned, but then my heart sank as Tara popped back into sight from behind Dean Celestine; her Invisibility Spell had reached its limit.

"Ma'am!!!!" Professor Morran called out to Dean Celestine from the stands after catching on.

"BEHIND YOU!" Professor Kravitz blurted out.

Dean Celestine spun on her heel to see Tara only feet from the orb, desperately sprinting closer to it.

Now was my chance! I could no longer sense the presence of her Shield Spell around the orb.

With just fifteen seconds left, I threw my hand out to try and pull it to me using telekinesis.

Dean Celestine must have noticed, though, as she spun back around and shot me with her own Telekinesis Spell, blasting me backward.

Any residue of hope seemed to leave my body as it roughly tumbled and scuffed along the hard surface.

That was it. We had surely failed. I let Tara and Sakura down, and now we'd have to wait an entire semester to try again. . .

I waited helplessly to hear the loud buzzer, signaling that time had run out, but I instead heard a girl's voice gleefully shouting something from the distance. It was Tara's and she was yelling, "I GOT IT! I GOT IT!!! WE DID IT!!!!"

Flat on my back, I craned my neck to scan the field. There Tara was, lying on the ground across the field. She was holding up the red orb, gazing admirably at it.

It must have happened during the split second when Dean Celestine turned to hit me with her Telekinesis Spell.

Tara had made it to the orb just in time. Against all odds, we had passed.

Chapter Twenty-Two

"WE DID IT! WE DID IT!" Tara repeated, and I could tell from her tone that she didn't fully believe the words coming out of her mouth.

"We did it . . . we did it . . ." I tiredly groaned to myself while the cheers of celebrations rang out from the girls across the field.

Now that my adrenaline was simmering down, I was quickly becoming aware of all the blows I took during the match, and I painfully gazed at the sky to see it spinning. That final blast from Dean Celestine did a number on me. Regardless though, nobody could take away the smile that was plastered on my face, no matter how feeble it may have been.

The next time I opened my eyes, I was greeted with a sight that only made my smile widen, all three girls were standing over me, gazing down exquisitely.

"Shit," I muttered, "looks like I'll be seeing gramps again sooner than I thought. I'm ready, angels . . . take me away."

Tara, Sakura, and Dawn all exchanged curious looks before bursting into giggles.

"Hold on there, cowboy," said Tara, wiping a tear of amusement from her eye and passing the red orb to Sakura before bending down and putting her glowing hands on my chest, "I'll get you feeling like a new man here in a minute."

"Thanks, Tara," I rasped, "those hands of yours are magical."

She rolled her eyes and tried to suppress a smile, but her pink cheeks gave her true thoughts away, while the swooshing from her Healing Spell sounded out.

It couldn't have even been a minute before I started to feel my energy replenishing, the many dull and sharp pains throughout my body fading away, making it all feel like it had just been a rough dream.

"That should do the trick!" said Tara, propping me up and giving me a warm, grateful smile.

"Wow, you weren't kidding about the 'new man' thing!" I said, springing up to my feet and stretching out my arms.

"Well done, Questers!" Dean Celestine's voice echoed out to my left, and I turned to see her with Professor Morran and Professor Kravitz, one looking just as proud as Dean Celestine, while the latter a grumpy mess.

"Congratulations, you three," said Professor Morran.

"Thank you, Professor!" we simultaneously said.

"I must say," continued Dean Celestine, "I am quite impressed with the level of skill, but most importantly, the team chemistry demonstrated by your group, especially considering how last-minute it was formed. Very impressive, indeed. I say it'd be wise that you all stick together throughout your careers. Team synergy can be a much rarer thing than you would think it to be in this field."

All of us shot each other quick glances of appreciation.

"And that includes you, too, Miss Hillman," Dean Celestine gestured to Dawn. "I understand you are in the Guard, and are doing a fine job with it, but there aren't many members of the Guard who are so willing to passionately cheer for a few Questers the way I saw you doing in those stands today."

Dawn brushed her bangs out of her eyes and turned a subtle shade of pink.

"Well, with that," Dean Celestine announced, "I hereby inaugurate the three of you into the—"

"Selene!" snapped Kravitz.

"Yes, Professor?"

"Surely, you cannot induct this group into the Quester program after this one's," he gestured to me, "*unethical* methods of completing the task at hand!"

"However," Dean Celestine sharply said, "he did *complete* the task at hand, just as you so kindly admitted."

"Well—yes, but—" the burly man stammered, and I couldn't help my lips from curling a little.

"As I know you are aware, Professor, all that matters when on a quest is that the quest gets completed. The means of completion is frivolous, even if it was a bit . . . *eccentric*." She grinned at me.

Kravitz had clearly heard enough. He stormed through the group, red in the face, and made his way off the field and through the tunnels, never once turning back.

"I'd say," Dean Celestine broke the silence, "he's just a tad bit upset over being confined to that earth prison you so skillfully conjured up, Mr. Gannon."

I tried my best to suppress a grin as Dean Celestine continued on.

"As I was saying," she proclaimed, in the same formal tone she had before getting interrupted, "I, Dean Celestine, hereby induct the three of you into the Quester program! Congratulations, and I look forward to seeing your progress." She smiled warmly at us while Professor Morran clapped behind her. The girls and I joined in on the cheering and embraced each other.

We were all just about to leave the field together when Dean Celestine called out, "Mr. Gannon, a quick word?"

The others paused and looked curiously before continuing their way out, but Tara hung back for just a second.

"Nate, I . . . I just," she uttered beneath her breath while Dean Celestine patiently waited, "I just wanted to say thank you—for everything— for what you said, and for believing in me." She beamed up at me, her eyes gleaming behind her glasses.

"Well, of course! I knew you had it in you." I smiled. "But I should be the one thanking you. You're the one that got that orb for us. You never gave up. To be honest, I thought our plan was a bust when Dean Celestine caught on. But you never missed a beat. You kept after it. That's who you are, and why we succeeded."

Her eyes glistened as her smile broadened, before giving me a quick but passionate kiss. "I love you so much, Nate. Thank you for just . . . being you." And then she turned to join the others across the field in front of the tunnel.

"Nice girl," said Dean Celestine, while I admired them all from afar, "they all are, really."

"They're the best," I softly said, finally managing to tear my gaze away from them and back to Dean Celestine.

"So," she started, grinning, "it would seem that you have now mastered the art of cloning others, haven't you?"

I chuckled. "I wouldn't have done it if I thought there was any other way to make you drop your guard, Professor!" I pleaded, but she raised a hand to stop me, still smiling.

"I have no qualms with it. I'm actually quite impressed. That was a very creative strategy, I must admit."

"Well, thanks!" I shrugged. "I try."

"Indeed, you do. I'm just curious how you got those fine gentlemen's mytosome structures to copy in the first place."

"I made a last-minute trip into Hearthvale yesterday," I explained with a smirk. "Figured there would be plenty of men that are your type at the bars in town. And it was like you said in class, the hardest part of the Cloning Spell was initially learning it. Cloning others was actually pretty easy in comparison, especially once I figured out how to sense out others' mytosomes."

"Very impressive, Nate, very impressive, indeed."

"I even ran into that Kevin guy at the Bronze Dragon!"

"I noticed," she added with a smirk, to which I sheepishly smiled.

"Nice guy, Kevin!" I went on. "I told him the situation, and he was more than happy to let me copy his mytosomes. He thought my plan was hilarious and only asked me to take a picture of your face when it happened."

"Is that so?" she joined in on my laughter. Thankfully, Dean Celestine was a good sport and shared the same type of humor as me. "Well, I'm going to have to have a word with Kevin next time I see him!"

"Give him my thanks!" I chuckled.

"Yeah, I'll be giving him *something*," she expressed with a wink.

"As for the other two dudes," I added, ignoring that gesture, "I may have . . . sort of, well, sneakily borrowed their myto-some structures. It was all for the cause, after all." I shrugged.

Dean Celestine raised her hands. "Hey, what happens between S-tiers, stays between S-tiers."

I couldn't help genuinely appreciating her at this moment. It was hard to believe this was the same lady who had me prac-tically drowning in a sphere of water only a few minutes prior.

"Well, I must say, Nate," she continued, looking past me at the tunnels, "I am very impressed with your progress, unsur-prising as it may be. But that said, even *I* must admit that you pulled off a couple of feats today which caught me off guard, something that doesn't happen often, I not-so-humbly admit."

"Thanks, Professor." I rubbed the back of my head as I tried my best to appear modest.

"I mean that, Nate," she reiterated. "Everything I threw at you today, you countered admirably, all while improving and learning new skills as the match went on. That alone speaks volumes to the type of sorcerer you can be one day. I'd even go as far to say that perhaps the life of a Quester would be beneath someone of your potential."

Hearing someone of her stature say that really meant a lot to me, though I truly wasn't expecting that last part, and I wasn't entirely sure what she meant by it either. It made me curious.

"More than . . .?"

"Perhaps a conversation for next year," Dean Celestine calmly said, not pushing the topic any further. "For now, I want you to enjoy this moment. So with that, I'd just like to again congratulate you, Nate. You've done quite well here today, this entire year even. It's been a pleasure watching you progress, and I must admit that I'm quite eager to continue *reading your story*."

"You mean—you're still reading my mind?!"

"No, no." She raised her hand and chuckled. "Your Shield Spell has improved as well, unfortunately for me. I just mean to say, I'm looking forward to watching you continue to progress." She winked at me. "Now, go join your girl-friends over there! I'd imagine you all have much to celebrate with the year being over."

I said my thanks and nodded before starting to head across the field toward the others, but then Dean Celestine's voice sounded out again, stopping me in my tracks.

"Oh! And one last thing, Nate!"

I spun on my heel to face her.

"If you *ever* use my first name again in public, I will destroy you."

I stood frozen in place, wide-eyed at her while she glared through me. But then her face finally gave way to a smirk and a spitting laugh.

"That never gets old!" she breathed and gasped as she slapped at her knee. "An entire year with me, and I'm still able to get you like it's the first day we met!"

I forced an awkward laugh. "Yeah, right."

"Oh, my," she said in between bouts of laughter. "Your face —you should have seen it! My, oh, my, that was good. Run along, Nate—go enjoy your summer!"

"Wait, you guys really aren't staying here over the summer?" Dawn asked, giving me and Tara a look of sheer disappointment with those dark eyes.

It was later that same day. And just as I had promised Tara, we agreed to celebrate at the Bronze Dragon, after perhaps the most relaxing shower of my life, of course.

"I'm sorry, Dawn." Tara murmured. "It's my fault—I just can't leave my family for good, you know? If I stayed for summer, then I'd never see them."

"Eh, who cares! They're just a bunch of Lackers anyway," blurted Dawn with a grin.

"Hey!"

"I kid, I kid," pleaded Dawn. "I'm really gonna miss that spunk of yours, Tara."

"Sure you will," said Tara flatly while rolling her eyes, but then her lips curled to a smile. "But I'll miss you, too. And I'm sorry that I'm stealing Nate from you for a few months."

"Yeah! What's up with that?!" Dawn reacted, and I felt both their gazes suddenly pierce through me.

"I'm sorry, Dawn. But I stayed with you during Winter Break, remember?"

"Yes, yes," she quickly said from across the table, drumming her fingers against it, "but that was just for a month! This is three!" She contorted her face into a somewhat exaggerated frown.

"I know, but hey—we'll still be able to come visit through the Magic Gateway!" I pointed out. "I'll rent out an apartment around campus to make sure that I can—"

"Oh," interrupted Dawn, her face now genuinely frowning, "you guys didn't know? The Magic Gateway closes for the summer, and Glendor's, too. You won't be able to return to the Rune Realm for a few months."

My mouth fell open after hearing this, and I could tell from the silence to my left that Tara was just as struck over the news.

"There aren't any other rune points near the Magic Gateway?" asked Tara, desperately.

Dawn shook her head, cringing apprehensively. "I'm sorry, guys. I didn't mean to ruin your day, and it's been such a good one so far!"

But I was still left at a loss for words as I now pondered my decision of returning to a world where Tara was the only person still emotionally binding me to it. I had already committed to going back with her, though, so it wouldn't be right to back out now. Not only that, but I really would miss her. I'd never been away from Tara for more than a month and I couldn't imagine being separated any longer than that.

"Well," I broke the silence, noticing Tara's guilty expression, "it's only three months. Time goes like *that* anymore, anyway." I caressed Tara's thigh underneath the table, so that she knew I was with her on this one. "And we aren't about to let that ruin our day. Not today! We did it. We passed, all thanks to Tara!"

Dawn gave a "Woot! Woot!" while I affectionately squeezed her thigh.

"Oh, please!" Tara waved. "I barely did a damn thing, and you guys know it. It was all you and Sakura. I'd say even Dawn did more than me from her cheering in the stands!"

We all laughed at that, and I was about to tell Tara not to sell herself short when my favorite waitress in the Realm came scampering toward us.

415

"And speaking of Sakura!" added Tara.

"Hey, there's our fox girl!" shouted Dawn with a smile.

"Hi, guys," she quietly replied, beaming at us as she placed a pitcher of runic ale and a dragon-shaped pretzel on our table. "I hope you enjoy your drinks and pretzel," she squealed and started to stride off.

"Hey! Hey!" Dawn called to Sakura, making her spin on her heel with a concerned expression. "Where do you think you're going, missy?" She waved her back.

"Oh, is everything okay?"

"Of course it is," added Tara, "but there's still one thing missing!"

"Oh?" She looked a little flustered. "I'm sorry, I—"

"It's you, Sakura," I calmly concluded, giving her a welcoming smile. "We're here to celebrate us officially being in the Quester program, and that would have never happened without you!"

"Yeah, you're a total badass, girl!" said Dawn.

"You really are," Tara agreed with a chuckle.

Sakura stood there, her mouth open and her eyes (which were now blue) glistening as her glossy lips gave way to a big smile. "Um, okay. Yes, of course! Thank you!"

"Don't sweat it!" said Dawn, as she slid over to make room while patting the seat in a gesture for Sakura to sit next to her. "Hey, waiter!" she hollered out to one of Sakura's co-workers, who came running over. Another glass for the fine lady here, please?" Dawn was smiling innocently.

"But she's—" he stammered.

"Our friend!" Just like that, her innocent smile had immediately disappeared. "So get my girl a damn glass!"

Me and Tara exchanged looks and tried to suppress our grins (Dawn was currently emanating similar vibes to the time when she slapped the werewolf on the beach) while Sakura's eyes remained glued to the table, her cheeks matching the color of her hair once again.

"Ye-yes, of course!" replied the waiter before stumbling off.

"Idiot," Dawn muttered underneath her breath while Tara and I snickered.

"I'm starting to think *you* have a frenzy state yourself, there, Dawn," I joked.

"Hey," she shrugged her shoulders,"I *did* hang out with Zula quite a bit last year. Maybe it rubbed off on me!"

We all laughed at that, and I halfway opened my mouth to say something back when a scene across the room caught my attention.

My brow furrowed at the sight. "Hey, isn't that Kravitz?" I discreetly gestured with my head, but then all the girls turned to stare, defeating the purpose of the whole *discreet* thing.

"Oh, yeah," muttered Tara. "Wonder what he's doing at a fun place like this?"

"Probably still trying to get over the beating you guys handed him earlier," scoffed Dawn. "Not sure there's enough runic ale in all of Hearthvale, though, to cure the embarrassment of being immobilized by dirt."

But I was only half-listening. Kravitz was no longer what had my attention. He was sitting with another man—an elf who looked to be around my age. Perhaps a student at Magic Rune Academy. Or rather, a future student, based off of the recruiting pamphlet placed on his side of the table, and the fact I hadn't seen him before.

There was something very different about this elf, though, and it wasn't just that he looked a bit odd, with his red eyes and red hair that spiked up to a point (something not all that common among the elves I've seen throughout my time in the Realm).

No, it was the fact that his pool of internal rune was so vast that it was practically radiating off him, making it almost difficult for me *not* to sense it. If I wasn't mistaken, it even surpassed Kravitz's levels of internal rune while in his berserker form. But the guy seemed completely calm and aware, clearly not in any sort of berserker state.

I had to do it, curiosity had gotten the best of me. I sensed out his mytosome count, using his noticeable internal rune as my guide.

And they hit me like a truck—leagues higher than anything I had sensed from the girls, or even the strangers that I sensed out during my preparation in Hearthvale.

I wasn't absolutely certain, but based on the density and activity level of his mytosomes, I'd say they maybe even rivaled my own.

At that moment, the elf glanced over, and we locked eyes. Perhaps he knew I was sensing him out, but I didn't really care. I made sure that my expression remained unwavering.

"You okay, Nate?" asked Tara, pulling my attention back to the table. "You look all intense all of a sudden."

"Uh, yeah, of course," I stammered. "Just ready to dive into this pretzel! You know how I get around food. And I need the nourishment after this morning."

"Why was I even surprised," chuckled Tara.

But Dawn was staring at me, knowingly, and I was reminded of the fact that she could also sense out mytosomes: it was what made her thrive at the Guard.

I looked back at her, and it was like we silently exchanged the same thought. Kravitz was recruiting a student, but not just any student—a student with an extremely high mytosome count, a count so rare that he'd be just the third runic on campus with it. This elf was an S-tiered runic.

The two men must have finished their conversation, because at that moment they stood up to take their leave. The elf was just as tall as the large Kravitz, but not quite as hulking of a man. He was leaner, but by no means skinny, like so many elves were. He was wearing a traveling cloak, so I couldn't tell exactly what class he was, but given his huge pool of internal rune and the fact he was with Kravitz, I'd bet the rest of my savings that he was a rune-knight.

He trailed behind Kravitz as they made their way toward the exit. And when Kravitz had already walked through the door, leaving the tavern, the elf paused. As he did so, he turned to look directly at me, smirking fiercely.

I stared right back at him, straight-faced. His red eyes and hair were only more pronounced by the way they contrasted against his dark purple skin, which almost looked black underneath the dim lighting of the tavern.

It was like he was studying me, and I was just starting to wonder how long this would go on for (it was starting to get a bit awkward) when he finally pushed his way through the door, leaving the restaurant, and me to stare at the now vacant exit, deep in thought.

In my peripherals, I noticed Dawn still gazing at me while Tara and Sakura were conversing about something I hadn't been paying attention to. And it wasn't until our waiter came back with the extra glass for Sakura, when I shot Dawn one last apprehensive glance and finally made the decision to push that whole encounter out of my head. It wasn't worth dawning over, not today.

Dawn seemed to be on the same page, too, as she thanked the nervous waiter and promptly poured the pitcher of light-blue beer into the four glasses.

And as we sipped on our beers and snacked on the pretzel, I took in the surrounding scene. It was like the whole thing with that elf never even happened. Any feelings of tension were eventually replaced by an overwhelming sense of gratitude. I had so much to be thankful for. Thankful for being introduced to this amazing world that was the Rune Realm, thankful for being enrolled in one of the finest institutions—Magic Rune Academy, and most thankful for these three amazing girls sitting around me.

"Well," I raised my glass of runic ale, the three girls beaming at me eagerly. "I just wanted to say that I am a truly blessed man." They all chuckled. "I know it may sound corny or whatever, but I really do mean it," I emphasized. "It's hard to believe that less than a year ago I had no clue that any of this even existed. And to be honest, I've never felt more at home than I have over the past year. I thought that was because of the Realm itself, but it's not. It's because of you three, all of you." I glanced at Sakura, to make sure she knew she was included in that. "Again, I am a blessed man, because I'm currently sitting here—a good ass beer in my hand, surrounded by three of the most beautiful girls in the Realm!"

They all blushed and gazed at me rapturously.

"Well," breathed Dawn, "I will *definitely* toast to that." She gave me one of those classic *Dawn winks.*

"Definitely!" Tara agreed with a warm smile.

"Yes, me too!" piped up Sakura, as she hastily raised her own glass.

"Cheers—to an amazing year, and an even better one next time!" I declared as the four of us clanged our glasses together, having much to celebrate, and even more to look forward to next time.

Afterword

Thank you for reading the first book in the Magic Rune Academy series! We really hope you enjoyed the beginning of Nate's story. Our plans are to take this book to a trilogy, which means there is so much more ground left to cover.

The idea for MRA came about because two good friends decided to write a harem novel together. We wanted something that blended slice-of-life elements with an academy setting, and the end result is something we both feel a lot of pride in. It's even more exciting because it's Adam's first foray into the world of haremlit, and this is just going to be the first of many books coming down the line.

As far as book two, we are already working on it, and as soon as we have a firm date for the ETA, we'll put out a message on social media. If you haven't already, please follow our author pages on Amazon and/or friend us on Facebook so we can keep in touch.

Thank you again for your support!

Friend Landon on Facebook.

Friend Adam on Facebook.

Also by Landon Scott

Goblin Girl Maid Service – A Slice-of-Life Fantasy Adventure

Build our business, beat the competition, and fall for a goblin girl (or three).

My life definitely wasn't going according to plan, but that all changed the moment I died unexpectedly. Now I've been reborn into the fantasy metropolis of Dragonmont City, where I get a second chance to flourish.

A twist of fate brings me into contact with Paulina, the proud but troubled owner of Goblin Girl Maid Service. Together with her slightly crazy best friend Kennedi, these two insanely beautiful goblin girls are trying to get their struggling business off the ground.

But the competition, in the form of bearded dwarf ladies with a serious attitude problem, has never been stiffer.

I'm going to do everything I can to help these lovely green ladies build the life of their dreams. Maybe I just might find something that always eluded me in my old life—a place to call home.

Click here to find the omnibus on Amazon.

Shifter Girl Summer – A Slice of Life Urban Fantasy

Sun, surf, and sultry shifter girls . . .

The beachside town of Oyster Cove had everything a man could want—endless white sand beaches, plentiful summer activities, and of course, more beautiful women than you could shake a tail at. I came to Oyster Cove to enjoy a leisurely summer of surf and sun, but I find out pretty quickly that there's more to this town than meets the eye.

My next door neighbor has eyes that are very similar to a cat's, and I could have sworn the gorgeous waitress at my favorite food spot has scales on her legs. Maybe I've been out in the sun too long, but when a foxy redhead asks me to join her volleyball team, I get pulled into a world that I never knew existed.

And for some reason, all these shifter girls are interested in me.

It looks like my summer is going to heat up quickly.

Click here to find the first book on Amazon.

Afterword

<u>Thank you for reading!</u>
<u>If you enjoyed this book, please leave a review.</u>
<u>Reviews are so important to authors.</u>

<u>Join Royal Guard Publishing Discord to</u>
<u>participate in tons of giveaways, extra content,</u>
<u>and chat with all our authors and narrators.</u>

Follow Landon Scott on Amazon here
For more Harem Lit Adventures:

www.royalguardpublishing.com
https://www.facebook.com/RoyalGuard2020
https://www.facebook.com/marcus.sloss.524
https://www.facebook.com/groups/dukesofharem
https://www.reddit.com/r/haremfantasynovels/

Made in United States
Troutdale, OR
12/29/2024

27250595R20239